DISAGREEABLY DISCHARGED

A Novel by John D. Meyer

© July 2013 by John Meyer. All Rights Reserved
978-1-304-27520-2

With many thanks to Paul Park and Amadee Meyer

1

If it hadn't been for the game of bridge, Edmond Beil's life would have taken a different turn and this story could not have been told. Looking back on it, it is hard to believe that something as simple as a game of cards could change a life so much, but it did, like a door you walk through where everything is different on the other side. Many fates are hidden in the cards we are dealt, but one's true destiny is in the hands of the player. Only a bridge master can thread the needle of what is possible or impossible, deciding what does or does not come out. Because of this my father, Edmond Beil, lived the most peculiar of lives.

Edmond Beil had been on the navy destroyer now for three weeks, not knowing where he was going except that it was dangerous and he might die...lost in thought, he lit another cigarette off of the last one throwing the butt into the sea where it got caught by the current never to be seen again; the prefect metaphor for his life ever since he had been drafted into the fucking war. It was hard to believe that only three months ago he had graduated summa cum laude from the University of Pennsylvania expecting to go to graduate school. The old saying was true. War is hell.

To find some peace, he let his mind drift back to the posting he had seen on the ship's bulletin board: open bridge tournament next week. Bridge was his passion and despite the bleak circumstances, it was all he could think about.

With a new sense of excitement he took a last drag on his cigarette and chucked the burning butt into the black hole whirlpool below. Again, mesmerized like a moth, he watched it spiral downward, whirling toward the trapped abyss of destiny. Immediately his melancholy returned, as he was once more reminded of his own plight on the death ship. There was no escape, and Beil knew it. But just as he was about to turn away, the butt abruptly broke free of the sinking hole and floated to the surface.

2

"I didn't think there were going to be this many," General Charlie 'Chuck' Vois said, the excitement evident in his voice.

"Neither did I," Major John Dewey answered back. They were standing near the back of the mess, which had been quickly converted when it became apparent that the bridge room they had set up in was too small. The hastily-cleared tables were now crowded with men eager for the tournament to begin. The two officers watched as Captain Jim Moss went over to the microphone.

"Gentlemen, welcome," he said as he surveyed the crowd, looking into the young faces, seeing nothing but fear. "First we will play a few hands amongst the various groups, changing partners every so often. Then we will make the first of the cuts." After speaking he went over to the other two officers.

"Let's hope we find ourselves a great player," the general squealed in delight. Chuck Vois was fifty-four, five foot ten inches and very fit. He and his entourage were only going to be on the boat for a few more days. At some point they were to rendezvous with a sub that would head them toward China. Their mission was to set up an intelligence operation to monitor Japanese movement on the mainland. But on the way, Chuck's best friend, Staff Sergeant Drum, had died. They had lost their bridge foursome and the general's playing partner. They had been very disappointed that they had been unable to find a sergeant in Pearl Harbor that was a good enough player to bring to China.

"Very good idea, not settling for that old fartbat," Major Dewey chuckled, thinking about the look on the poor bastard's face as they left their newly-assigned sergeant at the dock in Pearl. "That sergeant couldn't play as good as the dummy." They all laughed.

"Yes, very good thinking, sir, not to bring him," the captain added. It had been his inspiration to have the tournament. "But he was not too happy. Did you see his face? He wanted something bad to go to China."

"Well, that's what rank's for," the general chuckled as they observed the players at the tables. They were surprised by the turnout.

Their plan was to make the winner a staff sergeant. Then bring him to China so they would have a fourth and a new partner for General Vois. They did not mind if the winner was a private, because to be truly great in bridge you have to be very smart and catch on quick, both good qualities in a potential intelligence operator. They hoped there would be a great player amongst the enlisted men.

Edmond Beil looked at the player across from him knowing the man knew nothing about bridge, other then there were thirteen cards in a hand. He would have to carry the game by himself. It was like playing a dummy hand only worse, because you had a dummy playing a live hand. But this did not matter to Beil, who had been captain of the bridge club at the University of Pennsylvania. Still, Edmond was angered when his partner trumped his ten-high finesse with the queen. He was not surprised when they lost the first game of the rubber.

It was in super-frustration that he watched his partner in the next hand lead the queen of hearts, which was quickly covered by the king in the dummy, making what would have been a sure trick if he had just waited. Instead they were sent into defeat. The rubber was over. The only consolation was that Beil was not the only one who was frustrated.

All over the room many hands were being played like that, as if bridge were a game of nothing but luck. Oh yes, there was lady luck, but she was a very small part of it. Bridge was all about playing the hand you had. Making that hand better than it was by working with the cards to deliver what was and was not there.

For the three officers covert action was very much like bridge. They would go into a country and play it, only using their trump card— the good old U.S.—when they ran out of local solutions.

Unfortunately, though, America was like most of the men in the room, playing their hands wildly and only from strength. They had all been watching when the man had played the futile queen, covering his partner's finesse—very powerful overkill, and doomed. The three officers were not looking for John Wayne. They were looking for another master, one who could change with the change until the change was changed.

The reason so many people had showed up, even ones who had never played bridge, was because of the rumor that whoever won the tournament would be saved. All the men had seen the three officers come on board when the ship docked in Pearl Harbor for refueling, and had overheard that they were going to transship somewhere in the Pacific. It did not take too long for the men to put two and two together, so it was no wonder half the boat showed up.

"None of these men know anything about bridge," the general lamented about an hour into the tournament. It was chaos. No one knew how to bid, to make a contract or even play the simplest of cards.

"I think there are some good players here, sir. We just have to find them," Captain Jim said, not at all confident.

"Word must have leaked out," Major Dewey answered in frustration.

An hour later Beil was finally dealt a strong hand where he was going to make game regardless of who was playing.

"Three no trump," he said, cutting off all bidding, going for game. The frustration he was feeling did not show on his face. He could not believe how stupid most of the men were. He knew the general had been watching him a few hands ago.

What the general had picked up was his coolness. The man barely broke a sweat. The general had watched him long enough to know that he knew how to play cards. He could see that the man's poker face revealed nothing, even when the partner played wrong card after wrong card. The only sign of stress was the chain-smoking, but everybody did that.

"Four hearts," the man to Beil's left said, forced to overbid a classic three heart hand, nine trump, queen high. Beil's clueless partner passed.

"Six hearts." The man to Beil's right raised the bid from the four hearts his partner had bid. The general watched Beil's brows frown, but only momentarily. Just then the major and the captain joined him.

"I like this player," the general said. "Those two against him are decent." The general had walked around and seen the hands. He knew that the other team held twelve of the trump cards but not the ace, which was sitting in Beil's hand. He also knew that Beil was holding a strong enough hand for game, but lacked the powerhouse for the slam...that is, without some luck. He had a definite loser in the ace of diamonds, and would have to finesse a few cards. The general was pleased when he heard six no trump.

"Seven hearts," the next man said, confident that his partner had very strong hearts to have bid up his weak three bid. The two men had been playing bridge together for a few years, and both knew each other well. It was no accident that they were here at this table at the end of the games. The three watchers huddled together; all turned their eyes on Beil.

"Seven no trump," Beil said, gambling that his partner held the missing ace of diamonds that would doom the contract which was already doomed. Beil sighed to himself, waiting in the silence. It would take a certain dance of the deal to press the overbid slam. Besides the one ace loser, all he knew for certain was that the weaker hearts lay to his left, the stronger to his right and that his two opponents had played bridge together before. The game was now beyond skill—that could only take you so far. He was in the hands of the murky unpredictable cards of luck, the grey in the storm of life, as he liked to call it. Beil felt grand, his stomached twisted in the exquisite uncertainty of the cloudy unknown.

He lit another cigarette, savoring the smoke as he waited for the heart to be led. The excitement ran through him, replacing the doom he had felt when he had first got on the boat of death. The boat was still moving ever closer to hell, but now everything was alive with the cards of chance that had given him a way out. Beil was focused, ready to play the hand that he knew was like a card river bounded by suits of fate, with destiny lying within the thirteen tricks, his lucky number. He let out the smoke that had curled in his lungs as the man to his left tossed out the seven of hearts.

The three officers felt that they were watching a fish bowl. They all inwardly gasped when the dummy hand was laid down and there were no hearts. Beil saw that too, but mostly he saw the ace of diamonds sitting there in an otherwise weak hand. The next man played the king. All were surprised when Beil covered it with the ace.

He led the queen of diamonds, hoping the king was sitting to his left. The man played a lower card in a way that let Beil know he was doomed, but he showed none of it, still the confidant face of hope. He thought about it as the time passed: when you played something thinking you knew what would happen, but still there was a chance for something else. He knew that all you could do was wait and be ready. It was time standing still, where man was in the eye of God, a God that Beil did not believe in. He was going down, it was inevitable. He played the three off the dummy and waited. He felt a shot of adrenaline when he saw the seven.

"Very nice finesse," the major said to the general, both of them smiling. Both of them knew that skill combined with luck could catapult things to heaven, and that bridge was a lot like life.

"I thought he was doomed."

"You wouldn't know it from his face." They looked over at Beil and saw the impassive face; the ever-present cigarette, but on the inside Beil knew that he would have to have more luck or he was a goner. He needed the spades to be evenly divided in a three-three split or he would go down, as he was missing the jack. He made the decision to test fate and led the ace, then the king again. The others both had trump. He lit another cigarette and played the queen, knowing it was up to luck. The man on the left played the nine, and he played the three from the dummy. Time stood still. Everybody let out a breath when the jack fell. The slam was his.

"We have our man," the general said to his friends. And Beil, who had been headed for certain death on some bloody island was now on his way to China.

This was the story that I heard many times while growing up. How my father had won the bridge tournament and escaped storming some beach where eight of ten men died. So as you can imagine my struggle at the bridge table was one of the biggest disappointments in his life.

"How could you be so stupid?" he would yell into my face every time I tried to bid, as if the game were a game of life and death. Or worse, he would throw his hands up in frustration, then light another cigarette and give me the biggest and most subtle insult a bridge player can give. "You must be a good hearts player," he would say when I bid wrong but played right. Of course I would get into an argument with him and then he would flare up in rage, so different from his usually calm self.

There was only one time when he told me I played great bridge. But that is getting ahead of the story.

What I would like to say at this point is that if in this novel I misspeak about bridge and offend any great player out there, causing my father's pent-up rage to rise in them, then I apologize. It is not because of anything, except my lack of understanding of that special club to which my father belonged.

3

Newly promoted to staff sergeant, Beil could feel the hatred, the envy in the faceless eyes as word spread that he was leaving. Not that he knew any of them or they knew him, but all knew he was the lucky one and that suited Beil just fine. He had studied his three officers trying to understand them. For two days they played bridge non-stop, only taking time to eat and sleep. The food was much better at the officers' table, where there was also beer and hard liquor. It was here that he was introduced to a drink that would become his signature.

"What is that, sir?" he asked the general who was always his partner, the old man who despite his power had kind deep penetrating eyes.

"It's called a bull's eye. Made with vodka, beef broth, and a squeeze of lime." The general took his glass and handed it to Beil. "Here, have a sip."

"That's really good."

"Private," the general called out. "Get the sergeant one of these." As the private hustled to comply, the four of them turned their attention back to the card game, where after some great hands, Beil and the general won the rubber. When it was over the older man pulled out his cigar box.

"So tell us your life, Edmond," the general asked as the four of them enjoyed the fine Cuban tobacco. The general had marveled at Beil's card-playing skill. How it clicked with his. He had looked at the young man's dossier and found that at age twenty he had graduated from college with top honors.

"I was born in 1921 in Brooklyn, then moved to Long Island where I grew up. My next-door neighbor was my father's brother, who had two girls a little older than me. The three of us were inseparable."

"How is it that you graduated college two years early?

"Oh," Beil said, blushing a little. The drink was going to his head, and in any case he wasn't used to talking about himself. "I guess it was because of my temper and not taking no for an answer."

"What do you mean?" the major asked as he leaned in. None of the officers had yet seen the slightest sign of his temper, but all of them knew that you can find out a lot about someone by listening and asking questions.

"Oh, I was sitting around one afternoon with my two cousins when their mom came in. Dot my older cousin was going into second grade and my aunt Minnie told us that the younger one, Nellie, was going to skip first grade and go into the same class with her. I was supposed to start kindergarten, but I put up such a fuss that to stop my tantrum they moved me into second grade with them."

These were the kind of conversations the four men held around the bridge table. After two days of them, the three officers and Staff Sergeant Beil crammed into the skiff and the boson took off. Soon he called out that they were approaching the sub. The four men scrambled up the steel ladder and entered the hatch.

4

After a week in the claustrophobic confines of the sub it finally surfaced in the busy harbor of the Indian city of Bombay. The four men were met by a jeep and driven to an air base where they boarded a plane and took off into the wild blue yonder.

"These are the Himalayan Mountains," Capt. Moss said to Beil as they looked out of the window. The huge mountains were snow-capped, jagged, beautiful, and dangerous. The range was solitary, other-worldly, and it lent itself to silence and awe. The peaks seemed to jut up to the sky. One in particular seemed almost to extend to outer space. It was surreal to be flying on top of the world, over a place that man was not meant to be.

"That big one is Everest." The general pointed out the window.

"I wonder if anyone will ever climb it." Major Dewey said

"No, those peaks are too high. Look at the snow-cover—it goes on and on."

"And it reaches to the sky. There must be no oxygen up there."

"Yeah, it would take a madman. No normal person would want to get too close."

"I wouldn't want to get too close to any of those peaks," Beil said just as the plane started to shake violently and lose altitude. A few bags fell from the overhead rack. The plane swerved to the left, pushing Beil against the window. He looked over his shoulder. The pilot was white-fisted, straining to keep control. This did not give him any sense of confidence. Still Beil remained calm except for the chain smoking. There was nothing he could do, except to get ready for what happened next. Time stretched to a stop. He felt alive because of the danger below. He knew they were in trouble but within trouble there still was calm if one had the nerve. He looked over at the general and the other two, who were just as calm as he. The turbulence lasted less then five minutes. The pilot gained control of the plane, regaining altitude only a few hundred yards above the snow-capped peaks.

"Welcome to the famous hump." The general exhaled, breaking the silence. Beil along with the others all giggled. Then everyone including the pilot broke out in an uncontrollable primal howl, feeling fresh, alive, and reborn. Beil still hadn't asked where they were going, but he had figured it out: China, the great land of mystery that Beil had often dreamed of as a kid. He peered out of the window as they started over the other side of the mountains. His excitement grew. In a couple of hours they landed in an airfield. As they came down, Beil saw that the noses of all the planes were painted to look like great tiger sharks.

"Those are the Flying Tigers," the general said as they touched down. "We are in Kunming."

5

Kunming was the Allies' base in China. It had not been overrun by the Japanese. It was where a secret war was being fought, even before Pearl Harbor.

As soon as the plane landed the four men disembarked. Beil got his first smell of Asia. The hot tropic scent was full of the stink of ginger, garlic, lotus, and burning incense. The exotic mix of smells came upon him like a thunderbolt. He took out a cigarette and lit it. The sun was bearing down and soon the muggy, clothes-sticking heat of Asia was upon him. He looked over and saw the general was having a hard time with the humidity. The sweat was pouring off of him. A swarm of Chinese came up and grabbed their bags.

"Is it always like this?" Beil asked, looking at the general who now was being fanned by a Chinese coolie. The day got hotter. He thought back to the humid days on Long Island, out in Flanders, which until then he had thought was the hottest place on earth.

"Yes, Edmond, just like this. You either get used to it and love it or you are like the general, who is only here to do a job," Major Dewey answered.

"Yes, I'll feel better when we are in the aircon of the barracks," the general agreed. "We'll meet for bridge at seven." The three officers left Beil in the hands of another sergeant.

"Welcome to Kunming, sergeant," the balding man said to Beil while fixing his hat in a jaunty twist. The man's name was Hank Hammer. He was thirty-one. He looked at the young sergeant and saw the extra stripe on his sleeve. "How long have you been in the army?"

"Two months," Beil replied, noticing the look in the other man's eyes.

"Two months and you're the ranking enlisted man here."

"Am I?" Beil answered, not caring anything about rank, or about the Army and the way it worked, now that he was well away from hitting the beaches.

"What are you and the top brass here for?" the sergeant said.

"It's none of your business," Beil answered back while lighting a cigarette, not really knowing what he was there for, but knowing that it was a secret. He was very good at keeping secrets. What he did know was that his life had been saved and he was playing bridge. But he knew his mission could not only be about bridge. So far playing bridge was all that they had done, but he couldn't let that show. Instead he let his eyes wander around the busy airstrip.

"So sergeant, tell me something about this place," Beil said offering the man a smoke.

The man saw the pack of Marlboros, not the cheap Chinese tobacco he had been smoking. He grabbed one. "What do you want to know?" he asked, impressed by the young man's coolness, liking him despite being outranked. Hammer was sweating like a pig on the fourth of July and this man was neat and trim, shirt tucked in and not a bead of sweat at all.

"How long have you been here?"

"I've been here since before the war, unofficially of course, until a few months ago. We were supporting the Chinese in a not-so-secret war against the Japanese invaders."

"But now it's a real war," Beil said, but did not see any sign of fighting. He let his eyes wander over the landscape. All over the airfield were stall after stall of Chinese vendors, selling snacks, cheap cigarettes, and knick-knacks. "Though you wouldn't know it from looking around here," Beil said.

"Yes, the war is sort of in limbo. The fighters go out and come back, while the rest of us wait, but who knows what we are waiting for? Have you ever been to China before?"

"No," Beil said, but inside he was feeling like he was home. It was like a dream, a dream where the light twirled and shone like a pinwheel, the pinwheel of life where the sun danced, the sky exploded and everything was familiar.

6

Kunming, the home of the Flying Tigers, was where the CIA got its start. President Roosevelt had been concerned about the lack of military intelligence coming out of China, and had formed the Office of Strategic Services. The three officers and the newly-arrived Beil were the OSS in this area, on a top-secret mission to establish an insurgency to defeat the Japanese and drive them from Asia.

"Perhaps we should tell you what we are here for, Edmond," Major Dewey said as the four of them finished a rubber. They were sitting back enjoying a smoke and drinking shots of Johnny Walker Red, which the captain had found on the black market.

"I thought we're here just to play bridge," Edmond dead-panned. The officers laughed at the remark.

"Eh, I wish it was a simple as that. How well do you type?" Major Dewey asked.

"Fifty words a minute with no mistakes."

"That will more than do," said the General.

"We begin tomorrow to drive the Japs out of South-East Asia," the Captain said to Edmond, who was just lighting another cigarette.

That prompted the major to interrupt. "Hey, Sergeant Beil, that's pretty good to type fifty words a minutes and still smoke. Imagine how fast you'd be if you didn't smoke."

"Then I would only be able to type twenty words." All of them laughed as the smoke curled from his lips. "Besides, smoking's good for you."

"Three no trump," said the General as the men got back to the game.

7

"I know a short cut back home," Sergeant Hammer said as the two men slumped together, both of them almost falling. They had been drinking hot, potent rice wine in a Chinese restaurant. Now they were in the shanty-town near the barracks. If they went by the road they would have to pass in front of all the buildings. But if they went to the back and cut across the barren fields they would save twenty minutes.

They crossed behind the building and into the darkness. Off in the distance they could see where they wanted to go.

"God, I can't see a thing," the sergeant said.

"Neither can I, Hank," Beil said. He took out the Tiffany lighter that his father had given him and lit it. That did nothing but blind them further and now both of them in their drunken state became more disoriented. All of a sudden a hot wind came up.

"What's that smell?" Beil asked. "The place smells like a sewer."

"Better keep away from it," said Hank as he took another step and slipped on the side of an open channel. "Shit" he yelled as he tumbled into the murk.

Beil stood there laughing, until Sergeant Hammer reached up, grabbed him, and pulled him in. Beil felt his cigarette go out as his head slid into the foul canal. He came up gasping for air.

Both men started laughing and started throwing the slop on each other as they climbed out together.

"Holy shit, we better run back to the barracks and get into the showers, before we get cholera or worse!" Hank said. They ran all the way back to the barracks, where they shed their clothes and ran into the shower. Both of them were still very drunk, trying to hold each other up under the cascading water. Beil was surprised to find himself aroused. He looked down and saw that Hank was too.

"Wish there were some girls here," the virgin Beil said to break his nervousness. He wanted a cigarette.

"Oh, we can pretend," the other man said as he started to stroke himself. Beil watched in fascination as the slimy liquid rushed out of the

19

man and hit him. Hank then reached over and stroked Beil until he came. He was about to say something when he noticed that Hank had passed out on the shower floor. Beil left him there to find a cigarette.

8

That night Beil had the strangest dreams. He was seven years old and on a sleep-over with his cousins. It was late at night. They were all in the same bed. Beil was dressed like the girls in a night-gown. His older cousin Dot had gone into her mother's purse and gotten out her makeup bag. All of them had painted their lips and put color on their eyes.

"Don't you wish that you could be like this all the time?" Nellie asked as they lay together in bed. In the dream Beil felt how good it was to put on girl things and how he liked the games girls played. He was just about to answer when the dream changed.

He was now in a house with lots of older girls. Only he wasn't a girl anymore, but one of the guys. They were all lined up in rows, the women in evening dresses, the men in black tie.

"I didn't ever think you would come, darling." A young woman appeared in front of him and took his hand and led him away from the line of men. She had a grey streak in her hair

"But I like boys," he said pointing to the men.

"Well, you can like girls too," the woman replied. Next the dream moved to the jungle where there were all kinds of wild beasts grabbing at him. They all had huge penises except for one who had a giant vagina. That one was just about to eat him when he awoke.

When Beil ran into Sergeant Hammer later that day, Hank was sporting a huge hangover. "God, my head is on fire. How much did we drink last night?"

"Lots."

"Oh my lord, my head feels like an ocean is washing around in there. I don't remember a thing. Edmond, can you do me favor? Today is payroll and I don't think I can do much but sit here. The men will get antsy if they are not paid. Can you go and pay them?"

"Sure," Beil replied, wanting to talk about last night. But the sergeant did not remember.

9

It was a month later and Beil had found shower-room C. He had heard the rumor floating around the base that certain things would go on there after a certain hour. He had walked by it a few times at the hour but had never ventured in. Over the course of the next few weeks he had watched from his hiding spot by the side of the next building. He saw that a man would occasionally enter it, but never more than one at a time. He noticed that they were dressed in civilian clothes, with hats pulled low over their faces. He watched one man walk by him just as the light of the moon came from behind the cloud. Beil was surprised to see the face of the general.

Finally, one night Beil had the courage to enter. The steam was thick like fog. It was hard to see anything clearly. Water cascaded off the bodies of naked men who were touching each other. Not a word was spoken. Beil felt someone touch him on the back. He turned and touched back. When he got back to his barracks he showered again.

A month later, Beil was a regular at the showers. It was as if no one there knew each other, though Beil would recognize some of the men during the day. He often wondered if they recognized him. He would always arrive early at the showers to wait outside to see if the general would arrive, knowing the general was a creature of habit and if he came, it would be early. In that case Beil would walk away. He wanted to avoid a confrontation at all costs.

One day a few months later he was walking by the airstrip of the Flying Tigers when he heard some loud screaming. He went over thinking someone was hurt but instead he saw Captain Larry Haggard, whom Beil recognized as someone from the showers. "I'm going to report you, you worthless faggot," Haggard was shouting at a younger man whom Beil also recognized from the baths.

"But sir," the man said. "I was only being friendly. I didn't mean anything by it."

"I hate fucking faggots." The captain was enraged that this weeping faggot had tried to touch him. The man loathed homosexuals in his real macho life. Only in his sordid inner world did his actions make sense. He was fucking the faggots to teach them a lesson. Haggard was a very violent man, the Flying Tigers' best pilot, and the tiger with the most kills because he was unpredictable. Beil remembered how violent he had been the one time they had teamed up at the bath. After that, Beil cut him a wide birth.

10

"Edmond, go commandeer a jeep and pick me up and let's explore this city. I just heard of this great local flea market," the general said after breakfast. An hour later they were in a busy market with stall after stall with barely any room for people to pass by. There were strange smells wafting up around them, burning garlic, lavender, and other spices Beil had never smelled before. Little children ran by laughing while old women gathered around tables playing some sort of game.

"What are they playing, sir?" Beil asked the general.

"Mah jong. It is a betting game that they enjoy as much as we like bridge." The game had chips that were sort of like dominoes but had strange writing on them.

They moved down the alley. On either side vendors had laid blankets on the ground where they had placed objects for sale. There were piles of green jade, porcelain, and strange smelling wood carvings. The general stopped by one of the booths and saw a carved figure that looked like a female but also like a male. After some gesturing and pidgin English the general bought it. He handed it to Beil so he could look at it.

"This is an eighteenth-century figure of Kwan Yin. Do you know who that is, Edmond? It is the female side of man."

"It looks more like a woman that a man."

"Yes, but it is a man. See, it has no breasts but a feminine face. According to the Chinese there are two kinds of energy that flow through us. One is yang, the male energy. The other is yin, the female energy. All of us are made of both."

When the general said that, Beil could not help thinking of the other night when he had seen the general come out of shower-room C. As they walked, Beil saw a similar figure at another stall.

"What about this figure? It has breasts."

"Oh, that is because it is a later one. The Chinese are good at borrowing from other cultures, so when the missionaries came, Kwan Yin started to become more female, because of the Virgin Mary."

"How did you learn all this, sir?' Beil asked, seeing a side of the general that he had not experienced before. At the same time he was thinking about what he said. It was so logical. Everybody was both female and male. It was so simple. He liked the idea of men being both female and male. It was a way to make sense of his desires.

"Oh, it is because I am collector of things, especially antiques. I just love learning about a place through their works of art." The general smiled as they entered another booth. Beil saw a beautiful yellow bowl and mentioned it to the general. Immediately the general asked about it, bargained a price, and bought it for Beil.

"You have a good eye, Edmond. That is Chien Lung mark and period." Beil handled the bowl admiring that it was perfect in every aspect from the shape to the enameling.

"Thank you," he said warmly. He patted the general on the back.

The general returned the gesture. "I must warn you, collecting becomes very addicting. And you already have addictions." Beil felt the general's eyes bore into him, making him feel like the boy with his hand in the cookie jar.

23

11

The general was right, Beil thought as he lit another cigarette. He had addictions. Collecting was now one of them.

The very next day was payroll day. Again Beil was in charge, as Sergeant Hammer was sick with a cold. As soon as he got there he checked to see if there were any more Morgan silver dollars. He was happy when he saw a large bag of them. The last time Beil had done the payroll for Sergeant Hammer, the sergeant had told him to divide them equally among the men as they were more a nuisance than the bills. Beil remembered that the captain had remarked at how these Morgan dollars were a limited minting. Beil decided that he would take them and pay himself, the general, major, and captain with them.

"Very good sergeant," the captain said as they were playing bridge that night.

"Very smart and quick thinking," Major Dewey added.

"You will take over the payroll from now on," the general said.

So started my father's lust for collecting. I remembered him at his happiest when he found another bowl or carving to add to his collection. He always told that story of the Morgan dollars when he would take out his coin collection for my sister and I to admire. When we saw them it was twenty years or more since he had gotten them, and of course they had appreciated in value. He would always say that collecting was like treasure hunting. Wealth was hiding in plain sight but only an observant person would be able to see it.

12

Beil was sitting in on a top-secret meeting taking notes for the general. Captain Jim was talking to a French intelligence officer.

"It's now been more than six months and still nothing," Jim said, showing his frustration with the dark-mustached Frenchman. It was so hard to get anything done. It was almost as if the French in Indo-China didn't want to get rid of the Japanese at all.

"We are setting the seeds," the man answered back.

The French Vichy government still ran Vietnam, but also answered to the Japanese, whose army controlled the entire area. "Very well," the captain said. "We will meet next week. I hope you have more to report."

When the officer had left, the general said, "That fucking pompous asshole is no help at all. Nothing they have tried has worked. There's no drive, no passion. The Japanese are just as strong as when we got here."

"Yes, general. In fact I think the French are secretly on the Japanese side. They are more worried about losing their colony to Ho Chi Minh."

"Yes, they don't want to rock the boat. Interrupt their fancy food and all that."

"Well, their food is great," Beil said. Now that the French officer had left, he could talk with the officers.

"Yes, that was a fantastic dinner last night," admitted the major. After bridge, they had gone out to a French Chinese restaurant had frogs legs and chateaubriand for four followed by coffee and cognac. Now he sighed. "Get us a new deck of cards. We might as well vent our frustrations with the French."

"Yes to both ideas," the general answered back. "Edmond, would you be so good as to get us a fresh deck?" Beil left the room at once to go to his quarters for a new deck. As he walked out of the building he was approached by what he thought was a Chinese man.

"Sergeant, sir," the man asked. "Can I have a word with you?" He spoke perfect English in a British accent, but he was dressed like a coolie.

"What is it?" Beil asked, trying to hide his astonishment.

25

"We have an underground much more sophisticated than the impotent French. Tell your officers you should be speaking with us."

"Wait right here," said Beil, as he dashed off in a sprint to get the deck of cards. When he returned, he brought the man inside.

They studied the man with the eyes of intelligence officers, looking beyond the man's clothes, examining his manner, his posture, his teeth, his fingers. "Explain yourself," the major said.

"I am a Vietnamese and I live within the occupation. My friends and I can come and go. We have more desire to fight than the French, who are content to keep things as they are." All of them could see the man's hatred when he mentioned the French.

Beil had been reading a lot of intelligence manuals about the art of observing, how by waiting and watching many things were revealed not so much by someone's words but by how they said them.

"Where did you come to speak English so well?" the general asked.

The man's name was Hiu. "I was educated in Paris and then Oxford, London and all that," he said.

He had been sent by Ho Chi Minh to ask for American support for the Vietnamese resistance—arms and money for their great struggle, not the small one against the Japanese but the great struggle against their French colonial masters, so they could be free.

"How can you help us better than the French?" the general asked. Beil was to his left. Hidden by his frame so Hiu could not see him, Beil began to study the Vietnamese. First, he was very smart. Second, he was hiding something.

"Because we are fighting for our land, our independence. We hate the French who are nothing but feudal lords."

"But Vietnam belongs to the French," the Major commented.

"We are the people who live there!" Hiu answered loudly. "We grow all the food. We toil and endure. Without our support the occupiers cannot survive."

"What occupiers?" the general asked.

"All occupiers. We are like the water on the land. In the long run we will prevail."

Beil watched Hiu's passion knowing he spoke the truth. Later that night, around the bridge table, the officers were speaking about the events of the afternoon.

"Three no trump!" the general shouted, stopping the bidding. They all settled back to play the hand they knew would be made once the first trick was taken. "Do you think Ho Chi Minh is our man?" the general asked.

"Yes, sir!" the major answered. "Good going, Edmond," he said, "for finding us a liaison."

"I watched him. He's one cool character. I bet you he plays bridge. I could tell by the way he answered your questions."

"I got that same damn feeling," the general said. "Major, you and the sergeant go contact Mr. Hiu tomorrow."

13

The next day Major Dewey and Beil were out driving to the village where Hiu was staying. Beil was driving the jeep the general had commandeered for them. The road was narrow. The jungle encroached on it from both sides. There was a lot of traffic, mostly people on foot and a few ox-drawn carts. Theirs was the only car. People stared at them. They found Hiu easily, on the street outside his home.

"We would like to meet with Ho Chi Minh," Major Dewey said. Beil was watching Hiu. He detected no surprise.

"It will take some planning to set up a meeting, because Mr. Ho has many enemies," Hiu said.

"How long?" the major asked, sticking out like a sore thumb in his uniform.

"I don't know. I will let you know in a few days," Hiu said, his eyes shifting around to emphasize that the whole village was awash with political intrigue. "There are many eyes and spies here. Next time come in regular clothes."

Free of Japanese control, Kunming was a place where many enemies seemingly existed together, but only on the surface. The area was a stronghold for both the Kuomintang, Chiang Kai-shek's Nationalist Army and the Communists, who were supporting Mao Tse-tung. The place was teaming with spies, French, Vietnamese, and Chinese that made for constant undercurrents, strong ebbs and flows that were able to erupt at any moment. Some of these rivalries even existed with the Americans

As the Allies' only foothold in East Asia other than boats on the sea, the city was full of military brass. With too many chiefs and not enough Indians, no one could agree on much. All sorts of jealousies developed. The OSS's biggest rivals were the Flying Tigers, who had been there first and thought they ran the place.

Of the Flying Tigers, Captain Larry Haggard embodied the worst. He had been in Kunming since the beginning, flying mission after mission. He was a vile man who loved to kill. He would have been thrown out of the air force if it had not been for his skills at killing. He had an utter disrespect for Asians, whether they were Japanese or not.

Haggard got his violent streak from his father who would whip him in glee. He learned to hate at an early age. To satisfy his violent vein as a child he would burn caterpillars with a magnify glass; blow up frogs with fire crackers. War was perfect for him. He was fearless, reckless and because of that desire to destroy, the best killing machine in the Pacific. He had 57 kills, the most of any pilot in China, threefold.

The next week the general sent Beil to the meeting by himself. He met Mr. Hiu in Kunming so as not to attract attention.

"I thought we were all fighting the Japanese," he said as they met in a small French restaurant.

"We are all fighting the Japanese. But before the Japanese we were fighting each other," Hiu explained. He spoke in French, and when Beil answered in the same language, Hiu complimented him.

"It's nothing," Beil said. "You speak English, French, and probable Chinese very well besides."

"Yes, I have the gift of tongues. And you, sergeant?"

"I have it too. My family was German, so I speak that, French and some Spanish. But this Chinese is hard to learn."

"Oh, not so hard if you listen and get into the mind."

Beil asked the next question. "The general is very anxious to meet this Ho Chi Minh to enlist his support, so much so that we will travel to meet him." Beil was slightly surprised to see the slight flash of victory in Hiu's face, which he tried to mask by bringing out his lighter for Beil's cigarette.

At the same time Captain Larry Haggard was wildly walking the streets of Kunming having just found out he had not been promoted. He blamed everything on the OSS who did nothing but play bridge. They carried no guns other than pistols, never went on a mission, did not understand anything about this war, and were ungrateful, besides. When he had turned in the faggot private who had touched him on the ass, he had expected that he would be rewarded. He was fuming when he passed by the restaurant and saw the general's pet sergeant enjoying a nice meal with a gook. It upset him so much that he stormed in.

"Sergeant, what is the meaning of this?" he shouted in rage. He almost pulled Beil out of his seat, wanting him to salute. He hated the sergeant who seemed always to be looking down on him. This smug sergeant was part of the OSS team that did not understand who were the real heroes around here, or the real enemies.

Beil felt the fingers of the captain tighten on his arm. He was about to react when Hiu spoke in French. "No, don't do anything stupid."

"Captain." Beil rose. He saluted smartly and extra-correctly, catching himself from shoving back at the captain. "For what do I have the pleasure of your company?" he said politely, grabbing for a cigarette to calm himself down. Inwardly, he was furious, hating the asshole.

"This man is a gook, a Communist." Haggard eyed Hiu, looking at his well-tailored French clothes, his wire-rimmed glasses. "Why is he sitting at the table with you, Sergeant?"

"This man is my friend. He is a colonel in the army of the liberation of Vietnam." Beil continued in his best Ivy League accent just to infuriate Haggard. "May I introduce you to Colonel Hiu?"

Hiu offered his hand, but the captain refused it.

"That's the army of the Vietcong, run by the Communist Ho Chi Minh. Don't you understand, Communism is our real enemy. I won't shake his hand and you'd better have a good reason for meeting with him." Haggard stopped short of ordering Beil to leave, knowing that he must have been sent by the general. Power was the one thing that Haggard respected. He then turned and walked out.

"Quite a boorish man," Hiu said in his upper-class accented English. Then turning to French, he loudly cursed the bastard out. Switching back to English, he continued. "French is a good language to curse in. The words are so colorful."

"Yes I'm afraid no one taught this fellow manners. Nobody can stand him and the general says that if it weren't for his great flying ability, he would be long gone. He's a legend around here, most kills by a tiger."

14

It was later that same evening. The major and captain had just made the slam. It had been an exciting game where the outcome was not known until the final two tricks. Beil and the general had each kept the high heart but had been tricked when the major led the low spade from the dummy, which he took from his hand and then led back the two of spades. The general threw the jack and Beil slammed his card down in frustration.

"Great game, major. Beil, get us a round of drinks." After they had lit their smokes, the conversation turned to strategy as Beil gave them a detailed briefing of his encounter with Hiu and Haggard.

"I am afraid Captain Haggard has a profound hatred for the Vietnamese, even the Chinese," said the major. "Whenever he sees an American with one, his hair bristles."

"That's because Haggard hates Communists and he sees them as the enemy."

"He's right. And he's not alone. A lot of Americans think the Communists will be a bigger problem once this war is finished," lamented the general.

"It is attitudes like his that will ruin us all. Ruin all of South-East Asia for fifty years. If those attitudes win out, we'll have to play the hand of picking the wrong side." Major Dewey shook his head. "The fear of Communism and the fight to stop the spread of it will cloud everything."

"But Haggard is particularly violent," commented Captain Moss. "Some of the flyboys say he takes particular delight in machine-gunning the Jap pilots when they eject. I mean to kill for pleasure is not the same as killing for war."

"He does love killing," said the major.

"He is like a machine, like a dog machine. You get that kind of bloodlust and right and wrong just disappear. You hide behind ideas like democracy and Communism and violently kill for it."

"I would not want to be on his bad side," said Beil.

"We are already on his bad side." The general smiled.

"What do you think makes him tick?" Beil asked, still upset with the encounter with Hiu—not just Haggard's anger, but Hiu's as well. Too much passion in both of them. It was like bad fuel. "Why was he so vile to Hiu?"

"I think he knows he's Ho Chi Minh's man. And he thinks Ho, Mao, all these men are Communists hell-bent on taking over the world," explained Major Dewey.

"Well, he'd be right about that," the general said. "The new Intel is that Ho

Chi Minh has teamed up with known Communists—with Mao. I even hear some Russian advisers are with them."

"Hiu said the Chinese have been the Vietnamese's mortal enemy for centuries," Beil told them.

The general shrugged. "How ironic would it be if our actions made them allies?"

"In some ways the Japanese drove them together, forced them to put everything on hold until the end of the war. But then all truces will break apart. America will have to choose," predicted Dewey.

"How about Ho? Whom will he choose?" Beil asked, thinking of Hiu.

"It will depend on our actions, if we support him or not."

"If it's not us, it's the Communists, yes," said the general.

"Is he a Communist?" Beil took a drag from his cigarette.

"No. Mao yes, but not this Ho Chi Minh—not yet. He's for Vietnam, not for Communism," the major continued. "But he will use them, if he can't use us."

"That's what he wants?" asked Beil.

"Yes, but he's a Nationalist. The nationalists don't like the French, or Japanese or anyone that stands in their way. They are sort of like marching ants. They will turn against us, too, if they have to," Major Dewey lamented.

"Yes, this is war," the general added solemnly. "It makes for strange bed-fellows and strange alliances. Let's see what we can do to help our friend, Mr. Hiu."

15

My father was a life-long Republican who hated Communism. He thought it was an evil, was wrong. Why would you have a system where no one was allowed to make a profit?

Nevertheless, he always had a soft spot for Ho Chi Minh. He would often say that we had confused Communism with nationalism when we sided with the French. As a result, we succeeded in driving two natural enemies together. He was always quick to point out that the Chinese and Vietnamese hated each other. He would always say that America had made a mistake, that by not supporting Ho against the French we let the Communists win, and how he and others were against it at the time.

Here's how things developed: The general's decision to arm Ho Chi Minh had changed the dynamics of the war. By late 1944 Ho Chi Minh and his band of insurgents had become a leading force in the fight to drive the Japanese from South-East Asia. Only the French were furious, but they had little influence over the general's decision, having failed for so many years. The Vietnamese Nationalists were fierce fighters, succeeding beyond everyone's expectations. In the summer of 1945 the general was planning for a fall offensive when America dropped the atom bomb.

Immediately everything was thrown into chaos, especially in Kunming which was the center of it all. All the forces that had allied to fight the Japanese turned on each other, as Major Dewey had predicted. Mao Tse-tung and Chiang Kai-shek fought over China, in the vacuum left by the Japanese surrender. Ho Chi Minh and his guerrilla army asked for American help in throwing the French out of Vietnam. In addition you had the Flying Tigers, no longer occupied in fighting the Japanese. They were like pit bulls on a dog farm.

When the war ended, the general and his bridge partners had been in their office. "Let's open another bottle," he roared. They had raided the officer's club wine cellar and they were now on their fifth bottle. This one was a Chateau Margaux 1939.

"To the end of the war!" The captain raised his hand in a toast. They had been drinking ever since they got the word. They were sitting at the bridge table but they had not played a hand in over an hour.

"I'm afraid the end of the war is just the beginning," Major Dewey said.

He and Beil had been debriefing Hiu when the news of the war's end had come over the wire. The conversation had quickly changed.

"Will you help us with the French?" Hiu immediately asked.

"Of course we will," the major said. "We owe you that much at least. Of course it's not my decision, but I feel confident...." It was a glorious day. He took out his cigarette pack and passed it around.

Beil took out his Tiffany lighter and lit everyone up. "Hiu, the general thinks we should accompany you to Vietnam and look for any Americans that might be there."

"Of course. I think it would be a good idea for you to see our beautiful country and what the French have done to it."

16

It was a few weeks later. Beil and the major were in Vietnam. Beil was driving the jeep. They were lost. Instead of the general, Captain Haggard, who had flown them down, was with them.

They had been in Saigon for a few weeks, part of the OSS team which had been sent to help the French and British disarm the Japanese while searching for any downed pilots. In September, 1945, a month after the bomb, the French were very active in trying to get their colony back.

But Ho Chi Minh, who had become a national hero in the fight against the Japanese, had formed a movement of peasant workers to prevent them from taking back control. The French were quick to label him a Communist, as were the British. The work that he had done with the OSS during the war was of little importance to the French or British officials in charge.

"Indochina is no place for us to be," a disgusted Major Dewey said. Now they were off to meet up with Hiu. Everyone was in a bad mood, anxious to be at the rendezvous.

There was no question whom Dewey would support. Vietnam had made great sacrifices in their fight against the Japanese. To the major it seemed like a reasonable reward for the Vietnamese to receive their independence. It also made perfect sense. Allied with the US, Ho Chi Minh could be used as a wedge against the real Communist enemy, Russia. The major was afraid China might slip away, in which case America would need trusted friends.

"The Communists are taking over. We should kill this Ho instead of meeting with him," Haggard sputtered. He was particularly angered by this secret trip that the French and British knew nothing about. The stinking weather only added to his rage. It was so hot the sweat poured out of you. So far they had done almost nothing but waste time. He did not trust these gooks.

"These people are not Communists," the Major replied. But Haggard couldn't tell the difference. Beil kept his eyes on the road, keeping out of the conversation but listening to everything. Mostly he kept looking at Haggard in the rear-view mirror, hating him. He thought about the showers. Was the captain a homosexual? Was he? Once in Kunming, Beil had gone and bought the service of a lady from town but he did not feel the excitement that he felt with a man.

Finally they came into a small village. "Sergeant! Look over there," the major said, pointing to a group of men by the side of the road. This took Beil out of his reverie. He pulled up to them, recognizing Hiu immediately in his coolie clothes.

They got out of the jeep. "Welcome to Vietnam," Hiu said, leading them into a one-room house. "Are you hungry?" The men nodded, except for Haggard, who sneered. Hiu said something and food appeared.

"I am afraid we have no forks or other Western eating utensils. All we have is chop sticks." This was fine for everyone except Haggard. He fumbled with the sticks, aware of everyone watching him. He remembered Hiu from when they were in Kunming. He had been the bastard at the table with Beil. He had hated the uppity little guy then; he hated him now, even more now that he was dressed like a native. It reinforced his idea that these Asians were all alike. He looked over and saw everyone was having no trouble eating with the stupid sticks, especially Sergeant Beil who was eating like a native.

"Where is Ho Chi Minh?" the major asked. It had taken him and the general a long time to set this meeting up. He now wished they had left Haggard behind in Saigon. He put all of them on edge.

"Father Ho will be here soon," Hiu said. Beil guessed that Ho Chi Minh must be nearby, guessing that Hiu had met them without him in case there was a trap. You could never be too careful. The French had spies everywhere.

In time, Ho arrived, a small man with a beard. Beil studied him and made his assessment: polite, powerful presence, hard to read, just like a good bridge player. He saw in him a humble man who was kind, loyal to his people. After the introductions the major cleared the room of everyone except the two of them.

Hiu and Beil took a stroll down a path in the village, surrounded by fields of sugar cane and rice. While they were inside, there had been a sudden, brief rainstorm, but now the sun had just come out. They were by themselves. Captain Haggard had stayed outside the room with the OSS officer they had met in Saigon.

"So this is the future," Hiu said. Now that the war was over, they were looking at problems that were new and old at the same time. It was like the winter where the snow came and covered all the junk in the yard, keeping the mess out of sight, out of mind until the spring, when the snow melted. Then all the rusty things came out of hiding to turn the land ugly.

"You know if it were up to the general, he would help you kick the French out," Beil said.

"Yes, I know he thinks that. He knows the French were no good during the war. They sided with the Germans and the Japanese."

"No, that is not quite true."

"Close enough. And now they think they can have everything as it was before."

"But won't you miss the French food?" Beil said, remembering the great meals they had in the French restaurant in Kunming. There was always something you liked in what you despised.

"Well, we all have to make sacrifices. But if America throws its weight behind us, then we can smash the French."

"I hope so. But the general does not have the last say. There are people in America that think Ho Chi Minh is a Communist like Mao."

"Ho hates Mao. We Vietnamese hate the Chinese. Don't you understand?"

"I do understand. And I hope for the right outcome. But the French are doing their best to link you to the Communists," Beil said.

All of a sudden their conversation was interrupted when Haggard came up. "Sergeant, shouldn't you be guarding the jeep?" He hated the steely little man with the upper-class accent. It made his rage boil.

"We are among friends here, captain. There is no need for that," Hiu answered.

Beil added, "The Vietnamese are not the Japanese. They are our friends, who helped many pilots when they were shot down."

"No, you're wrong, sergeant. They are worse then the Japanese. I mean, look at them trying to overrun the French who helped them become civilized."

Beil saw the impassive face of Hiu turn angry, but only in the eyes. No one would have noticed it but him. It was like bridge, the knowing but not knowing. Beil was glad when the major finished his meeting.

17

A few days later they were back in Saigon at the old French embassy. "It has come to our attention that you have met with Ho Chi Minh," the British general roared. It did not matter to him that the French were fools. At least they were impotent fools, not like these Americans who thought they ran the world.

"Yes, we did," said Major Dewey. "Frankly, we all should meet him. No offence to my French friends here, but this is not their country. This country belongs to the Vietnamese, so it needs a Vietnamese solution. And Ho is a competent man. Your resistance to the Japanese was entirely ineffectual until he came in."

"You Americans are so naïve!" The French general could barely contain himself. His Gallic blood was at a boil at the not-so-subtle insult. What civilized person in his right mind would want to side with these slant-eyed natives? "You Americans don't understand! Ho is a Communist, fighting to take over the world. This is the new front."

"My French friend is right," the fat British general bellowed. "Look at how Russia came into the Eastern Theater at the end, after all the fighting was done. It was just to establish their influence in Asia. Now they are trying to ingrain themselves here."

"No! You two are wrong!" the major shouted, uncharacteristically emotional. Beil, who was recording the meeting, felt the anger and lit another cigarette. "Don't you understand? You are pushing Ho into the arms of the Communists. Indochina is going to burn!"

"You have been conniving with the enemy. You take this trip and meet with the son of bitch traitor Ho Chi Minh to undermine everything we are trying to do here!"

The French spoke in French, and the major replied in the same language. "Go to fucking hell, all of you! Do you fucking understand what's happening here? Your plan to achieve stability will turn this whole place into a battle zone." And with that Major Dewey walked out.

"Don't worry about him," Captain Haggard said after a momentary pause." He does not speak for the US. We hate Communism as much as you. Cooler heads will prevail."

Beil watched him. This whole meeting was like a card game, but in this case the cards were against them. It seemed that they were going to be trumped no matter how logical their argument. Beil thought about how one action would lead to another and that the goal you wanted to achieve would fail because of it. Haggard was less than a pawn. He had no clue, no understanding of the subtleties. Listening to him, Beil knew all the major's work was doomed. His attempt to separate Ho from the Communists was going to fail. Listening to Haggard was like playing bridge with a beginner who thought he knew it all. Beil hated him.

A few hours later all the Americans were having dinner at an elegant French restaurant in an old colonial building. Despite the sophistication, the place seemed like a prison. They watched the Vietnamese waiters move with a tension that was about to erupt. Outside they had heard gunshots.

Earlier that day, a French patrol had been ambushed and slaughtered. On the way to the restaurant, they had watched French soldiers rounding people up; tying them en masse to the lampposts. "I am afraid the meeting did not go well," the major said. Beil and the OSS captain chuckled, even though the situation was serious, especially with the ambush and the heavy-handed response. "That English idiot and the French asshole are like having the king and queen to your left holding only the jack, not to mention the wild-card Vietnamese. It is a huge mess."

They were drinking champagne, because of that the two officers forgot that Haggard was the enemy. Beil wanted them to stop talking, but it was no use. All he could do was to sit back and hope that Haggard was as out of it as the other two. Beil's only comfort was that the food, of course, was great.

"What do you want me to do?" the OSS captain said. He was new on this trip, not from this team.

"There is really nothing we can do. We can go back tomorrow. Try to convince the limey general to back us and throw out the fucking French."

"I don't trust those slant-eyes. Look at the way all these waiters are looking at us. If I was in the cockpit I would drop my bombs and wipe them all out," said Haggard.

"Do you play bridge?" The OSS captain nodded. Major Dewey looked over at Haggard.

"No, I have no time for silly little games."

Beil and the OSS captain saw the look in the major's eyes. "Well, that's too bad. You'll never know the meaning of life."

The next official meeting was two days off. The major asked Beil to meet with Hiu and give him an update as to what was happening. With all of the French spies around, it was impossible for the major to slip

39

off to another clandestine meeting. It would have to be finesse from now on. The OSS officers knew that they were not holding very good cards. Everything would have to fall into place for them to have any chance in Indochina. Beil kept remembering the major's words: "Indochina is going to burn."

18

"Edmond, this world is going crazy. No sooner do we throw out one tyrant than the other one comes back."

Hiu and Beil were in a café in Saigon, sipping coffee. "Does this really come from weasel crap?" Beil asked, to delay the conversation he knew had to take place.

"Not a weasel. It is a feral cat known as a civet cat. The coffee beans pass through its digestive system. They say the enzymes of the cat make it the richest coffee in the world."

"So the French are good for something."

Both men laughed. Then they got serious. "We are going to throw the French out whether you help us or not." Hiu's expression, narrowed in intensity, making a shiver run up Edmond's back.

"The major was afraid of that. He wishes me to say that there is very little hope the United States will support you and abandon the French."

Hiu sat for a moment in silence. Then he spoke. "Look at the French rounding up those people, chaining them to the lampposts like animals. They have no connection with the ones who ambushed their troops."

19

"Your services will no longer be necessary," the British general said quietly.

"What do you mean my services?" Major Dewey was angry. "We are not here for your benefit. We are here representing the United States of America. We aren't some weak little island or some country still living in the feudal times."

The general smiled. "Nevertheless, I am the ranking officer here, and I am asking you to leave. Yours is not the only American view. There are many here who think that your view will lead to Communism taking over the world."

"As I said before, Ho Chi Minh is not the enemy. French oppression is! How can you be so oblivious to this?" Dewey shouted. Beil was watching from the side, nervously chain-smoking, waiting anxiously. It was an abrupt exchange.

"Major, do I have to have you arrested, or will you leave immediately? Here, look at this." He displayed some grainy pictures of Ho Chi Minh next to a Chinese supply truck, talking to a Chinese officer. They could also see a man in a Russian uniform standing nearby.

"That is just the problem. You are driving them in that direction. What would you do if you were them?"

"Just today this morning a French patrol was ambushed right near here in the middle of Saigon. All their throats were slit!" the French officer shouted at Dewey.

"You deserve it, you fucking Gallic son of a bitch!"

"Are you going to go, or are you going to be arrested?" They all heard the finality in the English general's words. The military policemen at the door stood at attention.

"No I'm leaving. Remember this land is a powder keg and it is going to blow up and you will fail. The fucking worthless French will fail, and I hope America doesn't get involved in the wrong side and fail. It will be a quagmire!"

Beil saw the rage in Dewey. He saw the rage in all these faces. He was surprised when Haggard spoke. "General, you are right. Not all Americans agree with the major. I for one think it is a mistake to support this Ho. So he saved some pilots. He was well paid. I look at the arrogance of these people. They hate all of us. An iron hand is needed here. Not support. The French are right."

"Captain, stop talking," the major shouted in fury. "That is an order." And then he turned back to the French and British, and screamed at them: "This place will burn us all! Mark my words, this place will consume and burn us all." He looked at Beil. "Sergeant, go get the jeep ready. We are leaving now."

"Yes, sir," Beil said, heading outside. Waiting by the jeep was Hiu, dressed in his coolie clothes.

"Edmond, be careful. This place is very dangerous right now." Hiu looked worried, not his calm self. There was a mob forming over where the French had herded a gang of shackled prisoners. People were shouting at each other.

"We are leaving right now."

They looked over and saw the French sentries point their bayonets at the Vietnamese prisoners, forcing them to their feet. They watched as they were put up against a wall and blindfolded. The firing squad took aim. The prisoners started chanting. "Vietnam! Vietnam! Vietnam!"

The crowd surged forward, surrounding the French marksmen, picking up the chant. "Vietnam! Vietnam!" Then there was a sound of gunfire as the French soldiers executed their prisoners. The crowd moved forward. "Vietnam! Vietnam!" The French then turned their guns on the crowd.

Above them a fierce lightning-bolt exploded, followed by a clap of thunder and a violent rain. The sky turned black.

Just then Major Dewey came out of the building, followed by Captain Haggard. He was still fuming. "What's happening?" he shouted at Beil.

"The French just shot some Vietnamese," Beil said cigarette in his mouth. Next to him, Hiu hadn't said a word. Beil could see the shock on his face. Haggard saw it too, the open hatred. It made him boil. The fucking French are right, Haggard thought. Who are we kidding? These gooks are the enemy.

Then Hiu smiled at him making things worse. Then it came to Haggard. Hiu was part of what was going on, one of the leaders of the enemy, the Communists. He looked over and saw the French soldiers round up a few more of the troublemakers in the crowd and line them up against the wall. When he heard the gunfire through the pouring rain, it made something inside him snap. He felt like they were surrounded by the enemy. He turned to Hiu; again was greeted with the nervous, condescending smile of hatred. In rage he pulled out his pistol.

"Hey, you forgot this one!" Haggard shouted firing point blank into Hiu's wet face. Blood came spurting out.

"What the hell!" Beil shouted as the major slapped Haggard across the jaw. None of them saw a man running, fleeing, disappearing down the road.

"He won't be bothering us," said Haggard, touching his face. He was happy with what he'd done. The only good gook was a dead gook. But the assault on Hiu caused the mob to swing their way.

The storm had passed as quickly as it had come. "We will deal with you later, captain. Right now let's get the hell out of here," Major Dewey shouted. They left Hiu bleeding, and jumped into the jeep.

"Take the back way. Avoid this mob," the major ordered, as Beil sped around the courtyard across an open field. This road was not as developed as the main road. Soon they were in thick jungle on both sides. Just as the jeep rounded the corner, they spotted a group of Vietnamese near the road, fixing a tire. Blocking the road was a cart full of brush. The Major lost his patience and screamed out to them in French, "Get the hell out of the fucking road!"

That was when the Vietnamese opened fire. Beil had a hard time maintaining control of the jeep. He looked over into the passenger's seat seeing the major was hit and bleeding. Half his head was missing. Then the motor exploded and they coasted to a stop.

He and Captain Haggard jumped out of the jeep, and ran in the direction of the airport. Beil heard a shot, as the hat was blown off his head. Without thinking he picked up the hat, stunned to see a bullet hole through the crown. The bullet had lifted it off his head without touching him.

The French guarding the airport heard their shouts and came running. But as soon they appeared, the jungle went silent as the attackers melted back into the underbrush.

With the French soldiers, Beil went back to where Major Dewey had fallen. "Major! Major!" he called out, but Dewey's body was nowhere to be found.

Beil reached into his pocket and pulled out a cigarette. Captain Haggard came over and lit it from a book of matches. "Fucking little monkeys! But it served the major right for supporting them," Haggard shouted, his fingers shaking as he tried to hold the flame steady. "They are probably going to eat the body."

"It was your fault, captain. You and your stupidity ruined everything!"

Both of Beil's friends were dead, Hiu and Dewey. And the major's words were now prophetic. "This place will burn us all." He felt like he was watching a game of bridge where you were doomed, not by the cards but by the way that they were played.

"My fucking fault. You ignorant BASTARD. You don't know anything," sputtered Captain Haggard.

"You killed our contact, and because of that the major was killed," Beil spat back. "Everything you touch, you ruin. No wonder you don't play bridge. You have no idea of anything except killing. I'll see to it that the General knows the real truth of what happened."

"Why you faggot bastard!" Haggard shouted, and went to hit Beil, who ducked and side-stepped. Overbalanced, Haggard fell to the ground, landing in a pool of mud. He tried to get up but was restrained by the French soldiers.

20

Two weeks later and they were back in Kunming, which was starting to become like a ghost town, at least for the Americans who were leaving. Beil was with the general and captain. He had told them of the major's death and the three of them were in a local bar downing their sorrows, mourning the loss of their friend.

"To John," the general said as the all raised their shots of whiskey, John's favorite, Johnny Walker Red.

"So sad, Edmond," the captain said, feeling the pain of losing his best friend and bridge partner. The three men had not played bridge since his death. Everything was changing, including their mission which had ended.

"Yes, sad for the major. Sad that we are leaving."

"Tell us again how he died, Edmond."

Beil explained it all again to them, going over and over with it in his mind. Loathing Haggard even more after he finished, he said again, "That Haggard is a bastard."

"Well, his career is over," the general spouted. "I will make sure that he does not get past the rank of captain."

"But still as a captain he can make much trouble, trouble for all of us," Beil said, not knowing the full extent of it.

21

At the end of the war there was a rash of field promotions to honor the sacrifice and service of those members who had contributed to the American military. The China Theater was no exception. Beil himself was promoted to first sergeant. Captain Jim was now Major Jim. The general was given his fourth star while many of the pilots of the Flying Tigers were made major. The only exception was Haggard, who was not even mentioned. He was drinking heavily at the officer's bar, furious, vile. Over at the next table were a group of Tiger pilots who were celebrating.

"Haggard, come join us," one of them called out to him across the bar. Haggard's face showed his fury when he caught sight of the new major's badge, knowing this guy was not half the pilot as him: fewer kills, fewer missions, less of a man.

"How did you make major?" Haggard yelled across from the bar, putting the officers on edge from the power of his rage.

"Get Captain Haggard a whiskey," one of them shouted to the bartender, who fell over himself to get it.

Haggard slammed it down. He gestured to the bartender for another. When he finished that one he demanded another. The frightened bartender keep pouring. After the sixth or seventh shot Haggard took the shot glass and hurled it at the mirror behind the bar, shattering it. In the stunned silence he walked out to shower stall C where he forced himself on many, pounding home his rage, totally disgusted with all the fucking faggots.

Beil entered the shower room's outer door just as Haggard came stumbling out. He fell into Beil, eye to eye. "You fucking faggot sergeant going in there to get your perverted jollies, I see."

Beil tried to ignore the man, but in the close proximity that was impossible. "Good night, captain," he said as he tried to slip by. Haggard saw in this cocky sergeant everything that was wrong with the world. Just the way Beil said "captain" reminded Haggard that he was not the major he should be. Then he remembered Beil's words as they were leaving that hell-hole called Saigon. It became very clear. The little bastard had the general block him.

"It's because of you I didn't make major!" he screamed into Beil's face. "Well, I will get you. Out of my way!" he shouted as he shoved Beil aside.

An hour later, Beil was with a young lieutenant in the back of the shower when the MP busted in, catching them. "Get your clothes on, sergeant," the MP shouted. Unceremoniously Beil had his hands placed behind his back and cuffed. He was then sent to the brig along with seven or eight others.

22

The trial consisted of a military tribunal of three officers with the general presiding. Beil knew that he was going to be OK. Even though they had never spoken of it, Beil was sure that the general knew that he knew of his visits to shower stall C. He thought to himself how stupid it was to arrest him for something that most everyone knew about. If you don't want to go there, then don't. He lit another cigarette.

One of the officers was a captain from the regular army whom Beil had met only once. The other was a colonel who had just arrived from the States. Beil tried to catch the general's eye, but he could not. Very clever of the general, Beil thought, to not let anyone know that they were friends.

"Sergeant Beil," the general said after awhile. "It says that you were caught in a homosexual act which is not allowed under the sections in the military hand-book defining conduct befitting of a service man. The punishment if proven guilty is immediate dishonorable discharge from the military."

The general felt very bad inside. It was like a bridge game where you were going to go down. There was nothing that you could do but just sit back and play the cards. He would have been able to save Beil if it were not for the photos. But the MP had snapped pictures. Without the hard proof it would have been easy to confuse the witnesses; then dismiss the charges. It would have been a case of he said, he said, with all kinds of ways to paint the fog to find the grey that was needed.

The general thought to himself how hard it had been to keep his own gay life secret for his whole military career. He thought back to his last bridge partner, Sergeant Drum, whose death had been a knife in his heart. The general had known that Beil was gay for some time and on many occasions he had hinted to the sergeant about addictions, especially the importance of keeping them secret. But the problem was that it was very hard to keep this particular addiction secret, as there was always a shower or bath house on every base. It was the watering hole where all are vulnerable.

The general sighed to himself. This was going to be hard, having to ruin someone's career, someone's life. It was awful, very painful that he would have to be in charge of this hearing that now because of the pictures only had one outcome.

"Homosexuality is a sin, sergeant!" the state-side colonel shouted, startling all of them. "Against God and Jesus." The words made Beil cringe. He lit another cigarette off the last one. "You are a disgusting human not befitting an institution as great as the United States military. If it were up to me, I would throw you in the brig and throw away the key."

"Do you admit to being in the showers with these other men, engaged in a compromising act?" the general asked.

"No," Beil said, not feeling ashamed at all. Really what was the big deal? How did what he'd done affect these men in any way? How did it affect the military in any way? It didn't make him any less patriotic. It didn't make him type slower, eat less, smoke less, fight less, keep secrets less. In fact it made him better at keeping secrets.

"Very good, sergeant, will you leave the room? We will call you in when we have made our decision."

It was an hour later and Beil was still sitting in the other office. The heat of the day had permeated the room, so it was uncomfortable even with the windows wide open. The air seemed to be waiting like the rest of them. Beil was out of cigarettes and craving one. He began tapping his figures on the small table. Everything was going bad. The general would not help him. That made him feel weird, betrayed. He had assumed all would be washed aside, clouded in obscurity. The state-side colonel was like a barking dog full of hatred and God. Beil knew his hand was doomed, but part of him did not give up. There were always wild cards in the mix of life.

All of a sudden the door swung open. Beil was brought in the center of the room where the three officers were seated. The general started: "By order of the United States of America and the power vested this commission, you First Sergeant Edmond Beil have violated the military code of conduct and are hereby dishonorably discharged from the military, effective immediately."

The words hit Beil in his emotions as he struggled to hold it all in. God, how he wished he could have a cigarette. He tried to catch the general's eye, but saw that the old man had turned away. Beil felt that he had been betrayed by someone close. For the first time he hated the general, hated the military.

23

Beil was to be put on a flight the next day and flown back to the United States. He spent most of the rest of the day packing his bags, getting ready. When he was done he walked outside. Captain Haggard came running up to him.

"Serves you right, you fucking faggot. I made sure the MPs had a camera. Did you see the pictures?" Haggard screamed. "It's disgusting going to the showers. You got what you deserved!"

"Fuck you!" Beil screamed back, stunned that Haggard had alerted the MPs. Pictures—he tried to wrap his mind around it. He didn't know of the pictures until then. "Everybody knows the showers!" Beil shouted in fury.

"I'm not gay. How dare you think I am?" Haggard fired back. He hated homosexuals. But like many gay haters, he was addicted to gay sex. "Anyway, you got yours and your life is ruined!" Haggard chuckled. Beil turned to walk away, hating the fact that Haggard was right: Beil's life was now ruined. He was going back in disgrace, going back home with nothing. His anger was now directed at Haggard, not at the general who had not betrayed him—though that was of little comfort. The only good thing was that the matter was settled. The fresh air felt great on his face as he stood in the road. He lit a cigarette letting the late-afternoon hot Asian sun soak into his being. In time he was overcome by a feeling of melancholy. He was very sad that tomorrow he was going back to America.

He let his mind linger back over the last few years. In that time he had become very Asian, changed by the mysterious East, liking everything about it. It had gotten under his skin. He vowed to himself that after this mess was behind him he would come back here to live.

On the spur of the moment he decided to go to the Chinese restaurant that he had frequented so often with the general and Dewey. Poor Dewey whose life was lost, taken by the people he believed in. He went in, ordered a beer and a bowl of chow fun noodles, his favorite. He lit another cigarette letting his mind wander in and out. He thought he heard his name being called. He looked up surprised to see the general and Major Jim.

"Sergeant, we have been looking all over for you," said Jim as they sat down next to him. Beil tensed up, still feeling alone.

"Yes, Edmond. We came to say that we'll be going back with you tomorrow. Let's celebrate," the general added, not used to seeing his friend in a pensive, solemn mood.

"Celebrate?" Beil asked. Being discharged from the army was not something one would normally rejoice in.

"So how was the brig? No room service, I suppose." The way Major Jim said it made Beil laugh. He pulled out his cigarettes and offered them around.

"Sorry for making such a mess out of everything," he said, looking particularly at the general.

"It's silly that the army has such silly rules, silly that it has the policy that it does. You were a very good sergeant."

"It certainly has been a long and short three years, all the up and down, the end of the war. It's a let-down in some ways," said Major Jim.

"God, I need a game of bridge," Beil said, warmed by them coming to see him, beginning to feel better.

"Well, we'll have to wait till we get to Washington to find a fourth," the general said.

"Washington? But I live in Long Island," Beil reminded them. He was sad that he would no longer be part of this team.

"No, Edmond, you're going to Washington with us. I'm not going to let a great OSS agent, a seasoned Asia hand and most important, a great bridge player go because of some meaningless act of no concern."

"But they discharged me from the military."

"Yes, the military discharged you, but the OSS is no longer part of the military so we don't have their silly rules. You are to be part of our new agency, which the president says will be separate from the Department of Defense. We even have a new name."

"Oh, what's that?" Beil asked.

"CIA."

"CIA?"

"Yes, the Central Intelligence Agency."

So under these strange circumstances my father's next life was about to begin. Of course in keeping with my father's history of secrets, I did not know of his discharge until after his death, when my sister and I tried to get his military records.

At first they said there had been a fire and all his records had been destroyed. But finally after much pestering we were sent a letter that he had been dishonorably discharged for being caught in a homosexual act. When I called for details, the person on the phone said it was known then as being disagreeably discharged.

He hadn't done anything treasonous, or anything against America, or anything that was unpatriotic, nor did he do anything wrong except to have a private life, which our constitution is supposed to protect. This is still happening even today in this 21st century world. This homophobic insanity changes lives now as it changed his life then. It ended my father Edmond Beil's regular military career but started his next life, which is where this novel really begins.

24

It was now two years after the war. Beil and the general had been busy trying to formulate an Asian policy to stop the spread of Communism. This decision had been forced on them by Stalin's territory grab in Europe and by Mao's rise in China.

One of the unfortunate side effects of this newly named cold war against the Russians was the United States' decision to side with the French in Vietnam and abandon Ho Chi Minh. The general and Beil had argued in vain against what they thought was a grave mistake, but they were overridden by others inside the agency who saw Ho as a tool of China, which most people in the CIA thought was already lost.

In the two years since end of the war, Ho and the Vietminh army were on the move. Covert CIA operators had spotted Russian advisers among them. Aerial surveillance had uncovered a series of supply lines from China. This led many in the State Department to fear that this nationalist movement now draped in Communism would affect all of South-East Asia. Already places like Malaysia and Indonesia were seeing the rise of local strongmen who were looking to overthrow their colonial oppressors. In all of these countries were Communist movements that if left unchecked would spread like a cancer. America was scrambling to counter what it perceived as the Soviet march to take over the world.

"Edmond," the general said as they were ending work for the day. "I need you to go to Indonesia. As you know, there is this strongman named Sukarno who is about to overthrow the Dutch. I want you to go down there and live for a while. See what is happening down there and then we will figure out our best course."

Since the Japanese defeat, Indonesia had been a mess. There were various factions vying for power: the Dutch colonial government, the Dutch puppets, the PKI Communists, and Sukarno. Unlike the French, the Dutch knew that independence was going to happen and they were only trying to negotiate a smooth transition, one that would keep their interests intact.

"Yes sir. It looks like Vietnam all over again."

"Better than Vietnam because we have no French to deal with. No one is siding with the Dutch, so everything is possible. Most important are the new oil fields that we want to control. But the best part is this Sukarno and his allies have managed to defeat the PKI. We think that they will be a huge assistance in the fight against Communism."

Before that the United States had been suspicious of Sukarno, who was taking money from everybody, including the Soviet Union. But now with the crushing defeat of the Communists, the United States started to view him as an ally in this new type of war, a war that was being run without huge armies but rather with small band of agents like Beil.

"That gives us a chance to not confuse nationalism with Communism, as we have in Vietnam. Ho is going to defeat the French at some point, and we will lose the country to the Communists."

"Edmond—it will be worse than that in Indonesia, if we are not careful."

"What do you want me to do, sir?"

"I want you to enroll in Indonesian lessons right away. Here," the general said. "I have a new job for you. They have agreed to let you use their cover."

Beil looked at the pamphlet. It was a brochure for the Standard Oil Company of New Jersey.

"I know nothing about the oil business. What will I be doing there?"

"Oh, I imagine playing bridge in both real life and political life, finesse and all that. But first you will spent three months learning the oil business by going to work in the New York office. Then on to Indonesia, where you will be in charge of the operation."

25

Beil arrived for work in New York City dressed in a new suit and jacket, which made him look very smart and handsome. It had been a while since he had been in the city and he was invigorated by the hustle and pace. It was most evident on the street where the faceless crowds had an extra jump to their stride, conveying a new-found optimism that permeated the whole city now that the war was over. It was very contagious. Beil felt grand as he pushed through the revolving door and entered the building. He took the elevator to the top floor. There he found his way to the office of the director, Mr. Brogan. He approached the secretary who was seated at the desk right outside of the door.

"Hello, Edmond Beil to see Mr. Brogan," he said, catching a look at the secretary, thinking she looked familiar. She was very pretty in an unusual type of a way—skinny, conservatively well-dressed. Her hair was cut shoulder-length, parted on the side, which was the style. But the one thing that really stood out was the grey streak in the front of her hair. For Beil it was like deja-vu. She was so familiar. Fascinated, he watched her every move as she spoke into the intercom.

"A Mister Beil to see you, sir.... Yes, sir." She turned to Beil. Their eyes locked and they smiled awkwardly. Still looking at him, she spoke. "Mr. Brogan will see you now."

Agnes 'Aggie' Braun had been Mr. Brogan's secretary for three years, but it seemed to her like forever. She had not yet gotten over the death of her fiancé, and at age twenty-seven she thought that she would end up an old maid. It was not that she did not have suitors. But none of them could stand up to her Henry, who had died in Normandy.

After about an hour Beil came out of the office and saw Aggie typing away. He was going to go right out the door and not interrupt her but at the last moment he came over to her desk.

"Have you worked here long?"

"Since 1944," she answered, not interrupting her typing. "Sorry," she said. "I have to get this letter out right away."

"Oh, I won't bother you. Have a good day," he said as he left the room.

After he left Mr. Brogan came out. "Mr. Beil made a point of asking your name."

"Oh," Agnes said, all of sudden stopping her typing.

26

It was a month later. The general and his wife were up in New York staying at the Plaza and gave Beil a ring at the office.

"Edmond."

"General, you made it."

"Yes, dinner at the Oak Room; then bridge upstairs. Bring a date, and I don't mean a man."

"I'll try, sir."

"Don't try, Edmond. Do."

Beil hung up the phone to think about what the general had said. Then he called his mother and afterwards his two cousins. All were busy. On a whim, he walked out of his office and into Mr. Brogan's.

"Mr. Brogan is not here."

"I'm not here to see him. I'm here to see you, Miss Brown."

"Agnes Braun."

"Miss Braun. Sorry. I have a question for you."

"What's that?"

"Do you play bridge?"

"I love bridge. It's my favorite game," she said as her eyes lit up.

"Well then," Beil said. "My friend from Washington is up for the week, and I am going to have dinner with him tonight and then bridge. Would you like to come?" Beil looked her in the eyes, seeing very deep. They were very green, like emeralds.

27

Dinner was over and the four of them were sitting around the bridge table at the general's suite. Beil was playing with Aggie and the general was partnered with his wife Anne.

"So Miss Braun…"

"Call me Agnes. Or better yet my friends call me Aggie."

"Aggie, tells us about yourself," continued the general. They had just finished the first rubber and were sitting back enjoying smokes and cigars. The general's wife was smoking menthol.

"Here, try these. They're very good for you, especially if you have a cold. My doctor recommends them for this cold I just can't seem to quit."

"Thanks. Nothing really special. I grew up in Queens, went to school at William Smith College during the war. Met a wonderful man from Hobart. That's the men's school. We got engaged, and then he went away to the war and that was the last I heard from him."

"He just never came back?" Beil asked.

"No, he got killed at Normandy." Aggie started to tear up, but quickly recovered, but not before Beil saw something inside her.

"Whose turn is it to deal?" the general asked, anxious to get back to the game.

"Two no trump," Agnes said a moment later, sitting with a very strong hand. The general passed. Beil was impressed by the mandatory bid. He was holding only nine points but most of them were in spades, which he had six of. Having watched Agnes play, he realized that she was very conservative and that her two no trump bid would be an almost three no trump bid. His prudent bid would have been four no trump and let her decide, but he thought he would gamble and throw her into the game.

"Six no trump," he said, knowing he had overbid the hand, but wanting to see how this Miss Braun would play it.

"Pass," the general said. Agnes thought about what to do, whether to go for the big slam or leave it at the small slam. She studied

56

Beil, his eyes giving her nothing. She watched as he took another drag of the cigarette. She was not a gambler.

"Pass," she said. The general led a club. Beil put the dummy hand down and Agnes was very surprised to see only nine points. Beil saw it when her brow curled; most people would have missed it. She played a low club, trying to decide how to use his spades. She only had two but now was glad she had not pressed the full slam, as they did not have the king. One sure loser. She was also concerned with Beil's lack of clubs. He only had two and she had three of which only two, the ace and king were sure winners. She was very happy when the general's wife played the eight and she was able to take the trick with the ten.

Beil smiled to himself at her luck. He kept looking at her, liking her very much, perhaps even smitten. She reminded him of his younger cousin, somewhat reserved and timid—no, not timid, but passive, in a strong way. He was happy when she played the nine of spades and the general put down the six. Then she had to make a decision as what to play. She knew that besides the ace, the ten was out there but she went with luck and did not cover it but played the eight. She let out a small sigh when the general wife played the seven. All knew the slam was hers.

"Jolly good playing," the general said as the rubber ended. "Let's end the night with some champagne."

"Champagne!" Agnes exclaimed, somewhat out of character, emboldened from the rush of the slam. "That's my favorite. It makes me very bubbly."

"Then champagne it is," the general jubilantly confirmed.

"Yes! Yes!" they all agreed. Room service brought it up and the four of them took their glasses. "To health and wealth," the general said. As Beil and Agnes touched glasses, totally out of character she winked at him.

28

That night Beil had dreams again of giant penises and vaginas. In the dream a woman with a streak of grey in her hair came up to him. "Yes, darling, you can like both boys and girls. I will never tell," she said. Then the dream faded to being with his cousin.

"She is one of us," Nellie said as the three of them again found themselves in bed.

"Maybe you should think of yourself as the Kwan Yin, both male and female," the general said, walking into the room.

"Yes, darling," the woman with the grey streak in her hair said as she took his hand and led him away from the giant penises and into the giant vagina. "Here, have some champagne. It makes us all bubbly and different."

Then the dream changed to Asia, but not the Asia of China—more like Vietnam, lush, mysterious, inviting. He went down a path and came to a spring that turned into a river and then into an airplane where they were serving champagne.

"To health and wealth," the handsome, well-dressed steward said, winking at Beil who was surprised to find himself sitting next to the woman with the grey in her hair.

29

It was a few months later and Beil was with the general in Washington. The whole office was in turmoil. China was going to fall to the Communists, and there was nothing that could be done to prevent it.

"We backed the wrong horse," the general said, not his usually chipper self. "And it is going to have huge repercussions. Perhaps the domino effect that we were trying to prevent will come true. Mao is set to take power, and you know those Russkies. They want the world."

"I thought we wanted the world, too," Beil said. He thought about Major Dewey, Ho Chi Minh, and all the futile effort that goes into propping up the wrong person. "I hope we don't make the same mistakes."

"No, we are the CIA. We don't make mistakes. We try and fix the mistakes. That's why I called you here today. How is your Indonesian?"

"Bagus—good."

"Then it is time for you to go there. We now have your cover in place. The Agency wants you to go there and ingrate yourself with this Sukarno and his people. Find someone close to him. Establish a relationship."

"Yes, sir," Beil said. From Dewey he had moved on to thinking about his friend Hiu and the conversations he would have with him. How useful that friendship would be now. "This time I hope we will not confuse Nationalism with Communism."

"I hope not either. Our future relies on it," the General sighed. "There is one other thing, though, Edmond.

"What's that, sir?"

"It's time you thought about getting married."

"Married, sir? But you know my history."

"Yes, not so dissimilar to mine." The general knew that Beil knew about his secret, though he had never mentioned the subject. "How about this Miss Braun? The two of you seemed to get on pretty well."

"Yes, I do like her. We have played bridge a few times since you were up. She's a good player," Beil said, finding it strange the general would want to talk about this. He had found himself thinking more and more about Agnes, though he had not even tried to kiss her.

"I would like you to go to Indonesia as soon as possible and try to capitalize on this rift between Sukarno and the PKI before they try and close it."

"What about the Dutch? Won't they make a play for control?"

"Maybe they will, but they know they're finished. The President knows it too. We have learned our lesson with the French, I hope."

And so Beil got ready to make the move in a couple of months. He had to go back to New York and get his cover work assignment that only Brogan knew about. Everyone else in the company would think that his new job was the Director of Public Relations between the Indonesian government and Standard Oil.

30

That night Beil had another of his confusing dreams. This time he was riding a large horse with wings, only he was sitting in a cabin inside the horse, like inside a Trojan horse. He was sipping a glass of champagne and he was sitting in a seat that looked like a vagina with two penises as arms. Next to him was the woman with the grey patch in her hair.

"So, darling," the woman said, bringing her glass to her face. She was sitting next to him, but was in a chair that looked like a normal chair. "To us and to you for picking the grey and not going to the white."

"The grey not going for the white?" Beil said as the dream changed and he was now in the jungle. Around a big table were men that looked like Captain Haggard and his old friend Major Dewey.

"You have to choose one of us," they both said in union, arms around each other.

"Well, that is easy," Beil said.

"Don't be so sure."

"Oh, I am sure." But then they changed and Dewey became Haggard. They got up and sang a song, only just as they were about to jump on the table the woman with the streak in her hair appeared out of nowhere and pushed them both out of the dream. She had two champagne glasses in her hand.

"Here, darling. Remember, champagne makes me bubbly," she said, handing him the glass.

He woke up very confused.

31

Edmond and Agnes went out to dinner at the "21" Club. There was a silver bucket with a chilled bottle of champagne. Beil was in black tie, his hair slicked back. Aggie had on a simple evening gown of light chiffon with a corsage of frangipani.

"To what do I owe this great celebration?" Beil had just gotten back from Washington and had called her to say that he would pick here up and take her somewhere special. She had never imagined it would be "21." She was a frugal person. Just the price of the meal was a month's pay.

"Oh, I have something in mind," Beil said, fingering the ring in his pocket. He took out his cigarette pack and offered her one and then took out his lighter and lit them both. "Among other things, we are here to celebrate my promotion."

"Promotion?" For the last few months Aggie had looked forward to seeing Edmond, hoping he would ask her out on a real date instead of just bridge. She already knew how great a player he was. But she had started thinking about him more and more, seeing the little dimple in his face. He was such a handsome man.

"Yes, I am to be head of StanVac Indonesia focusing on public relations between the company and the Indonesian government."

"Oh, that's wonderful," she said.

"Yes, I'll be moving there next month," Beil said, looking at Aggie's face turn sad, even though she tried to mask her feelings. But Beil saw the disappointment. He saw her, saw into her, saw a slight tear well up in her.

"Then let's have a toast!" She forced a joviality she did not feel. Even though she did not know everything about this man, she felt that she could spend the rest of her life with him. He was kind, handsome smart, well dressed, and could cook. He loved flowers. The only thing was, he was a little secretive and shy. In all their time together he had not tried to kiss her. And now he was leaving. She flashed on the face of her fiancé the day he left for the war, the same look she now saw on Beil. She felt a foreboding well up in her. "To you Edmond, my darling," she said as their glasses touched.

Edmond flashed to his dream, the woman with the grey in her hair. Again he had a sense of deja-vu.

"I have another matter that I hope is a celebration also," he said as if in a dream. He took out the little box and gave it to her.

"What's this?"

"Will you marry me?" The words came out like music, and Aggie looked into Beil's eyes.

"Yes," she said, happy for really the first time since Tim's death.

"Great," Beil said, beaming. He poured more champagne. "To us." They touched glasses. "Great! It will make going to Indonesia easier knowing you are back home waiting. I will be leaving in two months; we can plan for our wedding when I get back after a year."

"After a year?"

"Yes, I'll go for a year and then I'll come…." Seeing the frown on Aggie's face, he stopped.

"No, that will not do. I am not going to wait again." Tim had said the exact same words to her, and now she was afraid she was doomed again; that she would really turn into an old maid. "No," she said. "No if I have to wait but yes if I come with you."

"But we don't know what it is like out there in that land. They are in the middle of a revolution and who knows how stable it is."

"I guess we will find out, darling," Aggie said, and she leaned in and their lips touched. Beil enjoyed it. It was a different type of passion than with men. He filled the glasses again.

"To us and to our new adventure half way around the world."

So this was the story I was told as a child, how my father proposed and how he wanted to go to Indonesia and make his fortune and then come back and get my mother in a year or two. But she told him she would not wait and wait she did not. They were married a month later and then instead of going on a honeymoon they boarded a DC 6 and flew to Indonesia first class. Finally after thirty-six hours they touched down at Jakarta airport, married and exhausted.

My mother at this time did not know of his secret lives, thinking he was just working for the oil company and also not knowing of his love of men. It was the type of thing that was the norm for gay men at the time. They got married, had children and had their secret lives. Nothing at this point was out of the closet. Everything was normal on the surface, but there were currents underneath that could not be revealed, just like in the bridge game that both of them loved. Each was playing their hand. My mother was just glad not to be an old maid, and my father had his cover. It was just like his other fronts, but sometimes a front can become the back, and the back can become the front, as the wave of life sometime changes everything. So in January 1949, Edmond and Agnes Beil began their life in the tropics.

32

"You must be Mr. and Mrs. Beil," the hunched man said, motioning for a couple of natives to take their bags. It was eight in the morning.

"Yes. I'm Edmond this is my wife Agnes," Beil said, taking out his cigarette pack and offering one. Agnes pulled out her pack of menthols.

"I'm Donald Finn, the plant manager." Don had been in Indonesia for a couple of years here in Sumatra, mostly in Palembang. "Our compound is on the other side of the river that divides Palembang from Sungaigerong. We don't have anybody like you. No one here really talks to any of these Indonesians other than business, so we keep pretty much to ourselves. I will tell you one thing from my dealings with them is that they are crooks, always wanting some payout."

As they were talking they reached two cars. "Mr. Beil, this is your car and driver. He'll be always at your call. He will take you and the Mrs. back to the compound while I go to work. Don't forget cocktails at five at the club. The driver speaks English." And with that Donald got into his car and took off.

"Apakabar—how are you?" Beil said in Bahasa, surprising the driver who answered in the same language.

"Bagus, tuan." The man smiled through his teeth, revealing the wide gap between them. "Apa Umar—I am you driver, Umar," he continued, still speaking in Bahasa to see if the new American had simply memorized a greeting, or whether he spoke the language for real. Beil asked a few more questions in Indonesian, and Umar realized that this was not the usual American from a place called Texas in the land called Marlboro.

"What's he saying, Edmond?" Agnes asked, but before Beil could answer Umar switched to English "He's asking me all sorts of questions about Indonesia. Do you have any questions, madam? My name is Umar." And then turning to Beil: "Let us speak in English from now on so the madam can understand."

They wound their way through the city, following the river that was surrounded by shacks built over the water. Children were everywhere on the riverbanks, laughing and playing in and out of the water. The road itself was full of overloaded trucks that belched black smoke. Both sides of the street were full of vendors setting up their booths in the hot sun. The heat brought back the same feelings Beil had when he had come to China years before.

They soon left the city traveling on a rural road where the rice fields were flooded with water. "What's that, Edmond?" Agnes asked.

"Oh, that's papaya!" he answered excitedly as they drove by a little wooden hut with fruit hanging outside. "Umar, stop here and buy Mrs. Beil some fruit."

"Yes, tuan," Umar said and got a huge basket of fruit of which Agnes recognized only the oranges and the bananas. There was one small red fruit that was all prickly outside. "Here, madam," Umar said, breaking it apart and handing it to Agnes. She took the fruit from his hands. It tasted just like a big ripe grape, nice and juicy.

"It's called a rambutan," Umar said as they left the fields to drive deeper and deeper into the thick encroaching jungle, hacked back from the road. It seemed as if they were going to be swallowed by the wilderness when all of a sudden they came upon a clear-cut swath of jungle and one of those developments that was much the rage in post-war New York. The clearing consisted of a single street and ten neatly-placed one-story tract houses on each side. They approached a front gate where they were met by a servant who opened it and waved them through. The whole compound was surrounded by an outer fence of barbed wire.

It was very strange to have such a thick jungle and then this little suburban street that looked like home, complete was manicured lawns and flowers. At the end of the compound was a big structure that housed the electrical generator needed to power the compound, especially the air-conditioners that most westerners could not live without.

"Your house is this one, Number 15," Umar said as they drove in the driveway to the carport. When they got there they saw a line of people all waiting for them by the front door.

"Welcome tuan and madam," an older man said, struggling to pronounce the painfully-rehearsed words. His relief was evident on his gnarled old face when Beil answered him in Indonesian.

"Selamat—welcome, my name is Seam and I am the head cook," the man said, his face changing to the wonderment of a child, full of joy that Allah had blessed them with a tuan who could speak their language. Seam's only foreign tongue was Dutch, because he had spent the last 15 years, before and after the war, with a Dutch family that had been forced to flee the independence fighting. He had gotten this job from his wife's brother, the head servant of the Finn household. Cheerfully he continued: "Let me introduce the rest of your staff." Beside himself there was the assistant cook, a cleaning woman, a laundry woman, a houseboy and a gardener. There were enough servants to run large palace, let alone a small ranch house. With a huge grin, the houseboy, a lad of about ten, opened the front door and motioned Beil and Agnes inside. The space was immaculately clean. Not a thing was out of place.

"Are these servants just for us, Edmond?" Agnes asked. Never had she seen such luxury. Everything was perfect as if it was a spread in a fancy magazine. "It must cost a lot," she said, hesitantly.

33

Umar checked the rear view mirror for any sign that he was being followed. Dusk was descending over the steaming river port of Palembang. He parked the Standard-Oil company car at its official spot in the parking garage and headed for the train station. He boarded a train for one stop, then got out, again looking over his shoulder. He hopped on another train that took him back to the same station he had left from, quickly darting into the darkness.

A few streets later he was by the river, walking by the slum houses that lined it. The area smelled of rotting fish at low tide. The river was full of garbage and broken boats. Finally he spotted what he was looking for, a white cloth tied to a tree, which signaled that the safe house was five houses away. For extra caution he walked by it and then circled back. Finally, he knocked the secret password. Quickly the door opened and he slipped inside.

There were blankets over the windows. No light escaped. The room was lit by a single oil lamp that reflected on the faces around the table.

"What do we do now?" someone was saying, the desperation evident in his voice. They had all been in hiding since September and their once mighty movement was in disarray. Just six months ago they had been close to taking power after their supreme leader, Musso, had triumphantly returned after twelve years in the Soviet Union. He had been ready to establish the PKI dream of a Communist state.

Believing they had the people on their side, they sought to force the moment by taking control of Medan in an attempted coup, killing the pro-government officers and waited for the masses to rise to their side.

Immediately the dog Sukarno had denounced the Medan coup ordering the army to launch a counter offensive to take back the city. Fierce fighting erupted and the PKI rebellion was put down when the masses they were counting on sided with Sukarno. A month later Musso was captured, then murdered, supposedly shot to death while trying to escape. Since then PKI members were being rounded up and slaughtered by Sukarno. All in all thirty-six thousand members had been killed and those who were left had gone underground to hide.

"We begin from the beginning and rebuild. We are still the voice of the people!" As he spoke, Umar thought about his new job as a driver for some American rich capitalist who spoke Bahasa.

Umar was thirty years old. He had grown up in Jakarta, fourth son in a large Muslim family, although he personally did not believe in God. He had caught the eye of a Dutch missionary when he was just six and was sent to a special Dutch school where he learned English among other languages. He started reading books at an early age and by the time he was fifteen he was devouring the writing of Karl Marx and Lenin. He believed in a classless society where everybody had the same chance. He joined the PKI to fight a guerrilla war against the Japanese. When that war ended he aligned himself with the new republic as a way for the PKI to take power.

The movement was making a strong advance in both the cities and rural areas and it seemed that with a little nudging that they would take power. Umar thought, they all thought they were so close to victory that they could taste it. But things never work out in war the way one thinks they will. All of them were blindsided when their revolt was crushed. Now they were all fugitives, hunted like dogs. Umar knew he had been lucky to find this job as driver for the new American oilman. Even though it was still a risk for him to go home every night to his house in the village, at least he was safe during the day. He thought it was ironic that a Communist like him was hiding out in the sanctuary of the oil company.

34

Beil soon discovered that the downside of his cover was the amount of company-related work that needed to be done daily. There were work orders and memos that kept piling up. He could not even identify the problems he was now in charge of; he had no idea about the oil business. At first he had put hope in Donald Finn, but quickly found out that the man was incompetent, unable to do much except to follow the simplest of orders.

It took Beil almost two weeks to find the perfect person to be his assistant. The man was Carl Dremmer, but the only problem with Carl was that he did not have the proper schooling to rise on his own.

Carl waited in the outer office, wondering why he had been sent for by the new boss. He tried to think of what he might have done, knowing from experience that to be summoned out of the blue was not a good sign. He had not spoken more than a few words to this new boss who seemed to always be watching. He was not usually a nervous fellow, but now he felt like a school child when the secretary called him in to Beil's office.

"It says here you're from Texas," Beil said, though the man didn't look like he was from Texas at all. He was not larger than life. He was only 5' 4" and had a Brooklyn accent.

"Yes sir, grew up in Houston." Carl had been here for three years. He knew everything there was to know about the oil business. He could almost smell the oil in the ground. He had worked at a rigger, a warehouse man, and now as chief supply man for the Indonesian fields.

"Why do you sound like you are from Brooklyn?" Beil asked matter-of-factly, pulling out his cigarette pack and offering Carl one.

"My mother, sir."

"Call me Edmond."

"My mother was from Coney Island, all her life, born and raised. And then she met my father who was a driller in Texas. It was love at first sight so she moved down there and brought her mother and father, both of whom I spent lots of time with—I guess the accent just rubbed off on me." Carl liked this new guy, even though he knew nothing about the oil business. Yet he was not a bumbling fool like Donald Finn who was worthless yet somehow the manager. Carl always thought how stupid it was to have someone in a white shirt in charge, someone who had no experience in running anything but his mouth. People like himself were so much more qualified, but lacked the right pedigree. Carl had never finished high school, never been to college and therefore was relegated to being what in the military would be an enlisted guy who knew everything but had no power.

"I'm promoting you too senior vice-president. From now on you will be in charge of running the oil side of this company."

"What did you say?"

"From now on you will be in charge of the day to day operations of the oil side of the business."

"Yes sir, I mean yes, Edmond!" Carl started to beam and then caught himself. "Did you run this by Donald?"

"No, but I don't have to. I'm in charge. From now on he will answer to you."

"Very good—now we can get some things done around here." Carl pumped Beil hand to show his appreciation.

"One last thing." Beil saw the guarded look come back into Carl's eyes. "I hear from Agnes that you and your wife play bridge."

The guard came back down. "Yes, we both love the game. My grandfather taught me."

35

Oil was first discovered in Indonesia in the 1890s. By 1920 Standard Oil, Dutch Shell, and others were all eagerly rushing to exploit the fields for their profit. The Japanese understood their importance and were quick to capture the oil fields of Sumatra during the war. Everybody seemed to benefit from the oil except the Indonesians.

After the war, the new Republic of Indonesia, vying for independence took over some of the Shell oil fields. The new director of operations was Nasul Rockman. He was thirty-seven and had been a major in the army that had fought against the Dutch. Now in the consolidation of power he was asked by others in the military to take over this very important operation. Part of his job was to closely monitor Standard Oil, spy on it. Today he was to be meeting the new head, a Mr. Beil.

"This is Nasul Rockman," said Donald Finn as he showed the man into Beil's office. Beil had dressed for the occasion in a suit, and was surprised that Rockman was dressed just as formally, with Italian shoes and a starched crisp white shirt.

With a nod of his head, Beil sent Finn away. "Good to meet you, Mr. Rockman," he said as he extended his hand, feeling the firm grip, military grip that Beil recognized from his time in the army. Because Rockman was in a suit, Beil changed his planned strategy. He decided not to bother with any boring etiquette, instead go right to the point, to try and put this Rockman on guard. He knew much is learned from body language, even more than words.

"So Mr. Rockman, where do you see your company in ten years?" Beil watched Rockman's brows and cheeks, glad that his question had startled this man, who had presumed that the meeting was just a formality.

"That is an interesting question," Nasul said, stalling for time. He could not tell the truth about what he wanted: all foreign dogs out of Indonesian oil. That was not possible. Their technical expertise was still needed. After a while he answered, "Ten more years of glorious partnership with Standard Oil!" His English fluent, though with a strong accent.

"Would you like a drink?" Beil asked, quickly changing the subject.

"Yes, please." Rockman needed one to calm himself. He was very conscious of this dangerous new American with the probing eyes, so unlike the bumbling idiot Mr. Finn. He was glad they were alone. If there had been an Indonesian, around he would have refused Beil's offer because Muslims were forbidden to drink. But he had seen the bar as he had walked in. He was surprised when Beil ordered into the intercom and a male servant came in carrying a tray with their drinks. After a while Beil came to the real point of the meeting.

"I would like you to pass a message on to Sukarno."

"I do not know if I will be able to do that. I am just the director of the oil company."

"I would imagine that makes you very powerful. If you are not able to do as I say, then you are not the man that I was told about." Beil changed to Indonesian: "We would like to hear the views of the new government. We here at the oil company feel that it is just a matter of time before you have complete independence and we want to be with you when that happens. We have a very close relationship with our own government and I am told privately that we will help you succeed. Perhaps we could arrange some help, very discreet help." Beil let the words linger. In the ensuing silence, both of them took sips at the same time. Finally Rockman spoke.

"Mr. Beil, I shall call on you next month."

36

Agnes was at lunch in her honor at the house of Dottie Finn. It was only one in the afternoon and the champagne was flowing like water. She was seated at the table, which had been decorated like it was a birthday. There were balloons everywhere and flowers like Agnes had never seen. Three servants were waiting on their every whim.

"Are your parties always like this?" Agnes asked. The champagne had gone to her head.

"Of course. There's not much to do here, no mail, no shopping. No house work." Agnes could hear the frustration in Dottie's voice.

"Dottie grew up on shopping," Sally Dremmer said. "There is no Bloomingdales here. Only the local markets. You have to go to Singapore before there is any real shopping, so all we do is have lunch and drink." Sally was a dark-haired Italian, very pretty.

"There is nothing to do here. We are like in prison surrounded by the jungle. I hate this place. I just hope for the day that Donald gets a transfer." Dottie was almost about to cry.

"Yes, the men at least they have work to go to. But all we have is each other," said Sally.

Agnes sipped her champagne. "There must be something you could do—a hobby, maybe get into the local culture? I mean this is a new country with many exotic things like the fruit I had the other day. What did they call them, 'rubattans?'"

"Rambutans, they are great. Have you had the purple fruit they call mangosteen?"

"No."

"Talner," Dottie yelled out. "Go get us some mangosteens." The servant hurried away. Another poured more champagne.

"Better pace yourself," Sally said as Agnes drank the glass in three sips. "We have dinner at my house after the men get back."

"Dinner?"

"Yes, get used to it. That is what we do. Have lunch drinks, have dinner drinks and then drinks again at night. It's like a full-time job."

37

Richal Abdullah got up from his mat after completing his morning prayers. It was still very early and the roosters where just starting to wake the non-believers. He had always assumed that once the great new Republic of Indonesia threw off the yoke of the infidel Dutch, all would embrace the true teaching of Islam. It infuriated him that Sukarno was embracing just the opposite and forming a secular society where true believers were being treated worse than pigs.

He felt the rage well up inside him, deep from the bottom of his toes. The hatred flowed like a river, gathered strength to possess him. How dare the republic water down the great teaching of the great profit Muhammad? It was so disrespectful. The mosque that should be full of worshipers was almost empty, with only a handful of true believers scattered about.

His blood was now racing like wild rapids about to boil. He thought of the corrupt Muslim brother in the silly western clothes who had taken a drink with the newly-arrived American dog. It made him feel defiled, dirty that he had to serve both of them. He was especially enraged by the mocking smirk on the well-dressed Indonesian's face. If that was the future, well then he would be glad to be martyred to prevent it from happening.

"Brother, you look so angry today," his friend Timal said as they moved to the entrance of the mosque. Both were dressed in simple traditional Muslim conservative clothing. They walked outside the mosque to where their wives and children were waiting. The wives were covered head to toe in burkas with only their eyes showing.

Richal heard the honk of a horn and noticed one of his sons was staring at the big sedan as it drove by. He looked over, angered to see the America dog and his whore wife out with their driver. He caught his son staring at the woman, who was dressed in short sleeves showing much of her arm. Viciously, Richal reached over to slap his son hard in the face.

"These western infidels are tempting our youth," he said to Timal, who made no move to contradict him. The boy needed the beating.

"You are right, Richal, it is all breaking down." Both of them were members of Daryl Islam, the newly formed movement to make Indonesia a Muslim state.

"We will wait out time, brother, and then we will rise, Allah willing."

38

"Edmond, this is the most fantastic market I have ever seen. It looks like it goes on forever. Thank you so much for taking me," Agnes said as they drove by stall after stall of vendors selling everything from car parts to food to antique treasures. Edmond had discovered the market about a week ago. Umar had told him that the best time to go was in the early morning right after the morning prayers, when it would be the most crowded. Agnes was just about to add more when she saw a man slap a young boy to the ground.

"What was that all about?" Agnes shouted in alarm. "Shouldn't we stop and help the poor youth? That man is going to kill that poor soul—he's just a kid."

"They are from the madrassas. They want to make Indonesia a strict Muslim state governed by barbaric Shariah laws where no one has any real rights, especially the women who are kept like slaves," Umar said. "They think they are doing God's work."

"I don't believe in God," Beil said, thinking of all the cruelty that goes on in God's name. How one can hide behind the idea of God to set one's own laws. It was the grand lie, where you can pass the buck to a mysterious entity that no one has seen. He thought he recognized the man beating the boy. He bore a strong resemblance to one of the servants at the office.

"I agree with you," Umar said. "There is no God."

But he was coming from a different place than Beil. There was no need for a God in Communism. How could the people be free under the yoke of religion? "He was beaten for looking at us," Umar said, not mentioning the real reason—Agnes and her dress. The orthodox Muslims were like loud big babies who could turn violent at any time. Umar hated them even more than then he hated westerners.

"Both of you are crazy. Of course there is a god," Agnes said. "Don't you believe in a higher power?"

"Yes, like nature and the natural order of things," Beil said as they parked and got out of the car, letting the smells of the market wafted over them—all kinds of spice and fruit and the burning of incense, mixed with the chatter of the crowd. It was all very intoxicating.

"Who needs God when you have all of this?" Umar said, liking both of them despite the fact that they were the enemy.

39

It was clear to Beil that the situation in Indonesia was very complex. It was not like Vietnam—compared to Indonesia, Vietnam was child's play. In Indonesia there were the Communists, who differed from the Nationalists. There were the Dutch, the Dutch sympathizers, the oil and mineral companies, and the religious fanatics. Finally there was the military that so far ran the show. Corruption was everywhere. Unlike Vietnam the sand was always shifting, so in the end no one could trust anyone. In addition to all this was the cult of Sukarno.

The DC 6 touched down on the tarmac and Beil landed in Singapore. He was met at the airport by the general who had thought it wise to meet in a different country, one that was controlled by the British and therefore secure for secret meetings. Beil had been in Sumatra for three months. This was his first briefing with the general and Major Jim.

"The only thing that is missing is the fourth," the General said as they sat down for a meal in an open market, away from the nearest table.

"That would be good," Beil said. "It would be much easier than the game being played south of here."

"Well, tell us about the situation so we can try and help."

So Beil briefed them on all the different strands, all held together by one man Sukarno whom even the military was unable to move against.

"This Sukarno is the key," the General said after a while. "He's our man. Can you get close to him?"

"That will be hard, sir." I have very little access to him, and he is unpredictable."

"Just like bridge," the major added. Everybody laughed.

"We will have to lead him rather that force him. You know a little of this, a little of that and so it will be."

"Agnes wanted me to give this to your wife," Beil said as he pulled out a little box. He saw the look change on the general's face.

"I suppose you didn't hear, Edmond. Anne passed away. That cold she had turned out to be consumption. Nothing seemed to help, not even the menthol cigarettes."

40

The two dark-clothed assassins entered the small village on the outskirts of Palembang. Aided by the moonless night, the two silently made their way to the house of Umar Rai. He was next on the list of PKI agents to be eliminated by the secret death squad with which Rockman was associated. Since the murder of Musso many PKI had gone into hiding, always living in fear, knowing they were being systematically hunted.

All of a sudden a loud clanging sound pierced the night air as one of the men tripped the wire of cans that Umar had arranged to guard his perimeter. Instantly he leaped to his feet, only having enough time to grab his always-ready escape bag before the men broke through the door, guns drawn. He dove out the window, frantically dashing for the thick jungle that was a few hundred yards away. He looked over his shoulder—the assassins had spotted him. With no time to put on his shoes, his bare feet were being cut by the bamboo stubs as he raced to the jungle. The pain forced him to slow down. The men were closing. He knew they would catch him before he reached the safety of the thick underbrush.

He changed course, knowing the long shot was his only hope. He crossed back toward Beil's car, parked in the road outside his house—as a special favor, after a late night, Beil had allowed him to drive it home the night before. He reached it mere seconds ahead of the assassins. He had just enough time to slam the door shut. He fumbled for the keys and started the engine. The two men jumped in front of the car to stop him, leveling their guns. Umar closed his eyes, thrust the car into first gear and stepped on the gas. He heard the screams as he sped away, knowing that he had run them over. Still in a panic he did not look back but kept going, only stopping when he reached Beil's compound where he waited for dawn.

When Beil appeared in the morning, dressed and ready for the office, Umar was washing the car down. Beil was impressed by the thoroughness of the man. He had watched Umar wash the car the day before. It was already spotless.

"Selamat, Tuan Bescar," Umar said, scrubbing the last of the remnants of the blood off the bumper. He was still shaking but his mind was racing ahead, trying to figure out where he would sleep. He knew full well that the secret death squads would come after him again. He had nowhere to go, nowhere to hide.

"Umar, you're up early today and already washing the car. You take good care of that car."

"Terima kasih, tuan." Umar spoke in Indonesian—not the usual English. Then he hatched the plan. "I thought we would speak Bahasa today and English the next day so we can both practice the language, and the Mrs., too."

"Bagus," Beil replied. Umar was a man that he would like to cultivate. In Indonesian he added, "I would like to go to the office."

While they were on the way, Umar said casually, "Last night I lost my home in a fire. I was wondering if it would be OK to move into the servant's quarter on the compound."

"Of course," Beil said, glad to be speaking Bahasa. He had been trying to think of a way to speak it more. Umar always would answer in English and ask a question in English almost like he did not want to speak Indonesian. He saw the smile in the man's eyes, mistaking it for gratitude instead of relief.

Umar let himself relax, knowing he was safe for a moment if he stuck with the American during the day and never ventured out of the compound at night.

41

Nasul Rockman was sipping a scotch and soda; Beil a bull's eye. The two were sitting in Beil's office. Finally after some small talk Rockman came to the point.

"Mr. Sukarno got your message." Rockman's eyes shifted as he spoke. He caught the eyes of the servant and got the feeling he was being watched.

"Good," Beil said. It was now the fall of 1949, just after the round table conference that produced the Republik Indonesia Serikat with Sukarno as president. Sovereignty was to be transferred by the end of the year. In the agreement Dutch investment was to be protected.

"I hear privately from my friends in government that we would be willing to send aid to the new Republic of Indonesia."

"We need aid very much."

"In this new cold war world, friends help friends," Beil said, getting to the heart of the negotiations.

"Yes, friends help friends," Rockman answered back, knowing the aid would have strings and conditions.

"America is always happy to help a struggling nation in its march to freedom. The Indonesian word for freedom—what is it?"

"Merdeka."

"Merdeka, that is such a nice word, but achieving it will be hard work. Words need deeds to back them up."

"Yes, there are many forces working against Merdeka. But with American help and our own hearts, we will be free."

There was vagueness to both men's words. But each knew what the other meant.

"Good, we will meet next month."

"Yes, next month, I look forward to it," Rockman said as he finished his drink. But when he got ready to leave, Beil stopped him.

"By the way, this is for you." Beil took an envelope from his desk. "It is a consulting fee from Standard Oil."

He watched as Rockman's eyes widened. He knew that Rockman was hooked. It was bridge, the finesse. Major Rockman was loyal to power, not ideas, just like Beil knew this Sukarno was. He had proven that when he had crushed the PKI revolt and killed what was reputed to be in the tens of thousands of people. This was the opening America needed to have an ally against the Communists—the best way to bind someone to power was through material excess. He had discovered in his secret inquires that Sukarno had personal vices ranging from women to art. He had heard of his insatiable taste for extravagance. This was good because without greed, ideas take over. And ideas in the end were like water, more powerful than greed.

"By the way, Mr. Beil," Rockman said after he had put the money in his pocket. "One other thing. I heard that the rupiah was to be devalued by half sometime in early spring."

42

Agnes and the rest of the ladies piled into the car. Umar was not happy at all. They were going to a performance of the wayang puppet theater in the heart of Palembang. While the ladies enjoyed the performance he would be out in the open waiting by the car, vulnerable. Umar, who as a young boy had always liked the shadow puppets, now felt like one of the puppets trapped in the shadows where there were many watchful eyes and much danger. Today he hated it.

"They are all the same," Dottie said as they were driving along, pouring the mint juleps that the servants had prepared for them.

"What do you mean, all the same?" Agnes questioned.

"The puppets are all the same, or a least look all the same and they all tell of some hedonistic tale from Indonesia folklore. They really are quite boring after a few minutes."

"Oh, come on now, Dottie," Sally Dremmer said. "You always pour water on everything."

"What is there to like here?" Dottie said, starting to slur her words. She had been drinking early on. They all saw the tears well up in her.

"What is it, Dottie? Why are you so sad today?" She started bawling.

"I just hate it here. I hate the food, I hate the heat. I hate being trapped so far from civilization."

"I find it very exciting here," Agnes said as the car pulled up to the open air market. They the saw the rush of natives and then it hit them that none of them spoke any Indonesian, and they would be lost in the crowd without it. So she turned to Umar.

"We will wait till you park the car. Then come with us to translate."

"Yes, madam," he said, liking this idea much better than sitting alone by the car. Now he would be surrounded by westerners, able to hide in plain sight.

"Tell us about the wayang theater," Agnes asked.

"Well, shadow puppets were first introduced by the Hindus to tell the story of the Ramayana, but through the years the tradition has changed because Indonesia is mostly a Muslim country. We kept the basic characters but have changed the stories, though people still perform the old tradition on the island of Bali."

"Why do they call them shadow puppets, when they are so detailed and painted?"

"Because in the Muslim religion it is not good to make images of God. So it was decided that if the plays were to continue, then they would only be able to see the shadow of the gods."

Because the women were the only group of westerners, all the Indonesians began watching them and soon they became the real show. The Indonesians were so enthralled by the rarity of seeing a group of white-skinned western women that they let them walk anywhere they wanted. Soon they were in front of the stage, a three-part wooden screen formed into a cube. In the middle screen was a large square of white fabric. Behind the fabric was an oil lamp. When the puppet moved in front of the lamp, it would cast a shadow on the cloth.

"But why are the puppets so beautiful and detailed if they are never seen?"

"It is an art form; there are many famous makers of these puppets. Some are made of leather and these are called wayang kulit. Some are made of wood and they are called wayang klitik, and others are made like the puppets of Europe and they are known as wayang golek."

"What are the plays about?"

"Some tell the great epic of the Ramayana and other Hindu texts, but most now just use the traditional puppets to tell invented stories, or ones they have borrowed like from your Shakespeare. Some of them tell about current events," said Umar as the gamelan music struck up and the first of the shadows was cast on the screen.

"Oh, how beautiful," the woman exclaimed as the shadows danced around the cloth. They all cried, "Oh" again as another puppet came onto the screen, the two shadows in a dance. A story was being told but Umar was sure the ladies would have no interest. They would only be mesmerized by the beautiful movement of the puppets, and by the idea of a tradition going back generations. But this play was modern.

This story told of the rebellion of the PKI and how the glorious forces of the new republic squashed it to save the republic from Communism. It made Umar look around nervously, but all eyes were turned on the western women and their funny clothes. He relaxed a bit.

"What is the story of the play?" Agnes asked him.

"Oh, it is the story of the struggle for independence," Umar said vaguely. He didn't want to tell her the real story of how the PKI was routed; Musso murdered.

"It seems to be very violent."

"Revolutions sometimes can be very violent," Umar said dryly. Neither of them saw the man in the back of the theater. When they drove away, he jumped into a car and followed them back to the western compound.

43

Life soon turned into to a routine of lunch and parties, dinners and parties, and more office parties. There was not much else to do or really anything else. The boredom affected people in many ways. Dottie had developed a depression that was contagious, as of course misery loves company. Others drank themselves into stupors, or else found other ways to deal with their situation.

Beil had become aware of an old craving. In some ways married life was great, because it supplied constant companionship. But it did not quell his secret desire, which came out in the most unexpected of places. Coming back from Singapore in the first-class cabin of the Pan Am Clipper, he had met Murray Timmons, the first steward. Murray was from Omaha, the very proper son of a Baptist minister. The two had flirted on the plane. Then after landing they had gone for drinks, and then more than just drinks.

As fate happens, Murray was going to be on the Pan Am charter that was going to take Sukarno on a state visit to India. Beil had met him at the airport where they were now in a bar waiting for his flight.

"You will have to tell me all about Sukarno," Beil said. He wondered how he could coach Murray on what to look for, without him guessing that Beil was using him.

"Like whether he likes men?" Murray laughed nervously as he reached over to light Beil's cigarette.

"That too, of course, but mostly I want to know what he eats, what he drinks, what kind of cologne he wore. Who went with him. Who did he have in his inner circle."

"You sound like you want me to be a spy."

"No, I just am fascinated. I've heard all kinds of stories. I just want to see if they are true." Just as Beil finished speaking, they saw the motorcade arrive outside the airport. The guards came out of the middle car waving machineguns. The street-crowd parted and Sukarno entered the main doors. He was wearing a traditional Javanese hat with a western suit. With him were his wife and three or four men whom Beil recognized from dossier photos.

"Well, got to go, Edmond. See you when I get back," Murray said as he put on his steward jacket.

"Don't forget, I want a full report," Beil said.

"Oh, don't worry, I'll give you a private one when I get back," Murray said with a wink. Then he made his way out of the bar towards the gate where the bus waited to take him out onto the tarmac.

Beil finished his drink. Then went to the parking lot where Umar was waiting. "Did you see Sukarno?" Beil asked him, wanting to get an Indonesian's take.

"Yes, he comes with all the trappings of power, all those guns and all that." In fact Umar had barely seen what was happening. He was a wanted man so had stayed low in the car, only poking his head above the dash. One could never be too careful.

"I hear he's the real hero of the revolution," Beil said, noticing the less-than-enthusiastic endorsement of the man most Indonesians considered the father of the country.

"There are others that were more important. He was just one of the lucky ones, not the best or the smartest, just lucky that the military supported him.

"Who were the other heroes?"

"Musso—now he was the real hero."

"But he was Communist."

"If that is what you want to call him. He was for the people, not this Sukarno who is for himself."

"How can someone as smart as you not be leading the revolution?" Beil asked, taking Umar by surprise. He was almost about to blurt out that he had been a high leader in the PKI, but because of Sukarno and the death squads he was forced to take refuge with the capitalist Americans.

"I stay out of politics. It really doesn't matter. The underprivileged are always going to be exploited."

"That's true. It's even true about Communism."

44

Richal Abdullah stared at the wife of the mandor as she walked out of the office, watching her get into the car. He couldn't believe how disgusting it was for the infidel to walk around half-clothed in shorts that showed her long gangly white legs. The sight of her drove him mad. He thought he should be punished for not be able to tear himself away from looking. He took the bag he was holding and hit himself hard in the head.

Everything about this office was full of vice, from the indecency to the chronic drinking, but the most defiling thing to Richal was the pig-roast at the company party last Saturday. He had to first endure the cooking of the putrid flesh, followed by serving it to the Americans who wolfed it down. When the horrible affair had finally ended he had to wash himself to get clean before he went to seek out his friend Timal.

"The world is becoming infected with filth."

"Yes, Richal, already Sukarno is flaunting his women. Pretty soon we will all be like the Balinese and eating pork."

"Whatever happened to the strong leaders of the Dari Islam? Even religion has lost its compass."

"Even our own children are tempted by this lack of morality."

"It has to be stopped. If no one will do it, we should do it. I had a dream last night. I was on a winged horse in the country of the shaitans, who were trying to destroy our world."

"Who were these shaitans?"

"The American infidels and their whores, they are the problem." Richal had thought long and hard about it. If not for oil or the money that it brought, all these evil vices would not be polluting everyday Indonesian minds like sponges of desire. Oil brought nothing but trouble. If the supply of it was not cut off, then there was no way Indonesia could move forward.

"It is also this dog Sukarno. He had the army purge our movement. My own son was killed with his hands bound, shot point blank in the head for embracing Islam." Timal did not tell Richal the truth, that the boy had run off, denounced their faith and was tending bar in Jakarta. Something had to happen. He thought Richal was reading his mind when he said:

"I think it time that we become martyrs."

45

Dottie Finn looked at herself in the mirror wanting to cry. She had now been in this hell-hole prison for three years. It was like a cruel trick where if you looked out the front door you saw a piece of America all manicured and perfect, until you got to the barbed-wire fence. There on the other side was the wild. The never ending jungle was full of snakes, spiders and even man-eating tigers. You couldn't venture out of the compound without fearing for your life.

The city was just as awful. The food was too spicy. The people were filthy. Open sewers ran down the center of Palembang. The smell mixed with the putrid trash fires that were everywhere. There were no normal department stores, no TV, few newspapers in English. Almost no one spoke anything but Indonesian, which every morning before dawn was blasted on loudspeakers from the mosques, calling the faithful to pray so loud that no one could sleep through it. Because of this, Dottie was always tired with bags under her eyes.

She wiped away her tears. There was nothing good to be found in this backward country. She thought of the old movie where the heroine crashes in the plane and ends up on some island where there is nothing to do but survive. It did not matter that she had a staff to cater to her every whim, or every type of liquor to satisfy her ever-growing habit. None of this eased her unhappiness with the fact that Donald had been demoted from plant manager to office manager.

"How could you let that happen, you idiot!" she had screamed at him last night.

"It's not so bad, dear. Now I have even less to do. No one listened to me anyway." Donald tried to comfort her, but it was hard to comfort someone in her state.

"And being replaced by Carl Dremmer! Why, he didn't even finish high school!" she shouted. Her life was really ruined. How was she going to face the rest of the ladies who she was sure would be gloating? "Carl Dremmer, how low class is that! My life is over. I hate this fucking place! I hate you!" she shrilled at him, then ran into her room. "Get me a drink," she shouted to her servant who scurried away. She looked at the elephant plant in her bathroom noticing that a big leaf had fallen, just like every thing else. She went to break it off but it would not break, so she bit it off. Two minutes later, her lips were the size of a hippopotamus and still swelling. When the servant came back with the drink she had lips almost the size of the leaf she had just eaten. Her throat started to swell. He quickly called the doctor.

46

Seam, the head of the Beil household, hated having Umar staying there. Until he moved in, everyone who lived in the servants' quarters had been a member of Seam's extended family.

"You should tell the tuan that this Umar is PKI and a trouble maker. I heard from my sister that he killed two men the other night and then fled here. The police are out looking for him. This is just a bad omen for this house," his wife Eto said, on a day Umar was out with Beil. Never would they have dared to say this when the tuan was around.

Eto was the cleaning-washer lady and head of the women in the house. She had a huge wart on her nose, which she considered sacred. She was not a fanatic like Richal, but she was devoted, and like most uneducated Indonesians she was superstitious to the point of irrationality. God had given her the ugly wart on her face for some reason. She did not know why, but she would not dare remove it because something bad might occur. She knew about bad luck. Umar was bad luck.

"The tuan has enough problems to think about," Seam said, not wanting to make trouble. He knew how lucky they were to have employment at all, especially since they had once worked for the hated Dutch. Without the Americans, life would be hard.

Umar did pose a problem. Seam was no longer the head man. He was now under Umar, who as the English-speaking driver was the most senior servant. Seam did not like the way Umar had come in demanding Seam's bedroom, the one near the back with the door that led not to the tuan's house but to the jungle. He thought that Umar had done this just to show his power, not knowing the driver had picked the room only because it made for an easier escape.

"You need to tell the tuan. What happens when he finds out that Umar is a Communist? The tuan will blame us for not fulfilling our duty by telling him."

"We don't know that for sure," Seam said, though he suspected it. That first night, when Umar had fallen asleep, Seam had gone out to check under the car. He had found some blood in a crevice of the bumper, which Umar had not managed to wash away that morning, now over a month ago.

"You must tell him or I will!" Eto said in a loud voice. Both were surprised that she had the strength to speak this way in a male-dominated society, but she was afraid, especially by the way her eldest daughter, a beautiful girl of eighteen, looked at Umar and the way he looked at her.

"No!" Seam shouted sternly. "You will do nothing of the kind or I will cut off your beauty mark and Allah will be furious with you. Do not speak of it again." But inside Seam knew she was right, that this Umar who had come on the same day that a black panther had arrived out of the jungle to kill a chicken was a powerful omen. Seam knew that omens are never good, always trouble, and usually unpredictable. Finally, after much inner thought, he said, "We will wait."

47

Sure enough, just like Rockman had said, the rupiah was devalued by half. Everybody was up in arms about it at the office except for Beil and Carl, who Beil had alerted. The two families were playing bridge at the Dremmer house which was three down on the opposite side of the street from Beil's. For the past three months they had played bridge two or three times a week where they usually had made a night of it with drinks and dinner. Tonight was no exception. They had all been drinking very heavily, even Agnes.

"So this is what it must have been like for our parents in the Great Depression," Carl was saying.

"No, in the Depression there was no inside warning, no little do-do bird to whisper in your ear."

"Oh, I'm sure there was. There had to be. I mean, some people made fortunes."

"Just like today." Dremmer and Beil had kept all their money in dollars for the last few weeks, only changing the little they needed to pay the bills, until today, when they had all gone to the money man to changed their dollars for twice as much. Beil had celebrated by giving all the servants an extra one thousand rupiah, which was nothing to Beil but a month's pay to them. All of them had been thankful, except Umar.

"I don't want it, tuan," Umar said, eyeing the bill that would go a long way to increase and make up the lost value of the money he was holding.

"Come on now, don't be so proud. Take it, take it and share in the good fortune." Beil felt somewhat guilty.

"The devaluation hurts the workers. Now the money is worth only half as much," Umar said. The Indonesian government did nothing for the people but make them suffer. If the PKI were in charge, they would have done it differently. He thought how it is always the worker who gets screwed. The foreigners, as far as he could see, must have had wind of this and had kept their money in dollars. He had heard from the shameless servants who had taken the money how the tuans had made out like bandits.

"But it also means that someone like me or an Indonesian who had kept their money in dollars will buy more, just like I did in the market."

Beil and Umar had had this conversation on the way back from the market, where Beil had bought all kinds of antiques from dealers before they had been able to adjust their price. He'd had a car full of treasures for half-price. Now Beil was drawn out of his musing by Carl, who had decided to imitate someone from the Great Depression. He had climbed drunkenly onto the widow sill.

"I am ruined!" he shouted at the top of his lungs in his thick Brooklyn accent, jumping off the sill right into a thorn bush.

"OH SHIT!" His screams could be heard in the whole compound. Beil, Agnes and Sally laughed till their jaws hurt, watching Carl moan on the ground, while a swarm of half-grinning servants rushed to him to begin the painful slow process of pulling out the three-inch thorns that were sticking out of his rear.

48

Nasul Rockman and other military brass both in uniform and others like him who were in quasi-private industry were also together that night. They also had benefited but in other ways. They had been buying dollars for the last few months and now today they had sold them on the black market where the rate was even better than at the bank. But that was not why they were gathered.

"There are still many mine fields for us to navigate," Major Suharto was saying. At the moment his official position was to counter what remained of the Dutch forces.

"Yes," Rockman said. "These are hard times. This time is like a flower that blooms, then wilts and blooms again. This money we make off the exchange should be able to fund our operations."

"That is the plan," Ures Jonas said. He was forty-five and the oldest of the men gathered. He was the coordinator of the death squads that ran on their own in the nether world.

"We lost two of our best men last month."

"How was that?"

"A PKI dog ran them over," Ures said, enraged.

"Do we know where this guy is?' Suharto asked.

"Yes, but he is protected by the Americans," Rockman said.

"They are protecting him?' Ures asked.

"Yes, he is living in their compound."

"Can we get to him?"

"We can always get to anybody," Rockman said. "I see him almost every day. He is the driver of this Mr. Beil I have told you about."

"The same one who has promised America's aid?"

"Yes, the same one."

"Shall we take him now?"

"No, that would upset Mr. Beil, and we want nothing to jeopardize the aid," Suharto said.

"I agree," Ures said. "We have him in a box. He cannot go anywhere."

"Yes," Rockman chuckled. "We know where he is all the time. He drives Beil around."

"Good. Then it is agreed. We watch him for now."

"So what did Sukarno eat?"

"He likes filet of beef with home-fried potatoes and Chivas Regal."

"Anything else?"

"Well," Murray chuckled, "he likes women."

"Did he bring his wife?"

"Oh no. She got off the plane in Singapore. He brought some singer from Jakarta. She was such a slut." They both laughed. Then Beil got serious.

"Did he speak of anything other than eating and women? Anything about what his plans are for Indonesia?"

"Why are you so interested in this?"

"Oh, I just get a compulsion some times, you know. I want to know everything about people."

"Like me?"

"Yes, like you."

"I do have some good news."

"What's that?"

"I can be your personal spy on this Sukarno." Murray was obviously joking, but Beil turned serious.

"How is that?" he questioned, opening a delicate line where you lead someone without them knowing it.

"He has asked me to be his personal steward, on call twenty-four hours a day, and for triple the money!"

"That's fantastic," Beil said, his mind churning. Now he would have a window on the man. He wondered if he would have to let Murray in on the operation, teach him to be a better spy, a more active spy. He would have to ask the general next time they met in Singapore.

50

Fortunately the elephant ear, or Colocasia Esculenta, is mostly an edible plant except for the raw sap, which sometimes can cause swelling and redness. But this was of no relief to Dottie, whose lips were as big as the elephant ears themselves. After being rushed to the hospital she was sent home with some lip balm and told to apply ice. The Dutch doctor said that the swelling might take days or weeks to go down.

"I hate you so much!" she screamed to Donald who had dropped everything and was by her side.

"Now dear." Donald was very upset, not just with Dottie but also with his new position, where he did nothing. He felt that Beil could see through him, knew his weaknesses. And he knew that when the stateside bosses came they would wonder why a high-school dropout, Carl Dremmer, had taken his job.

"I hate you. I hate this place. You have ruined my life. I hope you are happy." The tears stung Dottie's lips.

"In a week or so you will feel better."

"No, I want to go home," Dottie sobbed. "Bring me a drink," she screamed to the ever-present servants who rushed to obey. They were very upset to see their tuan this way. The master's unhappiness reflected on them. Already the other servants, especially in Seam's house, were joking about them, saying their tuan had been demoted and that the little man Carl was now running the show.

"We will have to find a way to make our tuan stronger," Talnor said.

"Maybe we should find the tuan a woman to make him strong."

"Good idea, but first I think we should consult a magic man and see what he says. Something has to done for the Mrs."

"Yes, we need to do something to get out from under this spell," Talnor said as he finished making the drink. He returned to the tuan and his wife, where he found her crying in Donald's arms, shrieking uncontrollably.

51

It was now the summer of 1951. Agnes was pregnant. She had not been feeling well for a few weeks and had first thought that it was all the parties she had been to, but when she missed her period she went to the doctor. She was waiting for Edmond to come back from the office so she could tell him the exciting news.

To get ready she had asked Seam to prepare Beil's favorite meal of chicken sate, crab and asparagus soup, and bami goreng—Indonesian noodles with vegetables. A bottle of champagne was already in the bucket. She took another drag of her menthol cigarette, thinking of the poor general's wife, but thinking also that there always was a death to make room for a birth. To be pregnant was a dream come true for someone who had been sure that she was going to be an old maid.

When Beil arrived he opened the door surprised that a table had been placed in the center of the tiled living room that was now lit by candlelight.

"What are we celebrating?" he asked, a little concerned, feeling a little guilty because of his secret tryst with Murray. Had he forgotten their anniversary? No, that was still a few days away. He saw Agnes was all dressed up, looking very pretty.

"Remember how I was telling you that I didn't feel very well the last couple of weeks? Well, we are celebrating the reason."

"What's that?"

"We are going to have a baby!" Agnes face exploded into a huge smile. Her happiness was contagious.

"A baby!" Beil shouted it again. "A baby! How wonderful!" Beil came over and hugged her. She handed him the champagne.

"To our family." They touched glasses.

"To our baby."

52

Indonesia like all Asian countries has a strong tradition of the supernatural, whether it is a folk cure or actual magic, where spells could be placed on people. Many cults flourished throughout the countryside. As in voodoo, if you were a believer, things did happen. Of course one has to wonder whether things really happened because of the spell or because people believed in the spell. But regardless of the reason, some things do happen that we can not explain. In Indonesia the common term for practitioners of traditional healing, magic, and sorcery is *dukun*.

Talnor, Donald and Dottie's head servant, was up in his home village near Boktingal, seeking out an audience with the shaman Windra Sychino, who was a very powerful dukun sàntet, or black-magic sorcerer.

"Master Windra," Talnor said, afraid, almost at the point of uncontrollable shaking. "I have come to request a sihir."

"Explain yourself," Master Windra said harshly. A sihir was no minor matter. It was a very serious matter. A sihir spell was used to kill a person, using a form of busung where the victim's belly would grow and grow with all sorts of devilments. It was well known that a busung spell would cause one's insides to turn to nails and pus, eventually exploding and ripping the unfortunate victim's belly apart. Once invoked it was almost always fatal.

"My household can no longer live with its shame. It started with the arrival of the new American who placed a spell on us."

"What do you mean?" the shaman asked. He had seen some of these Americans with amazing things like boxes that spoke or things you talked into and you heard voices. Such things were magic—not his kind of magic but very powerful nonetheless.

"When the new American arrived, things for my tuan started to go bad. First, his job was given to another less qualified tuan for no reason. Then my tuan's wife ate the leaf of the taro plant that the new tuan's wife had given them as a present, and her lips swelled up like an elephant and she had to be rushed to the hospital."

"Yes, that is odd," said the shaman, knowing that every part of the taro could be eaten. "The taro is a staple food, so someone must have put a spell on it."

"Yes, and since then our mistress has been possessed by evil spirits."

"By spirits?" the shaman asked. "How?"

"Last night she struck my wife for not making her drink strong enough. I made that drink. It was perfect. Now the tuan's wife just stays in her room all night and sobs. Things like this never would have happen before." Talnor was shaking as he remembered the screaming in the night, and the tuan wanting to leave.

"I can see this is very complicated and woven around many people. Whom do you want this busung cast upon?"

"The new American's wife. She was the one who gave the cursed plant. She is the one." It had become very clear now that Talnor was with the shaman who knew all. How clever this shaman was. He reached into his pocket to pull out the little box full of precious coins that all the servants had given him. It represented most of their combined saved wealth, but no expense was too great to combat the evil that was attacking them.

"I will do what you have asked, since you ask with such sincerity and are from this village. Villagers take care of villagers. This American—all Americans, I believe—must have strong powers, so what you ask will not be easy. Come back in one week and I will have the tonic that is needed to overcome the Americans' strong magic."

53

Umar was at the secret meeting in Palembang, after having left the safety of the compound. This meeting was to devise a new strategy—instead of fighting Sukarno, the PKI would try to work within his system to change from within.

It had not been their idea. But they had been approached by some officials within the Sukarno regime. Sukarno had become afraid of the power of the military and thought it might be useful to rehabilitate the PKI to counter this threat from people like Major Suharto. If they were content to work within the system, then the assassinations would stop.

"Why should we believe that?"

"It would be good for him. Would it be good for us?"

"The westerners have a name for it. They call it a quid pro quo," Umar answered having seen this term in one of the books that Beil had lent him. He could not believe that Beil would let him just, pick whatever book he wanted. How or why would someone give all the information away? There were books on all kinds of subjects ranging from birds to politics; not just capitalistic books but Communist books and books on Hitler. He had asked Beil how someone who was so anti-Communist could have so many books about it.

"It is always good to read all sides even though you believe in one," Beil said. That had been driven into him by the general: know your enemy. "That way you can understand the mind, because we human beings all have the same desires, though they get clouded by ideas. There are serious good men on both sides. There are serious bad men on both sides. The bad ones see everything as black and white. The good ones see it as grey." Umar began to think of things in that way, which was why he wanted to try this approach of working within the system to change the system.

"What is quid pro quo?"

The question brought him out of his reverie. "It is the idea that I will do something for you and you will do something in exchange for me. How an alliance or understanding can come about."

"Does it mean we change our views and agree with the government?"

"No, it means we work within the system on goals that are mutual for all of us. Instead of open fighting we go to the urban centers to help the people have better lives."

"But now Sukarno is now sucking up to the Americans. I hear they are giving him aid."

"Yes, but we can change the strings by moving them from within."

"I don't know if that is a good idea, but it is a good idea not to be hunted openly and allowed to have a say in the governing of the people."

"Yes, let us try or at least pretend, so we can move more freely. Await our time until we become strong enough to take power and make Indonesia a model for the entire world to see."

So the PKI abandoned open war with Sukarno and his forces, ordering their entire membership to work within the system to promote their ideas. Instead of Communism they would talk about Nationalism, but even so they knew that nothing really changed, except they would no longer be hunted.

54

Talnor had just returned from seeing the dukun santet. He had with him a potion that he would have to get the wife of the new American to drink. How he would do that was his dilemma. But then Mrs. Finn announced that they were going to have a party on Friday. She wanted the servants to cook the turkey that Donald had brought back from Singapore. Dottie thought that it would be great to have some western food instead of the Indonesian slop that she was sick of. The swelling had gone down and the new pills that the Dutch doctor had prescribed—something called speed—gave her so much energy that she actual looked forward to the day.

Talnor was very nervous. He would have to find some way to make Agnes drink the mixture. He was still thinking about this problem when the doorbell rang. It was Carl Dremmer and his wife. About ten minutes later the door rang again this time it was Beil and Agnes. Talnor shivered like he had seen a ghost. He looked away when she tried to catch his eye. His hand started to tremble.

"What is everybody drinking tonight?" Dottie asked, feeling very good. She had taken a few pills early in the day to rev herself up. She had also been drinking. There were trays of champagne around.

"What are you serving?" one of the ladies asked, knowing that the Finns were famous for keeping a well-stocked liquor cabinet.

"I think just about anything."

"Do you have Campari?"

"Yes, we do " Dottie replied. She and Donald prided themselves on having all kinds of liquors, even the very obscure.

"Very good. I'll have a Campari and soda."

"What do they taste like?" Sally Dremmer asked.

"Oh, they're very good."

"I'll try one."

"Good," said Dottie. "How about you, Agnes?"

"Sure, I'd love one."

"That settles it, we'll all have one. Talnor!" she sang out. "Please make us all Campari sodas."

"Certainly, madam."

Talnor could not believe his luck when he looked at the color of the bottle of Campari. It was red, the same color as the spell tonic that the dukun santet had given him. The red came from the blood of some animal that was used in the mixture. He could tell just by holding the vial that this was powerful magic. He made up a tray of cocktails with one special one.

He came back into the room and handed the first to Dottie, who had almost grabbed Agnes's from the tray; only a sudden movement on his part avoided that catastrophe. He next went to Agnes and handed her the special glass. After serving the rest of the women he waited in the room with the empty tray.

"Let have a toast, someone shouted as they all raised their glasses. Talnor watched as Agnes brought the glass up to her lips. His heart started to pound with a ringing sound that erupted in his ears. He felt sick. The room began to spin as he started to lose his balance. Staggering to catch himself, the silver tray slid from his hands crashing to the floor with a loud bang. Everybody turned his way. He recovered immediately but that did not stop the guests and the servants from coming to help him. Agnes and Dottie were the first to reach him, after having put down their glasses on the small table.

When they came back, Dottie picked up Agnes's glass. It had all happened so quickly that none of the servants had seen the switch. In no time the mess was cleaned up and the party got back on track. Talnor anxiously watched from the side of the room. All of the servants were watching, because it was too hard to keep a secret like this. The whole room was silent. Time stopped.

"To health," Donald said.

"To health," they all answered back; brought their glasses to their lips and drank. The servants were watching Agnes, grinning as they saw her take one big sip, then another. They were thrilled when they heard her say, "I just love these!" as she downed her glass. None of them were watching as Dottie slugged hers down.

55

"I overheard Sukarno tell his aides that his government was going to recognize the New People's Republic of China," Murray said to Beil at the American Club bar in Jakarta.

This did not surprise Beil. The general had forewarned him. Beil had also heard from Rockman that there was a truce with the PKI, that the army was worried about this but did not have the power to stop Sukarno, who was consolidating power. This latest move just confirmed what they had been thinking.

"What else did you hear?" Beil asked, his mind thinking about all the ramifications of this move and how to counter it by nudging. The one rift that he wanted to exploit was Sukarno's relationship with the fundamentalist Muslims in Aceh. At the general's suggestion, Beil had arranged for a shipment of small arms and some money that had been delivered by boat, though the fundamentalists had no idea that the money had come from the US.

"That this Sukarno joined the mile high club."

"Oh, that's very interesting."

"Yes, you should have heard them. We had on the intercom. He was so loud and they were drinking. He's quite well endowed, it appeared. She was some model from Jakarta."

"Did you get any pictures?" Beil asked. Maybe there was a way to compromise Sukarno to make the rift with the fundamentalists even bigger.

"Maybe I should have some pictures of us." Murray smiled at him, winking his eyes.

"That would not be a very good idea," Beil said as he lit both of them a cigarette. Then he added, "When do you travel with him again?"

"Next month."

"Next time you go, here is a present so you can remember everything," Beil said, giving him a new tape recorder that was the size of a handbag and took a cassette tape instead of a reel-to-reel.

"Are you sure, that I'm not a spy and you are not the head spy?"

"Of course not," Beil said lightly. "I am just collecting information to write a novel I have been thinking about. Bartender! Get us another round of drinks!"

56

Richal and Timal had been studying the compound for several months. They had followed Beil home one night and discovered the western compound in the heart of the jungle. It made them furious to think that the great white Satans were living in the jungle in a den of decadence. Since that day they had taken turns watching the comings and goings like it was a full time job.

"Disgusting, brother," Timal said as they were watching the women swim in the compound pool. Some of them had on the new style two-piece swimwear called the bikini.

"What are we watching for? They are nothing but disgusting." Both of them were so repulsed by the white skin that they could not tear their eyes off of it.

"We should cut all their eyes out."

"Yes, and feed them to the dogs."

"We should also kill Sukarno, who I hear has attacked in Aceh."

"Yes, I hear they are calling for a jihad."

"We should go there and fight."

Just then they saw a servant bring a round of drinks to the women. "It is so humiliating for one of our brothers to have to serve them in their den of vice. I don't know how you do it," Timal said.

"I can barely tolerate it." They watched as the servant served the women, and watched as the pasty hands took the drink.

Talnor handed Agnes the drink. It was a month later and the women were eating lunch. He saw that her belly was growing. He inwardly squealed in delight, knowing the curse had taken effect.

The busung, once started, was an awful fate. The most common symptom was a growing belly that over the course of a few months would grow to a grotesque size and then eventually explode. Inside the unfortunate sufferers, it was common to find all sorts of strange objects that would grow from the seeds of black magic. Stomachs of busung victims would be full of objects such as rusty nails, glass and animal feces. He thanked Allah for the medicine of the dukun santet. He was so happy that he went over to his wife and spoke.

"The medicine is working."

"I can tell!" Suman squirmed. It was so obvious—anyone could tell.

"And I hear from Eto that the Mrs. has been feeling ill and throwing up." She beamed because luck was now changing for their masters. Except in one way: Dottie, who had seemed to be getting better, was now in constant stomach pain, complaining that she felt like pins were ripping her belly.

"The best part is that Tuan Beil and Mrs. think she is having a baby," Suman chuckled. "Eto said they are painting a room as a nursery."

"That is perfect. She will have no idea that anything is wrong until her stomach explodes." Talnor grinned, but soon his face changed. Outside the compound two men seemed to be staring their way.

"Who do you think those people are?" he said, pointing to them. His wife looked over.

"They are watching Tuan Beil's driver. They have been watching before. Seam said he has seen them many times."

"Why would they be watching Umar?" Talnor asked.

"Because he is PKI."

"PKI," Talnor whispered, the fear running up in him. If Umar was PKI, then these men were the dreaded secret police. It was very unnerving. Everyone knew the secret police lumped everyone together who harbored the PKI.

57

A few weeks later Beil was at the market in Palembang. He was on Surabaya Street, which was full of vendors selling everything from Chinese antiques to Indonesian antiques and everything in between, old and new. Unless you had experience, you would be taken. There were no set prices and when the vendor saw Americans, the prices would skyrocket. Beil was with Donald Finn who had never been to the market before. Beil was looking for Chinese things.

"Tidak barang baru—I don't want new things. Minta barang tua—I want old things," Beil shouted out.

"Tuan, tuan, barang tua!" The boy was holding a brand-new wayang puppet.

"Tidak, barang baru," Beil shouted back, cigarette in his mouth. The youth broke out in a huge smile. All the other Indonesians laughed too, conscious that this westerner knew old from new.

There was stall after stall of mostly the same things, but every once in a while there was something great. He walked into a stall and spotted a blanc de chine Kwan Yin.

"Berapa harga—how much?"

"200 US."

"Mahal—expensive."

"Tidak tuan—no, sir, it's cheap." Beil looked it over and saw that it was very old and had a mark, was hand made. It was just what the general collected. Beil bargained some more, then bought it.

"Where did you learn all the stuff?" Donald asked, having never even been to the market, not even knowing that it existed, even though he had lived in Indonesia for three years.

"Oh, from my friend back in the States," Beil said, thinking about the general whom he was to meet next week in Singapore.

"What do you think is in that can?" Donald asked as they went by a booth. There was one in the corner that had no label.

"I bet it is canned peas," Beil said studying the can and seeing that it looked American.

"No, I bet you it's something exotic, like maybe bamboo shoots."

"How about monkey brains? I hear they're really good."

"Let's buy it, have a bet, and find out."

"Berapa harga—how much is it?" Beil asked to the vendor.

"Three thousand rupiah," the man shouted, seeing that the crazy tuans wanted something so worthless. Beil was just about to shout at the man for his ridiculous price but before he could, Donald cut in front of him.

"Sold!" Donald happily shouted, then reached into his pocket handing the stunned man three thousand rupiah for the mystery can that if the label was still attached would cost a hundred rupiah, tops. It didn't take long for the news of the crazy American's action to spread. Soon the whole market was in various degrees of trying to control their laughter.

Umar was having a hard time not looking at Beil. Both of them were trying to stare at the ground. Umar had been on many buying trips with Beil, and even though he thought it very decadent to collect material things when people were starving, not to mention that he thought it was the height of bourgeois capitalism, he had marveled at what a great negotiator Beil was. Now to see this other American being so clueless put him on the verge of convulsions. All of a sudden the two men caught each other's eyes; both erupted into uncontrollable belly laughs.

"What's so funny?" Donald asked. Everybody was laughing but him.

"Oh," Beil said between fits. "Nothing, really. They were just commenting that they never thought their friend would be able to sell a can with no label."

Soon everybody in the market with a can with no label came running up. Some even tore the label off the cans and brought them up. All of a sudden there were a hundred or more cans. Beil was still laughing.

"They want to know if you want more."

"No," Donald said, really out of place and sorts. He just wanted to go back home.

"Tidak," Beil said, but stopped when he saw one seller with a few really old and rusty cans that looked like they could be pre-war. He had a sudden inspiration that they could have a party to bet what was in each can.

"Barapa?" he said, and the vendor named the same extravagance price per can. Beil laughed at him. Saying he was not a great rich tuan like Donald, he pointed to all of them. "One hundred rupiah for everything."

"Tidak tuan—no sir, 1500 rupiah."

"Tidak, one hundred rupiah."

"Tidak," the vendor said.

"Then no." And Beil called to Umar in Indonesian, "Get the car ready. We are leaving." He walked out of the stall, leaving a stunned look on the man's face. All the other Indonesians were watching, all knowing the cans were worthless. Even at a hundred rupiah it was found money.

"OK, tuan," the man said in panic as he raced out after him with the worthless cans.

Once in the car Donald asked, "How much did you pay for all that?"

"One hundred rupiah for all," Beil said laughing again, as did Umar. On the drive home Donald started laughing, too.

"This is Asia. You have to bargain. It is a way of life," Beil said, looking over at Umar. Umar nodded. It then came to Beil that the reason Donald was so ineffectual here was because he never embraced Asia or Asian things, instead dwelling on what was not here, not on what was.

58

Seam was very concerned looking over at the Madam who was getting bigger as the days went by. He had just been told by his wife that Talnor had contacted a dukun santet who had put a curse on Tuan Beil's wife.

"Where did you hear this?" Seam had asked in disbelief. But after grilling his wife, he found that it was true. One of the Dremmers' servants, whose sister worked for the Finns, had told her.

"We must find a way to help her," he said anxiously, though both of them knew there was nothing that could be done against such power.

"She thinks she is having a baby," his wife said sadly.

"We must keep her thinking that."

"Yes. So far the only symptom she has is a big belly with heaviness. She says she can feel the baby." But both of them knew that she was only mistaking this feeling for the nails and garbage that were growing inside of her.

"Maybe we can try and reverse the spell. Hire our own dukun?"

"I tried," said Seam's wife. "But the dukun said it was black magic, and because of that the spell can not be reversed. He said all we can do is make sure she does not know till the end."

"She will know soon. She thinks her baby will come in a couple of months, according to the Dutch doctors."

"What do they know? They are no match for this great magic."

"Yes, I agree," Seam said as they looked at Agnes. She was busily talking to the house carpenter who was painting the nursery.

"Yes, it is so sad."

59

Nasul Rockman was meeting with his group of military advisers. None of them were happy with Sukarno letting the PKI come back into power. Rockman was telling them about his meeting with Beil, during which Beil had suggested that they use the Muslims as a wedge to drive an opposition to Sukarno.

"Let me get this clear. The Americans want us to let them arm the Muslims secretly, with arms that will be used against us."

"Yes, the crazy Islamists hate the Communists."

"But they hate us, too."

"That is why we let them make some noise in Aceh, and squash them."

"That would strengthen our grip."

"Weaken Sukarno who has the power."

"He does until he loses it." Rockman smiled.

"And then we will be ready." They all chuckled, knowing they were patient and willing to wait, until they could take over the great Republic of Indonesia of which these officers were sure they were the future.

60

It was two weeks before her due date and Agnes looked like a beached whale on the tarmac waiting to board the DC 6 to begin the long flight back to the states. In the last month she felt like she had almost doubled in size. Everyday things like walking had become a painful chore, made worse by the oppressive heat of the tropics, which had not bothered her before she was pregnant. Each day was more uncomfortable than the last. The baby inside seemed to sense this and was kicking non-stop, to the point where she could not wait for the little brat to pop out.

The plan was for her to travel home by herself, get settled at her mother's house, and wait for the baby. Edmond was going to accompany her as far as Singapore and then meet her back in the states after finishing some business first in Singapore, then in Vietnam.

The servants were all lined up wailing, not a dry eye among them. They had insisted on seeing her off. Agnes thought that it was over the top and very childlike to show so much intense emotion. She didn't understand that they were wailing because this was the last time they were going to see her alive.

"It's so sad," Eto lamented, her head buried in Seam's shoulder.

"It is better this way," Seam said. He had his arm around her trying to comfort her uncontrollable sobbing. Both knew that the end was near. That she was about to burst. It was better that they would not have to see it.

"I know. But the Mrs. is so pretty. It is so unfair that this would happen to someone so nice."

"I hear the Finn woman is very sick too."

"What do you mean?"

"I hear that she stays awake at night with her stomach on fire and has not had any sleep in weeks. They say that last night she saw spiders coming to get her and had to be taken to the hospital."

"That does not make me feel any better, knowing that Talnor's household is suffering too."

"Yes, but sometimes they say that happens with the curse. Because it is such strong magic it is unpredictable and can possess someone who only touches the potion. Maybe the Finn woman touched the potion somehow."

"But that won't save our madam."

"Yes, that is true," Seam admitted solemnly. Agnes looked very flushed with the sweat pouring off of her. The servants watched as Beil came up to her with the camera motioning to Umar to take a shot of them. Then Beil called all the servants to say goodbye to Agnes. Most of the women grabbed hold of some part of her.

Umar was ready to snap the picture but none of the servants could stop crying. After a while he gave up and took the picture anyway. Even Agnes had started to sob. After the photo she tried to move toward the plane but they would not let go of her. They grabbed her even tighter when the cabin attendant came out of the plane to begin the boarding. Finally Beil took her by the hand, and together they climbed the ladder.

"So, on to Singapore and then home where I'll see you in New York in a couple of weeks."

"Yes darling," she said tearfully. She felt hot and light-headed. The sky started to twirl. She felt as if she were going to faint. All of a sudden a new wave of sadness rushed through her. She felt she was going to pop from the pressure.

"They are like children, very much like them. They don't handle their emotions at all. You would think that someone was about to die," Beil said. He hugged her tight. As she was about to enter the cabin door, she felt something break inside her. She looked down as a flood of water came running out, drenching her dress. This was soon followed by a small contraction.

"Edmond, I think it is happening now," she said. Overcome by a huge contraction, she fell, only to be caught by Beil's quick hands.

"Hurry, help," he called out to the flight crew. "Umar!" he shouted. "Get the car. We have to go to the hospital."

The servants watched in stunned disbelief, fearful that the Mrs. was going to burst in front of them. The females intensified their wailing. "Let's hope she goes quickly," Seam said. He saw the anxious look on Beil's face; the pained look on Agnes's. He could see her belly moving up and down. Her dress was wet, tinged with red.

Umar brought the car right next to the plane. Beil and the captain took Agnes by each arm, half-carrying her down the ladder and into the car. Beil got in next to her and Umar sped off for the hospital, leaving all the servants sobbing on the tarmac.

61

It was midnight when Richal and Timal got off of the ferry. They had just returned from Java where they had been in training for the last few months.

"We will be home in a matter of hours," Richal said to his friend as they walked off the wharf into the Palembang streets. The first thing they saw were various ladies of the night, mostly Chinese dressed with slitted cheosang dresses. They watched as the cars pulled up to them.

"Nothing has changed here," Timal said as he felt the rage well up. Life here was so much different than it had been in the mountains of West Java. There the small villages were under Shariah law.

"Yes, the old fornicating ways are still among us," they said as they kept walking. In West Java they had learned that it was every Muslim's duty to move Islam forward to save Indonesia before it became a land of debauchery and lust. They had with them two guns that had been smuggled in from Malaysia or the Philippines. It was rumored that the guns had been stolen from an American base.

They went down another street seeing more ladies of the night and also young men dressed like woman. It disgusted them that they had to walk through this. They felt like pulling out their guns and killing everyone, but that was not the mission they had been given.

They were winding their way down the street when out of a bar came a man dressed like a woman, hand in hand with a western man. The man in drag was very drunk and lost his step. Richal gasped when he recognized his son.

"What are you doing?" he shouted. His son turned white under his make-up. He tried to break away but Richal was quicker and soon had his son in a headlock. "How dare you disgrace me and Allah like this, you disgusting whore?"

"Father," his son tried to say as Richal's clenched fist struck him in the upper jaw and then his nose. Soon blood was dripping.

"You have shamed us! You are no longer my son."

"I don't want to be your fucking son. You are wrong! Allah is wrong! There is no god!" The boy managed to turn his head and spit in his father's face.

"Why you wormless dog," Richal screamed. He raised his fist to smash him again. But the westerner grabbed his arm, deflecting the blow.

"Stop it!" he screamed in an American accent. Richal momentarily relaxed his grip on his son's neck. The boy saw his opening and bolted away, running for his life.

"Come back here!" his father shouted at the top of his lungs. "Come back here, you fucking whore!" Timal, who was standing nearby, saw the son race down the street. The fucking whore was getting away. Furious over the youth's disrespect, he reached into his pocket, pulled out his gun, waving it in the air, into the face of the American, freezing him.

"Hurry, hurry Timal. He's getting away!" he heard his friend shout. He turned the barrel on his friend's son, taking aim. The sound of the blast pierced the night as the bullet hit the boy in the back, sending him reeling to the ground.

"What the fuck!" screamed the American. "HELP! HELP!" he shouted. Soon the air was full of sirens as police cars raced their way. Richal turned and pointed his gun into the American's face, about to pull the trigger, then stopped as he saw the first of the angry mob now only a hundred feet away.

"Forget him and run!" Timal shouted as he took off down the street with the mob right behind him. Richal passed the body of his son who was moaning on the ground slamming his boot heel into the boy's disgusting face, right on the nose, driving splinters up into the brain. Then he spat on the vile urchin that used to be his son.

62

Beil was pacing up and down the hospital hallway, chain-smoking, feeling uncharacteristically nervous. He thought it a silly rule that fathers were not allowed into the room to watch a birth. But this was a hospital rule even he could not get around. There was absolutely nothing for him to do, but wait. Hour after hour had come and gone. He reached in his pocket for another cigarette but found the pack empty. So he went outside of the nursery to the main floor, heading for the little store downstairs in the outer lobby. As he entered the lobby he saw someone being rushed in on a stretcher amid lots of clamoring. He was surprised to see Murray in the crowd.

"Two men shot him right in front of me. It was awful," Murray stammered. He looked very disheveled, not his usual neat self, and on the verge of tears. Beil looked over spotting the poor girl lying on the stretcher, face smashed in, nose battered to a pulp, blooding oozing from her chest. He knew that the poor soul was not going to make it. He wondered who the person was. This was a Dutch hospital that did not normally treat an Indonesian unless he was a VIP.

"Who is she?"

"He's a friend of mine," Murray said his guard down, horrified that anyone could be so cruel to someone so soft and caring.

"Somebody important?" Beil said, putting two and two together.

"No, just a friend I see time to time." Murray left it at that. Beil did not probe any further. He did not ask why the boy was dressed like a girl.

63

In room eighteen Agnes was nearing the end of her labor. She was tired, in much pain, but had refused any type of pill, wanting to be present when the birth came.

The pain reminded her of going to the dentist. But the contractions lasted much longer than any cavity she had ever had filled; the pain kept getting worse. For a while she wished she had taken the advice of the old Dutch nurse who had told her she was crazy not to be knocked out.

"Push dear, push...." She heard the nurse's gentle voice. It brought her back into her body. She felt pressure like a wave start to build in her. The contraction subsided.

"I can see the head!" the nurse exclaimed as she patted Agnes's forehead with a cold towel. Agnes thought back to when she was a girl playing with her dolls. She would line them all up to watch as she pretended she was giving birth. That long ago dream was soon to be true. Oh, how she wanted a boy. A boy to carry on Edmond's name.

She felt the surge start deep in her belly, deep down in the depth of the universe. It gathered like a nebulous cloud forming together, tighter and tighter. She felt like she was being drained. All her concentration came to one point. She arched her back. "Push, push harder," the nurse called. Agnes focused and pushed, and something slipped by. She let out a scream. Then all was silent. The pain was gone. She felt herself drifting on an ocean. Then she heard crying, loud eager wailing. She opened her eyes to see what was making the sound.

"It's a boy!" she heard the doctor call.

64

"It's a boy!" Beil shouted to Murray. Immediately he reached into his pocket and pulled out two cigars.

"That's great," Murray said sadly. A few minutes before Beil got the joyful news, Murray's young friend had died of his wounds. Not from the gunshot but from the boot that had broken his nose, pushing a spur of bone into the brain.

"Mr. Beil." The doctor came back out. "You can see your wife." Beil was now uncommonly nervous, maybe because of the pain he saw in Murray's face. Maybe it was because Murray was here, witnessing this powerful event in his other life. He thought about how one new life had come just as another one had left. How you can have many lives while living, even third or forth lives like circles, whirling circles, lies within lies, worlds like Communism and Nationalism, words like straight and gay. The boy had been killed because he was dressed like a girl. It made him think of Vietnam, Hiu and Major Dewey. His mind flashed on Haggard, the son of a bitch. Beil had been told Haggard was now flying planes covertly for the CIA somewhere in the Middle East. He wondered if these men who had killed the boy were like Haggard, just angry killing machines.

He took one last drag on his cigar, put it out, lit his more comfortable cigarette and walked through the door. On the other side he would be a father. He thought again of that poor boy, thought about his father who would no longer be able hold him. So senseless, the hate that exists in the world of love. Where to be yourself was not allowed.

"Edmond, come meet your son," Agnes said, holding the little chubby baby in her arms.

"He's so fat!" Beil said happily, his gloom evaporating at the sight of the boy nestled in Agnes's arms. He came over giving Agnes a kiss. She handed him his son. Beil was in love.

And that was how I was born in February of 1952 in Indonesia instead of America, in a land full of eastern souls that permeates my western body. With my birth I am now officially in this novel where once in a while I may or may not give my impression of what I remember, a child's view of life in the tropics. But that is getting ahead in this tale. All I will say now is that when I looked into my father's eyes that first time a few minutes after my birth, I did not know about his secret life. But I did know or rather felt his love and my mother's.

65

"The new tuan besar must be a powerful dukun," Eto told her husband as they watched Agnes and her new-born son get out of the car. There was no other explanation. The only way a dukun sentat curse could be stopped was by more powerful magic.

"Yes, we are so lucky," Seam answered. When they had first heard the word last week that the baby was a boy and very healthy, they thought it must be a mistake. But now they saw the miracle. They dropped to their knees to kiss the baby. Agnes was beaming, showing them the little angel that she had named William Philip Beil.

"I heard the young tuan has even put a spell on the Finn woman for her actions against him," Eto said, staring at the new-born who had the bluest of eyes. "Just look at his eyes—that is a sign," she exclaimed, interrupting herself. Finally she got back to her thought. "Talnor said the Finn madam is always with stomach pain. Even her pills don't work anymore."

"What else does he say?"

"He says that the Finn tuan is also getting ready to move back to America if she does not get better."

"Oh, that is powerful magic. It serves Talnor right."

"Yes, if the Finns leave, then he will have to ask to have the curse lifted."

"We are so lucky to have such a mandor."

"Yes, that is what we will call him, 'mandor,'" Eto said as Agnes handed her the baby. It made Seam say.

"He looks like the mandor."

"'Mandor?'" Agnes asked. "What does that mean?"

"It means the great boss, the leader."

"Mandor, it has a nice ring," Agnes said. Then turning to me she continued, "So my little mandor, welcome to your new home."

"Selamat mandor," the two servants said in unison as they bowed to me, wide-eyed and impressionable.

66

"Tuan, I have a question for you," Umar said as they were driving to Medan. It was mid-August of 1952 and the PKI was feeling very good about their decision to work within the system.

"What is that?" Beil answered back. They were going to Medan to shop the antique district that Umar said was the best in Sumatra. But each of them was using Beil's shopping expedition to cover the real reason.

"Where is this Marlboro country?" Umar asked, addicted now to Beil's Marlboros. Beil immediately cracked up.

"There is no Marlboro country. It is just advertising," Beil said.

"What do you mean, tuan, no Marlboro country?"

"It's just advertising. It's used to try to sell something."

"Tuan, you mean this Marlboro country is not a real place?"

"Yes, like in the way Nirvana or Shangri-La are not real places, but they stand for real places."

"You mean to say that this Texas is not in Marlboro country?"

"Oh it is, but not in a real way. Marlboro means a big open space where the mountains and plains go on forever."

"But not like this jungle," Umar said, still confused by this place that was a place but was not a place. To make him even more confused, Beil handed him a Marlboro. Both of them broke out laughing.

They still had hours on the road. When Umar had suggested to Beil that there were some good old barong in Medan, it gave Beil the cover he needed to meet secretly with Rockman to check out first-hand the rumors that he heard of the unrest in that city, where the PKI was calling for labor strikes.

"No, not like this jungle. This Marlboro land is wide open. Have you ever heard of the term, 'cowboy?'"

"Yes, tuan, I see him in the picture of this Marlboro country. But what is this cowboy?"

"The cowboy is the symbol of American freedom. He is confident, strong, and independent."

"But why does he carry guns?"

"He has guns because that way he will always be free and willing to fight for freedom."

"What does freedom mean to you, tuan?" Umar asked. Beil did not carry guns.

"It means the right to freedom of expression, freedom of speech, freedom to choose what you want, to be a democracy."

"But then why does your government meddle in affairs of other countries?" Umar said, knowing this was dangerous territory. Some of his sources in the government had caught wind that the Americans were funneling tons of secret aid to Sukarno, in addition to the aid that everyone knew about. He had heard that this secret aid was to stop the PKI and Communism.

"Our country does not meddle in other countries," Beil said with steely eyes. Then he added some clarification. "But we do have interests, and we help our friends who have similar views." He was thinking of Hiu. How America had failed in Vietnam. That place was getting worse by the day. Now the French were engaged in a civil war, which he hoped would not spread over here.

"But tuan, aren't you invading the country of Korea?" Umar asked. He had heard from some of the PKI members that there were thousands of US troops in that country.

"Yes, we came to their aid when the Communists tried to take over."

"But why does this thing called Communism scare America so much?"

"Because it wants everyone to be equal, and not let anyone have freedom."

Just as he was about to expound on this, they saw the road-block a few hundred yards ahead. Immediately, the fear welled in Umar. There in the road, army soldiers were manning a checkpoint, stopping every car to check IDs. There was no hope. He was trapped. He would have to give his papers and he would be caught. He knew he only had a few minutes more of freedom. He looked over and saw Beil staring at him, his eyes bearing down. He reached the line of cars…stopped…waiting. He saw to his dismay that thirty more cars had filed in behind them, trapping them.

Beil studied the change in Umar, realizing what the servants had been hinting for the last year must be true. Umar was PKI.

They heard shouting in front of them. A car in line tried to swerve out, gunning past the roadblock. Soldiers screamed for them to stop. The car ignored them. The soldiers opened fire. The machine gun blasts brought Beil back to the war, to Saigon, to Hiu, Haggard, Dewey. They watched in horror as the car stopped. They saw the slumped bodies. Then watched as an officer extracted a man from inside.

"Merdeka, merdeka!" the man shouted. Another soldier came over and pistol-whipped him in the face until the blood poured down.

"When we get to the checkpoint, let me do the talking," Beil commanded. "Keep looking ahead and when they ask you for papers, say nothing. But do not get mad. And when I say go, drive forward but do not look back."

As they waited in line now, everything was quiet, very tense. Umar was trembling when he approached the checkpoint.

"Tuan Beil," Beil said as he flashed his American passport to the guard, who stuck the barrel of the machine gun in through the window. Beil could see the man was around twenty, perfect age for a killing machine. But Beil also knew that at that age, even with a gun in your hands, you could be manipulated. The youth was stunned when Beil started spattering at him in Indonesian.

"What is the meaning of this holdup? Don't you know that I am here on official business? Let me through, now!" Beil commanded, seeing the desired hesitation in the boys face. Just when he was about to falter another soldier came up, this time an officer who peered in.

"What business are you on?" he asked.

"None of your concern, now get out of my way or I will tell my friend Sukarno that you detained me," Beil said imperialistically, dismissively, very much the ugly American. But he knew his pose would be effective, because Indonesians hated scenes. To reinforce his anger he shoved his passport in the man's face. Beside him Umar cringed, unfamiliar with this side of Beil, though it was very much like his bargaining style. If Umar had tried what Beil was doing, he would have been shot like a dog.

The officer saw the car was very fancy. This foreign tuan was furious. An American was rare in these parts and therefore must be on important business, especially a tuan that spoke fluent Bahasa. He did not want to guess wrong and stop this man; it could be very bad for him. Still he felt he needed to check the driver's ID.

"Who is this man?"

"My driver! Who do you think he is?"

"Can I have his papers?"

"He's with me. He does not need papers. Here are his papers," Beil said, again shoving his passport into the officer's face. "This is ridiculous. I have no time for this. Of course he is with me. Now that's the end of it. I am leaving. I have waited long enough." Then he switched to English "Umar get the fuck out of here."

Umar stepped on the gas and drove ahead, expecting the gun shots at any time, but they did not come. Still he did not breathe until they were a few hundred yards away.

67

Dottie Finn had a pain in her gut worse than anything she had ever experienced, so bad that she commanded her driver to take her to the hospital. Once there she was rushed into surgery for an obstruction of the colon. After three hours the two Dutch doctors emerged and walked over to a very worried Donald Finn.

"Your wife is going to be fine," the older doctor told Donald.

"What was it?" Donald asked, the relief evident in his voice.

"It was an obstruction of the colon. She will be fine in a few weeks or so," the other doctor answered, still in shock from what they had found.

"Has your wife been eating anything strange that you know of?" the first doctor asked. When they had cut her open they had expected her colon to be obstructed by the usually bile and feces.

"No, nothing out of the ordinary, although she has been complaining for the past few weeks."

"Did she say what the pain felt like?"

"She said it felt like someone was sticking pins in her," Donald said seeing the startled look on the doctors' faces. "What was it?" he asked them.

"Oh, when cut her open to remove the obstruction we were surprised to find the cause...."

"What did you find?" Donald asked, trying to remember if Dottie had eaten anything strange.

"Three pounds of rusty nails...."

68

Nasul Rockman greeted Beil in the presidential suite of the Medan Palace Hotel for a clandestine meeting.

"Good to see you." Rockman said, extending his hand and motioning to the table where a few other men were already assembled. Among them was Suharto.

"How was the trip?" Ures Jonas asked him. All the Indonesians knew about his altercation at the guard checkpoint. All had been impressed by his finesse. It did not matter to them that his PKI driver had escaped. He was just a small fish in a pond that could be caught later.

"Quite long, but interesting going through all the villages." Beil said.

"Very good to hear that," Rockman said, offering Beil a cigarette, ready to get down to the real business.

"We have received your funds and are using them to finance the Daryl Islam," Suharto said. No one outside of this small group of men knew about this.

"Yes," Rockman added. "We are using them without them knowing, letting this colonel in Aceh lead the rebellion, which of course we will put down when the time is right."

Beil saw the seriousness in his eyes, knowing that since 1945, Rockman and these men had a hand in toppling all the fledgling governments. The only person they had been unable to control was Sukarno.

"I hear the PKI is working with Sukarno and that this city is under their control and the unrest is because of them," Beil confidently guessed, lighting another cigarette. It was obvious that Sukarno was going to be a problem just as the general had told him years before. Now the key was how to use him, how to mold him to do what the US wanted.

"Yes, they have been clever and growing, but we will deal with them as we have in the past. Tomorrow we will squash this strike. Kill a few, arrest a few, though they are like weeds and will come back again."

"Good, then your interests are ours," Beil said, confident that these men would understand that any continued aid would be contingent on not allowing the Communists to grab a foothold. He also knew that things were not quite in control.

He thought back to his friend Hiu, his understanding of Nationalism, how it could mutate into many things. He also knew that he had to work with what he had. When the Dutch had left there was a huge vacuum, with no group able to consolidate power, except the military.

One thing he had learned about Indonesians was that they were very emotional. Another problem was that there was not any real Indonesian upper class or middle class. Except for men like these, most of the country was stuck in feudal times. It was six years after the revolution. The Dutch still controlled most of the businesses and money. There was still no Indonesian solution.

69

Umar dropped Beil off for the night, parked the car, and now was making his way to the safe house, still trembling from his sure capture and narrow escape, numb that he was still free. He marveled at the tuan's audacity, the guile of the American dog. It made him think that words could be stronger than guns. When the guard was waving the machine gun in his face he had thought his life was over.

Tomorrow was to be the test of power. For the last few months the PKI had taken advantages of the unrest of the villagers and city workers who found themselves not much better off than under the Dutch. His near-capture gave him extra clarity. He now saw how the PKI could exploit the fever of the masses that had risen and overthrown the Dutch for a better life that was still eluding them.

"We will take to the streets after prayers," Jindal Ostan said as the small group of men sat around the earth-floored room lit by an old oil lamp. It made their faces appear distorted, as if they were in a wayang play. Jindal was about the same age as Umar. In fact all of the men were around his age; the older members had either been arrested or were dead. These new men were in some cases third-generation Communists and had not been bridled by the defeat of their movement. Their only defeat was the slaughter of Musso. None of them had been trained in the Soviet Union. Therefore their idea of Marxism had an Indonesian influence.

Another member spoke. "Are you sure we are not trying to move to quickly?"

"No brother," Jindal said, buoyed by the last few months in which their movement had spread in the ghettos and poor villages. But he was unaware that sometimes your strength turns into your weakness and the exuberance that you feel is the thing that pulls you down.

"The roads heading to the city were full of checkpoints. They were checking everyone's ID," Umar said. The light of the oil lamp flickered in a sudden wind.

"They must know," someone whispered.

"Of course they know," Jindal said, trying to rally their spirits. It was always a risk that the enemy would know. There were many spies and eyes. People talk, but he was confidant that this time the people would move with them. Their plan was to create a confrontation, one that would encourage the workers to take to the streets throughout Indonesia. In Sumatra, Medan had been picked because of its huge unemployment and the fact that there was a large Chinese population that was always supportive of the cause.

"The plan is to riot in the streets. Then hope that the masses come out with us," someone said.

"Yes, we will be the match that the flame will follow," Jindal added confidently.

70

The poor little elephant was found wandering the jungle just outside the compound, looking lost and forlorn.

"Look, an elephant—she can't be more than a few days old," Sally Dremmer said to Agnes who was over showing off her new son. Sally had a two-year-old and the women were just finishing up lunch.

"An elephant!" Agnes said. The women ran over to the fence and peered over.

"I wonder where its mother is?" Sally asked. She had a lifetime love of elephants. As a little girl she had wanted one as a pet. But she had grown up in New York City. "Eman," she called to her gardener. "Go outside and bring that poor little elephant in. It must be so hungry."

Eman went outside but the elephant had gone back into the woods. He went in after it and immediately smelt the stink. There in front of him was the dead mother, her tusks hacked off. The little elephant was by her side. He took the rope he had brought with him, threw it over the elephant's head, and brought it back into the compound.

"Mrs. Tuan," he said. "The baby's mother is dead. That was the stink we have been smelling for the last few days."

"Oh, then the poor elephant has no one. Eman, get me some milk." Sally could see the fear in the little one's eyes. Eman brought the milk in a bottle and soon the elephant was hungrily drinking it down.

"I think you have a new pet," Agnes said, as both women started laughing because Sally's childhood dream had come true.

71

The strike started out peacefully enough. The huge crowd was marching down the street. The strikers were protesting that despite overthrowing the Dutch, all the businesses were still owned by foreigners with the help of a few well paid figurehead Indonesians like Rockman. There was much anger that after all those years of fighting for the revolution, it was clear that freedom was in name only.

"This is our land. We are the rightful owners," the mostly young men shouted to each other, pumping themselves up, determined.

Umar was watching from the sidelines as the mob started to form, taking on a life of its own. It was hard for him to remain still and not jump out to join crowd, but he knew that as one of the leaders it was better for him to remain in the background in case violence took place. Beil was with him. They had arrived on the street early, right after going to the antique market, where they had pretended to shop. After buying very little, Beil suggested that they walk the streets, as he had never been to the city before. Though they did not say it, both of them were anxious to get to the main thoroughfare. They parked the car. Then walk to the central district where they pretended to be surprised by the strike.

Now it was an hour later, Beil and Umar were in deep in conversation. The excitement had started to build. The air was thick and humid. The humanity was also thick. Now there were no spaces between the various groups. The avenue of people looked like a huge serpent. Shop merchants had closed their window and were fretfully watching from the cracks in the shades. Beil could feel the rumbling of anger as the crowd continued to swell, now emboldened by the large numbers.

"What are they striking for?" Beil asked Umar as if he had no idea.

"They want a share, a rightful share of the labor that they do. All the industry is owned by foreigners," Umar said, the gathering emotion gripping him as the crowd turned more vociferous.

"But Indonesia does own the businesses. They are just run by the western companies that have the expertise," Beil said.

A spontaneous chant erupted: "Merdeka, freedom, freedom." A policeman got pushed and then another.

Then someone in the back of the crowd lobbed a grenade into an office building. All pandemonium broke out.

The police, who had been on the side-line watching, raced to the sound of the blast, guns waving. The crowd swelled to meet them, buoyed by the defiant act. The shouting intensified: "Merdeka, merdeka, freedom, freedom."

Over by the still-burning building a few men were staggering out, bloody, the smell of acrid smoke filling the air. The screams of the wounded added to the mayhem. The police tried to cordon off the area but the crowd surge stop them. It was impossible to move.

Jindal was trying to melt into the background, but before he could slip into the crowd, someone shouted, "That's him! That's the man who threw the bomb."

"STOP! STOP!" the police screamed, but Jindal ignored them and kept running for safety, trying to be swallowed up by the crowd. One of the young policemen started firing in his direction. The shots could be heard all over. The crowd panicked and stampeded. Someone started a fire in an overturned car.

The first soldiers fired warning shots that did nothing to dispel the crowd. The mob pressed forward. Then it happened: a soldier fired into the crowd. And then another. Soon all of them were shooting to kill. It sent the crowd scattering, running for their lives.

Jindal was resting by the side of a building, exhausted, bleeding, knowing that capture was imminent. He saw the wound in his leg had ruptured a major artery. His strength was ebbing. His life would be over soon, but he hoped to lash out at some soldiers in one more act of defiance. That was when he spotted Umar talking to a westerner. Killing the foreign dog would be his last living act.

The revolution would be proud of him. Last night he had wanted to tell them all about the grenade but he had not, afraid of spies. Now, seeing Umar watching the riot from the sidelines with this capitalistic dog, it was very clear. Umar was the spy. Allah willing, both of them would die.

Beil and Umar were pressed up next to the building trying to hide. They listened to the sound of gunfire. Then the screams of the wounded as the mob retreated, leaving the dead and dying in the streets.

Gathering the last of his strength, Jindal approached the two men. He had a knife that had been given to him by his father, who had been murdered by the Dutch before the war. Merdeka, freedom, freedom of the soul. He thought of his father, how his father would be proud. Stealthily he approached, now only twenty feet away.

"Tuan, we should make our way back to the car," Umar said, dejected by the way things had turned out, never expecting the violence. They had tried so hard to keep the demonstration peaceful. It pained him to see the innocent people lying in the streets.

"Yes," Beil said solemnly, brought back to Hiu, to Vietnam. The mob had gone out of control. The army had gone in just like they said they would. It was then that they turned and saw the madman with the long knife rushing at them, only a yard away.

Jindal would have stabbed Beil in the throat if Umar had not pushed him away. This gave Beil time to recover able to side-step the next blow. He grabbed hold of the man's arm shoving him to the ground, but the fellow still held the knife. Gathering his ebbing strength, he lashed out.

Umar was momentarily frozen by the realization that Jindal was the madman trying to kill them. By the time he recovered, Jindal was upon him. It was too late. In desperation Umar put his hands up in a futile attempt to protect himself, but just as Jindal was about to plunge the knife into Umar's breast, he started to black out. He felt the strength drip out of him, instead of plunging the knife deep into the enemy traitor, he collapsed harmlessly to the ground and died.

"Let's get out of here, tuan," Umar muttered. Beil took one last look around. The streets were now deserted except for the army, the bodies, and those captured. Fifty or more lay dead but the army had control. Beil lit two cigarettes, placing one in Umar's quivering lips. Umar sucked in the smoke, feeling very strange that he had protected Beil who was his enemy but also his friend.

72

Richal and Timal were again in their hiding place watching the compound of the American dog that had corrupted his son. It was all their fault. Timal was forced to kill Richal's son to save him from perversion. American morals were like a cancer that had festered in the boy like a godless egg where all the vileness of the world could hatch. It was unforgivable. Both wanted revenge on them all.

"Next week the head tuan wants me to help them have a pig roast in the compound." Richal spat in disgust that he would have to be there with the fornicators.

"That would be perfect," Timal answered. That would get them inside the compound where they could kill the infidels to become martyrs. He looked at Richal, both of them smiled.

"Yes, I had not thought of that. I will see the head tuan and tell him that I will be bringing my friend to help."

"Yes, Allah has answered. We will kill as many of the tuans as we can."

"And their women—that will stir up a hornet's nest. My son's death will be avenged." They were in the middle of talking, so they did not see the arrival of Seam, who was helping the Dremmers' head servant bring in the baby elephant that had been adopted as a pet. Earlier it had crashed through the fence. The servants were bringing it back when they noticed the strange men.

"What are they doing here?" Seam's friend asked.

Richal and Timal fled into the jungle before they could be recognized. Seam turned to his friend. "They must be the secret police watching the tuan's driver."

"Secret police? That is very bad. They will blame all of us. You should tell the tuan."

73

Dottie Finn was finally recovered and looking forward to the Sunday party of the Bowling Club. It had been a hard three months, one in the hospital two at home mostly in bed. Donald only had six more months left on his contract. She had talked him into not renewing. It was like a dream come true, and now because of it she could enjoy the last few months.

"Agnes, what a cute son you have," said Dottie as they arrived at the Beil house, where the bowling party was to take place. Why it was named the bowling party was not really clear. But it had been a tradition that the newest family in the compound would hold it. Some thought that it had to do with bowls of planter's punch that were served, others thought that it had to do with the manicured lawns, but regardless it was always the best party of the year. One thing it featured was a chorus line of men dressed as women.

"Thank you. I think he looks like Edmond. You're looking good yourself." Besides the punch Agnes had a champagne fountain that had started early to get them in the mood. "Come with me. Everybody's out back. Edmond's showing off the pork pit." All of a sudden the baby started to cry as he saw Donald Finn.

"Oh, I don't have much luck with babies," he said amiably, though somewhat put on edge.

"He's hungry," Agnes said, just as gracious. She motioned to the ever-present servants. Immediately Ina, my nanny, came up and took me away. Agnes grabbed hold of the Finns' arms and they walked out back where the others were gathered around the pit.

They watched as the men began to dig out the sand that covered the pit. Under it were the banana leaves that had been soaked with water but were now black. Inside of them was the pig that was wrapped in its own banana leaves. All the men and women were gathered around, smoking. Agnes joined Beil who was chatting with Murray.

"Dottie, let me introduce to you my friend Murray Timmons," Beil said. He and the steward were already drunk, having quickly downed three of the very potent punches.

"Good to meet you," Murray said, putting out his hand. It had been his first time out anywhere since the incident on the streets of Palembang. Other than working he had been staying inside, afraid that he might see that man again whose eyes he would never forget. He had only come tonight because he had run into Edmond at the airport earlier in the day.

"Quick, ladies!" Beil shouted. "The chefs are untying the banana leaves and you will be the first to see." They gathered around as the men pulled back the leaves, exposing the perfectly-cooked suckling, grilled in the bottom charcoal.

One of the men tending the pig was Richal, disgusted as usual, about to puke from the sickly, tempting smell. Beside him was Timal, standing in for the regular cook. The men gave each other discreet looks, knowing that soon they would be martyred. They had both brought their guns and stashed them in the bushes just outside the house, where they could retrieve them later when the tuans and their whores were around the table, gorging themselves on the putrid flesh. Then they would rush in, guns blazing. Allah willing, they would shoot them all before escaping into the jungle.

Murray was looking at the pig, drinking in the fine aroma. He watched as Richal picked up the steaming roast with huge tongs, placing it on Timal's platter where he began cutting it. As the steam dissipated, Timal's face came out of the fog. From his angle Murray had an unobstructed view of the man and froze. His fear swelled. The face was unmistakable, the face of the killer from the other night. He yelled out: "That's the man! That's the man from the wharfs." Beil looked over as the man dropped the platter with the pig. In horror the man grabbed the carving knife.

Everybody dropped what they were doing. The other servants came running, while Beil and Carl cautiously approached the man.

"Be careful!" one of the wives shouted. Richal looked over at his friend, not sure what to do. He caught Timal's eye, motioning him to remain where he was.

"Allah Akhbar, Allah Akhbar, God is great," Timal shouted with the knife extended. He decided on the moment to make a run for it and get one of the infidel Satans on the way out. Allah willing he would escape to see another day. Timal looked for the man who had called out, recognizing him as Richal's son's corrupter. He wanted to kill him but that Satan was in the wrong direction for escape, so he chose the nearest person, poor Donald Finn. Timal stabbed him in the back then fled into the jungle.

The only one who chased after him was Richal. The rest were afraid of following a knife-wielding madman into the thick underbrush. Instead, the servants went and got their own knives and waited by the fence, hoping the man had run away. Inside the compound there was pandemonium.

"Donald! Donald!" Dottie cried as the women gathered around her. The men rushed to Donald's side.

"Umar, get the car!" Beil shouted as he tried to stem the blood that was squirting out of Donald's back. "Hurry! Hurry! We need to get him to the hospital!"

74

"The Finns' head servant wants us to talk to the young mandor to have him reverse the curse that he has so obviously put on his masters."

"It serves him right for putting on the curse to begin with," Eto said, though Talnor was her brother.

"He says he is sorry."

"He should be sorry. Lucky our young tuan has such power."

"He says he will pay the santet to come and give the mandor lessons. He says he was very happy that the mandor was with them. That night of the party when the Finn man was staring at our tuan, Ina, looked into the baby's eyes and saw the mandor was staring at the Finn tuan and that the mandor had singled him out."

"Tell him he will have to pay us also if he wants to do this," Seam said, wanting to make sure Talnor understood that what he had tried to do to their young tuan was malo, and that people have to pay in many ways for their shame.

75

Richal had been questioned by the police the day after the stabbing. At first he thought that all had gone well, so well that he was confident he had deceived them. But this confidence was shattered when they arrived back the next day to ask more questions, harder questions, giving him the feeling that they did not believe his story. Fear shocked him into action, fear that the police would soon find out the truth.

It was now dusk, Richal and Timal were at his house, both very nervous, pacing the floor, afraid to venture near the window, knowing they could not stay much longer. A police car had been around all day, circling and putting everybody on edge. Only a few minutes ago Timal had emerged from his hiding place. The old barrel was cramped. By the time he slipped out, his whole body ached. Now they were waiting for the cover of darkness to make their escape to Aceh, where they were going to join the rebellion already in progress.

"I wanted to get the American dog who twisted your son, but he was not in my line of escape," Timal lamented.

"All infidels are the same. The one you got was just as guilty," Richal said to comfort his friend. "You should have seen the tuan bleeding like a pig."

"I hope he dies."

"I'm sure he will," Richal said.

"Allah willing," both men said as they touched their foreheads while turned towards Mecca. They got up. It was time.

They were going off to Aceh where the charismatic and mysterious Kartosuwirjo was now very engaged in fighting for an Islamic state. They had even heard that new weapons were being supplied by other good Muslim brothers around the world. With this help both men were sure that soon they would be able to topple the government to finally rid Indonesia of all the Satans. Little did they know that they were being funded by the CIA, or that their revolution was being orchestrated by the likes of Nasul Rockman.

"Before I left I wrapped the guns in plastic and buried them near the compound so that when we get back we can try again," Richal said.

"Good." Timal smiled to his friend as both of them knelt down to pray for the last time before they fled into the night.

76

Donald Finn was lucky that the knife had just missed his lung. That would have been instant death. But the knife had harmlessly but painfully lodged in the muscle of his shoulder.

"You were very lucky," the Dutch doctor said to him as they were cleaning the wound.

"Yes," Donald said, still numb and scared. Dottie was by his side.

"Very unusual for a native to attack a foreigner. Did you know the man?"

"No," Donald said shakily.

"The fellow acted like a wild monkey," Dottie exclaimed, still not able to forget the look in the man's eyes as he stabbed her husband.

"This is going to hurt a bit," the doctor said as he began to sew up the deep wound. He didn't know that the trichinosis bacteria was on the end of the knife, from the pig that had not been well cooked.

"You can get your driver to take you home. Rest in bed and we will see you in two weeks."

But when Donald arrived to get the stitches out, he had the chills and was not feeling well. His whole body was one big itch and in some places he had rubbed himself raw. The most peculiar symptom was that his other shoulder that had not been affected by the knifing, ached like it had. When the doctor saw him he knew something was wrong.

At first he looked at the wound, surprised because it had healed perfectly and was obviously not the cause of these new symptoms. While he was at the hospital, Donald passed out. The Dutch doctor saw the rash and thought that it was a reaction to an infection. It took him a while, but he came finally to the right conclusion.

"Did you eat any undercooked pork?"

"Not that I can think of." Donald tried to remember. He did not care for pork, so he never had his servants cook it for him. The doctors looked at each other, perplexed, as they agreed he had the classic symptom for trichinosis. It was then that Donald cleared up the mystery.

"The only time they served it was at the party where I got stabbed, but we hadn't eaten yet."

The doctors looked at each other. They admitted Donald to the hospital and started treating him to kill the worms.

When Dottie came home and told the servants that Mr. Finn was in the hospital, Talnor rushed over to Seam to set up the meeting with the santet before things got more out of hand.

77

Umar and Beil were driving to the antiques market. All of a sudden they saw the whole road was lined with works of art.

"Look at all those carvings," Beil said, the collector part of him very excited. Umar stopped the car. The man who had been standing next to the road came by.

"Morning, tuan, I invite you to look at my wares," he said in rehearsed English. He had word from Seam that the Tuan was going to the market early, so he had decided to line the road with carvings.

"How much?" Beil inquired, a cigarette in his mouth.

"Which one, tuan?" the man asked.

"For everything."

"For all, tuan, let me see," the man said nervously. He named a price which was unrealistically high. Beil offered a lower one that was just as unrealistic. Or so he thought. But when he took a closer look at the stuff he realized that it was mostly junk. The man countered, but Beil held for his low price. They were at an impasse. But there was face involved. Beil knew that he would have to increase his offer. That walking away from the deal was not an option. The man rightly had won.

Inside Beil was angry at himself because he hadn't paid attention. It was like playing amateur bridge. There were many people watching the excitement. Finally after much talk Beil knew that he would have to go up, so he turned to the dealer.

"You want to pay this. I want to pay that. So we meet in the middle."

"Yes, tuan," the man said beaming, knowing that he had the better of the deal. With much fanfare he had his help put the overpriced junk in the car. Beil paid and they sped away.

"Why did you pay such a high price?" Umar asked, angry at the man who charged so much for such junk. "Why you pay it, tuan?"

"I did it because of face, and because sometimes it is better to be humble than to be angry. You stand out differently and are judge by your actions the next time."

"But they will bring you junk again, tuan."

"Yes they will, but I will look it over carefully and say no. Then there will be no face involved. You can learn from your mistakes. Like you and the PKI." The non sequitur remark made Umar's back tense up.

Beil had been looking for the right time to question him, having been told by the servants what he had already suspected.

"Me PKI no, tuan," Umar said unconvincingly.

"Malo, malo—shame, shame," Beil said, knowing that the invocation of that word had very many meanings for Indonesians. To be shamed was the greatest horror that one could imagine. To be shamed was the worst thing that could happen to an Indonesian. He started to stare at Umar. "Don't lie to me. I won't lie to you, so don't shame me."

"Yes, tuan." Umar decided to gamble. He could trust the tuan or not, but he would tell, getting ready to swerve the car and jump out, run if needed, kill the Tuan if needed. "I believe in the PKI what they do. They are for the workers, not for the big corporations like the one that you work for."

"You work for it, too. The company employs many Indonesians."

"Yes, tuan, but not the poor workers who are oppressed and have no guaranteed wage."

"Is that what the strikes were about in Medan?"

"Yes, tuan." But Umar knew it was more than that. Indonesia would never be free until the yoke of the foreigners was lifted. He did differ from his colleagues who had been in China, and who he found were secretly getting money from Russia. Umar had not been indoctrinated in a Communist country, but he did believe in rights for all Indonesians.

"I would like to hear more about your views. I was in China during the war and spent a lot of time in Vietnam. I had this friend who was a lot like you," Beil said, thinking of Hiu, thinking about Nationalism, thinking about Communism. He had watched Umar when his alert driving had saved him from the angry mob. Nothing was ever simple. Sometimes your enemies were your friends, and sometimes you needed to have a link to other lines of thought.

"Yes, tuan," Umar said as they reached the office. Beil was greeted by Carl Dremmer who came running out. This ended their conversation.

78

The dukun santet brought all kinds of objects and laid them out on a blanket and then had Ina place the young tuan down on it. Of course I do not remember any of this. I only remember the stories that the servants told me when I was old enough.

On the blanket was a mix of objects, some common ones from daily life but some more obscure. There were shiny objects that sparkled, very tempting for a baby. But these were not the ones that a future dukun santet would pick out. Among the thirty-six objects were six that if picked would confirm the power of the child. How powerful a dukun santet would be depended on the sequence. It was very rare for a child to pick the six objects; even rarer for him to pick them in the right order. Only a very few had the supreme gift to be able to do this. My nursemaid Ina said when I was placed on the mat I immediately picked six objects in a row, never hesitating at all.

"Ahh," the dukun santet said in disbelief. There was no mistake. "No wonder he reversed the spell," the dukun santet said with awe in his voice. "He is already a very high soul. One who understands the nature within the nature or the way the mind flows. You were very right in having me come."

"Thank you, sir," Seam said, beaming. He looked at his wife and the others and they were beaming also. The only one not beaming was Talnor, who had put the spell on Agnes.

"What else do you ask of me"? the santet asked, now that the first test was out of the way.

"We need to have the young tuan reverse the spell he put on Talnor's household to punish him for the curse." Seam asked this for Talnor, who was not able to ask the favor for himself.

"That will be up to the dukun santet, whether he reverses it or not. Since he is young I will leave ingredients for the ritual, which you will have to do on the rise of the new moon so all the magic can be completed. At that point, he will have to give you a sign. If he does not, then you will know he will not reverse the spell and nothing else will help the poor household. Putting a sihir spell on a person is a serious matter.

Sometimes dukun santets forgive, but sometimes they don't. Usually they do not. Then if you are lucky and he gives the sign, you will have to help him, as he is too young to mix the tonic himself."

"What kind of sign should we look for?" Seam asked.

"It can take on many forms, a lightening bolt, a strange wind. What it will be, no one can say, except that it will be out of the ordinary. You will know; there will be no confusion."

Just then, according to my nursemaid, I sat up and stared at the dukun santet. We locked eyes. Then I crawled over to him with one of the objects in my hand. When our hands touched there was a great spark and the object disappeared.

79

Carl Dremmer had been at the office very early waiting for Beil. "Mr. Rockman called," he said before he got out of the car. "He said it was urgent and he was coming over right away."

"Where is Richal, my office boy?" Beil asked. He wanted him in place to make Rockman drinks. It was all part of the game.

"Richal, he just disappeared. He hasn't been here since the party, when he ran after the madman," Carl said. "I hear that Donald is coming in today, first day back since he was knifed."

"That's great news. Trichinosis, I heard. Good thing we didn't eat the pig," Beil said, tongue in cheek, then added: "Oh, have somebody check on Richal. Send someone out to where he lives."

"Yes, done," Carl said. Days before, Beil had sent Umar to his village, but his wife and family did not know where he was. They seemed fearful, Umar had said. The last time anyone had seen him was chasing the attacker at the party. Beil feared that the madman had done him harm. Hopefully Carl Dremmer would have better results.

When Rockman arrived at the office, Beil was waiting with a drink and a cigarette. "What's so urgent?"

"The cabinet is going to fall. Someone has leaked out the details of the American aid package and we do not have the power to stop him," Rockman said as he relaxed with the drink Beil had made.

"When will this happen?" Beil asked.

"Soon, by next year at the latest. A few things are happening to set it up. First is the PKI. They suck up to Sukarno, whose ego is so big that he falls over them. Already most of the Medan agitators that were arrested have been freed.

The government is under pressure to refuse this American aid or at the very least modify the agreement. Sukarno I hear has begun secretly talking with other nations about what they are calling the unaligned movement." Rockman wiped his bow, nervous that this new development would allow the PKI to take more power. Both of them knew this current cabinet had been trying to stop the PKI.

"What will the army do?"

"We will wait, for now. But we need to know that we can count on our friends," Rockman said.

He was happy when Beil answered, "Yes, friends shall help friends in open seas; even under water." Beil used the image to let Rockman know that the USA was there when he asked. It was like finesse, the saying but not saying. It was like the murky sea where the real sharks lived.

"At some point you will have to control Sukarno more," Beil said, fully aware that Indonesia was full of various factions that could be used against the other. The falling of a government was nothing new. They came and went like waves. The only one that kept standing was Sukarno; now the most powerful man in the country. The fear was if he became more powerful than the military—not the official military but the secret one that Rockman was part of—then there would be no one able to ride Sukarno and they would all fail.

"Yes, but he has the people," Rockman said with some pride and some hate. For now he and his friends would stay on the sidelines and see how things worked out. That Sukarno did not want this aid or that the cabinet was going to be dissolved did not really bother them at all, at least not now. But he needed to preserve this contact with Beil, who could get them the secret money that they needed. He looked over and saw Beil in thought.

"Yes, when someone has the power of the masses it is best to slowly bend them to your side," Beil said, thinking of Ho Chi Minh and Vietnam where things were playing out badly. The general said the French were losing ground every day. To Beil Sukarno was a Nationalist, not a Communist. The US had to do something to keep him that way, before ideas turned into actions or events were put on track that could disable the whole country. He knew that Rockman was using him as he was using Rockman. He reached into his desk, pulled out the envelope. Rockman relaxed when he saw that everything was still normal.

"Here," Beil said. "Here is a token of how I value our friendship." Both knew that they were joined together on a rollercoaster.

80

It was the night of the new moon. The servants of every household were anxiously awaiting a sign from the young dukun santet to see if he had decided to reverse his curse.

"Why are they all just watching little William so intently?" Sally Dremmer asked as she, Agnes, and Dottie were having four o'clock tea.

"Oh, you know, the servants are like children," Dottie said, now recovered from her surgeries. Donald had just come home this morning. To her Indonesia didn't make sense, unless you realized that the Indonesians were just children with simple children's minds.

"It's because Will is so handsome," Agnes said as she stroked his hair. She looked around, feeling the eyes of everyone watching. The servants looked away, but as soon as she picked up her tea to listen to the other ladies, they went back to looking at me.

"When will the dukun give his sign?" Talnor asked.

"Soon," Seam said. "Did you get the ingredients ready?"

"Yes." Talnor had gotten the required hairs from Dottie and Donald by having his cousin, the cleaning woman, bring a few samples from their hair brushes. Then he had taken the left shoe from each of them. The hair and the shoes had been mixed with some special spices the old dukun had left with them. All the ingredients had been cooked together in a pot. All that was ready. What was not ready was the secret ingredient that the baby dukun would add once the sign was given. If it were given.

Another hour passed, and still nothing. Finally Ina informed them the baby tuan had fallen asleep.

"Oh, no," Talnor said to his wife. "We are doomed." The dark of night was fast approaching and everything was very, very normal.

"It serves you right!" his wife yelled at him, furious about the curse that had backfired, forgetting that it had been her idea. Time was short and their hope was slipping away. In about ten minutes the new moon would be up, after that all would be lost. Maybe the baby dukun would put even a greater curse on all of them. Talnor began to tremble.

Just as he had all but given up hope, a loud shriek permeated the compound, followed by the sound of thunderous footsteps. Sally's pet elephant was stampeding wildly around the compound with her trunk blasting a constant terrifying wail.

The servants dashed outside. To their amazement, a tiger had jumped over the fence and was sitting in the yard right in front of the Beil's house. Astonished, Talnor called to the female tuans who came running to see the very rare event. The cat looked at them for about two minutes, never making any kind of a move.

The Sumatran tiger was the rarest and most elusive animal in the jungle. Poor Beil, who was not there, had been actively trying to see one for years but never was lucky enough, despite having spent hours with Umar driving the jungle roads. All the women called for their cameras. When the servants rushed back with them, the women ventured as close as they dared and started snapping pictures. The flashes startled the great cat. They watched in awe as the great beast jumped over the fence, disappearing back into the jungle just as the slip of the moon appeared.

There was no doubt in any of the servants' minds that the young dukun had given his sign.

Quickly, Ina woke the baby and brought him to the servants' quarters so he could finish the spell. Talnor bowed to him and put the vessel with the liquid in front of him. To everybody's delight the young dukun took his pacifier out of his mouth and threw it into the brew while laughing.

"It is done," exclaimed a beaming Seam. He was happy for the power of the young dukun and the unmistakable sign he had given.

"Thank you, mandor," Talnor said as he knelt before the baby. The young boy looked into his eyes, unnerving Talnor with his power. It was all the servant could do to stumble away gratefully.

"Terima kasih—thank you," he said over and over.

Now he had to rush the mixture with the dukun's secret ingredient and get the Finns and everybody else in their household to drink some. Getting the servants to drink was easy but still somehow they had to get the tuan and his wife to do it too.

It was now before supper and Talnor had mixed up the drinks and put some of the liquid in. It was the Finns favorite air jeruk, or special limeade. Thankfully the color did not change, but the taste did. He handed a glass to Dottie and then to Donald. He was very relieved when they both took big sips, and were unable to spit the liquid out.

"The lime must be rotten!" Dottie yelled. The vile liquid tasted like a smelly shoe.

"Terrible," Donald remarked, "Talnor, make another pitcher and throw out this rotten batch."

"Sorry, tuan, I had no idea," Talnor said happy now that their luck was going to change.

It was now summer of 1953. Indonesia was about to send its first ambassador to China, which no longer was hostile to regimes that did not support their point of view. The Chinese were evolving; Indonesia was evolving with them.

The PKI was also evolving. There was a new split in the movement. This split was in Umar's mind as he headed to a meeting with Kusdi, who had recently arrived back in Indonesia after living in Russia and China for the last few years.

Past midnight, in the Palembang safe-house they all sat down together. "We need to storm the plantations and kill all the foreign dogs," Kusdi said. To Kusdi working within the system was too slow. Sukarno was too unpredictable. The military was not going to support the PKI unless it was forced by the will of the masses.

"What you propose is folly," Umar said. He had learned a lot from watching Beil: that you had to wait for things. He also began to think that there was good in both systems, communist and capitalist.

"What do you know? You have never been to the Soviet Union," Kusdi said. "You know nothing of life in a worker's paradise."

"It is folly. You were not here in 1948 when Musso tried that kind of direct action. He was so sure, but he was put down. We were crushed. It has only been in the last few years, working from within, that we have been able to further our cause.

"Oh Umar, you have become infected by the American dog you follow," Undara said. "We have been lulled into thinking we can change from within, but this Sukarno will put us down. We need to begin the battle. Take the fight to our enemies, now!"

"No, Umar is right," Natal said. He like Umar was young and idealistic, but had not been indoctrinated into Stalinism. "We need to make Sukarno our number one friend and make him do just what we want, make him think it was his own idea."

Just as they were about to continue, they heard the warning whistles. Then the rush of footsteps as the intruders approached. Quickly they climbed out of the floor-hole just as the first of the secret police came running in the door, but their enemies were waiting for them.

Umar struggled to break away. Another man came up and tried to grab him. But he was able to slap him in the face, pushing him into the man who had hold of his other hand. This gave Umar the extra second he needed to break free, race out to the sidewalk, where he saw a few others running away, among them Kusdi. Those that got away ducked into an ally; the place was eerie, dark except for an occasional oil lamp that flickered like a firefly. Behind them they could hear shouting and the crackle of gunfire.

Still they raced on, crossing over a little stream following it until it got to the muddy Musi River, where they stole a boat and floated off into the night. On the other side they split up, vanishing with the approaching dawn.

82

Agnes had to eventually find out about Beil's secret desires, because even someone very careful had to take chances. No one can be in two places at the same time.

In January of 1954, it was time for another famous Standard Oil bowling party by the communal garden of the compound. All day long all the servants from the various households had carefully cleaned and trimmed and set up a huge tent in anticipation of the grand event.

The first of the guests started to arrive around five. There was the usual punch fountain, along with an open bar. The servants were busy bringing tray after tray of appetizers, sate and shrimp wrapped in cilantro, to be dipped into peanut sauce.

In the far corner of the yard there was the cooking tent that sat next to the fire pit. This year instead of the pig, Beil had gotten a side of Australian prime beef, which was still being slow-roasted in the pit.

The women wore dresses and the men wore Hawaiian shirts. For the first time an Indonesian had been invited. For the last year Sukarno had been in the process of nationalizing many of the foreign businesses, especially the remaining Dutch businesses. Rockman was here to reassure them that in principal everything would remain the same.

"Thank you," Rockman said, introducing his wife. She was dressed in western style.

"Ahh…" Eto raised her eyes to the matronly Indonesian woman dripping in gold, but clad in a western dress that made her look like something in the comic section of the newspapers that arrived from America.

"They must be very important," Seam said as he was preparing a new batch of punch.

"I hear that he is very powerful in the army," Umar said. He knew all about Rockman. He consciously retreated to the background, still unnerved by his near-capture by the secret police a few months earlier.

Those arrested had never been seen again. The good news was that PKI members caught by the regular police or army were mostly released, not like in 1948 when they also would have disappeared. But the situation was in flux now with the PKI's infiltration into Sukarno's good graces. The turning point had been when Sukarno had stood up against the military.

This was back in the fall of 1952 when the army had rebelled and taken to the streets to protest the disbanding of some of their units. Sukarno had faced them down thanks to the PKI, who had orchestrated the crowds. Sukarno intensified his power by having the people rise to his support, so that together they were greater than the army.

The only real problem for the PKI was the secret army that Rockman was part of. Umar did not want to take any chances.

"Nasul, this is my wife, Agnes."

"Good to meet you, madam," Rockman said in his accented English. He found Beil's wife a little too skinny. Rockman's wife was beside him, very glad to be invited, very glad to be flaunting her gold in front of the servants. She was pleased to see their open jealousy, confident no one would know she had grown up poor, like them.

"This is my wife, Saya."

"Saya, what a pretty name," Agnes said taking the woman by the arm. "Here, let me introduce you to the rest of the wives. Dottie, let me introduce to you Mrs. Rockman."

The servants watched, amazed that their madam would greet this common woman like a westerner. They were even more shocked when Saya took the glass of champagne that was offered to her, and raised it in a toast toward them. It was almost as if she wanted all of them to see.

Over by the pit the men gathered, watching the beef come out. They watched as the sand was shoveled off the pit, exposing the outer layer of banana leaves. The steam and flavor started escaping and soon the smells that had been kept inside now wafted over the crowd.

One of the chefs was a handsome young man that had gotten Beil's attention. Their eyes had met. The man winked. Beil winked back. Beil lit a cigarette as he fought hard to disguise his desire.

"Come, everybody get into line," Carl said drunkenly as the large slab of meat was carried to the carving table. The young chef was the head carver. Beside the beef there were salads, nasi goreng and many dishes of wonderful cooked vegetables. Rockman and his wife were next to Beil and Agnes as they waited their turn in line.

"We're having fun, darling," Agnes said. She and Saya had hit it off. Saya's English was not as good as Rockman's, so Agnes was speaking Indonesian, much to the delight of the servants.

"You'll have to come for lunch next week at the Stanvac club," Agnes said as they approached the line.

"I'd love too," Saya said, beaming. She saw the invisible faces of all the watching servants, which thrilled her.

Beil approached the carving station with anticipation in his mind. He thought about the showers back in Vietnam.

"What part would you like, tuan?" the young man asked demurely.

"I'd like some very red, with lots of that good fat from the rear," Beil said making sure that no one saw his eyes as he winked again.

"I have something very rare and will save you some when you come back for seconds," the young man answered back.

An hour later Beil came outside to get some fresh air. He lit a cigarette and headed for the rendezvous. He was happy to find his new friend out there waiting for him by the hibiscus bush. The rest of the barbeque crew had already gone home. Beil knew that they only had a few minutes before he would be missed at the party. They went behind the bush, which was on the side of the compound near the back yard.

Agnes was inside. Seam came up to her. "Sorry to bother Madam, but the young tuan is crying and will not stop until he sees you."

"Be right back," Agnes said to Saya and Sally Dremmer and headed to check on me, deciding to take the back way to the house. She was walking along the lane when she heard something coming from behind the Hibiscus. It sounded a little like the soft moan the baby elephant would make when the poor thing was hurt. She went over to see if she could help, but it was not the baby elephant. "Oh my," she said as she sped to the house.

83

That night Agnes had a dream where she was dressed like a native in a gold sarong being led up a mountain that was covered in flowers and banana trees. The flowers were shaped like vaginas; the bananas like penises. She walked ahead. There sitting under one of the banana trees between the penises and vaginas was Anne, the general's wife, smoking her beloved menthol cigarettes.

"Rather confusing isn't it?" she said as she took a drag and puffed out smoke that covered the whole jungle, turning everything grey. When the smoke cleared, Agnes found herself walking on a gold path toward a mountain peak. Anne was still by her side.

"You must have had the signs," Anne said. "There are always signs." Soon they had reached the mountain and at the top was a hut. Agnes knocked.

"Come in," the voice said through the door.

"I will leave you now," the general's wife said.

"Don't leave."

"Oh, don't worry." Anne took one more drag on her cigarette and blew a cloud of smoke. When it cleared, she was gone. The door became a giant door all painted green. She knocked again. The door opened. Sitting on the floor was a wise old man dressed in blue with a shaved head.

"You need to decide whether to live life or let life live you."

"What do you mean?"

"Life is but a dream of your own making."

"But I can never forget what I saw."

"Forget and forgive. You are to forgive for the rest of your life."

"The rest of my life…"

"Yes, do you want to throw away everything, forget everything because you can not forgive one thing?"

"How do I forget?"

"By accepting that everything is not what it means or seems."

Just as he was saying this, another cloud of smoke drifted over them. And when it cleared the monk was gone and Agnes and the general's wife were walking back down the mountain.

"The first time I found out, I was just like you, but then I realized that it was nothing but a dream, a dream that was only a nightmare if I let it be one." She took another puff and handed Agnes the cigarette.

"Here take a puff and you will see. It's not so bad. The first time is always the worst. It gets better until you are looking forward to it. Think about it. I did, and I had a wonderful life with the general."

Agnes woke up to find the sun out and her two-year-old son smiling at her.

84

Richal and Timal ducked behind the rubber tree, desperately trying to escape the rain of bullets. They had been ambushed an hour earlier and were fighting their way back into the jungle, fleeing a much larger and better-equipped enemy. Already half of their sixty men had been martyred and of those frantically fleeing many were seriously wounded.

"Don't they understand?" Richal screamed.

"They are possessed by the devil," Timal shouted back.

It began to rain. The sound of the torrent pouring from the forest canopy mixed with the thud of the bullets, making it almost impossible for them to hear. It was a stark change from the euphoria they had felt when they first arrived.

The two men had now been away from their home for over a year, living in one jungle camp after another, following the elusive and charismatic Kartosuwirjo, who had become a major distraction of both time and money for the new republic. He was particularly dangerous when his Daryl Islam movement formed an alliance with a more moderate Muslim party that had their own reasons to rebel.

The secret army of Rockman had debated what to do, finally deciding to unleash the regular army to drive these two groups apart; crush them before they got organized. Never mind that it was their idea to tolerate, even foster the small Islamic movement to use as a weapon against the central government, if needed. They had not anticipated that the whole north end of Sumatra would revolt. They were very concerned that the radical Muslim movement might spread to other places.

"I can't believe this Sukarno dog did not join us," Richal said between bursts of gunfire, still stunned that any Muslim would want to abandon Shariah law. For the last few months Daryl Islam had been fighting a guerrilla war, swooping down from their mountain camps and attacking. This time, though, the army had been waiting.

Now their band of sixty was reduced to ten. They made their way blindly through the jungle, stumbling in the underbrush, shocked that the army was still after them. They soon lost their way. An hour later they came to the edge of a cliff that had been carved by the raging river 200 feet below. They were trapped.

"What shall we do?" someone said, lifting his head to peer over the foliage. The bullet came out of nowhere. Richal felt the hot brains land on him. They must surrender or die.

"Oh shit, I'm out of ammunition!" Timal shouted, his head and hand covered in blood from the jungle thorns. There was a thick grime of gun powder on his face, mixed with his hot sweat. Just then another of the rebels shouted he was out of ammo, then another. It was like Allah had abandoned them.

"We have nothing to be martyred with!" Richal shouted. But no one wanted to lose his life, now that death was so close.

"We have our hands and knives." The brave words rang hollow. The rebels were no match for the heavy machine guns or the superior numbers. The first of them surrendered. The rest watched him step out of his hiding place, hands over his head, and start to walk toward the army. He was shot dead as soon as he took his first step—the army was not going to take prisoners. Richal, Timal and the rest of them backed up against the cliff. They heard the battle cry as the army charged the last fifty yards, peppering the jungle with machine-gun fire.

"Jump, brother, Allah will protect us," Richal said as he leaped off the cliff. Timal followed with two of the others. But two remained cowering on the cliffs, afraid to jump to a certain death. One of the officers came up shot them each in the head. Then he shouted orders to his men, who flung the bodies off the cliff. They struck the water just as Richal surfaced, almost crushing him. But thankfully Allah had provided. Where they jumped was a very deep area of the river. Richal swam up to one of the corpses. The blood was pouring out of the dead man's head. Still Richal hung on to him to help him swim. They went through a few rapids together, before he spotted Timal on a boulder with a long stick in his hand. Richal grabbed it and joined him on the rock where they waited for the others that never came.

"Allah saved us."

"Yes, it was not our time to be martyred"

"I think it is time to go back home."

"To be where we are supposed to be martyred."

"At the compound of the infidels."

85

Beil had spent the morning at the antique market. The events of the last night weighed heavy on his mind. It was just like being caught in the showers and facing another court martial, a trial of his life with Agnes. He knew that nothing could be put back into a bottle. His secret was in the open.

Right after she had spotted them, he'd chased after her. But after she had rushed to quiet me, she had rejoined the party as if nothing had happened. He watched the surrealistic drama of her drinking champagne while making small talk with the rest of the women. Whenever he tried to approach, she would hand him her glass calling out for all to hear, "Oh darling, go get me some more champagne." And he would go and get some. No one had any suspicion that anything was amiss, not even the servants.

After about an hour of non-stop drinking she had passed out and was still sleeping when Beil had left early for the market with Umar.

"Why are you so sad today, tuan?" Umar asked as they were driving.

"Oh, I'm just tired," he said, trying to think his way out of things. It was like a circle had returned, bringing back the same feelings of when he had been thrown out of the army.

"Well, my friend told me of this new dealer who comes from Jakarta. He has just arrived with many antiques."

"Let's go." Beil interest was revived. The solution with Agnes had not come to him yet. He thought about his feelings, how despite his attraction for men he did love her. As they were driving, his mind flashed on his own dreams of the woman in the penis chair, hoping that somewhere within that was the solution. His musing brought him back to the present as they arrived at the dealer's house.

The dealer laid out his wares. They were mostly Chinese porcelain of various qualities, but one thing attracted Beil immediately. It was the little figure of a praying monk dressed in blue robes. Next to him was a nice foo dog protector. The way they looked together reminded him of Agnes, and with no bargaining bought them for her.

When they got back to the compound Beil headed for the house, feeling very nervous, not knowing what to expect. It was all very strange because the servants still had no idea that anything was amiss. As he entered the living room she called to him. "Come over to the porch, darling." She spoke in a strong, excited voice. Beil had expected to see her in a funk, staring at the floor, or furious. He went to the porch, where she was directing the servants who were putting up a wall of fish tanks.

"I thought that I would get some fish." She looked at him, with very little emotion. There were lots and lots of fish. There was tank after tank, some with many fish of the same kind, some with many types of fish, and some with only one fish each.

"Did you have a good day?" Agnes asked. She came over to hand him a glass of champagne. Still, he could not read her. This was like a bridge game where he was playing with last night's hand. This was not the reaction he had expected; he was at a loss. He tried to look into her face, but she was like a master poker player.

"Which fish is your favorite?" he asked, looking over the tanks, marveling at the wall of fish.

"It depends on what my mood is for the day," she said. "Last night I would have liked the school in this tank where there are many varieties and all of them live in harmony together. But today I like this one." She pointed to one by itself, very handsome but alone in its tank. It was like the monk in her dream, almost human-looking, and dressed as if in cloths of blue and white.

"The Seamese fighting fish spends its whole life alone, because when it is with others it is always fighting," Beil said.

"Do you like to fight, Edmond?" She was surprised how well she was keeping it all in. She must have gotten her stiff upper lip from her

Scottish mother. She had decided that she did not want to end up like the fighting fish, alone. Watching the fish, she had been thinking that life was like swimming in a fish bowl, the water and the tank made of morals that were formed by generation after generation.

"No. I don't like to fight," Edmond said. "I am sorry."

"Do you have other secrets?" she asked him. She looked right at him. He thought he saw a little moisture in her eyes.

"Only in business."

"I want the truth," Agnes said, eyes level.

"That is the truth," Beil said. "I thought that you understood."

"Do you love me, Edmond?" she asked.

"Yes, I do." He came up and hugged her. "I do, I do."

"I don't want to be like that fighting fish."

"Neither do I," he said.

"How deep is this desire in you?"

"Very deep."

"Is there love involved?"

"No, not love. Desire. It is different. I love you, not them." Beil felt the tears rise up in him. He paused and thought. The men he most cared about—like the general, Dewey, Hiu, Umar, and Rockman—he did not desire.

"Here, this is for you." Beil took the wrapped figures from the antique market. Agnes opened the package. There it was, the figure of her dream with a dog to guard it. The last barrier was broken; she would forgive his desire.

"Thank you, darling," she said, "but I have one rule: not near me. If you have your fun: not near here. Away is all I ask. Be discreet, darling, but remember when I drink champagne I get bubbly."

"Yes dear," Beil said, emotion coming out of him. Hugging her, they both started to cry. And then laugh and then uncontrollably laugh.

Agnes called out to the ever-watching servants, "Get us more champagne!"

1954, and the nightmare of Major Dewey came true. The first of the dominoes had fallen. The French had been defeated at Dien Bien Phu. Hanoi and northern Vietnam were in the hands of Ho Chi Minh. America was scrambling to prop up the South Vietnamese with an influx of American advisers, both civilian and military.

Now with the division of the country, the CIA wanted to do something more forceful to defeat the ever-growing force of Communism. To meet this challenge, the General and all others in the Asian theater were called to a summit in Singapore.

Beil arrived at the hotel on Orchard Street and headed for the boardroom where the meeting was already in progress. When Beil opened the door, he bristled with instant rage. There was Larry Haggard.

"Captain Haggard, good to see you," he said in his most condescending voice, even though his major stripe was evident. "To what do we owe the pleasure of your company?"

"I'm on loan to the agency, have been for a couple of years, flying operations inside Vietnam and other places. I'm a major now. You may address me as that, sergeant."

"Oh, I'm not in the military so I think I'll just call you Haggard. It's more fitting."

"It's Major Haggard."

"Yes, Haggard, I can see."

"I am a Major, God damn it!"

"Yes, Haggard, you said it, a major's major."

"Enough of that," the general barked out, inwardly amused that Beil had parried the man, amused also that Haggard, despite his anger, was oblivious of the putdown. There were several others in the room that also caught the clever insult.

"I'm Tim Johnson," said the handsome man to Beil's left. He was tall with his hair combed back, very well dressed—something Beil noticed right away.

153

The general was summing up. "Vietnam has fallen. Ho has taken over the north. There is no way we are going to get it back, but the south is still free and the US government has drawn a line from where it will defend the freedom of the rest of Vietnam." His words made Beil muse on Hiu, on Dewey, but most of all he mused on the misunderstanding that was about to drag America into the very hell that they had tried so hard to avoid.

"Good. Now it's time to take it back," Haggard growled, confirming to Beil that the ruthless idiot had not changed and was still a top-gun killing machine. Haggard turned to Beil, loathing him, sick that he was here, disgusted by the knowledge that just by being here this faggot was high up in the game. He thought about back then, reliving the pleasure of putting his gun to Beil's gook friend's face then pulling the fucking trigger. "You were right about one thing, Sergeant, the fucking French were worthless. Now those gooks will watch what it's like to fight a real army. We'll take the country back."

The general sighed, furious that Haggard was here at all. The man was not qualified, had no finesse, and was only here because someone in Washington had used him to fly covert planes in South America and then a few in Vietnam. Now with the French falling there was a rush to find experienced operatives. The general had voiced his extreme objection but had been overruled by the wave of panic that was sweeping over the entire government.

"It's very important to go slowly according to our long range plans. We do not need to get swept up with the rest of them and go in like cowboys firing at everything. Vietnam will become the military's responsibility with help from us, but the other countries in South East Asia will be ours to hold."

After a few hours the meeting was over. It had been more of a pep talk than anything else. For Beil, the only important thing to come out of the meeting was the discovery that Tim was an avid bridge player. Dinner was over and Beil, Tim, Major Jim and the general were in his hotel suite, relaxing after having just finished a rubber.

"Tim is in charge of Thailand," the general said. "Like you he is running the show almost alone."

"Thailand is as important as Vietnam."

"Soon it will be even more important than it is now. It will be a staging point for Vietnam," Tim said.

"Do you think Thailand is in danger?" the general asked him.

"No, they are natural enemies with the Vietcong, so that will not be a problem."

"But so are the Chinese and the Vietnamese," the general commented. Then he turned Beil's way. "What about Indonesia?"

"It's much more complicated. First, the colonial powers are now mostly out. They are starting to nationalize the Dutch industries. The Communist Party, the PKI, is recruiting many people, but lots of them are nationalist, not Communist. Then there is Sukarno, who tries to use everybody while they all try to use him. The wild cards are the Muslims, whom we keep as a check on the government's power. But we can't let them take over, or make Indonesia into a Muslim state—that has its own problems. All this is on the surface, but within the military is the shadow power. I am confident that if the PKI tries another coup, the shadow military will be able to shut it down with our help. It's going to need finesse."

"Yes, finesse will be needed, but some of our problem will be to keep the Haggards of the world from rushing in and messing it all up," the general said somewhat sadly as the game and night came to an end.

As they were going, Tim Johnson came to shake Beil's s hand. "If you ever come to Thailand, look me up. I'm not hard to find." He gave him his card and a wink—Tim Johnson, Fine Antiques.

His cover was as an international antiques dealer.

87

During the power struggle for Indonesia in the summer of 1954, something happened that worried Beil: The Indonesian economy was falling apart due to the end of the Korean War. Resources such as rubber and tin were no longer in such demand, leaving many people out of work.

It started with the smallest of events. Beil and Umar were driving through the city of Palembang after visiting the antique market. As they were driving back to the compound, they passed by a rubber plantation where a mob of angry men were standing by the entrance gate.

"Merdeka—freedom," they were yelling. On the inside there was an armed westerner, a Dutch man who was waving his gun at the crowd. Only a small part of the gate was open. In the gap were another westerner and a few Indonesians who were having the men queue up in single file. Some were admitted, but most were turned away.

"What do you think is happening?" Beil asked Umar, though he knew the reason already: huge unemployment. It was strange to him how everything was intertwined, how the end of a war in Korea led to unemployment and unrest in Indonesia.

"There is no work," Umar said while both of them watched. Umar knew that this was fertile land for the PKI. They were active all over the country fomenting strife and strikes. He was sure there were members in this crowd who were organizing the peasants.

"I hear a lot has to do with the Dutch in Irian Jaya. There is much anti-Dutch, anti-western feeling developing."

"Yes, tuan, soon Indonesia will start to move on its own," Umar said, knowing he should not be telling Beil anything.

"I hear the Chinese Communists are funding a lot of the unrest," Beil said, semi-guessing, wanting to gauge the situation to see if the rumors were true. In 1953 when the Red Chinese had started to court nations, Indonesia had been high on its list. Officially they just wanted to be friends, but the Chinese way, Beil knew, was not so simple. For generations they would send members of their families all over the world to start businesses. They would adapt to the local customs. Grow those businesses but at the same time still be Chinese.

"I would not know about that," Umar said unconvincingly, sure that Beil knew he was lying. This new money did bother him. It was frustrating that money was needed. Money always had strings, whether it was from the capitalistic dogs or hard-line Communists. He saw that even though it allowed them to reach more people, it threatened to change the PKI so that it was no longer an Indonesian phenomenon.

All of a sudden they saw a man break though the crowd and rush at the man with the gun. The armed man was faster and slammed him in the face with the butt. Even from where Umar and Beil were standing they saw blood and teeth fly into the air. The crowd rushed forward, pressed on by their anger about to tear down the gates. Umar and Beil cowered in the car waiting for the violence to erupt. Shots rang out. The guards shot in rapid secession over the crowd, turning them into a panic as they all stampeded away. One of the stray bullets pieced the windshield, passing inches between Beil and Umar.

"Let's get out of here!" Beil shouted as Umar slammed the car into first and sped away.

88

Three weeks later a rogue Dutch major and his band of men, fed up with everything, went on a rampage of murder and plunder. Incited by the near-riots they began attacking army bases and robbing banks as they moved through Java. His name was Ton Van Derstock and he had been fighting a losing battle since the Japanese invasion. If only the homeland had listened they could have done what his grandfather did, just killed enough people until there was no dissent for a generation.

They were moving up into the mountains, playing a cat and mouse game with the army that was following them. So far they had stayed ahead, but everyone knew it was just a matter of time. No one would be coming to their aid. Most of his men had grown up in Indonesia and even though they were not of native blood they felt native. They were now near the tea plantations around Mega Mendung.

That evening they held up in an old farmhouse building near the Stanvac country house. In the morning when they awoke, a loudspeaker blasted at them in Dutch: "We have you surrounded. Give up and no one will be hurt."

"What should we do, sir? Should we surrender?"

"You want to surrender?" the major said.

"No, sir."

"Any man who wants to is free to, but they will not treat you well. For the rest of us, the time has come to make a stand," the major said, knowing that they were low on ammo and the chances of getting out were zero.

"What should we do with all the treasure, sir?"

"Bury it in the corner and throw those old boards over it. Don't want them to get it. Then let's break out the last of the whiskey and make sure everyone gets enough. Then we fight to the death. We'll show the fucking Indonesians how tough the Dutch really are."

"No one wastes their bullets," his sergeant shouted. To emphasize his point he put his rifle to the window, picked out a target, and fired. They all cheered as the man went down. Immediately bullets started to fly all around them.

Two hours later only the major and his sergeant were left. Both were wounded but both were happy seeing all the dead bodies outside.

"It's been a good run, sergeant," Ton said.

"Yes sir, a pleasure to serve you, you were right to fight, sir."

89

By the time I was three my fame as the white dukun had spread so much that many people came to seek out my services. Some of my earlier memories were being in the servants' quarters. I remember incense was burning while I was perched atop the ceremonial chair Seam had carved for me. I do not recall much of what I did but I do remember people giving me all kinds of sweet treats. My favorite was the very sweet sticky coconut candy wrapped in banana leaves. To keep this secret from my parents the servants taught me a little-known Sumatran dialect so they could speak to me without my parents having any idea of what we were talking about. My fame as a dukun can all be traced back to a single event. I have no recollection of it except for what was told to me by those servants who witnessed the supposed miracle.

My nursemaid's sister's child was in a terrible way with a rash that was spreading over her whole body. She was delirious with a raging fever, obviously possessed by black magic. Her parents were at their wits' end. Everyone knew that it would take a miracle to save her life. I was her last desperate hope, as they had already sought out several dukuns whos spells had failed.

As I was still new to this dukun business, the servants provided me a basin where I would place things in that they would then boil into a thick paste which the people would either spread on their bodies or drink, depending on the circumstance. In this basin I put all kinds of things ranging from toys to leaves to bugs to even bird eggs that I would find during the day.

On this particular day I had had broken into my mother's medicine cabinet and had managed to open several of her tubes of antibiotic cream. When the servants brought the basin, I smeared the globs of cream from my hands into it.

Later that day the hysterical woman brought her barely-conscious young daughter, totally covered in a fiery rash that made her look like a slab of raw meat. As bad as it was, the rash was something that a western doctor would easily heal if it was treated in time, but time was running out. Unfortunately the mother was from the countryside and did not believe in doctors, just folk cures.

The servants say that when I saw the girl, I got off of the seat and dipped my hands into the basin and spread the cream all over her body. Then I pointed to the rest of stuff in the basin, which the servants took as a sign from me that the woman was to spread it on her daughter in the coming days.

Three days later, the woman returned, convinced that the miracle was the work of the white dukun with the magic powers. Her whole village accompanied her in hopes of getting a glimpse of me.

So this is what happens when superstition and fate intertwine with modern medicine. Even though it was luck that I had gone into the medicine cabinet that day and there was a natural explanation as to why she was cured, the girl would have died had I not seen her.

90

Nasul Rockman huddled with the rest of the leadership of the secret army trying to understand what was happening; how far they should let it happen, or whether they could stop it from happening. It was now the fall of 1955 and it seemed like nothing was going right. The uprising they had fomented in Aceh had now turned into a protracted battle that was a thorn in their sides, sucking money. The PKI was now working relentlessly to reach out to the farmers, thus growing their base outside of the city. It did not help that Indonesia had runaway inflation with huge unemployment. It seemed that problems were like plants in a rain-soaked valley, sprouting up anywhere and everywhere.

But these problems were nothing compared to the growing power of Sukarno. He was now the father of Indonesia. All the people were his children. Twice the secret army had tried to move against him, but both times they were forced to retreat at the last moment. He was unpredictable, sometimes ruthless, and whenever he was cornered he would appeal to the people and be saved.

"The situation is like a wave that could break at any time," Rockman said. For the first time he was worried that they could lose control. What startled him the most was the slow but sure infiltration by the Chinese. It had made them all aware of the vast power of the wave: that the Chinese would use Sukarno without him knowing. Already Indonesia was moving away from the US, which was something that Beil had told them in their last meeting. He had conveyed to Rockman that his government was very upset with the direction of Sukarno's new unaligned movement. The meeting last month that Chou En Lai attended, had put the fear of God in them all—so much so that they all now had Swiss bank accounts.

"Maybe it is time to remove the dog once and for all."

"That would lead to chaos that we might not be able to control."

"I agree," Suharto said. "The best way is to wait until we have the opportunity, and then act. Tell Mr. Beil that we want a meeting to discuss the unofficial American ideas as well as our unofficial ideas."

The men around the table chuckled. Despite being somewhat out of control, the times were exciting. The feeling that welled up inside of them was indescribable.

91

Agnes's first trip to the island of Bali was like going to wonderland. As exotic as Sumatra was, Bali was ten times more. From the very moment that the DC 3 touched down, she was very excited.

"We should have gone here before, darling," she said. Edmond looked at the smile on his wife's face and felt the excitement. He had been to Bali a few times before. It was a completely different part of Indonesia. The most important difference was the religion. Instead of Muslim, the island was Hindu. This Hindu culture fostered a more communal or socialistic style of living. Village elders ran communities that were self contained and shared everything. They would farm together, sow together. Everybody got a share. Because of this it was fertile ground for the PKI, who had a considerable presence. Beil had seen the movement grow from a few thousand to now hundreds of thousands.

"The Stanvac house has just opened and we are the first to stay in it. Wait till we get there. It is right on the beach," Beil said, patting the head of William who was seated between them.

"Can we look for fish and shells?" William asked, now a young inquisitive boy of 4. He had a fascination with fish, thanks to Agnes, who now had over a hundred tanks with two full-time servants—cousins of Seam—to look after them. William had spent many hours staring at the fish. His dad had told him that there were reefs of beautiful coral that they could explore at low tide.

"Of course, son," Edmond said. It had been over a year since Agnes had discovered his secret life. She had forgiven him completely. He was so happy that he was still able to indulge his desires as long as he indulged them away from her. This was more than any man could hope for. It made his love for her even stronger.

When they got out of the airport, Umar was waiting for them. He had driven to the ferry and had arrived the night before. He was there in front of the tiny airport, smiling to see them.

"Selamat, tuan, madam and young mandor," he said, using William's nick-name. "Welcome to Bali," he added, eager to meet with the leader of Bali PKI to plan for the future. He had been unable to figure out a way to take the time to come to Bali, so when Beil had asked him if he would like to come on the trip, he jumped at the chance.

"Have you been to Bali much?" Agnes asked him.

"Yes, madam, I used to live here for a few years with my wife," Umar said, accepting the Marlboro that Beil handed him.

"I didn't know you were married," Beil said. It just proved that even though you think you know this or that about people and their lives, really there is so much you don't know.

"Yes, tuan, I was married to the most beautiful girl in the world." He answered, thinking of Yara who had gotten sick when they had moved out of this paradise into the slums of Jakarta right after the war. With her death his dreams of a family were over. In one way it was good that she had died, because now he could focus on the revolution.

"She died in my arms."

"Oh, I'm so sorry," Agnes said, grabbing hold of William's hand.

"It was very sad, but that is part of life. She was from Bali, and Bali is like a fragile flower that lives for the moment." They got into the car and drove out of the city of Denpasar. The first thing they noticed was that the woman did not wear any blouses and their breasts were exposed, both young and old. They were transfixed by this, especially young William. At first Agnes tried to shield his eyes but as they drove along she soon found that that was impossible.

The other thing they saw was cows walking around free and everywhere. "Why are there so many cows?" Beil asked.

"Because, tuan, Bali is Hindu and they worship the cow, so they are free to go everywhere, even in the city."

"Don't people eat them?"

"No, they do not eat them. They just are part of the landscape."

"Do they eat meat?"

"Yes, pork is the main food, and fish," Umar said. It was just the opposite in Sumatra and Java: they ate beef but not pork. Beil thought how foolish religion really was, how one dogma was the opposite of another, so therefore both were wrong. Like why do people think they need to believe so strongly in their view that they would kill for it thereby losing the real intention of God, if there was one?

Umar seemed to read his mind. "It is very funny, tuan, how because of religion things are made so difficult." He knew firsthand because of Yara, who was Hindu. He was born Muslim. The real reason she had gotten sick and died was because in Jakarta she had been a shunned outcast. That was why Umar hated religion.

Soon they arrived at the Stanvac house, right on the beach. It was like something out of a movie: lush, pristine, not another house in sight. When they drove up a host of smiling servants came scurrying out to help them in. Before they did, Umar turned to Beil and asked, "Tuan, do you mind if I leave tonight and go visit my wife's old village?"

"Sure, Umar, we will not need the car until the day after tomorrow. So take the car and come back then."

92

Haggard found the small airstrip cut out of a swath of the jungle—small, dicey, and not for amateurs. He was flying a P 47 without lights. The few torches on the runway gave him no idea of the type of terrain. Inside the cargo bay were the small arms and explosives that he had flown from a forward-operating base in the Philippines. It was his first trip into Indonesia.

His mission was to get in and out. Parties in the US government were going rogue and secretly supplying the Islamic rebels in Aceh. Officially within the agency, Beil's and Rockman's operation had been shut down when it became clear that fighters bound by the will of Allah were quite formidable, almost impossible to root out from their secret hideouts in the hills of the dense jungle.

Down below, Richal and Timal were waiting by the side of the runway, still hidden in the undergrowth to make sure that this was not a trap. For the last year they had been playing a cat-and-mouse game with the regular army, but now with the lack of weapons it was hard for them to keep their will. They still believed, but their morale was broken when the army last month had stormed one of their safe houses in town, taken out the faithful, lined them up against a wall and slaughtered them in front of their wives. The dogs even shot the women who came to bury them. The bodies were left to rot in the hot sun. The two longed to return home. No one was helping them. But just as they were about to give up hope, Allah answered their prayers with a shipment of guns. For the last three weeks they had been breaking their backs clearing this strip, so they could receive this new source of arms.

"It must be some Muslim brother," Richal said to his friend.

"Yes, Allah provides in many ways."

Haggard brought the plane down smoothly considering the roughness of the meadow. He had made so many similar landings that he had devised a system of coming off and going back down, and once you got the rhythm it was real smooth. He was glad he was out of the fucking military and working for this secret shadow military. The air force had not been good for him. He should have been a general by now.

Once landed, he focused on the ground. He had been shot at so many times that he had taken to carrying two loaded pistols. He saw two men run up out of the shadows. It put him on edge. Instinctively his fingers tightened their grip around the triggers. He didn't trust any Asians period, under no circumstances.

"Selamat, tuan," Richal said as the two barrels came out and press into his face.

"Dreamland!" he shouted nervously in the best English he could muster, having not spoken it for over a year. He thanked Allah he had remembered the password after recovering from his initial shock.

While he waited for them to unload the cargo Haggard was engulfed by the smell of the jungle. The experience brought him back to Vietnam, where he had gone with Beil and that dead idiot Dewey. The memory gave him sweats. He went back to that time, to the village with the smug Beil and the arrogant English-speaking Vietnamese aristocrat. He remembered his own pleasure when he had put the gun to the man's temple and pulled the trigger.

"I wonder what Beil would think of me being here?" He chuckled out loud, liking the words. He was far away from everybody. He was part of a secret team, from a different branch of the agency that did not like the way the general was handling things. Even the general did not know that he was supplying the rebels. It was all being accomplished through a Saudi-Arabian guy.

He headed back to the plane and taxied out. Then took off, flying perfectly into the night, like the night hell he was.

93

My next dukun moment was during that weekend in Bali when I went to the beach to walk the reefs. But before I did that, my father had an emergency phone call.

"Take the young tuan out to the reef," my father said to the guides, pointing to the boat. It was a catamaran about fifteen feet long, and when we hit the water it glided in the wind. The sea moved very quickly underneath the hull. The water was so clear that I could see the coral sometimes only a foot or two underneath as we skimmed across the lagoon. As I was looking at the reef, marveling at the beauty, the guides stopped and pointed to me to look down. There was the largest clam I had ever seen.

While I was looking at it, they began talking. "The whole village is in frenzy that we still do not have a gold cowry shell for the ceremony of the blessed."

"I know, I have been searching for two weeks now."

"Everybody has been looking."

"Shaot said that none of the other villages has found one yet. If we don't find one it will be very bad for the coming harvest." Just then they looked back to shore. My father standing there waving his hands, motioning to them.

"We'd better go back. The tuan has come back to the beach." They quickly turned the boat; caught the wind again and flew over the sea. They picked my father up and headed for the reef that was now exposed in the low tide. By the time we reached it, the tide had receded to the point that the coral had formed a bridge that you could walk on. My father made sure that we had sneakers on, so we would not be cut by the sharp and fragile coral. I had a net. He carried a small bucket in case we found anything.

"Be careful to step only on top where it is flat," he said to me. It was an amazing moment with the water rushing out. On either side of us the coral stretched away. We saw another giant clam and then some huge fish. Then I spotted a cowry shell there in one of the water pools and ran over to it, almost tripping on the sharp coral. I reached in to the pool and plucked out a spotted cowry. "William, what a great find." We turned it over and saw the mollusk had retreated into its shell. "We'll let it dry out on the porch," my father said. Then we explored all the little tide pools on the look-out for other shells.

"Did you know that the cowries were used as money?" my father said as he reached down and pulled one out himself. "But the real valuable ones are the gold ones."

"I sure wish we could find one of them!" I shouted as we continued walking the reef. For the next hour or so we explored all the little pools. Then the tide shifted and the water came rushing back. My father told me it was time to go. He signaled to the two guides that we would walk back to the boat. It was getting toward sunset. The light penetrated the water in such a way that it was clear all the way to the bottom. I saw something sparkle and reached down. I opened my fist. It was a gold cowry. I ran to the boat.

"Look what I found!" I shouted. The two guides huddled around me as I slowly opened my hand.

"Oh, tuan, you have such magic," they said, staring at the shell in disbelief. Now they were assured of a good harvest. We handed them the gold cowry, or rather my father did. I had found the shell, and wanted it.

"Thank you, tuan, thank you," one of the guides said, now believing what he had heard from his cousin that worked in the Seam household, about the young tuan. Now he had seen my power in person. Looking at me, he added, "Thank you, dukun."

94

The two boat guides insisted that Beil and his family, especially the young tuan, come to their village as guests of honor at the harvest celebration, which would include the village monkey dance. Agnes jumped at the opportunity. It was arranged that Umar would drive them out at dusk.

On the way out, Beil handed Umar a pack of Marlboros for each of the guides and then because he was in a happy mood he pulled out his new Marlboro lighter and handed it to Umar.

"Here, use my lighter for the evening. A Marlboro always tastes best when it is lit by a Marlboro lighter," Beil said as he lit one for each of them. Both of them savored the smoke.

When they got to the village, all anyone was talking about was the young dukun who had saved the day. Everybody gathered around as the family was led to the place of honor. It was a set of three carved chairs, painted in red with gold trim.

Umar said to Beil, "I am going to visit with my friend." He walked into the night, leaving Beil and his family. They were the only westerners there. The rest of the village was seated in a circle. Now that night had come, torches were lit. The whole place had a certain atmosphere that made everything appear exaggerated, more alive.

Inside the ring there were two sets of men dressed with flower headbands and no shirts. Some held drums, while others sat around a collection of gongs that Beil recognized as a gamelan. In the center of the ring was a stack of coconut shells. By the side but still in the circle was an old, wizened man who carried a pot with smoke coming out of it. Young William was very fascinated by this old man. He watched him come up under the noses of the men in the circle, waving the smoke up the men's nostrils. William saw the old man was staring at him, and even from the twenty feet or so he could see the deep penetrating eyes. The eye contact was broken when the stacked coconuts were lit and a fire erupted in the center. The two sets of men on either side of the blaze started chanting: "Cha, Cha, CHA, CHA!"

The old dukun stared at the youth, knowing that his lifelong dream had come true. From the instant word had reached him of the rare gold cowry, he had known it was time to pass the stone on. He dropped everything to prepare himself for the journey into the nether world. He bathed, changed into his white outfit, all the time fondling his special stone, a rough diamond that that been handed down for generations. He remembered when he was a young boy not much older then this white dukun how the stone had been passed down to him.

He was glad to be going. Ninety-six years in this body was enough. There were higher planes to explore. He laughed to himself; it had been he who had made the spell so that no one would find the gold cowry except the new dukun of his line, which was one of the most powerful lines in all the world. He then prepared the special smoke mixture which he put into a separate pot—not the one he would use for the dance trance. He had let the mixture ripen so when the time came, it would be ready. With a big smile on his face the wise old dukun got ready for the passing.

The whole village was now focused on the blazing coconut husks while the men chanted on either side. They started to form a rhythm.

One side would chant, and then the other, calling: "Cha! Cha! Cha! Cha! Cha! Cha! Cha! Cha, Cha, and Cha!"

The men started swaying. There must have been five hundred people. A man riding a horse puppet raced around the perimeter. Beil noticed his feet were bare. Then the chanting intensified from the other side. Quickly, the man raced to the sound, jumping on the fire, stamping on it. Sparks flew over the crowds as he danced over the embers with his bare feet.

"Cha, Cha, Cha, Cha, Cha!" The other side now called him. Again he raced over the blistering fire, jumping on it again, back and forth in a trance called by the pulse of the chanting. William, Agnes, and Beil had the best view and saw that the man's eyes were turned upward. Soon the fire was put out. The music stopped and the dance was over. Beil looked intently at the man's feet. He was astonished to see that they were not burnt, not even a blister.

Meanwhile as all this was going on, Umar was in his friend's house far from the ceremony. Like everybody else in the village, his hosts were talking about the young dukun finding the gold cowry.

"Did you know he was a dukun?" his old friend Angar said in glee. They had been drinking rice wine and smoking the Marlboros that Beil had given them.

"Yes, I have seen him work before," Umar said with pride. Even though he did not believe in God, he did believe in magic. There were just too many unexplained things in the world to think otherwise. He took out the Marlboro pack and handed his friend another, again pulling out the fancy lighter that Beil had given him. It was enameled metal with the logo of the Marlboro brand on it.

"Ahhya!" His friend sighed in pleasure, marveling at the lighter. He handed it back to his friend, both of them unaware that the lighter had a tape recorder with a camera in it. Just by clicking, he had turned it on.

"None of the other dukuns were able to find the shell?" Umar asked. It pleased him to offer the Marlboros, even if there wasn't a real Marlboro country, or that the name was just some capitalistic trick to get you to want to buy more.

"The young tuan must be very powerful."

The Indonesian belief in the supernatural was most prevalent in Bali, where huge decisions rested on the power of a dukun.

"His nick-name is the mandor," Umar said nervously. He knew that even talking about a dukun was not a good thing, because they had the power to listen to everything.

"Well, thank him again for this whole village," Angar said, savoring his drag on the cigarette, which was much better than the harsh cheroot that he was use to smoking. He had grown up in Bali but had lived in Jakarta and worked in a factory that was owned by the Dutch. The men worked in conditions that were not befitting a rat and their pay was nothing. When they had struck in 1948 shortly after Musso arrived, the police had been sent in and many were killed. Angar had been watching from the sidelines and had grabbed the gun from one of the policemen who had just shot his friend. He had killed the policeman and then fled to join Musso when he tried to take control. But the army had stepped in and most of the rebels were slaughtered. Angar had escaped with nothing. Somehow he made his way to Bali where he had been in hiding in his village. Because of its remoteness, he had heard very little news about what was happening in the movement.

"I bring good news from Jakarta," Umar said. "Sukarno has opened up many ties with China. Opened an embassy and sent delegations. This summer there was a meeting with the non-aligned countries that we hosted and it all went well. There is lots of secret aid coming in now from the Chinese."

"Better be careful about the Chinese," Angar said, like all Indonesians wary of these immigrants who owned everything and could be just as ruthless as the westerners.

"Yes, I agree with you," Umar said, remembering his arguments at the last few meetings of the PKI.

"Yes, we are fighting for Indonesia, not China or Russia."

"So that is what is happening." Umar did not mention his disagreement with other members of the group who wanted immediate change.

"I hope we have learned our lesson well, and we will not repeat the mistake that sent Musso to his grave."

"We have. That is why we are changing things from the inside, so much so that Sukarno does not know he is being changed at all."

"In Bali we now control most of Denpasar with our army of invisible warriors," Angar said. "We will wait till we have enough power for the tipping force."

"Yes, I agree and will report back to the others."

Just as the meeting was concluding they heard the gong calling them for the last event where the golden cowry was going to be placed in the hole on the sacred carving. The hole had been cut early in the year, so everyone was amazed that the gold cowry fit perfectly into its eye socket with no extra carving.

In the center of the ring now was the statue, surrounded by flowers on all sides. Eagerly the village started chanting as the statue was uncovered, complete with the golden-eye cowry. Everyone marveled at it, and many came up to touch the young dukun. Agnes patted William on the head.

"You are the hero, Willy," she said proudly, looking at me and then at Beil, who was beaming also. The gamelan music picked up. Soon the villagers all went back to their seats as the ceremony ended with me being made an honored member of the village.

At the end of the ceremony, the old man with the piercing eyes came forward. Agnes and Beil felt his power and came together to protect me, but were frozen, unable to do anything but watch. He came up to me. My eyes were transfixed into his. I did not know where I began or he ended. He was carrying his vessel with the smoke. He took out a wand, mixed the smoke, pouring it over me.

It came like a cloud. My head began to spin. I started to tremble. I felt many dreams enter me, like rushing down a river or a climbing a mountain or riding whales on the sea. All I was aware of were his eyes, now white and glistening. All sound had stopped. The earth seemed to slow down so time was bent into slow motion. His white eyes now became the size of the universe. Everything was so bright that I felt blinded. No, not blinded but permeated by the essence of universe within his eyes that were forever embedded into my soul. I watched transfixed as the old man came over to me and put the vessel down. He then rubbed his hands together, touching me on both temples where he tapped his fingers nine times. All the time he was staring at me in such a way that I felt as if he had entered me; instead of being a young boy I was an ancient pillar of grand light. Finally after what felt like an eternity he released his hands and then reached into his purse that hung from his side and spoke.

"To the finder of the golden eye, I give this stone before I die, for you to hold till you pass it on to a future dukun who lives on a farm." And with that the old man looked deep into my soul, shrieking three times until he collapsed at my feet. He was dead before he hit the ground.

I still have this stone, and I am waiting to pass it on whenever the time comes. I keep it in an old box under my bed.

95

Murray was beside himself, very nervous that he would blow it. He was head steward on the plane taking Sukarno on his first trip to America, but that was not what he was nervous about. What he was nervous about had started three months before when he and Beil had met in Jakarta.

"I think you are ready to become a real spy now," Beil had said to him as they were enjoying drinks in the captain's bar.

"I thought I already was a spy," Murray muttered jokingly, in a flirty way, but when he saw the seriousness on Beil's face he felt uneasy. "You're not kidding, are you?" It was one thing to pretend to be a spy; another to be one. Was Edmond really a spy? Or was it some exotic gay fantasy to make love to a secret agent?

"Yes, I think you would be real good at it," Beil said matter-of-factly, not sure at all because of Murray's nervousness. But sometimes you didn't have the luxury of everything being completely perfect. Beil had talked it over with the general. They agreed that with Sukarno on the plane and Murray on the plane too, it would be easy to listen in.

"Do I get to wear a gun?" Murray said, titillated now to be spy

"So you agree?"

"Yes. So do you want me to get a uniform?" Murray asked.

"No. You just do what you have been doing. Except now, when you come back I will debrief you completely."

"Don't I need to be wearing underpants for that?" Murray asked.

"Not if you don't want to. Now listen," Beil said, bringing forth a packet. "The only thing you have to do different is put this under Sukarno's seat and push this button," Beil said, showing him what looked like the flat inflatable life preserver that was placed under every seat. "And then when you get to New York the plane crew will take care of the rest."

"That's all?" Murray asked, somewhat disappointed. "There at the very least should be sunglasses, perhaps shoes that turned into wings or maybe a fast car." He saw Beil start to laugh.

"That, and listen to what he says, and watch who is on the plane. Who meets him. Where else you go after you leave America. Here is a bag with three more of these things."

Murray had laughed, too. It had all sounded so simple and exciting. But now that Murray was on the plane, he was nervous. He thought Sukarno was looking at him differently. More than once he almost confessed that he had been spying on him. Finally after twenty hours they touched down in Idlewild airport. A very relieved Murray ran for the nearest airport bar to have himself a double.

96

Rockman was very interested in what Beil had to say. They were in Beil's office sipping on bulls' eyes.

"We didn't know that the Chinese were so involved and funding the PKI," Beil said. "We knew they were getting something but not that much. Nor that Bali was the hub."

"Yes, it seems like they are maneuvering Sukarno toward their point of view."

"Do you think anyone will try a coup while he is gone?" Beil asked. He was fishing, looking very deep into the man like he was playing a bridge hand.

"A coup is a serious matter—not one for light comment," Rockman said calmly though inside Beil's words had put him on edge. He had not thought Beil would guess the topic of the last oh-so secret army meeting.

"Yes, that is true," Beil said. "But it is also true that to nip a bud is easier than cutting down a whole tree." It was good advice. If you cut down the poison ivy while it is young and vulnerable, it is easier than trying to kill it later. Like Vietnam, where things were going from bad to worse. But there the US had brought two enemies together by hacking at the wrong vine.

"But we will keep the PKI at bay. Sukarno has the masses, but does not have the fire power, so he hedges his bets. Does a little of this, a little of that," Rockman said, taking a big sip of his drink. How civilized, he thought. The ice, the beef broth, the vodka. It was so modern. A modern Indonesia is what he and his colleagues wanted, complete with all the luxuries that came with it. The idea relaxed him a bit.

He knew there was going to be a trial coup by some of the junior officers. It had very little chance of succeeding but he and the real power were going to let it develop. Then decide what to do.

"Be careful when you use someone that they are not using you," Beil said, well aware of the infiltration of the PKI into everyday things. Now the Communists were working for better schools, better working conditions. The yoke of the Dutch was finally thrown, and now Sukarno was visiting the United States, getting vast amounts of support both publicly and privately.

Beil said this more for his own benefit then anything else. He was of the opinion that what was happening was not bad, that you did not have to run a country to control it. That everything could be done by a nudge here, a nudge there.

"Speaking of being used," Rockman said, "we stopped funding the Islamicists two years ago. But they still are getting weapons. Our sources tell us they are from America."

"Impossible."

"No," Rockman said. "It has not stopped." He reached into his briefcase and brought out a grainy picture of a small plane. The next photo showed the plane being unloaded. The third and last photo made Beil boil. There, over by the trees, smoking on a cigarette, was a western pilot. Beil took the picture and studied it. He put it down. Then lit another cigarette, the picture still in his hand. The rage rose from the bottom of his toes. There in the picture was the SOB, Larry Haggard.

97

Agnes and Seam were doing a spring cleaning even though it was always summer. They came upon Beil's stash of old rusty cans with no labels. Agnes was now fluent in Indonesian, so they were yapping away.

"Oh yes, I remember these," Agnes said. "We were going to have a party with them, but never did. Well, there is no time like the present."

She beamed, showing off her big belly. She was seven months pregnant. "Seam, this weekend we will have a party for the cans. Let all the servants in the other households know."

By the weekend everybody was looking forward to the can-can party. Agnes and Sally had the servants get a collection of grass skirts and huge old bras.

"Agnes, this is going to be great," Beil said as they were getting dressed.

"Yes, darling, we will have the boys against the girls and who ever has the higher score will win, and the losers have to do a can-can in full costume, men or women complete with makeup and all that." She smiled.

It had now been a couple of years since her discovery of Beil's extra life, and she had learned to live in it. In some ways it was easier because she did not feel like Sally Dremmer, who complained that every time her husband looked at her, he wanted sex and she was beginning to feel like a sex slave. Agnes was free of that so when she and Beil had sex, it was she who would instigate it. Without the constant undercurrent, the two of them had developed a great friendship; a true love uncomplicated by the stink of sex.

The first of the guests arrived and the drinks were all passed around with the makan kecil, or finger food: small sates and peanuts roasted in garlic. The cans were all displayed on a table as if they were the crown jewels. There were twenty one cans in all, in all sizes and sorts, from square to round with even an oval one. The centerpiece was the can that Donald Finn had bought for such a high price that day at the market. The servants had placed a red cloth underneath it to highlight the rust. Next to it, also on a red cloth, was an ancient can that Beil had bought.

Everybody was gathered around the table looking over the cans. "What do you think is in that one?" Beil innocently asked Sally, wanting to get her opinion because she had grown up in a grocery.

"Don't tell him!" Agnes shouted, well aware of what Beil was trying to do.

"Nice try, Edmond." Carl said. Beside him was Donald Finn and his wife who had just arrived back in Sumatra. Part of today's party was to celebrate their arrival. After two years in the States they had taken another tour.

"Is that my can?" Donald asked, seeing the centerpiece.

"Yes," Beil said. "I figured the most valuable one should have a big price. So if you guess that one it will be worth three of the other cans."

"I can't wait to see you boys doing the can-can," Dottie laughed, glad she was back in Indonesia. She had to admit that as crazy as Indonesia was, being in the states was boring and not as comfortable. In fact life was so hard there that she hated it. After years of not lifting a finger, she was all of a sudden expected to do all the work of the household. There were no maids, no cooks, no servants, no help for the children and no time to relax. It came as a shock to realize that they were not rich unless they lived here. Much to Donald's delight it had been her idea to come back.

Two hours later, dinner had been cleared; everybody was drunk. Beil stood up, picked up a spoon, and started hitting the side of his glass until he got everybody's attention.

"Ladies and gentlemen, please gather around the table. Men on the left. Women on the right."

Quickly everybody took up their positions. "Here are the rules. We will start at one end. Make our guesses. Open that can and then move to the other end of the table, open that can, alternate back and forth until we are left with the grand centerpiece, the famous Finn can." Everybody applauded.

"And besides the official game, Carl here will be holding all side bet money. So if anyone wants to bid on a single can, go see him." Already Carl had a fistful of rupiah. The can getting the most action was Donald's very expensive can. Already he had gotten ribbed about it, and thanks to the liquor he was hamming it up.

"Yes it is one of a kind. Not another one like it in the whole world. Cost was no object. Look how grand it looks on the table. I just had to buy it before it was snapped up by sharp-eyed Edmond. Otherwise we would have nothing for the centerpiece and we wouldn't be having this great party."

"For the first of the cans, we need the official scorecard. So ladies and gentlemen please decide among yourself and then hand it to me." Beil pointed and bowed with great fanfare to a small, flat can. It was about four inches in diameter, one inch high, and not that rusty. It looked like it dated from maybe the late forties.

The two ballots were presented to Beil, the official judge, who according to the agreed-upon rules did not have a vote. After a proper amount of silence he spoke.

"The ladies say it is a can of tuna. The men say it is a can of pineapples. Let's have a drum roll." Everybody started clapping their hands and stamping their feet as Beil slowly started to open the can.

"It's a can of tuna!" Beil shouted. The ladies began hollering. The men groaned. It was one to nothing.

"Better start shaving your legs, gentlemen," Dottie shouted, very happy, now knowing that sometimes the place you hate is the place you love the most. Even the oppressive heat was comforting.

"Now for the second can," Beil bellowed as he was handed the official papers. "The women say it is a can of peas, and men are sticking with the pineapples." They all looked as Beil opened it. "It's a can of peaches; the men get a half a point." The men started clapping.

"Don't get so cocky," Sally Dremmer shouted. "You're still losing."

The next can was really a mess. Besides being labeless, it was dented and swollen so the original shape was hard to make out. The men and women huddled together in their respective groups. Even the servants were getting into it. Seam came up to the men. "Tuans, we think it is ox-tail soup."

"What makes you think that?"

"The top, tuan, it has the Australian top."

The men all looked at it as if they were examining the crown jewels, but no one was able to see anything other than the rust. Still, they did not have a better choice.

"The women think it is a can of pudding, the men a can of ox-tail soup." Beil opened the can. The contents shot out under pressure, sending a stream of foul liquid across the room, hitting poor Donald Finn in the face. "Yuk!" they all shouted before breaking into convulsions of laughter. After a moment, Beil finished opening the can.

"The men are right. It is ox-tail soup." There was much thunderous applause. The men had taken the lead.

The next can was tall and new, with only surface rust. Both teams guessed vegetables, the girls corn, the men peas—but it was beans, so no team got any points. Instead, according to the evolving rules, everybody had to do a mandatory shot of liquor.

"To the next can!" they all shouted in unison. The girls won the next one to take back the lead and then the men won the next three, giving them a two and a half point lead with two cans left.

"Looks like we are going to be winners," said Carl. Everyone was happy, especial since the rules had evolved again. Now the shots came out in never-ending trays, and the losers had to take one after each can, so the women were in almost constant hysterics.

"The men guess ham, the women peas." Beil opened the can. "Tunafish." The men shouted in glee.

"Now ladies and gentlemen, we have the last can, on the pedestal, the Donald Finn can." The place erupted in applause. "There has been a call for another shot, do I have second?"

"Second!" The servants passed the trays and soon all attention was focused on the can. Everybody was given a chance to hold it, though some declined, as it was the oldest-looking can by far in the bunch.

"It's from the caveman times!" Carl shouted, to everybody's instant laughter. The can was about six inches in height and four inches in diameter. Some of it was so rusty that many thought that it would not last the evening under the scrutiny of so many eyes.

After about ten more minutes and another shot, Beil was handed the two slips. "The men say it is a can of pineapple." He then opened the ladies' slip. "The ladies say it is a can of asparagus. Bring the can."

One of the servants came forward with a polished silver tray. He picked up the can, placed it carefully on the tray, and brought it over to Beil.

All eyes were on Beil as he slowly opened the Finn can. "You ladies are going to lose," someone shouted, and the men began to clap. The women joined in, but as soon as Beil had finished opening the can, the room fell silent.

"It's a can of asparagus!" A holler went up from the women and a groan from the men. "We have winner!" Beil shouted. "The women have won the first can-can party."

"Yes," Agnes shouted. "We have won, and now it is time for all the men to get into their outfits and dance the can-can for us."

"No, no," the men feebly protested, but the women had no pity as they led them to the changing room.

"You look so funny," Carl said to Don Finn, whose fat was sticking out over the grass skirt. On the top he had a large bra that made him look like cartoon character.

"You look pretty funny yourself," Donald said, laughing at the sight of the short Carl Dremmer with a matching skirt and a too-small bra to cover his man teats.

Soon all the men were dressed. They came out with pom-poms, but before they could start dancing, Sally yelled out, "They don't have makeup yet!" And then the women came at the men with lipstick and eyeliner and all this of course called for another shot. Finally the men were ready. They all climbed atop the large table and did their chorus line in as fine a can-can as anyone could imagine.

98

Rockman hadn't been completely forthright with Beil, since he had discovered the Americans were secretly arming the Islamic extremists in Aceh. He had been disappointed by Beil's actions when he had confronted him with the photo. Instead of admitting what was going on, Beil had feigned shock and surprise, denying any hand in it the operation. Even so, Rockman and others in his group thought it was good to occupy the regular army with the Islamic distraction, thus allowing the secret army to make the real power decisions.

Therefore he had not told Beil of the attempted plot that would be sprung when Sukarno was out of the country visiting the Soviet Union. They had found out about it but had done nothing, content to sit back and see what happened. They would let it develop until they finally had to make a decision. Well, that moment was now upon them.

"We wait," he said as he looked at the faces of the men sitting in the smoke-filled room. The first move had been made when the military commander of Celebes had declared a state of war, demanding autonomy. "This should send Sukarno a strong message. That he needs to pay attention and not step too far out of line."

"I think he will get the message, that flirting with the Americans is one thing, but flirting with the Russians and the Chinese is another thing."

"Yes, Rockman, we would not be very good Communists." The room erupted in laughter. "When do we need to tell Beil of our plans?"

"Later. Let it go for a while. So then it is agreed, we wait."

99

On the east coast of Sumatra Major Kanjor declared martial law and broke away from the Republic of Indonesia to form his own military state. He was twenty-two and had recently been promoted. He knew that what he was doing would have no sanction from anyone else in the military. He expected no help, yet he was more than willing to volunteer for the mission.

Sukarno was moving toward an embrace of the PKI and through them an embrace of Communist ideas, made all the more evident with his sweeping trip to Russia and China. It did not matter that Sukarno had also visited the United States on this journey. In Kanjor's mind, openly going to Communist countries was malo, especially China. The Chinese were the scourge of the earth. Chinese landlords had forced his parents out of their home in the slums of Jakarta, and when they had not left quick enough, they stole and sold all of their few meager possessions to settle a non-existent debt.

He was sitting at his command center. His loyal troops were commanding the streets and just now one of the captains was reporting to him.

"Merdeka—that is what the street is calling it," the even-younger captain said, buoyed by the bold actions that they were taking. Both of them were smoking cigarettes, full of confidence that they were going to secure their places in history.

"Very good, captain, have the men ready," the major said, now with nothing to do but wait for the official response.

100

Murray was handing out the hot towels as the plane reached cruising altitude on the trip back to Jakarta. Everything was in chaos and no one knew whether there was still a government, or whether they would all be arrested at the airport. There was scant news, and when he looked at Sukarno, he saw fear.

He could hardly wait to see Beil and show him the tapes, evidence of all the great spying he had done. It had been so much fun. When he was in New York he bought a pair of sunglasses and an attaché coat so he could look the part. He had almost blurted out his new vocation to Sukarno, who had commented on his new glasses and told him that he looked like a spy. Luckily he hadn't blown it. Now it was going to be so exciting. He looked at his watch—still six hours left.

"Murray." The word brought him out of is reverie.

"Yes, sir?"

"Come here and sit with me," Sukarno said.

"Sure."

"I need some advice."

"I don't think I am qualified to give you advice."

"That is the reason you are the only one I can confide in."

These words made Murray feel like a heel, because of the spying. "Well, I'll give you my opinion."

"I have just had word that there is rebellion going on in Sumatra and Celebes, and it is because I visited Russia. But the rebels don't know that I went there to get one hundred million dollars."

"That's a lot of money."

"It sure is. And it will go far toward helping Indonesia."

"Then you should go tell them, the people."

"Go to the people, you say."

"Yes, go tell the people."

"I will take what you say under advisement, Murray. Thanks."

101

Larry Haggard thought he had seen a ghost. He was in Singapore at the hotel bar drinking his cocktail when he turned around and saw an Asian man who looked uncannily like Beil's friend Hiu.

"What's an American doing in Singapore?" the man asked, very flirty, very sure of himself, having read Haggard's dossier. He knew Haggard was working for the CIA and his mission was to befriend him, knowing that Haggard liked men and rough sex.

"Oh, I can think of a number of things an American could be doing," Haggard said, still a little shocked by the man's appearance. Half of him wanted to reach into his hidden shoulder-pocket, pull out his gun, but he held back.

He was getting used to this new life, the below-water life as he called it. He had flown three more arms shipments into Sumatra, each time happy to be double-crossing Beil. He would like to see the look on the son of a bitch's faggot face. See that smug smile stripped away.

"I know a more private bar where we can go," the Asian man said demurely.

"Oh, are you some kind of faggot?" Haggard said gruffly, feeling the familiar rise in his loins, and the rise in violence which accompanied it. He grabbed the man by the ear whispering into his face.

"Show me this bar, you sick fuck."

102

Umar sat behind the wheel of the sedan, waiting for Beil to leave the office. Beil was late, which was unusual for him. Umar only had a little time to get to the hastily-called meeting. Finally Beil emerged with a frown on his face.

"Everything OK, tuan?" Umar asked as he put the car into first.

"Just the usual headaches of running an oil company," Beil said, though both of them knew this was a lie. Everything was falling apart. Secrets within secrets—and now the coup that Beil had predicted was upon them. He looked deep into Umar and saw the worry there. He decided to go fishing.

"I hear that the PKI leader Kusdi was in the Soviet Union the same time as Sukarno. Do you think it has anything to do with the hundred million aid package? I thought the PKI was more Chinese in their thinking. If I had to guess, it would seem to me like an internal rift were developing among the two camps."

"You have interesting ideas, tuan," Umar said nervously. Beil had guessed the reason for the secret meeting that he was now late for. Umar was furious that just when the PKI seemed to be winning, outside influences were threatening to tear them apart.

"You are going to lose your Indonesian flavor. You will fail because the Soviet Union and/or the Chinese will eat you up. Then you will understand that Communism is not the magic cure you think it is," Beil said with touch of anger. He saw the entrance of the Soviet Union into Indonesia as a chess move in the Cold War that escalated the already-tense situation.

Earlier in his office, Beil had brought out the grainy pictures of Haggard on the airfield, reliving the reaction of the general when the two had met last month in Singapore. He had watched the general's face, which did not show the surprise he had expected.

"Edmond, there is another team in the area. They operate independent from us. Our job is to support Rockman's secret army and to manage the PKI, theirs is to supply the Muslim extremists, to keep them effective as an agitation."

184

"But Haggard—that man is poison!"

"I agree, but I am not in charge." The general was lying. He had reluctantly approved the other mission under extreme pressure from the State Department, who wanted immediate results. They were going to fund anyone willing to overthrow Sukarno. Beil knew now that the game had become part of the Cold War. The game now was keeping the Russians and Chinese at bay and out of Indonesia at all costs.

"Tuan, Indonesia will have an Indonesian movement." Umar's voice crackled with anxiety, bringing Beil back to the immediate situation. Both of them were very aware that things were complicated, and both men worried that everything could unravel now that the coup was spreading to other areas.

103

Agnes pushed one last time and the baby slid out.

"It's a girl," the nurse shouted as she held the crying baby in her arms. Then she did something they had talked about in the clinic, something new and modern in the 1950s. Instead of taking the baby and immediately washing it, she instead put her onto Agnes's chest. This was a new technique that the Dutch were using in Holland, and the nurse believed that it would enable the baby and the mother to bond more closely.

"She has such tiny mules," Agnes said as she felt the warm baby on her, still with traces of blood and amniotic fluid. "Mules" were what her mother had called baby-cheeks. Agnes felt the love, joy, and understanding once again of motherhood.

Outside in the lobby Beil was pacing the floor. He stopped when the doors opened and the doctor came out. "Mr. Beil, you have a lovely daughter." The date was August 4, 1957. It was also Beil's birthday. He was 36.

He had rushed over from his meeting with Rockman when he had heard the news that Agnes was going into labor. The political situation was almost at a boiling point. Yet another army officer had broken away from the central government, so now the only part of the country still in Sukarno's hands was Jakarta, the capital, and some of Java. The militias of the various officers were fighting each other. Rockman and the secret army were ready to clamp down. Over the last few months, they had let events unwind. Now they had to do something or risk civil war.

At first Sukarno had appeased the rebels. He had sent emissaries to the various hot spots trying to defuse the situation. Rockman's secret group was conscious of his moves, but they knew that nothing he did would dampen the power of the PKI. It was a delicate situation. Rockman's group could not move publicly against Sukarno, because he still had the support of the people. Then there were the huge loans that he had extracted from the US, the Soviet Union, and China. He was using this money to buy the loyalty of the older generals, some of whom had been mentors to Rockman and his gang.

The months had gone by. The Rockman gang had even met with Sukarno, who had promised them that he was not a Communist, assuring them that the PKI was really a nationalistic worker's movement that did not answer to China or Russia. It was at one of these meetings that Rockman had suggested the means to come to a compromise, an understanding.

"Why don't you work in the framework of a democracy that we provide? A framework where we can pick and choose what we want, control what we want. Give only the freedoms we want; hold back the ones we don't want. Bring democracy to the people, only guided by you, the Father of Indonesia. Tell them you have their best interests at heart. Declare your support for freedom in what we can call a guided democracy." When he was finished, everyone in the room was laughing.

"Rockman, you mean a benevolent dictatorship."

"Oh, you make it sound so silly. You can't be serious. Guided Democracy?"

"No, it is a way to control things, like the press, like the PKI."

"And at the same time to let things like capitalism flourish...."

"What about the Communists, the PKI?"

"Well, they are part of Indonesia also. What do you suggest we do with them?"

"Kill them all!"

"How can you kill so many?"

"There are ways."

"Stop it! We aren't killing anyone!" Sukarno shouted, still unnerved at extreme power of these secret men. It was all he could do to appease them. All he had was the masses but no real power. All he was in control of was Jakarta. But if he accepted Rockman's idea, it would give him some breathing room. Guiding democracy with a firm hand—it was a brilliant oxymoron, and in the context of losing everything it was a good idea. The phrase had a nice ring. "Guided Democracy", letting democracy flourish by removing the unhealthy things. Yes, and they were right. He was the Father of Indonesia. He would guide the people in democracy.

104

Beil and Umar were having one of the philosophical conversations that they got into when they went for a long drive. They were going to Bengkulu to check out a collection of Majapahit sculptures that one of the local dealers had said his brother had.

"What do you feel about this guided democracy?" Beil asked. Many things were going through his mind: the baby girl, Haggard, the secret team arming the Islamists without telling him, the PKI, but mostly Rockman and his vision for the country. Brilliant, he thought. What a concept. Not such a bad idea to control freedom when it got out of hand. It gave you something to hide behind where one had a lever to control the flow of ideas.

"It is a bad idea, tuan," Umar said to him, surprised. Beil always seemed so well-informed. "They will shut down papers, shut down strikes, whatever they fancy."

"I hear they might nationalize all the western businesses," Beil said, knowing that there was a potential for disaster if the Communists were not controlled. Beil knew that the PKI was growing and hard to stop. He had to find a way to keep it nationalistic without allowing it to become Communist. He took drag on his cigarette.

"That would be a good thing."

"Why would that be a good thing?" Beil asked.

"Because it is the worker that spills his blood; toils his whole life for the riches that are exported to Holland or America. If Indonesia owned the businesses, then the wealth would be more even."

"How do you know that things would be better? How do you know that a corrupt Indonesian wouldn't grab the money?"

"I don't. But at least there would be a chance."

"What about a place like Russia? They have workers that toil for their bosses. You think Stalin was a good guy? He killed more people that Hitler."

"No, tuan, I don't think Stalin was good guy," Umar said, trying to cover his emotion, trying not to let Beil know that he had touched a nerve. He took another drag on the Marlboro.

"I think it has a lot to do with power."

"How, tuan, how power?"

"I think people come to power maybe with good intentions, but then at a certain point all they want to do is keep the power, not share it."

"I don't think the Dutch had good intentions. Their only intention was for them. Take what they could get."

"But it's not as simple as that. I mean the Dutch found the oil. They planted the rubber trees. Organized the business. Paved roads, built waste systems, employed millions of people who would not have jobs. How is that all bad?"

Umar thought for a moment, taking a drag on the ever-present Marlboro. How could something that oppressed the people also be good for them?" Indonesia had always been a crossroads. It made him think about the Majapahit artifacts that they were going to see. That had been a great empire, but one that had disappeared, overrun by the peaceful Buddhists, then the Muslims, and finally the Dutch. After another puff he answered Beil.

"Tuan, just because someone develops our resources, pays us nothing, and then makes huge money, does that make us modern? I mean, we could wait. Do nothing, and the oil would still be in the ground. You saw the riot in Medan. If the people were happy, if they were getting a decent wage, then none of that would be happening."

"But you have so many people that you need to feed. And to feed them in this modern world, you have to develop resources. To do that is not cheap. It cost thousands of millions of dollars."

"Tuan, why is it that the one who actually does the work does not get the money?"

Beil thought about that. He had to admit there really wasn't a good answer except that the worker did not have to put up any money or take any risk. "In the capitalist society, the one who runs the business gets more because of all the expense that he has to put out. The shareholder puts up the money, which he can lose all of with no guarantee. The worker puts up nothing and is paid for what he does."

"But they pay nothing, tuan, nothing."

"The company pays what it can to make a profit, and to pay back the people that took the risk. If they pay too much to the worker, then there would be no profit. Tell me, Umar, why if no one wants these jobs that you say pay nothing, then why are there thousands lined up to get them? They must have some value or no one would want them."

This question had always haunted Umar. It was true that even though these jobs paid nothing, people were afraid to lose them, even leading members of the PKI. They would not give up their jobs no matter how much they hated them.

"Because they have nothing, tuan, and bad work with little money is better then no work and starving to death."

"Do you mean to tell me that these people have no life at all? No fun, their kids don't go to school?" Beil said as they pulled into the dealer's compound and went inside.

105

The little river was just outside the compound only a few yards into the jungle, but the foliage was so thick that from the stream you felt lost. William was with three other boys from the first grade in the international school. Two of them were from the compound; the third was Rockman's son Amir. All of them were holding fishing nets. The nets were shaped like umbrellas that hung off a long pole, which allowed for them to be placed deep in the stream. Once the net was in the water, the boys would wait for a while. Then pull the net up, hopefully trapping the fish inside.

It was still monsoon season and with all the rain, the river was a swollen muddy mess. There was no way of seeing the fish. But that did not stop the boys from having fun dipping the nets in and out. So far they had caught no fish as they moved along the stream. Trailing a little way behind the boys were the ever present servants carrying the buckets for the so-far elusive fish.

"I hear the young tuan is a dukun," Rockman's servant said to Seam.

"Yes, and a very important one," Seam said proudly as they watched the boys dip their nets. Their conversation was cut short when they heard the excited scream.

"Look at all the fish!" Amir shouted in English as he lifted out his net. It was teeming with fish. He was Rockman's second child and first son, so according to Indonesian custom he was the Ida Bagus Rai. Amir, with Beil's help, was only one of a handful of Indonesians to go to the International School. As with the others, he was being groomed to be the next generation of leaders. Already at age seven he was fluent in Dutch as well as English, which he spoke with an American accent.

"Quick, get them before they get away," William called as the boys all scrambled over each other to get the fish. They were mud-colored like the river, and all of them had a top fin that looked like a prickly sail.

Another net was put in and pulled up teaming with more of these flopping fish. The boys lost track of time, of everything except the moment. They charged ahead, forgetting they were in the depths of a dangerous jungle. It started to rain. The water mixed with the heat turning the air to steam, making it hard to see. The servants got caught up in the excitement and let the boys run ahead, laughing and rushing to the next open spot in the river to dip their nets. They came upon a rocky area with a little waterfall, but before the servants could catch up to them the three boys ran for the bank. None of them saw the cobra until it raised its hood inches from the boys.

When the servants arrived, it was too late. There sitting on a rock right in front of the boys was a huge snake standing straight up, hood out. Just at that second the fog cleared and a ray of light hit the beast, making it appear red and fiery. The sudden blast of the sun startled the snake. It waved its great hood back and forth. The servants knew that a bite from this monster snake was instant death.

"Run," they shouted in panic as they rushed toward the boys. This further agitated the snake. He weaved around, bobbing his head.

All the boys except William dropped their nets and turned to run. But Amir slipped on the wet rocks, tumbling right in front of the snake. The poor boy began walling as he looked up from the rocks only inches away from the snake above him. He was helpless as the snake moved forward, tongue darting in and out.

Again the weather changed. The rain intensified. A violent burst spattered around them, causing the snake to hiss. It stretched its head forward, hovering above the poor screaming boy. The servants knew he was doomed. None of them could do anything but watch as the snake pulled back to begin its strike.

It was all over quickly. The net went over the snake in mid strike. William pulled down the net and covered the snake, causing it to thrash inside the net instead of striking Amir.

Rockman's servant rushed up to grab the trapped snake below its head. Seam took out his knife and severed it. He then stretched out the snake's body. They were aghast to see that the monster was the length of all the boys put together.

"Allah Akbar, God is great!" Rockman's servant shouted. "The young dukun saved my master's life!" Fishing was forgotten. Soon they were all running back to the safety of the compound to show off the huge snake. The boys had forgotten about the danger and ran up to Beil and Rockman on the lawn.

"Look at the snake we caught!" Smoking Marlboros, the men turned to see what the servants were carrying strung on sticks between them. The snake was fifteen feet long without the head, which Seam had wrapped in a banana leaf.

"William saved my life!" Amir shouted. Then the servants related that only the quick thinking magic of the dukun had kept Amir from certain death.

106

Timal and Richal got out of the ferry on the bank of the Musi River, setting foot back in Palembang for the first time in three years.

"Allah," the men exclaimed, touching the ground, thanking God for bringing them back safe. The whole voyage had been constant rain. Just as they were getting up from their prayers the sun suddenly broke free. The day began to sparkle, lighting the dirty shabby town like it was the crown jewel of the Orient.

"We are back," Timal said to his friend, feeling that they had come full circle. It was around midday. The hustle of the town began to flood into the streets. The rains had washed away all the polluted air.

"Yes, it is good," Richal said, just as they heard yelling from the riverbank. A huge crowd had gathered, and they spotted an infidel with one of those movie cameras. The two men walked down there to see what the commotion was all about.

Once they got to the edge of the crowd, they saw that there were a lot of foreign infidels there in the inside ring. They were looking at a strange-looking boat down by the riverbank. Even after three years, Richal instantly recognized Tuan Beil, but before he could run and hide, the man came over to him.

"Richal, Is that you?" Beil said in English. That way there would be no confusion, because he knew Richal spoke it very well.

"Yes, tuan," he answered, very nervous inside. He was glad that Timal had slinked to the back to be swallowed up by the crowd.

"My God, I was so worried about you. Where have you been?" Beil asked.

"I was off helping my brother in Java," Richal said, the lie coming easier than he thought it would. "And I just got back."

"Well, that is good timing," Beil said, happy because he liked Richal. "I expect you back at the office first thing Monday."

"Yes, tuan, thank you, tuan," Richal said, not having expected this at all, not having expected to run into the head tuan; furious that he had agreed to come first thing Monday.

"So, have you come to see the boat-car?" Beil asked.

"Boat-car, what do you mean, tuan?"

"A car that can drive on land and sea," Beil said, taking a drag on his cigarette. There by the bank of the river two men were standing by something that looked like a cross between a convertible and a speedboat. They were about to get in it and drive into the sea. Everyone watched as the two men took off, heading for the river. The crowd turned silent as the car boat raced into the water. Everyone expected it would sink but instead it floated and kept going until it was out of sight.

The crowd broke out in loud applause. Richal used the distraction to leave. On the way out he spotted the white tuan's whore dressed in a revealing two-piece dress, standing next to other similarly-clad women. He shook his head disgustedly. Nothing had changed. Then he remembered the hidden guns.

That Monday Richal was convinced that he had made the wrong decision. He had vacillated all weekend whether to come or not, but in the end he had decided that the tuan would come get him if he didn't. When he saw Donald Finn he nearly fainted.

"Richal, we thought you were dead," Donald said, coming up to him, pummeling his hand, causing his head to spin. "Where have you been?"

"I had to go to my family in Java," Richal said nervously, sure that Donald Finn was now a hantu, a nonbeing ghost. He stared up for a moment and caught Finn's eyes, knowing that Finn could see through him. Finn was not a human but an evil spirit that was out to get him.

"Mr. Beil wants me to show you around. Things have changed some since you were here. He wants me to get you acquainted with the new system."

"New system, tuan?" Richal asked, not knowing whether to run or stay. He felt his legs wobble.

"Yes. First thing is to change into these," Finn said, holding up a pair of overalls that had the oil company's insignia on them in garish red lettering. They were modeled after the gas station uniform in the States and someone state-side thought they would be fun for the staff servants to wear.

Beil was standing next to Donald Finn when Richal emerged with his new suit. Both men broke out in laughter. Richal was so slight that the overalls made him look like a girl.

"Richal, come with me," Beil said, forcing himself to take a drag on his cigarette so as not to laugh even more. Inside Richal was fuming, sure that this was part of the doings of this Donald Finn, who was dead but not dead.

When they got into Beil's office Rockman was waiting for him. Beil turned to Richal. "Get us a drink, two bulls' eyes." It was all Richal could do to check the hatred that welled up in him. He mixed the drinks for the infidel and Indonesian heretic, inside swearing silent vengeance to Allah.

"Edmond," Rockman said, now comfortable with calling Beil by his first name, knowing that he was an equal in many ways. It was now a few years since their first meeting and both men knew they had each grown much more powerful together, and that each had the same vision for Indonesia.

"I still want to do something for your son, for saving my son," Rockman said with more emotion than he would usually show. Amir was his first son and the love of his life. Just the thought of losing him was unthinkable. Despite being a very modern Indonesian, Rockman deep inside still believed in the thoughts and customs that had passed through generation after generation of his ancestors. Indonesia was such a mystical place where so many strange things happened, that to question the notion of dukun in the modern world was foolish. He thought back to the many times when the superstitions of the past would guide the future.

"It was very fortunate," Beil said proudly.

"Yes, it was. Do you know that the servants think your son is a dukun?" Rockman asked, still not knowing what to think himself.

"I heard that, but what does it mean?" Beil said. Every time he approached the servants about it they would act like they had no idea what he was talking about.

"It means that he is a master of magic," Rockman said in such a way that both men laughed.

"Do you believe that?" Beil said, thinking about the absurdity that this was the kind of magic they were talking about, when they should be talking about their kind of magic in shaping the world.

"I mean I do and I don't, just like the idea of God. Like I believe in him and I don't."

"I don't believe in God at all," Beil said. "But I do believe in drinks, and even fate, but not some God who controls everything." And as if to empathize his point he downed his drink. He called out to Richal, who had been standing by the door in case he was needed. "Get us more drinks."

Richal hurried to comply, furious with these two blasphemers, especially this Rockman person who was drinking liquor and did not defend Allah. Nothing had changed. He had spent the last few years fighting for something that had not happened. Didn't anybody else see the truth? When he got back with the drinks he went back to his perch to listen.

"Has your son ever met Sukarno?" Rockman asked.

"No."

"Well, Sukarno will be going to a school in this area, and has invited a group of kids that are not at the school to come along. Maybe I could take your son, and you and Madam could come too."

"I would like that," Beil said. The two men kept talking. Neither paid any attention to Richal.

108

It was a very sad telex, short and to the point. General Vois was dead. Beil immediately was overcome by emotion as he walked back to the car where Umar was waiting. Umar saw the tears streaming from Beil's eyes but did not ask why. Beil fumbled for a cigarette and kept striking the matches but was unable to get it lit. So Umar pulled out his Marlboro lighter that Beil had given him, the one with the recorder and camera. He lit it for him.

"Thanks," Beil said, letting his mind drift to thoughts of the general who had changed his life. Before he heard the news, he had already packed his bags and was preparing to head for Singapore to meet Colonel Jim for an urgent summit. Death, the general's death was so sudden; Beil remembered what a strong man he was. Beil had loved him as much as he loved anybody. He thought about their first bridge game. How the general had bellowed and poured them all another drink when they had won. He felt like his father had died. The motion of the car was like a tunnel that was closing in. He started to cry uncontrollably, so much so that Umar finally spoke.

"Tuan, what's the matter?" He had never seen his friend in such a vulnerable state. He had never seen his friend look like a little boy.

"My...my...." Beil finally got it out: "My friend has died, suddenly. He was very important to me. He taught me lots of things."

"What was he like, tuan?" Umar asked. He saw that Beil was again fumbling with his matches so Umar pulled his lighter out. The smoke helped Beil regain his composure.

"He was a great man in many ways. A general in the war, and a person that saved my life," Beil said. "Have you ever had a friend like that who saved your life?"

Umar thought about it. Not his father, not his mother nor anyone from the village. His life had been about himself. He was the one who saved himself. Saving a life, he'd had think more about it.... Wait, Beil had saved his life many times. Beil was only one who had been kind to him. He saw his friend there, so sad.

"You, tuan, you have saved my life." Umar felt his emotions well up in him and he put his hand on Beil's arm to comfort him, which was something that was not done in Indonesia. The gesture made Beil cry even more. The tears were contagious, and Umar's eyes began to stream. He thought of all who had died so far in the struggle and even though he hadn't even known most of them, he felt for them.

"This man the general was a great man. He would look at a person and know if he was good or bad," Beil said, feeling comforted by Umar. It did not matter to him that Umar was PKI. What Beil had learned from the general was that in wrong there is right and in right there is wrong, and how someone who was your enemy in some cases was really your friend, and someone who was your friend was sometimes really your enemy.

"Just like you, Umar," he said as he grabbed him tightly. "A great friend."

Haggard arrived in Singapore, checked into the Raffles Hotel and called the Asian boy. He was addicted to the rough tumbles, finding the fucking dirty Asian faggot whore was just as perverse and disgusting as he was addicted. He found himself longing for the sex as the hate welled up in him. It was just like shooting someone.

Haggard was there for the meeting. It had been two years since the last company meeting in Singapore. He was glad the general had died; the old fart was nothing but a son of a bitch. He wondered if the other son of a bitch, the general's protégé Beil would be at the meeting. His musing was interrupted by the knock at the door.

"Come here, you mealy-mouthed whore," Haggard yelled as he pulled the man inside and pushed him down on his knees.

Yang Foo studied the man as he opened his pants. He put aside what he had to. For the last year he had endured much, but had also learned much from the big ignorant idiot who talked in his sleep. The Chinese were happy for the information. They knew about the secret arming of the Islamists in Aceh. It played into their plans, so they did not tried to stop it.

"You, big man, important man," Yang said, after he was finished. He went over to fix Haggard a drink. He wanted to probe his ego after the abuse. One can learn so much when the head of power walks the line of desire.

"Yes. I big important man, you piece of Chink shit."

"You fly planes still to those Muslims in Indonesia?"

"Yes, they're even more shitty than you."

"Maybe you fly them even more weapons, make them very strong."

"Yes, now that the big shit head general has died," Haggard said, starting to stream information because of pill that Yang had slipped into his drink.

"General who? Do I know him?"

"No, he is like a spook, here or there."

"He must be a big man like you."

"A big dead man."

"Now who in charge of all this?"

"No one. That's why I'm here for the big meeting to see whom will be the head."

"Oh, I know you be head, big boss man."

"Maybe," Haggard thought, happy the general had died. The general had kept Haggard at the lowest rung, kept him out of the whole loop, having him fly in arms to these natives that barely wore any clothes and lived like monkeys, fighting other monkeys.

"Oh, I know so. You come back after and I give you good happy time." Yang looked over at Haggard who had passed out on the bed. Then he went though all his clothes trying to find more information. It was awful work but it had an end and the end would be to kill this son of bitch when he had been milked of all the information. Like who was at this meeting and who was this important general who had died.

He looked over, Haggard was snoring away, evil even in sleep. A tormented soul, wandering in the human hell. Yang fought the urge to pull his pistol and kill him. Instead he took a long swig on the open whisky bottle to try and wash away the vile filth he had to endure for his home, so they could be victorious in their quest to bring Indonesia into their red dawn.

110

Agnes and her two kids were over at the Finn house for lunch. Dottie's servants made the best bami goreng. Today's was to be extra special because the young dukun was coming over.

"AAAAYA!" Talnor's wife squealed in delight. "The dukun looks very happy with your bami."

"Yes, I put in extra shrimp which I heard from Seam is the boy's favorite."

"Very smart." Even so, both of them were just a little worried, because this was the first time the dukun had been in their house since he had lifted the curse. They were very surprised when he came over and addressed them in the dialect of their village:

"My mother says you are the cook."

"Yes."

"I just wanted to say that this is the best bami I have ever had." Bambi goreng is a special Indonesian dish of fried noodles made with soya and many secret ingredients that are passed down from person to person, generation to generation and is as closely guarded as how to make sate. "Can you please give me the recipe?"

The question was unusual for an eight-year-old, but Talnor knew this was a very unusual child. If it had been another Indonesian, he would not have told him, or if pressed he would have given an almost-recipe where something would be lacking.

"Tuan, it is very hard for anyone to make, especially someone so young like you," Talnor said, feeling the eyes of the dukun sink into him.

William had been looking at him, but only because he had noticed a pimple on the underside of his eye and like all young boys was fascinated by it. He kept staring at it, but Talnor thought the dukun was looking through him into his soul, where he would know if Talnor was lying. Talnor felt hopeless in his power, knowing that no matter what he did he would have to pass down the recipe that had been secret for generations of his family.

"I will have my father cook it with me. We have been practicing cooking Indonesian food, so when we go back home on furlough will be able to cook it for our relatives."

It was true that Beil and young William would spend time together cooking, much to the annoyance of Seam, for whom it was a question of face. He should be the one that cooked for the family.

All this time, William had been staring at the pimple, unnerving Talnor even more.

"OK, tuan, here is the recipe." And he began to give it. He planned to hold something back, but under the pressure of the dukun, he felt his knees begin to weaken. And so he told the real secret of undercooking the noodles and then quickly frying them to finish them off so they were never soggy.

Mrs. Rockman was also at the luncheon. "Oh, how do you like the international school?" Dottie asked, glad to be hosting the party.

"It is so wonderful," purred Saya Rockman, pinching herself, thrilled to be invited, basking in the tremendous face it gave her. She watched the servants from the corner of her eyes, reveling in their envy. "Young Ida Bagus Rai Amir, or Andy as he now calls himself, refuses to speak anything but English. It is driving the servants crazy." All the women laughed.

"He'll be happy about that later on," Dottie answered, pleased. It had been her idea to allow Indonesian students to attend.

"I really like the field trips. Especially when we go to something that is Indonesian so our kids learn about your culture," Agnes chimed in. She liked when the class went to the market or to a silk factory, where they could all see real life.

"Oh, I love them too!" Dottie's exuberance was echoed by Sally Dremmer and the others. Saya Rockman started to beam from ear to ear.

"Well, you are all in for a treat. I wasn't going to say it. It is not officially announced by the school, but Nasul has arranged a very special trip to another Indonesian school in Palembang."

"Well, that is marvelous," Dottie exclaimed.

"And to make it even more exciting, Sukarno is going to be there."

"Sukarno!"

"Yes, and all the children will get to meet him," Saya said very excitedly. "They will get to shake his hand and get a group photo," she added. On top of that Nasul had arranged for their son and the Beil boy to be in the official photo that was to be sent out on the AP wires around the world.

She was happy for all of it, but most of all she was happy for another reason. She could now properly thank the dukun for saving her son's life. When she had heard the frantic story from the servants about her Andy's certain death by snake bite and how the boy had saved him, she wanted to reward him. But it was hard to find a proper reward for a rich ex-pat's son who already had everything. She was delighted when she had found out from Andy that the dukun wanted to meet Sukarno.

111

The meeting took place again at the Raffles Hotel, in the presidential suite on the top floor. Beil had come early, meeting privately with the newly-promoted General Jim. When the others started to arrive, Beil was sitting off to one side, chain smoking. He was very happy to see Tim Johnson, the antiques dealer from Thailand enter the room. Then Haggard walked in. Beil's back tightened. This was the first time they had met since Beil discovered Haggard was flying secret missions, arming the insurgents. By the way Haggard looked at him, Beil knew that Haggard did not know he knew.

"Gentlemen, the general died," General Jim announced like it had just happened. Where the general had been strong, Jim was weak, unable to get a handle all the various factions in the room. The general had been privy to everybody's twists and turns. With him gone there was a huge vacuum where many jockeyed for position. Jim had absolutely no control. Even arranging the meeting had been a problem.

"So where do we move from here," Tim said, concerned about what they were going to do. He knew that everything was in a jumble because the United States was losing ground. Communism was growing everywhere, especially in South-East Asia.

"We'll kill all the fuckers," Haggard shouted, smoke curling from his lips. He was glad the general was dead. Now with him gone, things would go better. The general just did not understand that the only thing that worked was force. The only good enemy was a dead enemy and you should live by the rule of shoot first and ask questions later. Just take Indonesia, for instance. The general had pulled them back from toppling the government. Now all that could change. They would step up their arms shipment and take charge.

Haggard glanced over to Beil, loathing him and his stupid idea that he could work with the Indonesian leaders from the inside. Well, that was a failure. Seven years of meddling with nothing to show for it. This Sukarno was playing them for fools. The Communists were more powerful every year.

"Haggard, don't you ever change?" Beil asked. "Kill everybody, it's not that simple."

"Oh, it's very simple. You just take out a gun and shoot."

"That's just great. You shoot and then all is fine. What planet do you live on?"

"One where it is like nature, the survival of the fittest." Haggard felt like pulling his gun out and shooting Beil right then and there, but held his impulse.

"So when you kill all of them, then what do you do?" asked Tim Johnson. He saw the lost look on Haggard's face, just behind the violence. He thought to himself that that was the problem with people like Haggard. They had no solution other than force. If you wanted to use force, then use the army. They were not the army. They were what they were. They were subtle power like the wind that only needed to rustle the leaves to make them fall. They were the game inside the game.

"It will just take care of itself," Haggard said, furious at being questioned by this Beil-like clone.

"I'm afraid Mr. Haggard does not understand the subtleties. You know he doesn't play bridge." There was some stifled laughter in the room. It made Haggard tense. Beil was belittling him. Inadvertently he clenched his fists.

One thing was evident to all. The meeting without the general had no leader. Although people laughed at him, Haggard was not without his supporters. After all, who really cares what happens after you kill everybody. That was not their part of the game. Force and repression, kill them all, then install a dictator, like in South America or Iran to protect America's interests. Let them figure it out. The only other choice was to be like Russia and come in with your armies and purge. Sometimes you had to become what you were trying to destroy.

Some thought it was already too late for anything but extreme force. China was a new superpower that had beaten the US in Korea, and was full swing into the Cold War, arming nations such as Vietnam where secret games like theirs were now irrelevant. It was a big mess. All of them knew it.

"I think this meeting has gone off track. It is time for some serious discussion," Jim said, wishing that the general was still alive. All these groups and secrets within secrets that the general had managed. Now with him gone the anti-Communist sentiment sweeping the US was placing huge pressures on them to stop the advance sooner rather than later. There was no patience for long drawn-out games. "The first thing is to remember that we are all on the same team in a very complicated game. One that we play on many levels." Jim was looking at Beil, who had ingratiated himself into the Indonesian power stream, but so far outwardly without results. If anything, the influence of the PKI Communists kept growing. There had been a decision to let him proceed, but at the same time try a different, parallel track, because the State Department thought that the idea of this guided democracy had gone too far.

112

Later that night Beil was drinking in the lounge of the Raffles Hotel when Tim Johnson came up to him. "Mind if I sit here?"

"No," Beil said, in the dumps about everything. He was worried that General Jim would not be able to keep so many powerful factions together, let alone accommodate the mood in the States, where they were obsessed with stopping Communism at all costs.

"What are you drinking?"

"Bull's eyes."

"I haven't had one of those in ages. Bartender, make me one of those."

"Too many hot-heads in that room. I'm afraid that everything will burn up in smoke if we are not careful. Sometimes I think the whole world is insane. I keep thinking how we all stand behind an ideal, like freedom or Communism, but that really says nothing about what kind of a person you are."

"You mean like Haggard?"

"Like Haggard. Now there's a prick who believes in freedom."

"What do you think he thinks about? What does he like?"

"He likes killing, killing and more killing, and unfortunately he is very good at it."

Just as Beil completed this sentence, Haggard walked in. He did not see them because they were at the end of the bar. They watched as he sat down at a booth where an Asian man was waiting.

"I never though you would get here," Yang said, putting on his game face. He had been watching Beil and Tim intently, snapping pictures of them, not sure where and how they fit into this meeting that Haggard had attended.

"I get here when I want," Haggard said as he got up to go to the bar, where he now spotted Beil and the other faggot. He went straight over to them. "Things are going to change now that your general is dead. You won't have your way anymore."

Haggard chuckled. Beil and Johnson could see that he was already drunk, and loud. Both men said nothing, not wanting to rouse his fury. Instead they let him stand there, almost ignoring him. He shot down his drink and went back to his table.

"Who were those men? They were so rude to you."

"Oh, they are a couple of faggots," Haggard said off-guard.

"Where do you know them from?"

"Oh that one at the end was in the war with me, and the other I just met. He's some big shot in Bangkok. I know one thing: both of them are enemy."

Haggard got that look in his eye. "Let's get out of here," he continued. As they walked out Yang made sure they went past Beil and Tim Johnson, snapping close-ups of the both of them.

"That Haggard is a strange sort who hates Asians, but there he is walking out with one."

"Haggard hates everyone. That poor boy is lined up for hell," Beil said as they lit each other's cigarettes, at the same time snapping the pictures of the tall Asian with their secret cameras.

113

Timal and Richal had just finished praying. Both were thinking about the blasphemy of non believers, or worst yet believers who did not practice, like the whore Rockman who drank against Allah's laws. The day seemed to mirror their mood, as it was overcast with a dark sky, very bleak, as if there were no hope for their cause. Both men were frustrated that after having spent more than two years fighting, their nation was changing but not for the good. Stores selling all kinds of evil temptations were opening up. It was all because of the infidel foreigners, Sukarno and worst of all the Communists who hated God. It seemed like everyone and everything was ruining the word of Islam. They were outraged that the government had not made their religion mandatory, or that Indonesia was not yet governed by strict Shariah law.

"Nothing has changed since we have been gone," Richal said, smoking some cheap leaf that he had dried, because of not being able to afford expensive tobacco.

"It's the foreigners. We should go, get our weapons and kill them." Timal spat, thinking back to the last attempt to kill them that had gone so bad. His mood darkened.

"Yes, they're bad, but they are not the worst," Richal said, thinking of Rockman and having to serve him drinks with Tuan Beil. He had tasted the foul drink himself and spit it out. How could someone drink that? "I have an idea of how we can change all this."

"What idea?"

"That dog Rockman came by last week and while the two were talking I was listening," Richal said.

"What did they say?"

"That Sukarno was going to be visiting our old school." He pointed to the run-down school that was at the end of the road.

"When?"

"Soon."

"Can you find out?"

"Yes, of course."

"That's good."

"It is even better."

"How?"

"Rockman has arranged for all of the International School to be there visiting on the same day."

"The same day?"

"Yes, a very unique opportunity." Richal said as they both looked over at the old school, where an army of workers were busy making it ready. Both men smiled. And then they got the sign as a blinding light came upon them. They watched as the sun broke out of the clouds like a ray gun to shine only on the old building, showing the way to true believers like themselves. They felt reborn.

"Allah, so many prizes. What a unique opportunity indeed."

"Yes, Allah provides in many ways."

Umar was by the front doors waiting when Beil emerged from the airport. He noticed that the tuan still seemed sad and not himself.

"What's the matter, tuan? Still sad for your friend?" he asked as Beil settled down into the front seat.

"Oh, long hours, and yes, still sad that my friend died. I told you he was like a father to me," Beil said. That was all true, but not the reason for his somber mood. Nothing about the trip had gone well. When the group had met the next day it became clear to him that his mission was now one of several. It frustrated him that all the subtle maneuvering over the years was going to be put at risk in an attempt at instant gratification. He had not realized how Communist hunting had swept across America like an out of control plague, or panic. Panic—what the general had called the Achilles heel of reason.

"I'm sorry to hear that, tuan," Umar said, leaning over with his free hand and lighting the cigarette for Beil. Umar himself was in a good mood. The PKI was now firmly entrenched in the Sukarno government and poised to take more power in the upcoming elections.

"Thank you, Umar," Beil said, still lost in thought, still unnerved by the hail Mary attitude that had consumed the Singapore meeting. He thought of the absurdity of life. Here was Umar his friend, maybe his best friend, who was a member of the PKI, the same PKI that was now a popular nationalistic movement trying to march Indonesia toward Communism. A movement that was being secretly funded by the Chinese and now Russia in an effort to expand a new front in the Cold War. A movement that had every reactionary idiot in the agency scrambling to destroy it with no regard of the future or human life. At one point someone at the meeting had actually proposed dropping an atom bomb on Jakarta. Bottom line was, everything was falling apart. The PKI were very strong; demanding more and more.

To anyone on the outside, it did look like everything Beil had done was a complete failure. That was because no one knew of his secret weapon, except the general and whoever he might have told. Beil's trump card was Rockman's secret army, which Beil had been nurturing for years. His plan was based on finesse and not trying to force yourself, but

208

allowing freedom within reason and tolerating strikes, dissent, and even the recent nationalization of all the Dutch companies. In other words, Guided Democracy.

But letting events and ideas have some freedom was not without danger. Now there were spies from Russia and China running around Jakarta trying to assert their influence. Some had even been spotted attending PKI meetings. That was a troubling development. The strikes were getting more organized. Many in the PKI were tired of waiting to seize power. They were being egged on by the Russians and Chinese, each with their own agenda. Both countries had given huge official loans to Sukarno and unofficial loans to the PKI. Beil knew that all this money came with strings. These Communist countries were each trying to become the sole puppeteer in this new front of the Cold War. Beil wondered if any rifts between them had developed because of it.

He wanted to know what concessions were being made because of the money. How did the Indonesian members of the PKI feel about these concessions, or did it even matter to them? The quest for power corrupts and you can easily lose sight of why there was a movement in the first place.

Beil looked over to Umar. He decided to gamble. "I have heard that both Russia and China are now funding the PKI."

He saw Umar's eyes become guarded, his breath heavy as he sucked on his cigarette. "Money has to come from somewhere, tuan. You said so yourself many times."

Umar tried to hide his worried brow. Beil had struck a chord. Umar was furious about the outside influence, especially from the Russians. Their type of Communism was not the type Umar envisioned for his country. They were pushy and wanted control, both subtly and with an iron fist. It disheartened Umar that some of the leaders had bought into the models the Russians had provided, some were even starting to sound like them. Just last week he had been at a meeting where there had been advisers from both Russia and China. He felt they were there to protect their interests, not help Indonesia. And every time he spoke out, he felt like he was being watched like fish in a tank. Now he knew that even in a Communist state, dirty money was in control. He was very frustrated. It was hard enough controlling Sukarno, let alone controlling these outside forces.

Beil said, "Yes. But with money comes influence, whether it is overt or covert. For instance if I come into your village and give you a water buffalo for free and then come back to visit you and mention that I like rambutans, then someone in the village would see I got some. And then if I mentioned that perhaps they could plant more rambutans instead of something else, then when I arrived with more water buffalo the whole village would be planting rambutans and nothing else, thinking it was their idea. You have to be careful when there is money involved, even if you are using it to fund noble ideas."

Beil was content with the PKI if they were Indonesian. Once again, it was all back to words: Communism, nationalism. And nationalism wasn't such a bad idea, but like the general said it could turn into something bad if you weren't careful and not just Communism. It could also turn into fascism. Both men were lost in thought when they arrived at the compound.

115

"They are all rusted!" Richal shouted in frustration when he and Timal had opened the bag that they had left buried all those years before. During those years Mother Nature had penetrated the carefully-wrapped packages. The tropical rain had rusted the guns and melted the ammunition so it was a hard ball of useless waste.

"The infidels must pay!" Timal shouted irrationally. This had ruined all their plans. To go to the school without weapons was folly.

"There has to be another way." The frustration was evident in Richal's voice. Finding weapons would be hard if not impossible. They could try and steal some, or maybe find some Muslim true believer in the army to sell them some, but both options were long shots.

"How? We have no money," Timal said. And without weapons it would be even hard to steal weapons. The only ones available to them were knifes, which were not so effective when you were trying to kill a lot of people. "Do they have any weapons in the office of the infidels?"

"No." Richal shook his head. He had never seen one.

By this time they had returned to Palembang. Their conversation was interrupted by a loudspeaker blasting from a car that was driving through their street: "In the next four weeks this street will be torn up and paved. The fronts of all the houses will be painted for the visit by out father, Sukarno."

They went outside, feeling even more powerless. The visit to the school was gong to take place in four weeks. They watched the car come back toward them and Richal saw something that made him think. There on the back bumper was a sticker for the Ministry of Tourism, which listed all the districts of Sumatra, among them Aceh, where they had fought for so many years.

"Timal, did you see it?"

"See what?"

"The sign."

"What sign?"

"The sign from Allah." Timal shook his head.

"Did you see the sticker on the car that drove by? It was from Aceh," Richal said, very excited.

Timal felt the excitement, too. "Aceh, I had not thought of that. We can go there and get weapons."

"Yes, with four weeks there is plenty of time." The men smiled at each other. "Praise Allah for showing us the way."

116

Haggard touched down on the runway, noting that it was in much better condition than the last time.

"Welcome, sir," Richal said, acting as the emissary for the local warlord, Colonel Panti. Richal had arrived in Aceh with Timal one week earlier, disappointed that there were no weapons to be had until the American pilot arrived. In the three months they had been away, Colonel Panti had wrestled control from the various factions and was building himself a rich sheikdom based on Shariah law. The colonel remembered that Richal was fluent in English. He had sent Richal to show the infidel American his importance.

"Who is in charge here?" Haggard shouted, hand on his side, fingering his pistol in case this was a trap. It was his first mission since his promotion to theater director where he did not have to answer to anyone outside of Washington. After the general's death, it was clear inside the agency that what was happening in Indonesia was not working. But rather than shut Beil down completely, Haggard was given his own separate mission. The PKI was now very powerful. Many inside the agency thought that if they were not stopped, Indonesia would fall to the Communists. The president thought so, too. Haggard was eager to make his mark. He wanted to use the Aceh rebellion to overthrow the government.

"Colonel Panti is expecting you," Richal said, recognizing the foul-faced American instantly. "Come this way. I will take you to him." Richal led Haggard to a small building, empty except for a table and chairs. Behind it sat Colonel Panti in a military uniform with too many fake medals. Strong man. Warlord, Haggard thought, not at all displeased. It was the first time he had met the man. Nothing like a bloated ego to get a man to fight hard.

"Colonel, the time has come," Haggard said. He knew very little about him. The only important thing was the man was anti-Communist.

But the colonel was just a big fish in a small pond. "I have brought the arms you called for." Haggard was surprised that the colonel did not wait for his words to be translated.

"Excellent," the colonel said in English, having learned the language when he was a servant, before he had found his true calling. "I am quite fluent." Turning toward Richal, he added in English to emphasize the point. "You go organize the unloading of the weapons while we talk."

Richal could not believe his luck. He went over to the plane and opened the cargo doors. There were cases and cases of guns and ammunition. He went over to a crate and opened it. Inside were grenades. Perfect for bombing the school. He grabbed a few and quickly stuffed them under his shirt. Then he called for help for the rest of the unloading. He smiled to himself. Allah does supply.

Meanwhile Haggard was talking turkey to the colonel, making sure this new warlord knew what was expected of him in exchange for the arms. It was one thing to start a rebellion from here but another to have it spread and influence events throughout Indonesia. The PKI leadership was to be targeted to make up for wasted time. Beil had been in Sumatra for seven years and was a complete failure. All he had done was compile a list of PKI members as the movement grew. Haggard was determined to show results in a few months. He could not wait to see the look on Beil's face. Maybe he would even give him mocking credit. After all, it was because of him that they knew the names of the individuals in the PKI office in Jakarta where the leadership operated.

"How great is your reach into Jakarta?"

"We have friends everywhere," the colonel said confidently but he had no connections in Jakarta at all, other than the acquaintance of some low-level military officers. But then he remembered Richal, who had mentioned that he had learned much of his English working in the capital.

"Good. In return for these arms and the next shipments, I want you to blow up the PKI office in Jakarta," Haggard said. "Can that be done?"

"Yes, tuan, it will be easy. It will begin the real war. We will strike and declare ourselves independent and rid ourselves of these Communists."

"We want it to happen soon. Good. The PKI mission will be the catalyst. After that, you act." Haggard saw the ruthlessness in the colonel's eyes. It gave Haggard a rush at the thought of the violence.

117

"Umar I would like you to fly with me to Jakarta. I have arranged a car but they have no driver." Beil wanted to travel to Java to get a first-hand sense of the growing power of the PKI. Rockman had tried to crack down on them by shutting their newspapers, but they were bypassing him and going to the people. Their leadership was being infiltrated by the Russians and Chinese, who were providing new tactics. Everybody knew that it was about the money.

"Yes, tuan," Umar said, welcoming this unexpected opportunity to travel there and meet with the other cell leaders now that Jakarta was the hub.

But on the day that they were to be leaving, there had been a report that rebel army officers in Manado had broken with the government and had declared an autonomous state in North Sulawesi. This threw everything into chaos. As they drove to the airport, they passed a convoy of military trucks.

After parking the car, Umar found Beil on the tarmac. Together they walked up the first-class steps and took their seats. While they were looking out the window waiting for takeoff they saw the large caravan of official army vehicles come out of nowhere, surrounding their plane.

"What are they doing, tuan?" Umar whispered, feeling trapped in his first-class seat next to Beil.

"I don't know," Beil said, lighting a cigarette. The two watched as armed men in full uniform got out of the cars and started to come up the ramp and into the plane.

"There has been an emergency and the army is taking over this flight," an officer announced in both English and Indonesian. Umar slumped down further into his seat.

His panic increased when Beil jumped up and approached the officer, screaming in Indonesian. "I don't care if the others get off, but me and my driver are staying. I have to be in Jakarta for a very important meeting."

"Impossible, sir," the officer replied, shocked that the ill-mannered foreigner had the audacity to question his orders. He was just about to have his men throw the insolent man out of the plane when Rockman appeared.

"Oh, Edmond, what are you doing here?"

"I'm on my way to Jakarta for a few days. What's going on?"

"Oh, a show of force. We have been summoned back to the capital." Rockman looked knowingly at Beil.

The officer come up to him, very agitated with Beil's attitude. "I told him we were taking the plane but he refused to leave. Should I remove him?"

"No, Mr. Beil can stay."

"What about the man next to him?"

"He stays too. That's my driver," Beil said imperiously. Umar was afraid he would be recognized. He tried to slink deeper into his chair. The officer looked at Rockman who despite a lack of uniform was in charge.

"His driver can stay too," Rockman said, looking over at Umar who had no choice but to look back. His anxiety increased when a group of officers sat next to them, placing their machine guns at their sides. Umar expected to be arrested at any moment. He was relieved when the plane finally landed in Jakarta.

Richal got off the overloaded ferry with Timal. For the last three hours they had been packed like sardines, pressed against others in a putrid mass of poverty. It took all their faith in Allah to endure. There was so little room for them to move. For the whole voyage they were afraid someone would rub up against them and the grenades would explode from the pressure. When they finally made it off the ferry, they got down and prayed, surprised they were the only ones.

"Everybody here is living in sin," Richal said. Around them many men were drinking in corners gawking at the women of the night as they paraded their wares on the wharfs. Nowhere was there any sign of a good Muslim.

"This is what the Communists do. This is what Sukarno has allowed." Timal spat in disgust, seeing that Jakarta was a bigger cesspool than Sumatra, one giant slum of sin. "It is the Communists," he said. "They do not believe in God."

"How could one not believe in God?" They passed a mosque. A whore was standing by the doors.

"Allah," Timal cursed. They were even more infuriated when a foreign car pulled up. They watched a westerner get out and approach her. They were close enough to see the red thick lipstick; the long legs. The westerner asked how much in English thick with a Russian accent. The two men heard her answer and what she would do for the money. Both of them got aroused watching the evil filth, unable to take their eyes away until she had entered the car.

Finally after a few minutes Timal spoke. "It will be better when we are martyrs. It is disgusting how the rise of the Communists has led to this debauchery, broken down the boundaries so the foreign ways have come in to corrupt us."

Richal saw Timal about to pull out one of the grenades. He quickly grabbed his friend's hand. "Let us not be martyred here. Remember we have a plan. We shall be avenged. Our actions will help set Indonesia back to Shariah law," he said, conquering the lust he felt within, hating this tempting modern world that Sukarno had allowed.

Richal was happy with the plan. They had been given six grenades. Richal had stolen two more. Their official mission was to case the PKI headquarters for a few days. Then blow it up with the grenades when all of the PKI members were inside. That was the official plan. Both men were glad to do it, but they had additional plans, more elaborate plans. This was just the warm-up.

The first plan was to throw only a handful of the grenades. Run away before the police arrived. Their real plan, Allah willing, was to use the remaining grenades in the martyrdom attack on Sukarno at the school.

All of a sudden they saw another western car, this time with a driver. They saw a man lean out of the window and flick his cigarette out into the street. They had eye-contact for an instant in the surreal light. Richal was shocked that he recognized the face in the moonlight. He froze for a quick second then quickly covered his face and darted into the darkness of the alley, afraid they had been spotted.

"That man on the street looked just like Richal," Beil said as he rolled up the window.

"Many Indonesians look alike, tuan," Umar said, thinking to himself that all westerners looked alike, like all fish or dogs of the same breed. Beil pulled out two cigarettes and lit them, handing one to Umar.

"Yes, you're right. That would be impossible. Take me to the hotel." The two of them had landed a couple of hours ago and were in the car that had been arranged by the Stanvac Company. Umar took a drag on the butt. The nice mellow smoke was wonderful. Just what he needed to relax from the plane-ride where he had been on edge every second, sure he would be recognized and arrested. In a short time they arrived at the hotel.

"Where will you stay?" Beil asked him.

"Oh, with friends, tuan. Remember I used to live here," Umar said, leaning across the seat and lighting another cigarette with the Marlboro lighter Beil had given him.

"Goodnight then. See you at nine in the morning."

119

The PKI office was in the middle of a busy street lined with storefronts on either side. It seemed out of place in the capitalistic bustle that surrounded it. The street corners were full of vendors in small carts selling everything from sates to newspapers.

The movement had come a long way from its underground beginnings. Now with its access to Sukarno and its organizing strategy it was a very powerful force that could almost rival the military. It had evolved from the grass-roots with little help from outside, other than ideas. Until now. Now outside leaders attended regular meetings to discuss tactics.

Jakarta was now the power base. The influence of the PKI among the various trade unions was a constant pressure on the government. They were now advocating the nationalization of the Dutch businesses just as they had overthrown the Dutch government. Money was pouring in, both in official aid and covert money. In the back of the room were Russian and Chinese observers. They spoke to each other in English.

"Comrade Yang," the Russian said. "Soon Indonesia will be our prize."

"Yes, I agree," Yang said. He didn't trust this Russian. Neither of them trusted the other. Their countries wanted different things. When it had been found out that Yang spoke fluent Indonesian he been taken off watching Haggard, who it was decided was a minor player. Yang was rushed to Jakarta to look after Chinese interests now that the decision was made to actively finance the PKI.

"Why do we need this money," Umar asked, disgusted that the movement had become like the very dogs they were trying to overthrow. There was corruption that came from the money that both the Soviet Union and China was pouring into them. Each had a different brand of Communism, if it could be called that.

"Because without the money, then we will not have the resources to overthrow the government."

"Why do we need money? Everything should come from within."

"Umar, you have been away too long," Kusdi said. It had been a year or so since he or anyone had seen much of Umar, who was in Sumatra, which had become in terms of the movement somewhat of backwater. All orders now came from Jakarta. Kusdi had just come back from three intense weeks in China and was in favor of a hard-line position. He was convinced that they already had the people. All that was needed was bolder actions to prod the masses to rise up and complete the Communist take-over. In China he had been warned of dangers from within the movement. How differing views needed to be eliminated, especially the views of those who advocated compromise, which was weakness. Umar was standing in his way. "It is so naive to think that the people will just pour out into the streets with nothing, against guns. We tried that, and Musso was murdered by the same powers that still are in place."

"Oh, they cannot stop us now," Umar said, believing it, carried away with the passion of the moment. He had been in the movement from the start, long before it was anything but raw ideals. All this outside influence was no better than the imperial dogs they were trying to overthrow. How could they be allowing Russians and Chinese to attend the meetings? It was just as Beil said. They both wanted to take over the world. Beil had showed him some newspaper clippings relating how countries like Hungary and Poland had been invaded by troops from the Soviet Union, clamping down on freedom.

"They can stop us and will stop us if we are not strong and if we don't have money for guns we are weak," Kusdi said. People entrenched in power are going to fight to keep what they have. At some point it will come to extreme violence. The PKI had to be ready. That meant money for guns. Umar was too idealistic, too willing to wait. "Look at what's happening in Vietnam. Ho Chi Minh defeated the French and will defeat the Americans only because of money and arms."

"No, he has the people—nationalism. Without nationalism, Communism will fail. He is winning the struggle. The arms are nothing without the will." Umar felt his body shaking.

"You are wrong. His movement was nothing without money. He had no real power without the guns to back him up. Same as us. Without money, we have no arms. Without the arms, we have no power. We need arms to rise when the time comes. Umar, you are so naïve."

"Yes, Umar, he is right. It's all about the money. That's how it works," Yang said.

"Money. That's what you think. What about ideals, about making everything equal, everybody the same?"

"How can that be achieved without money? We are nothing without this money."

"But with this money they will want influence," Umar said, pointing to Yang and the Russian, who stared back angrily. "We will be indebted to these powers."

"No we will not. We will not let them!" Kusdi screamed.

"Say that to someone from East Germany or Hungary. They just tried to revolt and Russia came in with tanks." Someone from the Bali contingent spoke in support of Umar.

"That was because of capitalistic dogs trying to take them over," Kusdi said, near the boiling point. Umar's temper was also near breaking. It took all of his will not to punch the man in the face. The emotion was uncharacteristic of him, and set a wave through the room that led to rising tempers. If they continued on this path they would all be fighting each other.

"You have been indoctrinated, brainwashed into their system. This is Indonesia and this is how it has to be done. I've been here while you have been abroad. Look, everybody, there are Russian and Chinese guests here." Umar pointed over to the Russian and Yang. They tried to remain inconspicuous but had some difficulties, especially the Russian.

Umar finished his tirade and walked outside to clear his head. On the way out, he lit a cigarette with the Marlboro lighter just as he walked past Yang and the Russian. Unknowingly to them all, the secret camera snapped a photo of Yang close up.

The heat of the sun was bearing down outside the PKI office, forcing Umar to seek the shade on the other side of the street. He moved under the shadow of a tall teak tree and lit another cigarette. The meeting was not to his liking. He needed to calm down and think. He took another puff and let his eyes focus in on the changes that had taken place since he had last been to Jakarta. It was so much more modern than the last time. Compared to Palembang this was Paris or New York. Though he had not been to either, he had seen many pictures and read many articles from the magazines that Beil and his wife received from the States.

He walked down the street and saw in one shop some of the latest fashions that had been in the magazines. While he was peering into the window, two men passed by. One of them was as white as a ghost.

"That is Tuan Beil's driver!" Richal shivered, suddenly filled with apprehension. The two had been up very early in the morning praying to Allah for his blessing. They had left the mosque buoyed with confidence, but on the hour walk to the PKI office, the reality of what they were about to do eroded much of it. With each step they had become increasingly on edge. The grenades in their pockets suddenly felt heavy and cumbersome. The only comfort was that it would all be over soon. All that was left to do was pull the pins and lob them into the doorway of the building that was just down the street.

"Impossible," his friend said. "You are just nervous. Let Allah enter you and do his work."

"No, it is him."

"No, you are wrong. What in the world would he be doing here?"

Just as he said this, Umar turned around and look their way. It was true. The man was Beil's driver. A wave of panic set in. Quickly both of them turned, increasing their strides, and continued toward the PKI office.

Umar looked at the men. He saw the flash of recognition in their eyes. Did he know them? He racked his mind. Although both looked familiar, he was unable to place them. Then it came to him. They were friends from Bali. Friends of his friend the woodcarver, Wari. The same Bali where socialism was a way of life. Where everyone shared as equals.

He started to calm down. Now he would have more allies, ones who would understand how outside money would have strings, just like Dutch money or American money. It was so clear to him. Indonesia needed an Indonesian solution. It was so simple. Bali was the model. He lit another cigarette. Now he could talk some sense into the others, especially the leadership who was overrun by the money. Quickly he raced to catch up with his friends.

Timal turned around and saw Umar racing toward them like a madman.

"Quick, Richal! We've been spotted!" Both men broke into a sprint. They were around one hundred feet from the office doors. Their plan had been to case the joint. See who was inside. There was no time for that now.

They reached into their pockets, fingering the grenades as they raced the final yards. Timal was ahead of Richal now in an open sprint for the door, afraid that Umar would catch them. Timal pulled a grenade from his pocket and tried to pull the pin a few yards before he got to the doorway. The sweat ran down his fingers, making the grenade slip harmlessly from his hand and hit the street.

Umar saw the grenade hit the ground. These were not friends, but enemies. He dashed to close the final few yards. He watched the man scramble to reach the grenade. Umar sprinted for it, tackling the man as he reached it. The two men rolled around on the ground, but Umar was stronger and was able to wrestle the bomb from Timal's hand.

Richal pulled two grenades from his pockets. Richal did not have any problems pulling the two pins. He reached the door that was open in the heat of the day, and lobbed both of them inside and raced on, not knowing that Timal had fallen down. The explosion was loud and blasted the door and windows into the street.

Smoke and fire engulfed the burning building. Scattered glass was everywhere. Inside, screaming men stampeded to reach the only exit through the fiery hot door. Blood was everywhere.

Umar had finally subdued Timal and now had the grenade in his hand. Shocked by the sudden blast, he turned, his hands trembling. He saw the agony and screams. He watched one man rush out, missing both his hands, blood spurting out. He watched the man stagger a few yards, then fall.

This gave Timal his opening. He twisted free and got to his feet. Tried to sprint away, but tripped and sprawled on the ground.

"Stop him! Stop him!" Umar screamed.

"There he is!" someone shouted. "Look, he has grenades in his hand."

"Get him! Get him!" The mob began to race toward Umar, who looked up and saw them coming after him. Quickly he raced away, frightened for his life. The angry mob was on his heels. He raced down the corner and into an alley. The sounds of ambulances and police sirens were in the air.

Timal was still on the ground as the crowd rushed by him in their frenzy to get to Umar. He waited for them to pass by. Then got to his feet, and raced away toward the park where Richal would be waiting for him.

120

"Tuan, I need to speak to you," Umar said, waiting by the entrance to the hotel with the other drivers. He had not slept at all the previous night, having spent his time on the move, afraid he would be caught. He felt like a hunted tiger. The city was the jungle. Every alley was a path of danger. By this time news had spread of the bombing at the PKI headquarters. Many people, especially in the slums of Jakarta, were out for revenge. He had heard that fifteen people had been killed and another hundred wounded in the bombing, some really awfully.

"Sure, what do you want?" Beil said, stunned by Umar's appearance. His boyish face was haggard, with big black circles under eyes that were full of fear.

"No, not here, tuan, wait till we are in the car." Beil followed him in silence. It had already been a chaotic morning dealing with the aftermath of the bombing. The most unnerving thing was the unexpectedly angry call from Rockman wanting to know if any Americans were behind it.

"Tuan, the man who did the bombing was the same man who stabbed Tuan Finn years ago at your party," Umar said. He had struggled over whether to tell Beil this or not. But finally he had come to the conclusion that Beil was the only one he could tell. He could not go to the police with the grenade. They would be arrest him. He could not go back to the PKI safe-house, because he was afraid that someone had seen his face, especially after his public fight with Kusdi only a few minutes before the bombing.

"The same man?" Impossible, Beil thought. Then Umar reached over and unlocked the glove compartment.

"And this, tuan. This is American-made." Umar handed the grenade to Beil, who kept his eyes fixed, not wanting to let Umar see his shock. There, clearly printed on the grenade, was the USMC stamp and serial number.

"How did you get this?" Beil asked, trying to appear calm. But inside his mind was in turmoil, full of thoughts, all of them leading back to Haggard and Singapore, especially the look on Haggard's mocking face as he spoke of Beil's seven-year failure, while all the time hinting that his mission was not the only one.

"From the man. He was with another man. I saw them and followed them," Umar said, not revealing to Beil that he had been at the meeting. "And when he approached the office they both pulled out the grenades. But I was able to tackle the one man before he was able to throw his. I wrestled it away from him, but the other man threw two in the office. It was awful, tuan, so many people died, the blood, the smoke, it was all around. As I was wrestling the assassin, people started streaming out, some with no arms and blood everywhere. Then the mob turned on me, because they thought I was the bomber because of the grenade. But I'd taken it from the man, the same man from the party."

"Drive me to the blast site and let's have a look around," Beil said. They got to the place and saw the policemen and the soldiers. Beil spotted Rockman. "Wait here, Umar, while I find out what happened."

Rockman saw Beil get out of the car. Rockman had been there most of the night, trying to determine the million dollar question. Who had ordered this?

"Oh Mr. Beil, what brings you here?" Rockman said, playing cool in front of the other soldiers, not wanting to let on that the two of them were close friends. You had to be careful associating with a foreigner.

"Terrible," Beil said as he surveyed the scene.

"Yes, fifteen dead, many wounded," Rockman said, giving no information except what was in the paper. To Beil it was like bidding in bridge, the gradual increase, subtle, finesse, the telling but not telling.

Beil got excited. He decided to increase his bid. "Do you have that picture of the man on the airfield?"

"Yes, why?" Rockman said, not expecting this line. He was aware that the grenades were American-made. His intelligence had heard that the order for the bombing had been given in Sumatra. He called for his aide to bring him his briefcase from the car. He noticed that Beil's driver was sitting scared in Beil's car, parked nearby. He should be scared, Rockman thought, trying to decide if now was the time to continue with an all-out attack on the PKI. He opened his briefcase and got out the picture.

Beil examined the grainy picture of Haggard; then the two Indonesians with him. One was in profile but the other was full-face. He looked hard at this man—it was true. There he was, the man from the party who had stabbed Donald Finn.

He looked over to Umar in the car and motioned for him to come forward. Umar got out of the car, trying to calm the shakes. It did not help that Rockman stared at him or that there were so many around with guns. He had the grenade in his pocket just in case.

"Umar, look at this picture." Umar looked. There was the man he had wrestled, clear even in the grainy photo.

"That's him, tuan, that's the man, the bomber, the Finn man."

121

Timal and Richal were by the docks waiting for the ferry to take them to safety. They'd gotten no sleep either. There were many eyes about. The two of them felt like they were being watched. Both of them were nervous. But they had seen the morning papers, rejoicing over so many dead and wounded. Allah had provided.

"Too bad Beil's driver intercepted you and took your grenade," Richal spat, throwing his cigarette on the ground.

"Yes, what were the chances of seeing him? I should have killed him," Timal said without conviction. He knew that if it had not been for the mob that mistook Umar for the bomber, he would have been captured.

"But you will not have to worry about him. I am sure the mob got to him," Richal said as the ferry approached.

"But what if they did not?"

"Then we'll have to stay out of sight until we kill Sukarno," Richal answered as the two men boarded the ferry to safety.

122

"Excellent!" Haggard exclaimed as he got the second-hand report after he had landed with more arms and equipment. It was a grand success. The final total was thirty-two dead. The office had been blown apart, but the very best thing was that the blast had been blamed on internal fighting within the PKI.

"Yes, my men were very successful," Colonel Panti said, looking ridiculous in his new green army uniform with patches and medals that made him look like a bulletin board.

"I think you will be happy with these new weapons," Haggard said as the colonel's men began to unload the plane. There were some new machine guns, a very heavy model. Haggard picked one up from the crate. Loaded it and shot it into the jungle. The force of the bullets cut the thick underbrush as if it were paper. He handed it to the colonel, who took aim. But he was not prepared for the kick and fell back spraying bullets, hitting a group of coolies, cutting one of them in two. Haggard felt the death-wish rise in him. It took all of his power not to grab the gun out of the colonel's hand and make this a real killing field.

"Very powerful!" the colonel exclaimed as he got to his feet. With these new weapons he would be able to mount the insurrection to save Indonesia. "These will bring us victory."

"Yes, the time is approaching. Everything will be in place soon. Then it will be time to act," Haggard said, the killing with the sweet smell of blood in the air making him excited. Now with the general dead, he was free to move without any interference, especially because of the anti-Communist sentiment that was sweeping America. Thank God for patriots like the McCarthy fellow. Because of men like him there was all kinds of money. It had been very easy to convince the agency about his plan. The coup would go on, using this idiot as a puppet. Haggard would show them all. Not like in Vietnam, where they let that worm Ho get too powerful.

Yes, very soon, Haggard thought to himself. The last piece of the puzzle was a surprise attack to destroy the entire Indonesian air force in one day. The planes for that attack were being readied at a secret base in Malaysia.

123

When Beil got to the office there was an urgent telegraph from Murray to meet him at the airport. It had been a week since the bombing of the PKI office and things were starting to settle down. Umar was in semi-hiding, staying close to Beil, very aware of the whispers that he was the bomber. Beil and Rockman felt it was best to exploit that thought. At this point, it was better to keep Umar a hunted man than to let the real truth come out that the bombers were radical Islamists. Beil felt bad about Umar, but if he stayed close to Beil he would be safe.

"Umar, to the airport," Beil said, lighting a cigarette.

"Yes, tuan," Umar said somewhat dejected, the victim of circumstance. The truth was he had saved further carnage. Had the perpetrator been able to detonate his grenade, the death count would have been higher. Unfortunately the man had been able to slip away from Umar's grasp, aided by the very mob that was after him now.

"Umar, you need to move on. Regroup. You saved many lives. You are a hero."

"No, they think I am the traitor, the one who did the bombing. The press has printed a description, and it fits me. My life is over now."

"No, Umar that is crazy. The real bombers will be caught and you will be cleared. Rockman knows you did not do it. All they have is a description of you."

"But the police have no power in the PKI. The PKI think it was me. They saw me with the grenade," Umar shouted in frustration. Beil did not understand, he thought. Rockman only made matters worse. Rockman was playing him like a fish. Being seen with Rockman would just make the PKI surer that he was the traitor. He thought about his arguments with Kusdi. How he had left in a very public huff. Very angry in his position that the movement had to be brought back under Indonesian control. He was a hunted man. It would be just matter of time.

When they got to the airport, Murray was waiting for them. They chit-chatted as spies do until Umar dropped them off at Murray's apartment.

"Edmond, I found out Sukarno has no real power except for in Jakarta and that many rogue officers are like kings in their part of the jungle," Murray said, now used to being a spy and liking it. He had made sure to be hovering just out of sight but not ear-shot to take pictures with a special little camera Beil had given him. He had taken some very good kinky pictures of Sukarno with a bevy of women, some of them white. "He also is using the plane as his personal brothel. The whole plane stinks of sex."

"And that's bad?" Beil asked.

"Well, that kind of sex, yes," Murray answered as he chewed on the ice of the gin and tonic.

"I also heard that he is taking money from us, the Soviets and the Chinese, promising nothing but hinting at everything."

"What else's did you hear?" Beil said wondering if Rockman knew all this. Or was Sukarno just hedging his bets. He must know that he was in a box.

"There is one thing that he is passionate about."

"Oh, what is that?"

"He is furious that the British are going to give independence to Malaysia."

This was the first Beil had heard of this. He wondered how this could be used, but first things first. First, the bombing had the mark of Haggard, no finesse. Second, Sukarno was playing all the sides against each other. He wondered if any of them knew of his link to Rockman. He was brought out of his musing as Murray reached over and touched him.

"Edmond, enough of spying," Murray said. "I want to know if you missed me."

124

A new outfit had been delivered by Mrs. Rockman's driver for William to wear on the field trip to the native school next week.

"Oh, doesn't this look great!" Agnes said to William, after he had changed into the light blue shirt and tan pants.

"Yes, mommy," William said, anxious to get outside and play. Seam had promised to take him down behind the generator where yesterday one of servants had seen a swarm of giant grasshoppers.

"Why are you in such a hurry?" Agnes asked.

"I'm going out to catch grasshoppers, mommy."

"OK, then run along. But change out of the clothes first so you don't get them dirty." But William did not listen and raced outside where Seam was waiting for him.

"Come on, mandor," Seam said. Out behind the generator was a fence that separated the jungle from civilization. It was a forgotten part of the compound where only Sally's pet elephant went. The grass was waist-high on the fence. There above the grass, clinging to the fence was the biggest grasshopper that William had ever seen. He caught it in his net.

"Wow, look at the size of the thing." It was four times the size of a normal hopper.

"Good going, young tuan," Seam shouted.

"Bagus—good, it is so big," William exclaimed.

"Ya, bagus, good tuan, but there are even bigger ones, double this size."

"Where Seam, where can we get bigger ones?"

"Not here, but near the school on the other side of the Musi river, where you are going to see Sukarno. That is where the really big ones live."

"How much bigger are they?"

"Oh, double, maybe even triple the size."

"Maybe I can catch one."

"Maybe you can, tuan."

Seam saw William pick the grasshopper up by the wings, and turn it toward him, but before he could shout out a warning the giant insect let loose a stinking torrent of orange ink that splashed all over William's nice new clothes.

"Oh no!" William screamed as he looked down at the mess. "Mommy will kill me."

He saw his mother come out to see what all the shouting was about. Then she saw the ruined clothes. "William Beil, come here right now," she said. Seam came with him. Eto appeared with a change of clothes, quickly taking the soiled ones to get rid of the stain.

"Sorry, mommy," William said. "It won't happen again."

125

Allah has provided and Allah willing we will be martyred very soon," Richal said ecstatically.

"Yes," Timal answered, both of them still shocked that they had not been captured. But such is Allah's way. Both had just renewed their vows to become martyred and find their reward in heaven where the virgins would be waiting. It was time. Richal was ready to end the suffering that had started with the death of his son. He would be avenged doing Allah's work.

They got off of the bus in front of the school in their old neighborhood. It had been freshly painted and stood out, looking somewhat out of place in the otherwise run-down neighborhood. In front of the school the open sewer had been covered by fresh plantings of flowers. They walked into the reception hall, surprised by the size of the crowd that had already formed up near the front by the podium. They were able to find a place near to the side where Sukarno was to speak.

"This is the place," Timal said as he fingered the pin on the grenades that he carried. He turned to look out the window. Saw a caravan approach, a line of big foreign cars. Beil's driver was behind the wheel of one. Timal quickly turned away.

Umar had dreaded this day for two weeks but there was no way that he could avoid it. Ever since the description of the man with the grenade had appeared in the paper, he felt like a wanted man. He had to talk to the police on more than one occasion, which had made him feel worse than a caged bird. In some of the meetings Rockman was there, probing him with questions on many subjects. He knew that there were spies everywhere. That just being with Rockman was dangerous. He was under constant fear that someone might identify him. It was bad enough that he was Beil's driver. Already Kusdi's allies in the PKI were suspicious of him.

"Where should I go, tuan?" he asked Beil, who was next to him in the front seat. The back seat was full of loud children. The noise added to his edginess.

"Rockman said to pull up to the back room where the children can change into their uniforms," Beil said, having thought it better they change at the school in case they spilled something on themselves. Given William's track record, Beil didn't want anything to ruin the arranged photo shoot with Sukarno. Beil was glad to act as chaperone. It gave him the chance to observe Sukarno close up.

When they got to the back room, there was no sign of Rockman, so Beil had the children change. Once they were changed, they got impatient and loud. Just as they were about to explode with anticipation, Rockman approached.

"Sukarno is going to be half an hour late," Rockman said through the window.

His son was with him. "Andy," Rockman said. "Take the children to the swings in the back and wait there." Soon we were all running toward the swings. Near the swings was a fence that led to an open lot.

"Look!" William shouted. There clinging to the fence was the largest grasshopper in the world.

"Quick, William, don't let it get away." Andy shouted as the boys in their nice clothes ran up to the fence. William steadied his hand. The huge grasshopper twitched and started to rise, but William was faster and clamped his hand down. The grasshopper was so big that he had to wrap both hands over it. The boys crowded next to him.

"Be careful not to get too close," William said. He turned the insect in his hands in such a way that if it did spray the foul liquid, it would not get his new uniform wet. All the boys took turns holding it and then it was given back to William.

Sukarno's motorcade finally arrived and pulled up in front of the school. The press started snapping photos. Sukarno was dressed in an ironed white shit, western pants, but with an Indonesian hat. There were armed guards everywhere. Rockman approached the car.

"Hello, Mr. President, before you go tour the school, I have my son's class here from the International School. We have arranged for you to take a photo with them."

Sukarno motioned for him to lead the way. Before William or any of the others could see him, he was upon them.

"Come here, boys," Rockman ordered, motioning for them to line up near the side of the podium. People broke out into a chant: "Father! Father!" William was still holding the giant grasshopper.

Over near the podium the microphone crackled in anticipation. The crowd now surged as the swell swarmed tighter and tighter toward the stage. Richal and Timal had split up and were on opposite sides of the podium, having changed their plan at the last moment. Now they were both going to lob grenades at Sukarno, hoping to escape in the confusion. Umar was standing in the back on the same side as Timal. He was waiting for Beil. He had never seen Sukarno up close. He started walking toward the front.

"This is William Beil," Rockman said as Sukarno came forwarded. William was about to bring his hand out but the grasshopper was still there.

"Let me see that," Sukarno said. He looked into the boy's hand and saw the huge grasshopper. He reached to touch it but it squirted all over his white shirt. Brown goo gushed out like an ice-cream cone dripping in the hot sun.

"I'm sorry," William said in Indonesian. He was in trouble. The guards around Sukarno gripped the triggers of their guns.

"Apology accepted," Sukarno said and started laughing, prepared for anything but not this, even though he remembered those insects from when he was a boy. He called to his assistant that was hovering nearby. "Get me another shirt," he barked as he moved into a backstage antechamber to wait for the fresh shirt.

"Now tell me where you caught that thing," he said to William.

233

Over near the podium, Timal was very nervous. He looked around behind him. Umar was only ten feet away. His hand fingered the grenade in his pocket. Ten minutes passed, still no Sukarno. He looked down at his watch. Where was the dog? He began to panic as the fear of waiting overtook him. He grabbed another quick glance behind him as the crowd surged toward the stage, pushing Umar closer, close enough that he could touch him.

Richal on the other side was just as nervous. There was a line of school children behind the podium who broke out into the Indonesian anthem. Young girls and boys. He looked past them and saw Beil standing by the side of the curtain. The two had eye contact and Beil waved a hello.

At the same time, Umar looked in front of him and did a double-take. There was the bomber from the PKI office. The same one who had stabbed Donald Finn. He reached over and tried to grab him. Timal turned and parried and was able to break free to slither his way toward the stage.

"Stop him!" Umar shouted. He tried to follow but he could not break through the crowd. A police officer on the stage heard him and moved in his direction, but did not know what he was looking for. He called to another guard who rushed to help.

Timal saw the guards move his way. Sukarno had just started to approach from the back of the stage. The guards began questioning people next to him. It was just a matter of time before he was captured. He made an instant decision. He put both hands in his pocket and pulled the pins. He rushed the stage, knowing that the time was now.

Sukarno saw the young western boy with the grasshopper as he walked toward the podium. The boy looked so sad. It touched a nerve with Sukarno, who wanted to tell the lad that it was ok. He remembered his own childhood. He stopped his march to the stage and came up to William, affectionately patting him on the head.

"Stop him! Stop him!" Umar shouted again, pointing to the rushing man. The two guards were now right behind him, guns drawn. Timal took the grenades out of his pocket and slammed them together. "Allah Akbar, God is great!"

The room exploded. A thick black smoke engulfed it. Everyone was screaming. The smell of blood was in the air. Other guards rushed over to where Sukarno was standing still next to young William. To their relief, he was fine.

As the smoke started to clear, everybody saw the destruction. There were body parts everywhere. Beil rushed over to William, almost tripping on the severed head of a young girl, still with her hair nicely pulled back. It made his stomach turn. He made it to William and embraced his son.

Richal made his way out of the building, shell-shocked and furious that Sukarno had escaped the trap. That Timal had acted alone. The only thing that pleased him was the vast destruction and death. He had been looking at the school children, especially the girls who did not wear burkas, who were flaunting their skin in public. At least they had been made into an example. But Sukarno had survived because he had stopped to talk to the young tuan, son of Beil, the evil infidel.

Then he began to calm down as he remembered the first plan. He still had his grenades. Now more than ever he would carry out the plan and attack the tuan compound to have his revenge.

126

"The dukun saved his life," a proud Seam told the rest of the servants. Umar had told him the story.

"His fame will grow. Because of this we'll be able to raise his fee," Eto said.

"How clever of him to make it seem so innocent. A flying grasshopper ruining his white shirt so he would have to change it," Talnor chuckled, now part of the circle. He had made his peace, and because he was Eto's brother, he was entitled to forgiveness and a share.

"Yes, I can't believe the Mrs. punished him for it." When William had come home he had been sent to his room and made to write

Sukarno an apology note. He had been sent to bed without supper. Little did Agnes know that later the servants had brought him a plate of all his favorite foods.

Now they heard footsteps approach. It was the Mrs. They quickly changed their conversation. Both stood at attention, ready to serve the madam. Happy they had been speaking a dialect that no one except the young Tuan understood. But still they were nervous when the two women—Agnes and Dottie Finn—appeared.

"We are moving to Jakarta," Agnes said.

"Us too, Talnor," Dottie said. "We are moving there in the next few months. Away from this jungle and into civilization. Did you hear there is a new Fitzpatrick store?"

127

Yang thought back to the PKI bombing, knowing he had been very lucky to escape. Fortunately, he had been by the entrance looking at the door when he saw the grenades lobbed in. He immediately rushed out the door and was twenty yards away when the blast went off. He was the first to see Umar wrestling with the bomber. He was going to help, but stopped when he saw that Umar had gotten control of the grenade. It pleased him when the crowd chased after Umar. That fit perfectly into China's plans. Umar was a dissenter who had a following. Yang knew it was very dangerous to have him around. Umar was for Indonesia. He was not for helping Chinese interests. Fortunately there were many Chinese who had been in Indonesia for centuries. They would run Indonesia under the umbrella of the motherland.

I know it was him," Yang said to Kusdi, who had also escaped injury.

"How can you be sure? Why would he bomb our offices? Many of those who died were his friends. Luki from Bali says the crowd got it wrong. He says that Umar was a hero for wrestling the grenade from the bomber. He had no choice but to run when the crowd rushed after him."

"He had the grenade in his hand. No one can deny that. I was one of the first to escape. All I saw was the grenade."

"It just doesn't make sense."

"It makes perfect sense. He wants to weaken everything, now that we are winning. He is not a true Communist. You saw him storm out, angry and disgusted. All I saw was the grenade in his hand. No one else was around," Yang repeated. "He cannot be trusted."

"Yes, he cannot be trusted," Kusdi sighed, content to let the doubt linger, but for other reasons.

"I have to be going now," Yang said. He was going back to his other job: getting information from the ugly perverted American to see who was really behind the blast.

128

Haggard smiled to himself when he read the account of the attempt on Sukarno's life. Some deranged Islamist nut wanting an orthodox Indonesia. Some nut-case who believed there was something other than this life. He was going to hell anyway so he might as well have fun.

Haggard was not aware that the suicide-bomber was one of the assassins he had sent to do the PKI job. It would have been better if he had succeeded in killing Sukarno, but nevertheless Haggard was ecstatic with the unplanned follow-up to the PKI bombing.

Soon, he thought to himself, they would be ready to launch the attack. He had flown over the Indonesian air force base, astounded to find their entire fleet of planes was all in one location. It would be no problem knocking them out in the first few minutes of the war. Then at the same time Colonel Panti would declare a new republic and take over, stemming the tide of Communism. After that it would be on to Vietnam.

It was good that people like him were taking over the agency. Then these operations would be accomplished the right way, with sufficient force. Thank God the general is dead, he thought again. The general and Beil had done nothing but lose. Gather facts and sit around. Who were they kidding? The only kinds of facts to gather were what he was doing. Scout out the enemy's strength. Then kill him with a swift knock-out punch. It was oh so simple.

Now he was busy hiring a crew of mercenary pilots who would eventually fly combat missions out of the small covert field, where he was assembling a secret air force for the soon-to-be declared independent Indonesia. Already he had five planes, which had been easy to procure from where they had been mothballed after the war. Crews were busy painting them. Getting rid of any kind of marking. However long all of that took, that would be the launching point.

129

Richal got up from his mat after morning prayer, crushed by the loss of his friend. He knew he should be happy for Timal, who was now in heaven with virgins everywhere. But his heart was broken. It was hard for Richal to make it through one hour without thinking of his friend.

At the time of the bombing Richal's hands were in his pockets, fingering the pins as he waited for Sukarno to come to the podium. He had frozen for a second when Timal jumped up on to the stage yelling, "Allah Akbar!" By the time he was able to move, Timal had slammed the two grenades together, causing a huge explosion that had picked Richal up like he was a kite, throwing him back. He got back on his feet, dazed, blood everywhere, only to see the dog Sukarno escaping through the back. He tried to get to him, but the panic of the disaster had caused a stampede. Before he knew it, he was out on the street in front of the school, watching as Sukarno drove away.

Richal had waited around numbly as the dead were carried outside. The dead were mostly schoolgirls dressed in uniforms with pretty ribbons still in their hair. Still in uniforms that even in death were disgusting because of the amount of flesh they showed. He then saw the body or rather the body-parts of his friend, very glad to see a big smile on Timal's face.

The next few days were surreal. He walked around in semi-shock, not knowing if he had been spotted or whether to go back to work for the dogs. He had stayed at the mosques deep in prayer, disappointed in himself for failing. His friend had been so brave.

He had been furious that the paper had portrayed the bomber as a radical religious fanatic who was trying to stop Indonesia from becoming part of the modern world. He had mulled this over, stewing by himself. Finally he had come to the conclusion that his friend must be avenged. It especially infuriated him when he read in the papers that Sukarno had been saved because one of the international students attending the event had caught a large grasshopper that had soiled Sukarno's shirt so he was late in getting to the stage. He lost his temper when he found out that the student was Beil's son, who had been on a field trip arranged by the dog Rockman. If it had not been for that, Sukarno would be dead. Indonesia would be back on its way to becoming a Muslim state.

He blamed the foreign dogs for Timal's death. He walked out of the mosque determined that today was the day for his friend to be avenged. He had woken up early in the morning and shaved all his body hair. Then he bathed just like he had the day Sukarno had escaped with his friend who had been martyred. Richal was ready. Today he would succeed, and by night, Allah willing, all the foreigners—especially Beil and his son—would be dead and Richal would be in heaven with Timal having their way with virgins.

He went into his house, got the grenades and headed out the door on the mission that would take him to glory. All the way he fantasized about heaven and Timal. Allah Akbar--God is great. By the time he reached the walled compound, his will was made of iron.

It would not be long, he thought to himself as he approached the unmanned gate. Inside, though, he started to worry. Where is everybody?

The compound seemed deserted. The usually-manicured lawns were overgrown. No one was around. Finally he came upon some workers in the back who were dismantling the generator.

"Where are all the tuans?" Richal asked, fingering the grenades in his pocket.

"Oh, all the tuans have moved to Jakarta."

When he heard these words, the misery of living once again pressed into him.

130

Aren't these houses great?" Dottie Finn gushed as she and Agnes walked into their new homes with no jungle is sight.

"Makes you feel that you have come up in the world," Agnes said as they moved from house to house. The company had hired a stateside architect to build an all-American-style street. It was modeled after a new design called a ranch home: everything was on one floor. After coming from the jungle where you could only walk inside the fenced compound, this was freedom. There were so many interesting things to do. Nearby was a street market where at all hours vendors would be selling their special sates or nasi goreng by an oil lamp. Peddlers with baskets would knock on your door, trying to sell everything from native crafts to fine antiques. The only person sad about leaving the jungle was Sally Dremmer, who had to give up her baby elephant.

"I am going to miss her so much," she said, lamenting the look on the elephant's face, who was so sad and seemed to know what was going on.

"Oh, you can visit it again sometime," Dottie said.

"Yes," Agnes added. "They say that an elephant never forgets. I am sure the boys will take us back for a visit. They had arranged for the elephant to be put in a zoo in Palembang, as it could no longer live in the wild.

"Yes, I'm sure you're right, but I felt so bad."

"But don't be sad," Agnes said, just then getting an idea. "You know what we can do? We can have a remembering Palembang party this weekend."

"Oh, that's a marvelous idea. I'll have Carl bring all the movies that he took over the years," Sally said. "He even has some pictures of the elephant!"

"I even know where we can have it," Agnes said. "Edmond told me of this Chinese restaurant in town called the Moon Palace. Edmond says it is the best. We can take over the whole restaurant and show the movies there."

"Yes, we can even dress up in Chinese clothes for the occasion."

"Yes, I wonder if we can make the boys do the can-can again."

"No, I think we will have to think of something else."

"Like what?"

"Like we can pretend we are empresses of China and the boys can be our slaves."

"Yes, and we can order all the disgusting dishes that no one would eat and make them eat them."

"No, I have the idea for the evening. We will go as mandarins and the boys will go dressed as empresses of China," Agnes said, beaming to all her friends.

"Then we will have to go to Fitzpatrick's and finds ourselves some costumes." The women giggled and went into the new Beil house in the center of the compound for tea and some of Seam's famous peanuts and garlic.

131

Beil arrived at the house on the outskirts of Kuala Lumpur very early in the morning, having flown first to the Philippines where he boarded an unmarked plane. The secret meeting had been authorized at the highest level. Beil had no idea where he was going until he had arrived at the airport. He knocked on the door.

"Oh, Edmond, good to see you," Tim Johnson said as he opened the door. "Follow me," he said as he led Beil into the basement to an old cupboard which he moved out of place to reveal a secret door. This led to a tunnel; the two men scrambled about a hundred yards in the pitch darkness. They could see filtered light in front of them. When they reached it they pushed out the brush that had been piled up, finding themselves in an overgrown lot. Neither had a hair out of place. They moved through the trees until they came to a car parked along an empty road. Tim found the keys and they set off in the dawn light. In no time they were knocking at another door. There inside was General Jim.

"Glad you two could make it," he said, shaking Beil's hand.

"Why all the cloak and dagger?" Beil asked. He looked around the room. All the windows were heavily draped. No light could get out.

"You can't be too careful," Jim said as he shook Tim's hand. Then he began. "We are the unofficial official mission. Hot-heads have prevailed, with the paranoid desire to turn over every rock to find a Communist plot. So now we are what you might call semi-rogue. Very few know of our mission, now that another plan has been formulated."

"What other plan?" Beil asked, taking out a cigarette, already knowing the answer. He had heard the rumors that the agency was already arming a rogue officer in Sumatra with arms. He knew that the grenades used in both the PKI bombing and Sukarno assignation attempt had come from the US."

"The heavy handed approach, with no finesse," Tim said.

"Yes," Jim added. "The general would not approve."

"That is the problem when you get someone who can't play bridge. All they want to do is take a hammer and pound away."

242

"Yes, and we all know that hammers are only good to build house or tear them apart, not to keep the peace."

"Still," said General Jim. "There are cooler heads in the government, people who can't come out openly, but are turning a blind eye, wanting us to continue. The difference between force and power, it gets confused. We are about to get more involved in Vietnam. Our current strategy is not working. The only way to prop the southern government is to send in the army."

"They will fail," Beil and Tim said in unison.

"Yes, but folly is the result of bad advice."

"If only we had supported Ho after the war. We would be in much better shape," Beil said, thinking again about his friend Hiu.

"We are out to fight our secret war which has no rules. So what is happening is that in your different theaters there will be other operations counter to yours. So you have to find a way to make sure that the official operation either works if it is in keeping with your plan or fails if it is not. Nothing in between."

Tim and Beil looked at each other. "Our enemies are already in the game," Tim said, bringing out the picture of Yang that he had snapped when they all had last met in Singapore. "I have found out that this is Kong Yang Foo, thirty-five years old, spy, fluent in many languages."

"That's very interesting you would mention him," General Jim said, taking out his own photo. "Seems this Yang is a very busy fellow besides, befriending Haggard. He showed up in Jakarta right before the PKI bombing. He was in the office when the bomb went off."

Tim and Beil were aghast at this development. "This fellow will be a problem, I am sure," said Beil.

"What about Haggard? Do we tell him Yang is a Chinese agent?" asked Tim.

"No we don't. After all, we might need one enemy to control the other. Haggard is our enemy, though unfortunately he has the ears of the official mission. For now we just follow this Yang. Keep Haggard out of the loop and hope that some god comes down and makes everything all right."

"I don't believe in God," Beil said.

"Then you have to become God if we are to succeed, said General Jim. "Thailand will become a base to launch any Vietnam mission, so you're going to have to make deals with the Thai military."

"I have. I will make sure to exploit the hatred between the Vietnamese and the Thais."

"Good. And you, Edmond?"

"I will continue my path with Rockman and his gang, and I will let the game play out."

"Then that is it, gentlemen. Time to go back and play our hands."

132

It was very funny seeing the tuans dressed like Chinese empresses and the madams dressed like Taipans. It was all Umar could do not to break out laughing. They were in a caravan with the other drivers headed for the Moon Palace restaurant. He looked over at Beil, who had lipstick on, eye makeup that made his eyes look slanted, and a long black wig. The only thing that was still the same about him was the cigarette.

Umar was glad of the move to Jakarta. It gave him more of an opportunity to try to clear his name. A couple of days ago he had been to a meeting where he had been accused of having a part in the bombing. Kusdi had made the suggestion in a very subtle way that left room for doubt but emphasized the circumstantial evidence. But there were people on Umar's side as well.

Umar was parked on the side of an alley off the busy street where he could be out of the way but still have a view of the restaurant in case Tuan Beil came out and needed him. He had just lit a Marlboro. When he looked up, two men were walking past his windshield. He recognized them immediately—Kusdi and the Chinese agent, Yang. For some reason a wave of fear swept over him. In a panic he slid down in his seat so that they didn't see him. Once they passed, he peered up over the dash and watched them turn into the Moon Palace.

"This is the best Chinese food in all of Chinatown", Kusdi said as they walked through the door. The place was packed. The owner said the restaurant was more crowded then usual because some mad foreigners had reserved the whole balcony for the unheard-of sum of a hundred thousand rupiah plus food and drinks. Yang and Kusdi were seated at the only table left, the one nearest the entrance of the balcony. The noise coming from the Americans was deafening.

"OK, now it's the boys'—oh, I mean the girls'—turn." Dottie Finn laughed as the women had just downed their shots. She tried to talk in a loud deep voice, the false moustache falling off. Just then the waiter appeared with the first of the courses.

"What are these?" Sally asked, pointing at the plate of what looked like tiny chicken legs.

"Oh, those are my favorite," Beil said as he popped one into his painted lips. "Here, have one," he said, passing one to Dottie, who normally would not eat much of anything, but in her man costume was more adventuresome.

"They are great!" she exclaimed.

"Yes, they are good, darling," Agnes said. "But what are they?"

"They are frog legs," Beil bellowed.

"Frog legs!" Dottie screamed, forgetting her man voice. "You mean I just ate a frog?"

"No," Donald said. "You're in costume, so Dalton ate a frog." All of them had taken different names for the night.

"Well, if that's the case, Dalton will have another," Dottie exclaimed. Beil started laughing. He looked up, noticing the two men seated at the empty table. All of a sudden his senses went up.

"Excuse me," he said. "I have to use the bathroom."

"Which room will you use?" Carl asked sweetly, looking ridiculous with his five-o'clock shadow poking through his makeup.

"Whatever one you're not." Beil laughed, got up, and then turned serious. He walked by the table where the two men were in deep conversation. Beil recognized both of them immediately from photographs. One was Kusdi, the leader of the PKI and the other was Yang.

The two men stopped their conversation to stare at the absurd American as he came into view. Beil pulled out a cigarette and lit it with his lighter just as he passed them.

When Beil got back to the table, the next course had arrived and there was a bottle of champagne. "Remember, champagne makes me bubbly," Agnes said, looking like a handsome gentleman in her white shirt and tie, her hair dyed black for the occasion. The next course was a specialty of the restaurant, Ayam Shanghai, which consisted of a thick Chinese pancake sliced into strips. On each strip was some hoisin sauce and then a scallion, and on top of that fried-chicken skin with a little bit of meat. They were so delicious that the party ordered three more plates.

Over at the other table Yang and Kusdi heard the loud clanging of chopsticks as another round of shots was brought to the Americans' table. They were reminded of why they hated capitalism so much.

"Disgusting," Kusdi said to Yang, watching the group where the men were dressed like women and the women dressed like men. It was such silly nonsense, just a privileged excess.

"Yes, they come in like they own the place with no regard for anything," Yang said, though secretly both of them were captivated that the Americans could be so open and lustful in their enjoyment.

"It will be very good when Indonesia is Communist and a friend of China. Then we can drive these nuts out." The two paid their check and headed out into the night. Umar wondered if Beil had noticed them.

He had been thinking about the book Beil had told him about, *The Art of War*. One saying kept coming back to him. "The seeds of your own destruction come from within." A random thought entered his mind. Were these two enemies the seeds within the cause? He was thinking about it when he saw Beil and the madam stagger out of the restaurant with the rest of the drunken tuans.

"Hi, Umar," Beil said as he got in to the car. He was about to take off his wig. But Agnes reached over and stopped him.

"No, I want you to keep it on, darling."

"Why?"

"Oh, because I've been drinking champagne and I am very bubbly," she said leaning over and kissing him.

133

Beil was in his new Jakarta office. Rockman had just arrived. Each was sipping a bull's eye. A lot had been happening in the few months after the attempt on Sukarno's life. The radical Islamists took the cause of the martyr to heart and were making trouble again in Aceh. And then there was the colonel who had recently declared independence and was calling for an over throw of Sukarno. These factions were allied, and both were very anti-Communist.

"So I hear you have some problems," Beil stated to Rockman by way of an opening bid.

"Oh, you mean the PKI," Rockman said, knowing that was not the issue. The PKI was working with Sukarno, but that was the same as before.

"No, I was more thinking about the problems in Aceh and the rest of Sumatra."

"Oh those, they are just some inconveniences," Rockman said. Still, he was worried about the Islamists. To brainwash was to control. There was nothing more controlling than religion. No one more brainwashed than religious fanatics. Still, they could be used.

Both men were waiting for the other to up the ante. Beil decided he would go for it. "Oh," he said innocently. "I thought you might like this." He pulled out the photo of Yang and Kusdi.

"Where did you get that?" Rockman asked. He tried to keep his face flat but Beil noticed the eyes open wide.

"What do you know about the Chinaman?" Beil asked.

"How do you know I know anything about him?"

"Because you know everything and what you don't know you can find out."

"Oh, you flatter me too much, Mr. Beil." The way Rockman said it, both of them burst out laughing. "Yes, I do know of him. His name is Kong Yang Foo, and he is an attaché to the Chinese embassy."

"You mean a spy."

"Yes, a spy."

"He seems to be everywhere." Beil brought out another photo he had gotten from General Jim, this one of the PKI meeting.

"How did you get the picture?" Rockman asked.

"Oh, a little smoke and mirror."

"I thought you were running an oil company."

"I thought you were running one, too." Both men again broke out in nervous laughter.

"I hear your air force is all together in one place just like having all your eggs in one basket," Beil said picking his words carefully. He was getting to the real intention of the meeting.

"Oh, I would not know of those matters. As you said, I'm running an oil company just like you." But then he added as a way of thanks, "Maybe they should all fly out soon to check out if there is oil on Aceh."

"I think that would be a good idea," Beil said.

Rockman finished his drink and made for the door. "This Chinaman comes and goes. He has diplomatic immunity, but we have our ways of keeping track. We have heard he frequents Singapore and has a American friend." Rockman gave the quid pro quo as best he could: "But don't worry, Mr. Beil, we will see he is no problem to you."

134

Haggard was in the lead plane, flying in tight triangle formation. This was the start of Panti's revolution. The first mission was to take out the Indonesian air force in one giant strike. Haggard and the three had taken off from the secret field in Sumatra. All the identifying insignia had been taken off the planes. Then they had been painted gray so they would be less visible in the sky.

For the last three months Haggard had split his time between Malaya via Singapore and Sumatra, giving the colonel with the too many medals a pep talk so when the day was upon them, he would be ready to strike. He hoped the colonel would be able to attack unopposed from the air when the real offensive started next week.

As they neared the target Haggard got aroused as usual. He wished that his Asian whipping boy was between his legs. He remembered their last interlude when he had gotten out his whips. The son of a bitch had loved it.

"You can't hurt me, big boy!" Yang had shouted. That had just made Haggard more hard, more aggressive.

"I'll show you," he had said as he jumped on Yang.

"Why do you hate Asians so much?"

"I'm just going to kill them all."

"How are you going to do that? What are you going to do, fight a war?"

"Yes, I'm going to take an entire country," Haggard shouted, consumed with lust.

"Oh, you must be pretending to be a big boy!" Yang shouted back.

"No, not pretending. Soon I'll be killing thousands of you."

"With what, your hard dick?" Yang said, driving Haggard wild.

"No I'll be killing with machine-guns and bombs from the air, taking out the whole air force of some Asian country. You just wait and see, little mealy-mouthed whore!" Haggard had shouted. After that he didn't remember much of the conversation. In his plane he checked the coordinates. They were hiding out of sight above the clouds.

"Time to go for the kill!" He radioed the others. He watched as the bombs pierced the clouds on the way to their targets. A few minutes later the three planes broke through to swoop in low to check out the carnage and machine-gun any plane or person that had escaped. All were shocked to find the runway deserted.

135

Richal took the ferry to Jakarta. It was now a few months since his attempt to kill the tuans had failed. But Ramadan had helped him to become whole. He had flagellated himself with needles and chains, enduring vast pain for the right to another chance to be martyred.

The ferry landed and the slums of east Jakarta engulfed him. He wandered around aimlessly for most of the morning until he finally summoned the inner courage to take a bus downtown to the new office of the Standard Oil Company. There again he loitered around the entrance until he had gathered enough courage to walk up to the security gate, where the guards summoned the ghost, Donald Finn.

"Richal, I can't believe you're here," Finn exclaimed. Richal shivered as the hantu, the non-being shook his hand. The only thing that made Richal overcome his fear was the knowledge that he was going to kill him a second time.

"Yes, I have been away with family," Richal explained, the lie coming easily, almost sounding like the truth.

"Are you looking for work?" Donald asked. He was desperate to find English-speakers. He would have thought that English would be prevalent in Jakarta, but that was not the case. People spoke Dutch.

"Mr. Beil!" Donald called out. As part of the new rules Jakarta, formality was now in force.

"Richal, well I'll be damned. You keep turning up like a cat," Beil said, then turned to Donald. "Mr. Finn, see that Richal gets a new uniform and give him the job of office boy."

The new uniform was very proper, a far cry from the cute gas-station jump suit décor from the Palembang office. It pleased Beil to present a more formal appearance when they had visiting guests. Today the chairman of Dutch Shell was coming by for a urgent meeting.

"Hello, Mr. Van Roon," Beil said. Carl Dremmer was with him in case any technical oil-related matters would come out. After coffee and small talk the meeting started.

"Thank you so much for the information about the coming nationalization," Van Roon said, feeling somewhat in a box having to rely on the Americans for his information. When Sukarno had begun the nationalization of all Dutch businesses, the situation had seemed bleak. But after the initial public fanfare there had been some fruitful back-room discussions.

When Rockman had first told Beil that Indonesia was going to nationalize all the Dutch companies, Beil had asked him who the Indonesians had in place to run them. The stunned looked on Rockman face told it all. Indonesia was in no position to run these companies. The businesses would collapse. So Beil came upon a plan that could satisfy everyone. Why not lease the companies back to the Dutch? It was a simple face-saving solution.

"I was told that you could lease the field and equipment and still have your people run it," Beil said, not caring or knowing anything about the technical details. That was for them to figure out.

"It was made clear to our government that all our things were confiscated and that we would all have to leave," Van Roon said.

"Many things get said that are regretted later. Half the time our job is just trying to get around the new situation," Beil said, studying the man before him. He saw a slight smile appear on Van Roon's lips.

"Do you have any of the particulars?" the man asked, thinking Beil was like him a powerful outsider, the head of Standard Oil in Indonesia. He didn't know that he was one of the guiding hands in the country's subtle transition into the modern world. He didn't know that the one thing all factions agreed on—Sukarno, the PKI, the Islamists, the rebels, Haggard, or Beil—was that the Dutch were going to be kicked out of their former roles.

"As you know, I have overseen the formation of the Bagus Oil Company. Most of the board are far-sighted thinkers, committed to a modern, free Indonesia. I think you will find then very reasonable."

"But what about the riots in the streets?"

"Oh, that is the masses stoked by nationalism and other forces. Sukarno organizes them to remain popular. My advice would be to evacuate all non-essential personnel. Then tell the others to take a very low profile. I am sure in a few months it will be business as usual."

"Very well, how will this arrangement work?"

"Everything that you own in Indonesia becomes Indonesian property which they lease back to you."

"Does that include the oil fields?"

"Yes, everything, but on very good insider terms."

"Thank you, Mr. Beil, for arranging this. It is so much clearer," Van Roon said as they shook hands.

136

Umar had settled into his new life in Jakarta. He now had his own apartment near the Stanvac compound where he could keep the car and come and go without having to stay with Beil. It was a better life where he was more in touch with the pulse of Indonesia. He was amazed at how modern everything had gotten since he had last lived here. New stores. A huge shopping complex.

He was glad the Dutch had finally been driven out, that the Dutch businesses nationalized. Now they were owned by Indonesians instead of the exploiters. It was a euphoric moment for those who had been in the struggle for so many years. At the last PKI meeting they had celebrated, but also remained determined to increase the pressure. Most of that pressure would be coming from those like Kusdi who were eager for Indonesia to embrace the hard-line Soviet or Chinese model. Those two camps were actively pushing, even demanding that Indonesia become Communist as soon as possible. They already had Sukarno's blessing. It seemed just a matter of time before everything moved in that direction.

Umar was somewhat concerned with the fast pace of change. He felt that Indonesia should remain unaligned, continue independent. Not rush into embracing foreign models. He could see there was a divide within the party as they grappled with their new power. This underlining problem was threatening to split the movement into those who were nationalists and those that were fervent Communists.

Still, Umar knew there were many obstacles blocking their path. He had recently heard some rumblings of a coup in Sumatra. That some unknown colonel had declared independence. Umar did not know much about it except that it was in an isolated area that posed no immediate threat to what was happening in Jakarta. The only real threat to the PKI was the army.

The only part of his job that he did not like was being lent out as a driver for the newly-formed Bagus Oil company, whose director was Nasul Rockman. For two days a week he had to drive Rockman around. Each day he felt like he was being interrogated, forced into volunteering more that he wanted. Rockman's eyes were penetrating. His smile was the coldest Umar had ever seen.

"Where do you see Indonesia in ten years?" Rockman asked in English, the language that both of them were more comfortable speaking to each other. It gave them both something to hide behind. Rockman knew of Umar's PKI activities, but he had listened to Beil's suggestion that there was much to learn from him. He knew Umar was reasonable, a nationalist; not a full-fledged ideologue like Kusdi.

"I am just a driver, so I imagine I'll be driving some car around," Umar said. Ten years. It had been more than ten years since Musso's death and still things were almost the same.

"Well, that is what I want, a common man's opinion," Rockman said, keeping up with the game. What he really wanted was an inside view of what was happening in the PKI. "Like for instance what are your feeling on the nationalization of all Dutch businesses?"

"I think that is a good thing. All the Dutch have done is exploit us."

"Do you think Indonesia should nationalize all companies, even the Americans?"

"That would not be a bad idea either," Umar said knowing he was on dangerous ground.

"Why would that be a good thing?" Rockman's group was asking itself this very question, trying to balance all the outside influence under the guiding principle of anti-Communism.

"Because then Indonesia will be dependent on Indonesia. I mean we can all disagree, but in the end we have to be Indonesian."

"Well, what about all the Chinese and Russian advisors coming to the PKI meetings?"

"That is a bad thing," Umar said, thankful that they had reached the building.

137

"Can we get them?" William asked, pleading with his father to buy him a pair of squirrels for sale from the bazaar. Beil, William, and Umar were out in the garden district of Jakarta where there were all sorts of exotic plants, flowers, rocks and animals. Beil had discovered the market a few weeks ago. Since then he had visited a few times to buy interesting plants to landscape his yard.

"Umar, do you think the servants will want to be chasing them around?"

"I think if the young tuan wants them, then the servants will be honored to take care of them."

They were speaking in Bahasa. The shop keeper was pretending not to listen. "Oh please, father, please. We could keep them with the fish."

"OK. We can if we can arrive at a cheaper price", Beil said. He wanted the vendor to include the cage with the two squirrels.

"Bagus, very good." The vendor took the two red squirrels out of the cage and handed them to William. Soon they were playing around his shoulders, but then a dog on a leash came by and began barking. The squirrels jumped out of his hands, racing for a nearby tree.

"Oh no, they have escaped!" William shouted.

"Never fear, young tuan," the vendor said with a smile on his face. "I have trained them to come back with the lure of a certain fruit which I keep just for this reason. The fruit is very rare and has to be imported. Something about this fruit drives the squirrels crazy. I think it must be their favorite food. Come closer and watch."

William, Beil and even Umar huddled around the man, who brought forth a basket tightly covered with a cloth. But first he brought out a blanket and motioned for all of them to gather under it. When they did he carefully removed the cloth. Inside the basket was a pineapple the size of a huge chicken egg. It was a type that none of them had ever seen.

"Why do we have to be under this blanket?"

"So the squirrels don't see it until we have put it in their cage."

"Why does it matter that they see it or not?"

"Because they go crazy at the sight of it."

"What do they do?" Beil asked, seeing how tame the squirrels had appeared.

The vendor showed them his hand with the middle finger missing. "This is what can happen when they see the fruit. It makes them very crazy. They will stop at nothing to get to it." The vendor pulled out another blanket and covered the cage. He quickly picked up the palm-sized pineapple and placed it in the cage, leaving the door open. As soon as he removed the blanket, the two squirrels saw the fruit and began a frantic chatter. At once they raced like possessed demons into the cage, almost killing each other in their fight to get the fruit.

The vessel was a sitting duck and Haggard knew it. He was like a cat playing with a mouse, toying with it, deciding when he should make the kill. He was in the cockpit of his plane. It had been two months since the launch of the revolution. Very little had happened expect for a bombing here and there. All that was about to change as the only modern destroyer in the fledgling Indonesian navy was right in his path. He got ready. The day was overcast with a thick upper-altitude cloud cover in which to hide. The poor ship did not know he was even up there. After a few minutes of savoring the impending excitement of the massive kill, Haggard plunged through the clouds like a white shark jumping for it prey. He readied his hand on the trigger, enjoying the exquisite pleasure of death and destruction, confident that in a matter of seconds the bombs would be on their way to destruction.

KABANG!!.... The sudden blast ripped through his plane, causing it to twirl wildly around end to end. In the next second he was in a life and death struggle, fighting for control. He looked back. Saw he was on fire. Another plane was in the sky with him. He recovered his wits, knowing that a less-experienced pilot would have already died.

Frantically he grabbed the throttle, trying to keep from crashing. He was losing altitude. He was going down. His survival skills took over. He was over land now. He searched the ground for any opening in the jungle canopy. He found none.

That left only one option. He turned back toward the sea. It was his only chance. The plane was very hard to steer. He fought, almost willed the plane to keep level, knowing that if he went into a spiral he was gone. He checked behind him. The flames had now engulfed the whole rear fuselage. It was only a matter of seconds, not minutes, before he was burned to death.

With the heat of the flames at his back, he held on, using all of his will to endure the pain. As he reached the water, the plane started to wobble. He managed to hold it near level as he hit the sea in a belly flop, skimming across the surface until finally coming to a stop. Immediately he felt the water rushing in as the back of the plane broke open. Quickly he undid his seat belt and leapt into the sea, trying to dive under the surface so as not to be burned by the oily flames spreading out on the water.

He did not remember how he got to the shore. He awoke to find himself half in the water and half out on the sand. His shirt was burned, and even though the blistering sun was hot, he was shivering.

He got up, surprised that he was able to move everything except his left arm, which was broken. The salt water caused him to grimace in pain. His shoulders were badly burned and beginning to blister in the hot sun. He had to find help soon. He surveyed the coastline. Except for the thin band of sand, the rest was thick jungle. He started to walk down the shoreline, not even sure what island he was on.

About a mile later he came upon a small fishing village where the boats were coming in. "Help! Help!" he cried as he stumbled toward them. They came running, thinking this was an omen. They had never seen a westerner before in this very remote village on the Sumatran coast. One of the fishermen ran to get the village elder as the rest of them got a sail and made a makeshift stretcher. As soon as Haggard was placed in it, he passed out.

139

When he awoke Haggard was surprised to find himself strapped down in a hospital bed. His arm was in a cast, but the bed was surrounded by guards with machine guns.

"What were you doing flying an unmarked plane?" Rockman questioned in English, seated behind Haggard so he could not see him.

"What plane?" Haggard said. He tried to remember—village he thought. Villagers—then his mind went blank. He had no idea that he was in Jakarta or that a week had passed. The villagers had not known what to do with him, so they had turned him over to the police who turned him over to the army. Finally he was turned over to Rockman and his people.

"Oh, come on, we are not stupid. You were shot down trying to attack an Indonesian naval vessel."

"I attacked nothing," Haggard said, feeling trapped, realizing he was with a professional interrogator, knowing it was only a matter of time before he would have to speak.

"What I want to know is this. Are you working for the United States or some mercenary group?" Rockman said. He kept thinking it all through. What was top? What was bottom?

"I was working on my own," Haggard said, not believing he was given an opening in which to lie, but unaware that by his words, he had confessed to the attack on the ship.

"You know attacking Indonesia, a free and sovereign land, is a death-penalty offence?" Rockman said, slowing the words like a torture. He summed up the American before him. Not at all like Beil, whom he knew was CIA. But Beil was a man he was able to work with. They respected each other. With Beil it was OK to play with the enemy—no, not enemy, but on different sides, working for common ground. Beil was all finesse, not like this boorish bigot in front of him.

"Well, fuck you! I'm not saying anything more." Haggard's venom spilled out. He tried to pull against the restraints, but all that did was shoot pain up his arm.

"Oh, I'm sure you will have lots to say."

"No, I won't."

Rockman turned to one of the guards and said in Indonesian, "Give the subject a shot to sleep. Then in an hour give him one to wake up. Continue this through the night. I will come back sometime in the late morning." Abruptly, he left.

The guard made sure that Haggard saw the syringe, purposely waving it across his face and then slowly going down to the arm. Haggard tried in vain to struggle. After a few minutes more of teasing, the guard plunged the needle in, putting Haggard into a violent quick sleep.

He dreamed of Beil's gook friend whom he had killed. Hiu was standing over him, shouting into his face, laughing. "You are not so strong big boy after all."

140

"We want him back," Beil said curtly, without ambiguity, no finesse.

"I don't know what you speak of. Who back?" Rockman answered just as coldly, aware that he was running out of time. It was a week since the capture. They needed a few more sessions to milk this Haggard of all his secrets. Rockman had been avoiding Beil's phone calls, which had been constant from the first day. Still, he had been unprepared when Beil barged in unannounced, almost shoving Rockman's secretary out of the way.

"Stop it!" Beil shouted, furious at this cat and mouse game. He knew Rockman was interrogating Haggard. Part of him hoped they were using real torture techniques. Haggard had been shot down trying to start a revolution. He had absolutely no idea what he was doing. That's all we need, thought Beil, some hot-head cowboy thinking he can save the world.

"OK, we have him," Rockman said, startled by Beil's directness. He had never seen him as mad as now.

"Good, that's better. Now we want him back before word gets out." Beil was under direct orders from the president himself to resolve this issue before it got into the news. So far nothing had come out, except for a few whispers from unreliable sources.

"It is out of my hands," Rockman said.

"Well, it better be back in your hand shortly, or—"

"Or what, Mr. Beil? He was shot down trying to overthrow the Indonesian government. That is treason!" Rockman shouted back.

"Many things are treason. Some would say some of what you've done is treason." Beil let that set in, hoping Rockman would understand that this was not a negotiation.

"I don't have complete power over this matter," Rockman answered, which was the truth.

"You owe me, and I am here to collect."

"Three days and you can have him, that's the best I can do. Sukarno knows about this and is furious."

"Who else knows?"

"I don't know for sure." Rockman's temper was now in check. "I am afraid, Edmond, that this is a very fluid situation beyond anyone's control."

141

Kusdi was huddled with Yang. They had just learned that an American pilot had been shot down and was in the hands of the Indonesian government.

"You need to go public with the information right now," Yang said.

"But we don't know if it is true," Kusdi said.

A couple of hours ago Umar had stopped by to tell them the news. He had been outside the door when he had heard the unaccustomed shouting coming from both men.

"In life sometimes we need to gamble," Yang observed. It was time to break this thing open to drag Sukarno over to the Communist side. First the assassination attack with US grenades. Then the fledgling revolution in Sumatra with American involvement. Finally, an America pilot in captivity.

"How to reveal it?" Kusdi asked.

"The best way would be to call all the papers. Then take to the streets, with banners, anti-American, anti-imperialist banners, also ones in support of the PKI, Indonesia, and Sukarno."

"Don't you think we should call a meeting?"

"No, Kusdi you are the new Indonesia, the man of destiny," Yang said, knowing Kusdi was the prefect pawn, expendable if necessary.

This information had to be acted on right away. It was Yang's fear that because the facts had remained secret till now the American and Indonesian government would work out a quiet trade and the opportunity would be lost.

142

Haggard awoke from his dream and was now lying on a table under lights that made him feel like he was sunburned. He thought that the table was surrounded by wild crows, spitting.

"Help! Help!" he cried out, all his training broken down.

"You can only help yourself." He heard the voice, the same voice as the other day…. He tried to remember, but there was nothing but the cry of the crows and the light.

"Who is your mother?" Another voice came through.

My mother, he thought. "My mother's name was Mabel," he said, not expecting this line of questioning. He felt a hot wind on his face. He was burning, choking. The air got hotter and hotter until he was unable to breathe. "Stop it, mommy," he cried out.

"Only you can stop," the first voice called out.

"What is your name?"

"Haggard. Larry Haggard." As he answered, the air became cooler.

"What plane were you flying?" Haggard did not answer. After ten seconds the hot choking air came back.

"No plane," he choked out. The heat intensified.

Again the question. "What plane were you flying?" Haggard could not stand it anymore. "It was a secret mission," he said as the cool air came again. He felt someone, one of the crows, come and bite his arm. They are eating me, he thought. Then he fell asleep as the assistant took the syringe out of his arm.

"One more session should do it," the interrogator said.

"We don't have much more time," Rockman answered. They had gotten quite a lot of information, but not the complete truth. The end was in sight. Each time Haggard was led down the same maze, again and again, slowly revealing more and more. But soon they'd have to give the pilot back.

143

The first public hint of the downed American pilot came when a piece of the fuselage was uncovered. The PKI rallied into the streets the next day, shutting all of Jakarta to voice their outrage. Then eye-witnesses came forward from the villages. A day later Sukarno came on state radio to announce to the world they had captured an American airman.

The US government denied this until a few days later when the prisoner was dragged in front of the cameras. Beil was in a hastily-arranged meeting with Rockman. The room was thick with smoke.

"I told you I did not control the events," Rockman said.

"Never mind that. It is now a State Department official inquiry, so the Jakarta embassy has jurisdiction. It is out of our hands."

But that was not the reason for this meeting. Instead, Beil wanted to focus on the power grab by the PKI. They rode the waves of anti-Americanism, which was also fueled by massive economic and military aid from China and the USSR.

"We want assurances that the PKI will be contained," Beil stated.

He had finally gotten to see Haggard the night before. Despite his hatred, he felt sorry for him.

"Beil, get me out of here," Haggard had cried, no longer the macho hero. Gone was the snide bravado. All had been replaced by this broken hump. Beil thought how strange it was that the human body can take on a mood, a depression that could turn it into a shell of itself.

"Soon," he had said, not knowing if transfer would be soon or not. The affair was now public; therefore beyond the control of anything but events. He looked deep into Haggard knowing that any information that he had inside of him was compromised.

The situation was not good. He drifted back to the present job. "Rockman, do not let this get out of hand."

"I will try my best," Rockman said. Many things were twisting inside of him. First there was the decision to crack down on the Colonel Panti and eliminate him as soon as possible. A revolution against Sukarno could only succeed if it had full popular support. If the people supported Sukarno, then the real army would not intervene. So Rockman's group had decided to take the aid from the Russian and Chinese, while at the same time working to slow the rising power of the PKI. One troubling development since the assassination attempt was the infiltration of PKI members into the military. The capture of the American airman played right into the PKI's hand.

"That is not a very confident answer to my question," Beil said, trying hard to keep the frustration off his face. Fucking Haggard with his ill-conceived plot. What madness and folly. He kept thinking back to the general's favorite book, the one he had lent to Umar about the Chinese art of war. He thought especially of one saying: The seeds of your own destruction come from within.

144

Beil and Umar were on their weekly trip to Jalan Surabaya, the famous flea market Beil had discovered a couple of months ago. It was a collector's dream. The whole street was lined with makeshift shacks that sold everything and anything. It was a great place because dealers from all over the Indonesian islands came to sell. You never knew what might turn up.

He had started collecting interesting wayang puppets, and this market was a very good place to find them.

"Tuan! Tuan!" they heard the dealer call. "I have a very rare puppet." He grinned as Beil walked by his stall. Beil watched as the dealer pulled a series of levers and the puppet started to move.

"Where did you get that?" Beil asked, knowing he was going to buy it. "Is that real tears coming out of its eyes?"

"No, it is lemon juice. It releases when I pull a certain string."

"Is it a wayang puppet?" Beil asked. It was so different from any he had seen.

"Yes it is, tuan," the dealer said, lying. It was not a wayang puppet but a gali-gali-man that the dealer had decorated to look like a wayang. But that was not the reason the dealer had painted it white. He had painted it because when it was black, it was very scary and the dealer thought that it was possessed. Little did he know that it was. The gali-gali was traditionally used to act as a child for the childless, and when they died to mourn them. After the ceremony it was burned. But this was a gali-gali from no ordinary funeral. It was from the funeral of a great and powerful dukun santet.

At the funeral the gali-gali revolted and started cursing his former master. The ground began to rumble and soon all the villagers were running for their lives. But before they were able to flee, a giant wave crashed onto shore, destroying the whole village before the gali-gali had been burned. The puppet was swept out to sea and landed on the Java coast, where it had eventually made its way to this market.

"Berapa harga?—how much?" Beil asked, thrilled to find such a thing even though he could tell the paint was new.

"Two hundred rupiah, tuan," the man said, giving the very low price because he and all the other dealers on the street knew he needed to get rid of the cursed puppet. Already at the market there had been strange fires; unexplained illnesses that had already claimed the life of one of the dealers. They had consulted a dukun who said the gali-gali was the cause of the problem. The dukun also said that no one could destroy it, because no one had the power to overcome its magic. All they could do was sell it before things got worse.

"Mahal—expensive," Beil said, covering his surprise at the already-low price. "One hundred rupiah."

"Yes, tuan." Beil was surprised at how quickly the dealer had agreed and how happy he looked. As he and Umar walked back with the puppet to their car, Beil thought it a little odd that the rest of the market had gathered around the dealer, clapping.

145

The CIA plot to over throw the Indonesian government had been a complete disaster. It climaxed when a dazed Haggard was brought in front of the press, forcing the US government to admit that they were meddling in Indonesian affairs. America quickly promised vast amounts of humanitarian aid, while the Soviet Union and China upped the ante by providing millions in military aid. Sukarno knew how to play this game, which was just fine with Rockman and his crowd as long as the president remained committed to an independent Indonesia and did not stray into Communism. The secret aid from Beil continued as before.

"We could embarrass him with the Muslims. Show them his womanizing and drinking," Beil said, conscious that Rockman was Muslim and also conscious that they drank at every meeting. But the idea was to stir up a hornet's-nest, and give the Islamicists a little more influence, to curb the power of the non-religious PKI. The order had come from higher up, to show that Sukarno was not the moral father of his country.

"Yes, that might work," Rockman said somewhat warily. It had been tough to crush the power of the Muslims, especially the fanatics. Still, it was an interesting idea to use one extreme against the other. As he sipped his drink, he was thankful that Indonesia was a series of islands where things could happen and stay out of the light. "Do it if you want. His girlfriends are common knowledge."

Rockman was well aware of his own transgressions. He wanted no part of this, but was willing to let it happen. He left the decision to Beil to implement the plan if he was so inclined.

Murray on the other hand jumped at the chance to be on a mission. It was a week later. Beil was with him at the airport lounge. In an hour Murray was about to take off for Bali with Sukarno.

"Now you know where to put the camera?" Beil asked, going over it again.

"What, you don't think I'm a good spy?" Murray said, indignant. It had now been four years or so since Beil had first asked him to spy. He fancied himself a professional. He even looked the part. When he wasn't wearing his steward's jacket, he would constantly be in safari outfit, complete with a safari hat.

"No, I think you are a good spy. But you need to put the camera focused on the bed, so when the girl arrives no matter where they are you will have pictures of it."

"I have even stayed in the room myself. I know exactly where to put it." Murray smiled naughtily, gulped his drink, and hurried off to prepare the first-class cabin for Sukarno.

"When will you be back?" Beil asked him.

"About a week."

146

Yang was going through old photos to see if there was any information he had missed. He was halfway through a stack he had taken in Singapore when he came upon one of Beil, recognizing the man as the one who had been instrumental in the behind-the-scenes release of Haggard. "So this man perhaps is the big fish in Indonesia," he said, pleased with himself. In the picture Beil was sitting next to another man.

The two were dressed very similarly, and Yang wondered if maybe they were brothers. He would pass the information on to his higher-ups.

It was now 1961. The US was expanding its role in Vietnam, sending advisers and hardware to prop up the South-Vietnamese government. All over Asia the Communists were winning. North Korea was already theirs. Vietnam would be next. In Yang's mind it was just a matter of time before this wave of glory would wash down into Indonesia and bring the island nation into their fold.

With the capture of Haggard, the whole world was forced to take off their rose-colored glasses and see America for the imperial dogs they were. He then went through another stack of photos that the PKI had sent. He was astonished to see numerous clandestine photos of Beil.

He heard a knock and froze. Then came the second secret knock. Yang relaxed and got up to open the door. There was Kusdi.

"Do you know this man?" Yang showed him a picture.

"Yes, that is Tuan Beil. He is the bossman of Standard Oil."

"Do, you know anything about him?"

"No. I know only that we are going to nationalize his oil company so he won't like us much," Kusdi said with glee, heady from the recent gains, excited by the new push to infiltrate the military and purge it of anti-Communists. He was confident the movement was unstoppable now that more than seventy percent of the people supported them.

"Does anybody know anything about this Beil?" Yang asked.

"Umar is his driver. We know that."

147

By the early sixties Indonesia was facing staggering unemployment and inflation. The nationalization of foreign companies had been too abrupt. The bitter lesson was that while the policy sounded good, the actual implementation was not so easy. It got so bad that the rupiah had to be devaluated ten to one. To try and protect the poor, any bill over ten thousand was now worth a thousand, while those under a thousand were worth the same as before. Thanks to Rockman, Beil once again had found out well in advance, and had passed the information on the rest of the expats. All of them now had suitcase after suitcase filled with the smaller bills, so many suitcases that they could use them to build a wall.

It was Carl Dremmer who had the inspiration for the next big party, a devaluation party where Carl would reprise his role of the Wall Street banker jumping out the window. In addition there was to be a mixed bridge tournament where the prize was a suitcase of the smaller bills.

The party started hours before it was supposed to with the surprise announcement that there had been major oil discovery in the Java sea. In celebration the boys had closed down shop and started drinking, eventually ending up at Beil's house. By the time the guests who did not live in the compound started to appear, most of their hosts were three sheets to the wind.

Mr. and Mrs. Rockman arrived at the party dressed in western clothes. Mrs. Rockman had on a new blouse and skirt that she had bought in Singapore. The style was very modern and quite daring, with a skirt that showed most of her knees.

"Oh, Rockman," Beil said, slightly slurring his words. Agnes was by his side. "So glad you could make it."

"Yes, welcome," Agnes added, grabbing Mrs. Rockman by the arm. "Let me show you around the house. All us girls are out back on the veranda drinking bubbly." She giggled as the two walked out the room, leaving Beil with Rockman. A servant came by with a tray of champagne and offered Rockman one.

"Are these any good?" he asked Beil in English. It would have been beneath him to be speaking Indonesian at this western party.

"See for yourself," Beil said, picking up two and handing one to Rockman. "Cheers." Rockman tasted this liquid and found it bubbly and tart.

"No, I think I'll stick to the bull's eyes," he said.

"Seam, get Mr. Rockman a bull's eye."

Just then Agnes came running up. "Mr. Rockman, your delightful wife tells us you two play bridge."

"I didn't know you played bridge," Beil said, excited but dumbfounded. How was it possible to know someone so long and still not know everything about them?

"Yes," Mrs. Rockman added. "Nasul won the Mideast Classic Tournament when we went to Iraq a few years ago. He is a master."

"Yes, I love bridge. I believe it has a lot to tell us about the world, and how the hand becomes the world if played correctly."

"I have entered them in the tournament!" announced Agnes.

"Fantastic," Beil said, looking forward to some competition. He and Agnes were much better than any of the others.

Over in the back the servants were talking about the Rockmans.

"Do you see the way his wife is dressed? She looks so silly."

"She looks just like a madam and he a tuan."

"No, worse than a tuan," Eto said. All of them knew that being a servant to a white tuan was much better than being a servant to another Indonesian. To work for them was more like being a slave.

"Mr. Rockman likes to drink," Talnor said when he came back.

"I see he has already had four and is catching up to the other tuans."

"And the Mrs., she likes the bubbling wine called champagne, just like the rest of the women. See, she has taken another one." Eto shook her head disapprovingly.

Mrs. Rockman was conscious of the servants watching her as she put the drink to her lips. It had only been a few months since she had tried any type of the alcohol. It had taken her a long time to overcome her Muslim inhibitions. But Rockman had convinced her that he and she were part of modern Indonesia, where Islam that would have to change to fit the modern world.

Carl Dremmer came over to join the women. He was already dressed in his too-tight vintage banker's suit that he had bought at the market. It was black and white and made him look like a stuffed penguin, especially in his wobbly state. He was laughing at anything. His wife was trying to tell Mrs. Rockman about all the wonderful books she had read.

"Do you read English?" Sally asked.

"Yes."

"Good. Then I will lend you some of my favorites."

"Oh really? That would be lovely," Mrs. Rockman bubbled, very happy with the warmth of the western women, not to mention the champagne that was going to her head.

"I wrote a book once," Carl cracked.

"Oh, what about?"

"About a whale," Carl said, catching Sally's eye.

"What kind of a whale?" Mrs. Rockman inquired enthusiastically.

"A white whale," Carl said after a long pause. Mrs. Rockman continued to hang on every word. Sally had to choke down another laugh. Agnes and Dottie were forced to look away and avoid eye contact.

"Oh, a white whale! How marvelous! That is my favorite color," Mrs. Rockman declared. "Was it a big whale?"

"Yes, a very big whale," Carl answered seriously just as Dottie could no longer contain herself, and burst out laughing.

"Champagne it makes everyone laugh," Agnes said, covering for others. All were thankful when the dinner bell rang.

When they all sat down, Beil banged on his glass. When he got their attention he began: "Welcome to the reenactment party of the first devaluation of the rupiah. Mr. Dremmer will at some point after dinner reenact his famous role by jumping out of the first floor window." Beil pointed outside to the false façade that the servants had constructed out in the yard. What no one knew except for Beil and the servants was that it had been constructed over the pool, so when Carl jumped out the window he would get very wet.

"Here, here!" someone yelled. They brought their drinks to their lips. "To us!" they toasted. The servants started to bring out the food.

"AYAH, did you see Mrs. Rockman is still drinking?" Eto exclaimed to Seam as he came back with the dishes.

"I know. She is like Mrs. Beil, the way she drinks the champagne." Just then Umar came in from the PKI meeting in downtown Jakarta. The two servants stopped their talk. Umar was in a strange, sullen mood. They watched him walk by and go straight to his room.

"What's wrong with him?" Eto said. Then she went back to watching the party.

"I didn't know this champagne stuff could make you so happy," Mrs. Rockman said.

Dinner was cleared. Soon everybody had left the table and gone outside. Torches illuminated the stage where a very wobbly, drunk Carl Dremmer took one last puff on his cigarette by the makeshift window. He turned to the crowd, and pulled out of his pockets a huge wad of bills.

"I am ruined!" he cried out at the top of his lungs. Laughter erupted from the crowd. He stood on the window sill.

"No, don't do it!" someone yelled.

"There is no hope. I am wiped out," Carl shouted as he leaped out. Everyone heard the giant splash as he hit the water. The yell was followed up by a primordial swear: "SHIT." Carl was floundering in the water like a drowned penguin. Quickly servants pulled him out.

"Why, I'll get whoever did this," Carl laughed, still clutching a soggy handful of bills.

The champagne came around again. Agnes and Mrs. Rockman were the first to take theirs.

"Ladies and gentlemen, it is time for the bridge game to begin!" announced Beil.

"No, the ladies don't want to play." Agnes said, reeling from the champagne. Mrs. Rockman had passed out and was lying on the ground.

"Yes," Dottie said. "The ladies have decided to keep drinking champagne."

"Yes, the men too," Carl said, now changed into shorts and a tee-shirt.

"Well, I guess the bridge game will not be happening," Beil said, lighting a cigarette.

"Yes, I was looking forward to it," Rockman said. "But I was wondering, there is a bridge tournament next week in Singapore. I was thinking of going but did not have a partner."

"Singapore. Why yes, that would be fantastic."

148

Meanwhile Umar was in his room, unable to fall asleep. He heard the mad laughter coming from outside. He took a puff on his Marlboro and blew out the smoke, watching the rings as they hung in the air.

At the meeting he had spoken to Kusdi and the ever-present Yang. What they had told him was astonishing: Beil was the head CIA man in Indonesia—yes, he had already guessed that much. But they wanted him to drive him to some remote place where he would be kidnapped, and disappear forever.

Umar was trapped. They had told him to prove that he was innocent of the fire bombing of the PKI office. In order to prove his loyalty, he needed to lure Beil into a situation where he could be captured.

Umar needed to think, but the loud constant giggle from the party put him on edge. All he could do was sit in bed inhaling smoke after smoke. He fumbled for his lighter, but it wouldn't spark. There was a replacement kit in the glove compartment of the car—Beil kept it there in case they ran out of flints or fluid. He got up and walked to the carport and got the kit, deciding not to bother Beil, who usually reloaded the lighter for him.

After he had replaced the flint, Umar took another drag on his cigarette. His whole world was upside-down. There in his palm he held the tiny tape recorder camera.

149

Richal had been working at the office now for three months with only one thing in mind, revenge. He had been assigned to work with the hantu Donald Finn. Each day he had to overcome his fear. He knew he was being tested by Allah, but his unwavering faith enabled him to endure this hell for the chance to become a martyr.

It had taken a month for him to even find where the Stanvac expats lived. Once he located them, he had to fight the desire to rush right over there and blow them up. But he knew that things take time and Allah would provide. He thought about blowing up the office, but decided against it. He wanted to kill the whores who flaunted their disgusting flesh.

Once he had found where they lived, he became obsessed with visiting the Stanvac houses to plan how he was going to carry out his attack. Over the next few weeks he came to the conclusion that one of their debauched crowded parties would be the perfect setting. Every day he went to the office, waiting for the sign from Allah.

"Richal."

"Yes, tuan," Richal answered, coming back from his daydream.

"I would like for you to help me with a party to celebrate my son's tenth birthday. He has requested a pig roast and I remember from years ago that you are an expert in cooking pigs."

"Yes, I am good at that. Sure, tuan, I will be honored." Surely handling the vile pig flesh was Allah's last test.

"Good," Beil said. "Of course I will pay you extra."

"Oh, that won't be necessary," Richal said, trying to contain his excitement. "You pay me enough already. When will this be?"

"Next month."

"I now have something to look forward to," Richal said. He meant it. Allah had answered him.

150

For the last few months William had been having a reoccurring nightmare. The dream had started when a huge box had been carried in from the car and locked into the closet in the living room. As soon as he saw the box he felt the fear well up in him. His heart started to race. He found he could not walk by the closet without panic. That first night he had the dream that afterwards came every night.

He saw a wave in the ocean, slapping at the shore that was not a real shore but instead a shore of fire. The wave grew into a tsunami and put the fire out. William found himself hanging on to a log that turned into a figure, charred with fire but not burned. William was unable to break out of its spell.

"You are the one," the figure said, sending another bolt of fear.

"The one for what?" William answered in his dream, now not quite a dream. His eyes were open, but the world was different. He was in the sea with fire all around him, but he was not burned.

"You are the one I have been waiting for."

"Waiting for what?"

"Waiting to set me free."

"What if I don't?"

"Then the world will end." The figure started to laugh. Now it was a puppet whose eyes were full of tears.

The first morning William had woke up screaming, by the end of the week he was petrified. One night he woke up to go to the bathroom and walked by the locked closet. He heard voices coming from inside. He mustered all his courage and peered into the keyhole.

"AHHHAH!" he screamed, running back into his room and throwing the covers over his face. There inside the closet was the figure of the dreams.

That night the figure came again. "I see we have met. But you can't touch me until I'm yours. Do you know what to do?"

William shook his head.

"You will have to burn me before you are ten. Otherwise your doom cannot be avoided." William woke up with a start.

151

After three days of almost non-stop playing in the banquet room of the Raffles Garden Hotel on Orchard Street, the tournament was down to the last two teams. Beil and Rockman were one of them. In three days the two men had learned a lot about each other. They seemed to have an intuitive sense of each other that was, Beil thought, even deeper than what he had shared with the general. Rockman was not afraid to deviate from the normal progression of bids. After a few hands, the others at the table would think that they were bidding the opposite of what they were thinking. By the second day of playing it was obvious that they were the best of the very good players.

"One no trump," the player to the right of Beil said. It was now the last rubber and Beil and Rockman were in a hole; down one game and the other team had a leg up. The cards they had been getting were miserable. The fate of the universe was against them. Beil looked down again at his very weak hand. All he had was the queen and jack of hearts. He knew he had no business bidding at all.

"Two hearts," he said, hoping Rockman would know he had a terrible hand, hoping he would know also that he had only three points and that they were in hearts.

"Three no trump," the next player squealed, barely able to keep in his excitement.

"Four hearts," Rockman said, sitting there holding only four points, the ace of hearts, in an otherwise dismal hand.

"Five no trump," the first bidder said.

"Pass," Beil said.

"Six clubs."

"Pass," Rockman said.

"Six no trump," the first player said, cutting off the bidding. He knew that they would lose only the one trick because of the missing ace. Which he thought he knew was sitting in Beil's hand.

"Double," Beil half-shouted, knowing that they were doomed but trying to intimidate the other party with his audacity. If they were to go down, then it was fate. He played the queen. It was covered by the king from the dummy. Beil watched as Rockman covered it with the ace. He led back the four, his only other heart. The player next to him played the six. Beil covered with the jack. The game was theirs and the point count from the double was in their favor.

The next game they were rewarded. Both were dealt strong hands. As they made there way up to game, Beil bid six hearts, this time signaling that he had two aces. Rockman asked again: "Six no trump."

"Seven hearts," Beil said, and again they were covered.

"Seven no trump." It was almost a lay-down. Soon afterwards they were celebrating with fine wines at the awards dinner. They were being toasted by the rest of the players.

"To hearts!" Rockman held up the goblet. He was happy, having been introduced to a proper martini at the banquet. "My mother had a saying; six hearts leads the night into day."

"In America we have a saying, that things happen in threes," Beil said as the waiter handed him another drink. He and Rockman clinked glasses.

"Then to the next game of bridge, to the six hearts that will lead night into day."

152

Umar still had not made his final decision. Part of him felt betrayed; he was very hurt. His friend Beil was spying on him every time he lit a cigarette. His first reaction was to quit smoking, but after an hour the cravings were so bad, he had one. Then he went out and bought a local pack of the cheap Indonesian smokes, but after a few he gave into desire and went back to Marlboro country.

Beil was a spy. Umar knew he was a spy. Beil knew Umar was PKI. Still, it was a violation to actually be spying on him.

"So, Umar, the plan is all in place," Kusdi said. Yang was with him to make sure that there was no deviating from the mission. The plan was to send in the special Chinese crew to extract Beil. Whisk him away, first by boat and then by plane to China, where they would milk Beil of all his information. What they did with him next was not Kusdi's concern, but he knew it would either be a dismal prison or death. Death would be better.

"Good," Umar said, not meaning it. Still, he was very angry at Beil, who had driven him to this.

"When do you think he will be going to the house in Mega Mendung?" Yang asked. Umar had told him of the company house. A day later Yang had gone to check it out. It was secluded, remote, with many places to hide a team and wait. It was perfect.

"I am not sure," Umar answered, feeling sick. He thought it strange that even though Beil had spied on him, he was more his friend than Yang. Again, he thought it strange you could hate the people that believed like you and love the ones that were your enemy. It made him see how complex the human situation was. It made him think about ideals, wondering if they were more important than friendship. How could Beil betray him, yet be so kind to him?

Never did he say a word about the lighter. But Beil must know, now that he had disabled the thing. Now he was being asked to betray Beil. To set him up to be kidnapped and taken to who knows where. He had asked Yang what would happen to Beil. Yang said he would be questioned and then released to the US government in a secret prison exchange. But he spoke in a way that made Umar know that he was lying. He remembered Beil, who had told him of the old saying: trust in God, but tie your camel.

"Well, find out as soon as possible!" Yang spat.

153

While Richal was waiting for his rendezvous with revenge, he settled into working at the new office. His job consisted mostly of getting supplies or serving drinks to the other tuans or the dog Rockman, who seemed like a constant fixture. In some way it gave him perverse pleasure mixing them strong drinks, especially Rockman, who was quickly becoming worse than an infidel. All his patience had paid off last week when he overheard Beil invite Rockman and his family to the party. He had almost squealed out in glee when Rockman had accepted. He came back out of his musing when he heard Beil calling his name.

"Yes, tuan," he said eagerly, a huge smile on his face. He had taken great care in storing the grenades so they would not be useless like the guns he and Timal had hidden so many years ago.

"Just want to remind you that next week will be the birthday party. I'll expect you there early. There is a lot to do."

"Yes, tuan, I am looking forward to celebrating the day."

"Good, then we're all set. When Mr. Murray comes, please send him in."

"Yes sir, right away."

Murray arrived wearing a new outfit that almost made Beil burst out in laughter. He had to light a cigarette to keep it in.

"You're looking very handsome," he managed to say. Murray looked just like Dick Tracy in his fedora.

"I got the pictures," Murray stated, bringing out a manila envelope, half-throwing it across the desk. Beil opened it. Inside were pictures of Sukarno with a whore. She was wearing too much makeup. In the first picture Sukarno and the woman were on the bed, he in western clothes; she in Indonesian.

"Where did you get the woman?" Beil asked. Everything about the pictures looked like a bizarre cartoon. The picture was so dark that Sukarno's face was hard to make out. The next series of pictures showed two bodies fitted together with almost no view of their faces. One picture showed a very big penis.

"Oh, I have friends that know friends," Murray said excitedly, mistaking Beil's question as praise. "You should have heard them," he added.

"You did well," Beil said kindly, knowing that no one their right mind would use these pictures for anything. They were disappointing, but Beil was under orders from above, so he had no choice. The plan was to leak them into the papers, especially the orthodox Muslim papers. Beil did not give the operation much hope. The hand was doomed, but Beil knew he had to play it as best that he could.

"When can I expect to see this in the papers?" Murray asked, reliving the excitement. It had been very dicey setting up the cameras without any one knowing.

Two weeks later and the pictures or rather picture of the woman and the figure that was purported to be Sukarno was in all the papers. For days it was the only thing anyone talked about. The plan to call attention to Sukarno's womanizing was successful beyond Beil's wildest dreams.

Unfortunately it had just the opposite result from what Beil and his superiors had wanted. The next day Beil was walking on the street having had lunch at a sate stand near the office. On the way back, he heard all the banter by the front door.

"Of course he loves women," a man said, the pride evident in his voice. The way he was dressed, Beil could tell he was a devoted Muslim. "This is known." In fact it had been an open secret for years. Every Muslim man lived through the president's actions, though they themselves would have to wait until heaven.

"Yes, he is the father of our country."

"Yes, I have seen the other pictures," one of Rockman aides said. "And I can attest that he is very well-endowed." All the men chuckled. Beil had to endure their stares as he walked by. Richal came running out to tell Beil that Rockman was inside waiting for him.

"Well, I see that the papers have all picked up your big story," Rockman said, then burst out laughing.

"Yes," Beil said, starting to laugh too. "How was I to know they were proud of him and his exploits?"

"Yes, he is esteemed now and there is a huge black market for that photo of his penis."

"Yes, to the best laid plans of mice and men," Beil said as they clicked their drinks.

"Yes, I am afraid, Edmond, that you will have to try something else."

154

It two days before his tenth birthday and William was having his nightmare, the same dream he'd had every night since the gali-gali man had been put into the hall closet. He heard the awful laugh. Then he saw the eyes. Then came the voice. "You can only stop me before you are ten."

William found out from his mother that he was born at seven in the evening. That would not give him much time. If this were like other birthdays, he would be given his presents when his father came home around five, which would only give him two hours to burn the thing. And how could he build the huge fire he would need? He felt a shaft of fear run through him, then another. He was doomed. His birthday was the next day.

"Tuan, there are huge grasshoppers by the furnace," Seam exclaimed later that morning. His words brought William back to the present. "They are just as big as in Sumatra!" Together they went to the back of the house. But the grasshoppers had left.

"They will be back, tuan. Come with me while I put coal into the furnace."

William followed him. Seam led him to the furnace and opened the door. Immediately they were both driven back by the heat inside. William had his answer. He would bring the puppet over here and burn it. All he had to do was figure out a way to get it there without the servants stopping him. He would need a diversion.

That night as he was going to sleep staring up at the ceiling, a vibration came and paralyzed him. Try as he might, William was unable to move his arms. He tried to scream for help but was unable to say anything. His whole body filled with dread. He watched as the gali-gali man entered his room and hung over him. The puppet's eyes were only a few inches from his own. He tried to scream again, but still no sound.

"One more day and we will know."

Know what? William thought. The evil face began to howl: "If you doubt my power, then you will die."

"I do not doubt it," William said, not knowing if he was awake or dreaming.

"Just so you understand, when you wake up in the morning you will hear of my power."

155

It was February 19, 1963. "The gods are mad at us," Seam said as he served the birthday breakfast of all the young tuan's favorites: rambutans, fried rice with egg.

"What do you mean?" Beil asked.

"Didn't you hear, tuan?"

"Hear what?"

"Gunung Agung in Bali erupted last night."

"Last night?"

"Yes, tuan, there was no warning. No smoke. Thousands were killed."

"Thousands killed?" Agnes asked.

William turned white. "Oh, don't worry," his mother reassured him. "Bali is a long way from here. Nothing is going to ruin your birthday today or the party tomorrow. Now eat your breakfast, and when father gets back then we will celebrate with your presents. He has gotten you a very special one."

For the rest of the day the gali-gali in the closet seemed to grow and grow. William kept hearing the voice from the previous night. The volcanic eruption was no coincidence. Throughout the day the voice became louder, sounding like a madman's laughter. Over and over the figure rambled in an obscure dialect, counting out the minutes till he could not be stopped. By late afternoon the first of the volcano's ash was raining down on of Jakarta, tangling up traffic. By the time Beil arrived home, William was in full-fledged panic.

Beil was an hour late getting back from the office. He had spent the whole day dealing with the volcano. At six o'clock, there was only an hour left! William then had to endure Beil taking a shower. When he finally came out, carrying all the presents, there were only thirty minutes left.

"Which one should he open first?" Agnes said.

"Well, the big one will be last," Beil responded, wanting to keep the surprise till the very end. William ripped open the rest of the presents, barely looking at anything to get to the gali-gali man. Finally it was the only one left.

Beil knew that William was going to be thrilled. He could hardly keep the joy off his face.

Trembling, William opened the cardboard box. In real life the puppet was even more frightening than in his dreams. "Thank you, father," he said, trying to lift it. It was heavy, very heavy. A servant came to help.

"Just three more minutes and you will officially turn ten," Agnes said, motioning to the servants to bring the cake. William was trapped. Now that all the servants were around, there was no way for him to grab the puppet and run. All the time its eyes bore into him.

"Here, son, let me show you how it works," Beil said happily. He'd had the servants put lemons in the eyes last night. Now Beil pulled down on the levers.

"See, son, how it moves!" Now even the servants were afraid. It was almost as if the figure were moving itself without the help from Beil.

William looked at the clock. Only two minutes left. He watched as the figure began to smile. Beil pushed the lever and the eyes started to tear.

The sight made the squirrels run around their cage in panic. The squirrels! The diversion! William opened the door of the cage, pretending to comfort them. They both jumped out and ran away.

"The squirrels!" William shouted. The servants all raced after them, leaving Beil with his son and Agnes. William overcame his fear of the figure that had come to life. Beil had stopped working it, but it was still moving. William came up to the figure and touched it.

"Thank you, father," he said, trying to pick it up. It was heavy, especially with the lever box. So instead of trying to lift the whole thing, he pulled it up, breaking the figure at the knees and running away with it.

"William!" Beil shouted. "What are you doing?" His son raced out the door with only seconds to spare. Beil took off after him, almost catching him as William reached the furnace door. There were now only a few seconds left. William took one last look at the figure whose face was twisted in a maniacal smile. As if through a trance, the figure spoke to him. "You are too late to stop tomorrow's doom."

"No I am not!" William screamed. "There is still time!" Just then the clock struck the first of the seven tones.

"William what are you doing?" Beil shouted again, furious. He watched in disbelief as William threw the puppet into the fire. Instantly it caught fire.

"Sorry, father," William said as Beil came up to him palm open, ready to spank but before he could William took off. All the servants who had been trying to catch the squirrels were now watching as Beil chased his son around the house, again and again. Everybody had been shocked that the young tuan had burned the puppet, but all of them were secretly glad.

Finally Beil got tired. The next time William rounded the house, he went the other direction. Beil was waiting around the corner, and when William came running by, he caught him easily.

"Don't you ever do that again!" Beil shouted as he struck the boy on his bottom a number of times. Then he lit a cigarette.

"Yes, father." William was afraid, but not of Beil. He was afraid that he had not killed the thing in time. "Tomorrow…" He thought of the creature's the last words. He would have to be ready for tomorrow.

Ina took William away now that the party was ruined.

"Tuan," Seam asked Beil. "We have none of the special pineapples to get the squirrels back in their cage. Should I send Umar to the market to get some?"

"No don't get them. Let the squirrels go wild. It will teach William a lesson."

156

Throughout that night William waited for the nightmare, but when no nightmare came he knew that the power of the puppet was no more. Yet early in the morning he was surprised when the gali-gali man came to him in a different dream.

"I see you were able to burn me up with only a second to spare," the puppet said to him, no longer looking like an evil thing. Instead it looked more like a kind man but with the same intensity in the eyes. But you did not burn the legs or the lever box, so that will pose a problem."

"A problem? Am I doomed?"

"Yes and no. It means that you could be little doomed, that is all."

"Little doomed?"

"Yes, little doomed. But you are a very powerful dukun, so you will find a way out."

William woke that morning unnerved but not remembering the dream. It was Saturday, the day of the huge party.

"I'm very sorry, father," William said. "But I kept having nightmares of that thing. I don't know what came into me."

"Well, son, you should be sorry," Beil said, furious and hurt that William had burned the puppet. If everything hadn't been already planned, he would have cancelled the whole party. It had been his first reaction, but after his fury Agnes had calmed Beil, telling him the servants had told her that the puppet he thought was a wayang was actually a gali-gali man that should have been burned at a funeral. The young tuan had just done what any Indonesian would have done. It was bad luck to have a gali-gali man in the house. It had great powers that were hard to control.

"Father, can we send Umar for the special pineapple now?" William was concerned for his squirrels, especially with all the stray cats around. He had just gone outside and seen the two squirrels high in a tree by the backyard near where the party was to be later in the afternoon. He had seen the neighbor's cat try to climb the tree, and had gone outside to chase it away.

"No, son, there has to be a punishment. What you did was wrong. It will serve as a lesson to you. Tomorrow maybe, if there are no more outbursts."

"But father, I was so scared of that thing. I had nightmares all the time that the puppet was alive and going to kill me."

"Puppets are not alive, son," Beil said, trying to drive away a fear that he was sure had come from the superstitious servants. Last night Agnes had told him of the nightmares. Beil was afraid that William's mind was like an Indonesian's, where the supernatural merged with reality so there was no clear line between them.

157

Richal woke early that morning before dawn praying to Allah that he would be strong and successful. He then bathed, shaving all his body hair except for his head so he would be clean when he entered heaven. He had the two grenades in his pocket as he walked to the Stanvac houses early in the morning to start the fire pit for the roast pig. He spent the morning with the young tuan and Seam digging the fire pit.

"What do you think of Mt. Agung erupting?" Richal asked the young tuan.

"Oh, I think it a bad omen," William said at once.

This alarmed Richal. "Why is that?"

"Because the power almost doomed us," William answered back. He was worried about his squirrels and had pleaded with Ina to get the pineapples. But she had come back empty-handed because they were out of season.

"Oh, there, young tuan, it is just a folk legend. Isn't that right, Seam?" Richal said, uncomfortable that the young tuan was looking at him so closely. He felt the intensity of the boy's eyes, as if he could see right through him; see the grenades hidden in his pocket. William just kept starring without blinking or thinking, in his own world.

"No, the young tuan is a dukun," Seam said proudly, and then caught himself, remembering that Richal was not part of the circle. All the servants knew the reason the dukun had burnt the puppet. Unbeknown to Beil and William, Seam had later that night burned the rest of it, the legs and box, frightened the whole time.

"A dukun?" Richal felt the jab of fear run through him. He saw the young tuan's eyes and recoiled again.

"No, not a real dukun," Seam said with pretend laugher. Still, Richal kept his distance the rest of the day. It was now late afternoon and many parents with kids had arrived. They were all in the back yard by the barbeque watching the last of the roasting. Richal was thinking about his plan. When the pig came out of the pit on its way to the cutting board, everybody would be right in front. It would be easy to throw the grenades and run. More important, it would be impossible for him to miss.

Mr. and Mrs. Rockman arrived with their son Andy. Richal was thrilled when he saw them.

"Hi, Edmond, Agnes," Mrs. Rockman called.

"Seam," Agnes said, "get us some champagne." In no time Seam came up with a tray. They both grabbed one.

"Nasul, what would you like?" Beil asked.

"Oh, I'll have a bull's eye." A few minutes later they had their drinks, and joined the gathering crowd over by the fire pit.

"Ten more minutes," Donald Finn informed them. Seeing Rockman, he tipped his drink to him, adding, "Mr. Rockman, it's good to see you. Have you ever seen a pig come out of the pit? If not, it is a wonderful sight." Donald had no idea of finesse and did not know that Rockman had only had pork a few times, and only with westerners.

"Never."

"Oh, then you must come to the front," Donald said as he led the Rockmans to the edge of the pit. Richal could not believe his luck.

Rockman would have no escape from his punishment for breaking the holy laws and leading Indonesia into decay. Richal felt the raging bliss of knowing that evil would be avenged. It would not be long before Richal would join his friend Timal, who would introduce him to the many virgins that they would enjoy together for eternity.

"Still no luck," Seam's son explained. The lad had been up the tree, coming down with only a few scratches on his arms to show for his effort. Both the squirrels had leapt into the underbrush.

"Where are they? Do you know where they are?" Seam asked his son.

"Yes, they are in the tree just above the pit. See?" the boy said, pointing. "They are hungry but won't come down in this crowd. I will try again when everybody has left."

Just then they heard a cry from Carl Dremmer, who had arrived in the costume of a painted puppet. He resembled the gali-gali man, complete with a wooden box to stand on. He had heard about the burning and could not resist.

"The pig is ready," Richal announced as he directed his two helpers. They lifted the pig out of the pit, bringing it to the banana leaf carving table. Richal felt a supreme gratitude in the depth of his soul as everybody surged forward in a tight ball. To his delight, all of the foreigners including the Hantu Donald Finn, the Beils, and the Dremmers were within his grasp, as well as the perfidious Rockmans. Allah was now flowing through him, guiding him in his moment of glory. Richal walked a few steps backwards to the base of the tree that he was going to use to shield himself from the explosion. He reached into his pockets, brought forth the grenades, and pulled the pins. He looked up to see the young dukun was staring at him. He froze the two grenades still in his hands. Everybody saw him.

"Richal!" Beil screamed. "What are you doing?" He tried to move forward but was stopped by the panicking crowd.

"Allah Akbar—God is great!" Richal yelled as he finally broke free of the young dukun's power. People had started to flee but it was too late. There was not enough time to run out of the way. Confidently he cocked both his arms back with the grenades, holding both of them over his head for the frightened crowd to see. For a second he savored the moment. Then his arms started their descent.

Up in the tree the starving squirrels saw the pineapples as soon as Richal pulled them from his pocket. When they saw him raise them up, the two went crazy. Just as Richal was about release the grenades, the squirrels leapt from the tree. Each of them grabbed a grenade and along with it parts of Richal's hands. The force and the surprise carried Richal backwards, causing him to fall with outstretch arms. Blood started flowing from his hands.

The squirrels raced away from the crowd toward the back of the house to enjoy their meal. Three seconds later the grenades exploded. The noise was deafening but the blast had lost most of its power. Nevertheless, no one moved except for Rockman and Beil who ran to Richal, lying there, knocked unconscious by the blast.

Richal was falling in slow motion as if he were in a dream. He was floating in a lazy river. He felt as if something were flowing out of him toward the great sea of paradise. He floated along on his new journey, confident he was a martyr. He rejoiced, knowing he soon would be in heaven. He knew he had done his part for Islam by ridding the world of filthy infidels. Soon he would have his reward.

The pain in his hands surprised him. The dream had ended, replaced by great blackness. He heard voices calling out his name. He waited for the virgins, but the pain intensified. He started to panic. All he felt was a burning in his hands, a ringing in his ears. Inside, the tide had turned. The river that was rushing out of him began to rush back in, bringing nothing with it but a sea of pain. He opened his eyes, shocked to find Beil and Rockman standing over him.

"Tuan!" Seam screamed as he came running up. "One of the fuel tanks has caught fire. Run tuans, run before the tanks blow up."

Together Rockman and Beil grabbed hold of Richal, but the man was dead weight, very cumbersome to carry. In their hurry they had only the most tenuous of grips. They heard another large explosion followed by a blast of hot air that pushed them back. The force caused both men to lose their grips. When they recovered, Richal lay on the ground a few yards away. They watched as the fire darted over him, engulfing him as it headed toward them. They ran for their lives, just able to reach the safety of the other side of the street as another tank exploded, sending more fire everywhere.

Richal felt the warmth. This must be heaven. He opened his eyes to embrace his new world.

"OOOOOha!" He screamed in agony as the flames caught his shirt, setting him afire. He began choking when the voice came with an all-encompassing laughter. It must be the virgins he thought, his mind clouded by the vast pain. Yet for a second his hope swelled. He turned toward the sound, embracing it.

In front of him was the gali-gali man. "Ha Ha Ha! There are no virgins in hell!" The menacing tide of evil surrounded him. The last thing Richal saw before he died was the gali-gali man's twisted face.

158

Haggard was back flying, though not in the way he had expected. The agency had banned him from any kind of leadership role. He would have been kicked out of the CIA for good if there had not been a shortage of good pilots. So now he was ferrying arms and ammunition to the anti-Communist rebels in Malaya, from a secret base in the Philippines.

It was 1964, and things were really going bad in Asia. The American presence in Vietnam was escalating in an attempt to counter the power of Communism not just there but in all of South-East Asia. Malaysia was now part of the battlefield, especially since Sukarno had declared that an independent Malaysia was unacceptable, claiming that it was part of Indonesia. Already secret and not-so-secret battles were taking place. The PKI and their sympathizers had formed small armed bands that would skirmish with the anti-Communist rebels.

Tim Johnson was in charge of driving the Communists out. The operation that had worked so well in Thailand was now carried down the peninsula into Malaysia. Because of the constant nationalistic rhetoric coming from Sukarno, war could break out at any moment. China with its ever-growing influence had openly offered to arm Indonesia in this conflict over Malaysia's independence. At the same time they were secretly arming the PKI.

Haggard saw the little clearing, just like all the hundreds of little clearings he had landed on over the years. He set the plane down perfectly. He waited to the side as the rebels unloaded the guns and ammo. He lit another cigarette, letting his mind drift back to the failed plot and his capture. He had been broken and humiliated. The first person he had seen while still under arrest was that faggot Beil. Haggard was sure Beil had had something to do with what had happened to him. Beil was the one who benefited the most from his plane going down. Haggard spit violently in disgust.

"Hurry, hurry," he barked. "I have no time to spare." He hated this new job. When Beil and the impotent General Jim had debriefed him, to his shock they told him that Yang was a Chinese spy. They were convinced that Yang had milked Haggard of vital information, but he had not. It was the evil, well-dressed Indonesian who had gotten the secrets out of him. He remembered the voice of the interrogator who was present in every session.

He lit another cigarette, continuing his musings. He had been so close to success. If he had been able to destroy the air force that should have been there, if he had been able to destroy the ship.... It was just bad luck that had put him back here, a glorified errand boy. He had thought about retiring, but Asia had gotten to him. He knew that a shitty job flying was better than none. It still provided all the perks.

159

"And to think the dukun let the squirrels go, right before he burned the gali-gali man," Seam said in awe to the other servants.

"How brilliant, and just in the nick of time."

"And no one expecting the reason."

"It was very wise of you to help the young tuan by burn the puppet box."

"Very clever, and no one sensed a thing."

"I do feel bad that the young tuan's squirrels had to perish, but that is a small cost compared to what would have happened."

"Yes, we are very blessed," Eto said. They stopped their conversations when Tuan Beil appeared. It was now two weeks later. The old furnace had already been replaced, the old shed torn down. After that a crew of gardeners had dug up all the grass and replaced it with new sod. Everything looked as it had before.

"Seam, call Umar for me," Beil said. Then he went inside to get ready for the meeting with Rockman. He had just gotten the word from Tim that arms were being smuggled into Indonesia via Malaysia by boat. But what worried him most was the pressure from the PKI on Sukarno to arm a new civil militia—essentially another army. Now with open aid from both the Soviets and Chinese to replace the curtailed military aid from the USA, America's influence was waning. Its only hope lay in the continued covert aid to Rockman's bunch. Beil had a lot on his mind.

Another armed faction would be catastrophic, especially if it was under the control of the PKI. The Communists were becoming much bolder because of the tensions surrounding Indonesia's objection to Malaysian independence. It was a very strange situation. No longer was it a simple internal game of chess between the PKI and the military. The popular desire for Indonesia to recover its land was almost universal and threatened to unbalance the whole region.

Complicating the problem, many leading generals shared the PKI's desire to go to war with Malaysia. Already the PKI was pouring out into the streets in huge numbers, trying to use this nationalistic fever to their advantage.

The situation had gotten out of hand a few days before. There had been a raid into the contested land of Sarawak by Indonesian special forces, who had misjudged the skill of the British Gurkhas. The Indonesians had been no match for the hardened British trained troops.

In retaliation the PKI had again taken to the streets, storming the British embassy, setting fire to it.

Beil was pulled out of his thoughts when Umar approached. "Yes, tuan?"

"Get the car ready. I need to go see Mr. Rockman at once."

On the way the two began talking. "Did you hear about the fighting in Sarawak?"

"No, tuan, what happened?"

"It seems that the Indonesian army overran a British base."

"Overran?" Umar said, somewhat excited, the pride coming up in him.

"Yes, but I got word that the British Gurkhas had retaken the base, and when the Indonesians ventured out they were slaughtered with no survivors," Beil said. He was lying: there had been a few survivors, but presumably they were being interrogated to find out who authorized this foolish attack. That was the reason he was going to pay Rockman an unexpected visit.

"Killed, tuan? All? That is awful." Umar was watching Beil, knowing that Beil had other information. It was clear that even though Beil was for certain good things in Indonesia, if push came to shove, he could not be relied on.

Over the past month Umar had wrestled with whether or not to set Beil up. He had tried to remain angry, but that soon faded. He had come to the realization that CIA or not, Beil was his friend.

"Yes, killed. One needs to think about the consequences before one gets too involved." Beil said this as a way of warning.

"What do you mean, tuan?"

"I mean pushing to arm the population is dangerous, a very dangerous game."

"I don't know of this, tuan," Umar lied. Many thought it was the only way for the PKI to succeed. They had the people. They had Sukarno, but they did not have their own army. Now it upset him that the Indonesian forces had been killed so easily.

"Be careful, Umar, there is a dangerous game going on right now," Beil said candidly. "But let us speak of other things. I will need you to take me to Mega Mendung," Beil said.

"Yes, tuan, of course," Umar said, now knowing he had to decide what to do. For support he took out the lighter, the one with the tape recorder that had caused all his doubts, and lit two cigarettes, one for Beil and one for himself.

160

"To what do I attribute your visit?" Rockman asked with his bridge face on. Beil was the last person he wanted to see. He had just received word of the debacle in Sarawak. The operation was stupid, but certain generals and Sukarno had pressed for it.

"Oh, I thought I would come and discuss a few private matters. First, I have brought this gift." Beil brought out a bottle of Chivas Regal and two crystal glasses. Before Rockman could protest, he had poured the both of them shots.

"To health," he said as they touched glasses.

"A gift for what?" Rockman asked, confused and flustered.

"For helping at the party and not letting the rash action by the madman get into the press and such. Did you find out much about the man?"

"Not much other than he was very devoted. A true believer who acted alone."

"Where did he get the grenades?"

"From you, I imagine," Rockman said.

"So they are from the same batch as the ones at the school and the PKI office?" Beil asked, tired of waiting to get to the point.

"Maybe they are, but what of it? They were from you, supplying that idiot Colonel Panti and his ill-fated revolution."

"Whose idea was it to attack the Sarawak base? That was brilliant." Beil spoke in disgust, watching Rockman's eyes as they shifted to anger.

"It was not my idea."

"Whose, then?"

"Generals, warlord generals, Sukarno, and the PKI. Circles inside circles. It is fucking dangerous right now, Edmond," Rockman said. The smoothness of the Scotch let his pent-up fury come to the surface. He was furious with the operation he had advised against. But he had been overruled by the egotistical old nationalistic generals. Some were his early mentors who in their ignorance had played into the hands of the PKI.

"How many generals?"

"Five or six."

"Connected to the PKI?"

"No, but not fanatical anti-Communist, either. Just weak, old and very corrupt. Be nice when they retire. The real danger is that they are desperate to remain in power," Rockman said with a calm he did not feel. Hopefully the ambush and the loss of life would diminish them. A victory would have been awful. Still, Rockman felt for the troops that had been lost.

Beil changed the subject. "The Chinese are now offering to arm a peasant militia in addition to the arms that are already being smuggled in. We can not allow that to happen."

"Yes, we will stop that," Rockman said. "But you know that is not enough. Everything is so unsettled. There is too much grey and too many twists. Sukarno, the PKI, the war, the famine, the inflation." He thought back to the speech Sukarno had given the previous week, in which he had used the phrase, "the year of living dangerously." It had been picked up by all the papers.

The slogan summed up things quite well. There were massive problems in Indonesia: crop failures, growing debt, volcanic eruptions, the PKI making its move, outside influences from China, Russia, and

America. He and his group were trying to keep the country together before it unraveled into anarchy, which was a very real possibility. They had the muscle but not the people. A peasant army would spell disaster.

"It is the year of living dangerously," he said, then went over to the bottle and poured two more shots.

"To the year of living dangerously."

"Then we are at bridge," Beil said, repeating the phrase that they had used since they had become bridge partners. Now they were playing the cards of a secret war in a game for the future.

Fueled by the exquisite calm of the alcohol, Rockman came over and picked up the bottle. Again he refilled the glasses, and handed one to Beil. They were about to play the most dangerous of games, where they might or might not have trump. Many things would have to be finessed.

"Six hearts," Beil said out of the blue as they touched glasses.

161

Haggard climbed out of the cockpit as soon as the Indonesian troops had been spotted, knowing that to take off would give away his position. Still, there had been time to camouflage the plane before slipping away with the four-man British special forces team and the well-trained Gurkhas. Silently they waited in the jungle, melting into the underbrush, positioned for ambush. In addition to his pistol, Haggard carried an M16 that had been given to him by one of the Gurkhas.

In the past month the pace of his flying had picked up in the cat-and-mouse game going on around the border between Sarawak and Kalimantan. Both sides were armed in a covert conflict that was gradually being pushed out into the open. With it, all-out war threatened to break out over Malaysian independence. In Indonesia, the PKI pushed the battle cry of "Konfrontasi," inspiring a national movement. Already many of their members had rushed to the border to defend Indonesia. In that time Haggard had gone from hating his new job to loving it.

The flying was dangerous and brought him back to a situation where killing was permitted; where the formal rules of war did not apply. His adrenaline was up. It was the danger that made him happy. He cocked his safety off of the gun and waited.

The Indonesian patrol approached the ambush. Haggard could see that they were well armed but, judging by the way they were walking, untrained. The sick sweet smell of the topics filled Haggard's nostrils. He would now get his revenge on the Indonesians who had ruined his life. It felt so much better because he would be able to see the whites of their eyes, kill from close up where the thrill would be better. The last time he had killed a man like this was in Vietnam many, many years ago. But now it felt like yesterday. Now he relived the pleasure of killing Beil's faggot friend with the wire-rim glasses.

The patrol was mostly made up of members of the PKI, eager to show that they were real Indonesian patriots. The leader of the mission was a young captain named Puri. He was from Jakarta, just twenty-seven. He was Kusdi's son, and one of the first PKI officers to serve in the army.

He surveyed the land ahead of him. The objective was to cross the border, sneak up on the British-backed Gurkhas, kill them, and then slip back. The mission was to avenge the brutal slaughter of the brave martyrs last month.

"Won't be long yet," his sergeant whispered. They were walking down the trail, having spotted smoke from a house in the trees. They had been in training for the last six months. This was their first combat mission. All were eager to get into the thick of it. They had on official uniforms, brand new. Each man looked forward to the day that Indonesia would be a part of the great communist world. The jungle was thick on both sides of the path, but that did not worry them. They would be in and out faster then a mongoose. None of them had killed anybody.

They were now only a hundred feet from the house and still they had not been spotted. Then they heard a dog bark, and saw a figure running from the house. Then another.

"Run, don't let them get away!" Puri shouted to his men as they chased after the figures in the trees. "Merdeka," they shouted in the press forward.

The ruse worked perfectly. The untrained Indonesians began shooting wildly, eyes straight ahead. The men in ambush waited until just after the patrol passed, so as to not get caught in the cross-fire. The Indonesians did not have a chance. It was all over in manner of minutes. All the Indonesians were dead except for three. One of these was Puri, the only officer.

"That was easy," Haggard exclaimed. He had fired deliberately and at close range, knowing he had killed a few.

"Yes," the British lieutenant said. One of the Gurkhas came up to him.

"What shall we do with the prisoners, sir?" he asked, pointing to the three trembling men.

"Oh, if I had my way I'd kill them all, but that would not do with the rules and all that. We need to get the information out of them. Who sent them. How many more."

A few more minutes and the British officer came back to where Haggard was uncovering his plane. "The fucking bastards are not saying a thing. We need that information. God damn all these rules of engagement."

"Oh, I have a way of dealing with that," Haggard said, lightening a cigarette. "Follow me." Haggard went over to the men and dragged them to their feet. "OK now tell us where you landed, where the rest of you are!" He yelled at them, feeling the rage overpower him. When they did not answer him he picked the young captain and slapped him in the face. When the captain did not respond, Haggard slapped him again.

"You will answer, God damn it!" He pulled out his pistol, and put it to the head of one of the other prisoners, and pulled the trigger. The blood splattered onto Puri's face. The other prisoner began to whimper.

"Now start talking!" Haggard screamed again into his face. When Puri hesitated, Haggard put the gun to his temple and cocked the trigger. Puri began to tremble uncontrollably. "Stop it!" Haggard shouted, pressing the gun into his temple, seeing the captain's eyes bulge out. "I'll give you something to stare at, you son of a bitch!" Haggard shouted as he turned the gun on the other prisoner and shot him down.

"No," cried Puri.

"Now will you start talking?" Haggard asked, overcoming the urge to blow his brains out too. He was reminded again of Beil and his dead side-kick, Hiu.

The frightened man began to blabber. Haggard waited about thirty seconds before he pulled the gun away from the man's face and fired into the jungle.

"He's all yours," Haggard said to the disgusted British officer.

162

Six months later Mt. Agung erupted again. This was a double bad omen. Things were going to get worse. The mountain had never erupted once, let alone twice, in recent history. With all the uncertainty in the air, the services of a dukun, especially the white dukun, were in demand. For a few hours every day, William would hold court in the servants' quarters. Seam and his gang ran the sessions.

Today's visitors were the servants who staffed the Stanvac vacation house in the tea plantation area known as Mega Mendung. They had a huge problem. Since they had taken over the post one year ago, they had nothing but bad luck. It was just one thing after another, broken legs, mysterious illnesses. Now one of the wives had become pregnant with twins, which was considered very bad luck, an especially bad omen. They were convinced that someone had put a curse on them.

"Young dukun, we ask you to cure this spell that someone has put on us."

"Dress two tuans like twins on the day after a full moon." William stared at them, saying the first thing that popped into his head, remembering a cartoon his grandmother had recently sent, in which twins were dressed alike, making it impossible for even their mother to tell them apart. He had learned through the years of doing this type of thing that he might just as well say anything that happened to come into his mind.

The Stanvac servants did not understand anything, except that the words were profound and they would follow them.

"Yes, but how will I know who they are?"

"When two guests arrive and one asks you for a cup of jasmine tea," William said, having read that jasmine tea was very popular in Singapore. Then he added another random thought as he remembered going with a servant to look for bullets in the abandoned building in the meadow where the Dutch had made a last stand during the battle for Indonesian independence. "Then in the morning of the next day go to the little house in the field and dig in the left corner until your dreams come true."

"Terima kasih, tuan, terima kasih," the servant said, thankful now that the curse would be lifted.

163

"Mr. Beil," Rockman said as he entered Beil's office with a somber look on his face. It had been a few days since the second botched foray into Malaysia.

"Mr. Rockman," Beil answered back, put on guard by the unusual formality. It always amazed Beil that the nature of a relationship could change at a drop of a hat.

"I need your help," Rockman said, lines heavy on his face from lack of sleep. "As you might know, there has been another skirmish with British troops in Sarawak."

"Yes," Beil said. "I know, it did not go very well." It had been another slaughter, untrained troops, mostly boys. He had heard that Haggard had been involved.

"I am afraid it is even worse than that. What has happened is that the PKI is trying to capitalize on the situation, using it to pressure Sukarno into officially arming the militia."

"That is unacceptable," Beil said, knowing he did not have any real power other than riding the wave, and nudging at the right time.

"Yes, but these unnecessary slaughters drive them to the point of insanity. The situation is worse than even two months ago. But that is not why I am here. I am here to have you arrange the release of Kusdi's son."

"His son," Beil said. He hadn't known who he was, only that there was one survivor who was talking like a bird.

"Yes, I have been sent here by Sukarno himself."

"Why come to me instead of the British?"

"Because you can get it done."

"Is it really Kusdi's son?" Beil thought about how blood was still thicker than ideals or anything else. To get the son freed, Kusdi, the PKI leader, would have had to go to Sukarno, who would have had to go to Rockman and then ask Beil, Kusdi's enemy, to help. It was the game in the game in the game.

"Yes," Rockman said. "It is very difficult now, too many things afloat, too many pressures. This idiotic war with Malaysia is just what the PKI wants. Not to mention the Chinese who are pushing for arming the PKI, suggesting it to Sukarno. They are feeling very bold."

"How many generals did you say are caught up in all of this?"

"Five or six, no more."

"Then it is time to think of six hearts," Beil said, the code for the secret plan they were developing if things went out of control. He pulled out a cigarette and offered Rockman one.

"The young officer could play very well into our game," Rockman stated, letting the smoke curl and linger.

"Yes," Beil said softly after a couple of silent drags. Both men were thinking the same thing. Nationalism and Communism were being united because of stupid pride. The Chinese were nudging them together. Kusdi's son a prisoner. Rockman needed to get him out. Sukarno was leaning closer and closer toward China. The USA had cancelled all official aid. Vietnam was going wrong, North Korea was still Communist. Both men knew they did not have trump or time.

"Six hearts, I never thought it might really be, but these are strange times. Edmond, get the boy back. We will need him. So I have more time before the flames grow beyond our control."

"I'll see what I can do."

164

As things happen, a small unrelated event well away from the present crisis became something that changed everything. In Indonesia Ramadan was coming to an end. Throughout the islands plans were made for lavish feasts and celebrations.

In the Sumatran city of Medan, the streets were filled with Muslims celebrating the end of a month of fasting. Everybody was in good spirits as night descended on the city. Already sate vendors were on their favorite corners. The smell of spice was heavy in the air.

A Muslim family had just walked out of their house to be part of the festivities. Father, mother, three sons and a most beautiful little girl, who was so happy wearing the new outfit she had been given by her father.

Down the street a bunch of Chinese were drinking hard. They were gathered around the motorbike one of them had bought with money he had earned over the last few years. It was an old motorbike. Between shots of whiskey they were trying to start it.

"Yi, you worthless son of a dog-owner, this thing is never going to start," one of them laughed as they passed the bottle around.

"Yes, you got ripped off," another said. Yi was on the bike. They were all smoking.

"No, you are wrong. I just said a prayer to the motor god," Yi shouted, slurring his words. He took another swing from the bottle, lit a cigarette, and slammed his foot down hard on the clutch. A puff of black smoke billowed out of the exhaust pipe as the engine started with a loud bang, rattling the neighborhood.

"Do you know how to ride this thing?" his friend asked as Yi let up on the clutch. The sudden movement caused the bike to lurch forward. Then it stalled.

"You are a dung head" one of them shouted, almost drowned out by the howl of laughter. Yi quickly got back on the bike. A friend handed him the bottle. He took another long gulp. The engine started right up. This time Yi slowly eased off the clutch, shifted, shifted again, and took off fast. He looked back at his friends.

"See who is a dung head now!" Yi yelled, turning his back just as the little girl stepped out into the road. The impact sent Yi head over heals into the open sewer twenty feet away.

The bike pinned the girl down, smothering her body so that all you could see of her was the batik pattern of the new dress on either side. The rest of her body was hidden under the motorbike making it look like grotesque butterfly with wings. Her pretty face was up against the muffler, the hot metal searing her cheek.

"AH!" the poor girl cried. Frantically her father and bothers raced to her side. The smell of gas was everywhere. The wind started to pick up.

"Get the cigarette!" someone shouted as a gust blew on the smoldering butt. Before they could get the bike off her, a fire erupted, the heat so intense it drove them back. All they could do was watch in horror. The girl's agonized screams wailed into the night.

"Help me, daddy!" the cries could be heard for blocks. Then the screams went silent. All that was left was the hissing of the blaze and the smell of cooking meat.

Dazed by the crash, Yi rose to find a crowd around him. All the other Chinese around knew to stay away, especially his friends who had melted into the crowd.

He's Chinese!" someone shouted. In his fury one of the brothers of the poor girl rushed forward and kicked him. The blow knocked Yi over, slamming him into the ground. Another family member threw a rock at him.

"You killed our little girl," the father cried as he threw a rock at Yi's face, breaking his nose. The next stone broke his jaw. Then another fell on his eye. He was long dead by the time they finished. When the last person had had his revenge, all that was left of Yi was a pile of broken bones and raw meat. Still that was not enough as they poured gasoline on him and lit him on fire. Then they went in search of other Chinese.

165

Yang and Kusdi were sitting in the back of the PKI offices when Umar came up to them. They had been discussing the release of Kusdi's son, which had been accomplished, Yang claimed, thanks to Chinese pressure. Captain Puri had told them about Haggard's brutality, his disrespect for any moral law.

"Did you hear what they did?" Kusdi asked. "The American came and shot the prisoners in the face just like an animal. CIA, we are told. Shot them just for pleasure, because we are winning this war."

"It confirms our speculations that the Americans are behind this. The CIA is running the British show," Yang said.

"Oh, that is awful," Umar said. Now there was proof that America was working directly against Indonesian interests. "How did you get him back?"

"Our Chinese friends pressured the American dogs into submission," Kusdi explained, turning to Yang.

Yang nodded. "Sukarno was very grateful."

"Yes, soon Sukarno will be ours completely, once we have armed the masses and gotten rid of the army that is being held in place by this same CIA that slaughtered those brave men," Kusdi said. But of course the Chinese had had absolutely had nothing to do with Puri's release. It was Beil who had arranged it. Without him the poor boy would be in a black hole prison or worse.

"Yes, and with support from us the arms will come for the final push towards liberation," Yang said, satisfied that soon Indonesia would be a Chinese puppet state. Then they would be able to get rid of people like Umar, who was a genuine threat, not like this pawn Kusdi.

"Merdeka!" Kusdi shouted suddenly.

"Merdeka! Merdeka for all!" Umar picked up the patriotic call.

"Let's get rid of the American dogs and avenge my son!"

"What about the CIA dog Beil? When will he be going to the country?" Yang asked. The team that was to capture him was already in place. They would take him to China, where he would disappear forever.

"The tuan will be in the country this weekend," Umar said, feeling a sickness in his heart the moment the words came out of his lips. He was betraying Beil. Seeing Yang's twisted smile made his skin tingle. He hated the man, loathed him, but there he was obeying him, betraying his friend, for what? For the good of the PKI, he thought, immediately regretting his decision.

"Good," Yang said, with a venom that belied his lack of emotion. "Soon the America dog will get his reward. Do you have the map of the area?"

"Yes," Umar said, his whole insides on fire. Why should it matter? One man, when there would be another to takes his place? He thought of Beil, who had yesterday surprised him with a carton of cigarettes and a new pair of shoes. He started to tremble, fumbling for his pack of cigarettes, wishing he could take everything back.

166

Murray was in the back seat with Beil. Umar was in front driving them to the Puncha, to the Stanvac house on Mega Mendung. They were going to spend the weekend. It was Friday afternoon and they would be together until Monday when Agnes arrived. Murray, who had never been to the house, was looking forward to his vacation.

It had worked out perfectly because Agnes was at a woman's bridge tournament until Sunday. She and William would come up after that for the rest of the week. Umar would drop off the two tuans, then drive back to Jakarta to pick Agnes up. Then he would turn around again and bring Murray back to Jakarta late Monday evening, so on Tuesday he could fly out with Sukarno.

Umar was very quiet in the front seat. He was glad that he would not have to see the tuan kidnapped, but he was still fighting the urge not to warn Beil. Many times on the ride he had almost blurted out a warning, and would have if it had not been for the ongoing conversation in the back seat. Seam had mixed a batch of planter's punch, which the tuans had started drinking as soon as Murray had been picked up at his house in Jakarta.

"I can't believe they let Sukarno get away with it," Murray said. He was dressed in his silly spy safari suit. He was already drunk.

"That's the problem with things once you try something. They have a life of their own. Sometimes they work, sometimes they don't work."

"But the pictures were great," Murray pouted defensively.

"Yes, especially the penis one," Beil answered, trying to stifle a laugh. He looked out the window to regain his composure. They were driving through mountains lined on either side with tea plantations. The sky was very blue.

"They are like children," Murray said.

"Yes," Beil answered, thinking it was mostly the servants who were like little kids.

"They really have no minds of their own," Murray said. "Not like America, where a man's a man."

"I thought you liked boys better," Beil said. They both started to laugh.

"I do, but all of them are so childlike. The Dutch never should have let them govern themselves. What a mess. And the PKI stuff, those people are nuts."

Murray rattled on, oblivious to Umar in the front seat. Beil wasn't. He watched Umar's body turn rigid, and watched his eyes and face through the rear view mirror.

"Umar doesn't agree with you. Isn't that right, Umar?" Beil said, breaking out in a huge belly laugh from all the drinks. Umar just sat there driving away, but inside was fuming.

"Oh, Umar, you are so wrong," Murray sniped. "The Dutch gave you everything, made you modern. You would be a bunch of backwater natives it wasn't for them."

"No tuan, we would not."

"Oh, you don't know what you're talking about. Look at the mess you're in. Just look at the streets: mass starvation, open sewers, no work. No, you need to grow up," Murray answered back, hot and bothered. Beil turned toward Murray in his funny suit and started another laughing fit. Umar was sure Tuan Beil was laughing at him.

Finally after another hour they pulled into the driveway where the servants were outside waiting for them. Selamat pagi, tuan," Dory the head servant called out as others scurried to take the bags out of the back. Murray was still in the back seat feeling sick. He had the whirlies from the high altitude combined with all the drinks he had consumed. His head throbbed; a wave of nausea welled up in him. He started to throw up all over the inside of the car. With help he staggered out into the bright sun where he was sick again.

"Can I get you anything, tuan?" Dory asked.

"Some aspirin and jasmine tea," Murray said before he passed out.

"Jasmine tea!" Reni, Dory's wife, exclaimed. "And on the full moon. Just like the dukun said."

"But now what do I do?" Dory asked. "This man the tuan brought is the tuan's size, but his clothes are so much different."

"I'll delay him with the aspirin and the tea. You search his stuff and see if there is anything that is like the tuan's and we'll substitute it with some of the tuan's clothes."

"Good idea," Dory said.

But there was nothing that was even similar, down to the underwear. The tuan wore boxers and this man wore briefs. The tuan wore v-neck tee-shirts with arms. His guest wore tee-shirts without arms. The list went on and on. The servants were beside themselves. Everything had to be done the night of the full moon. There was no room for error. The clothes had to be worn the next day when the tuan's guest got dressed.

"We will have to steal the clothes," Reni said. It was getting late and still nothing had come to them.

"No, that is impossible. Think of something else."

"I know. I am washing the clothes the man got sick in. I'll take his bag and wash it all and by mistake put in bleach and ruin everything. Then he will have to wear the tuan's clothes and the curse will be lifted!"

When Murray woke up the next morning he was surprised to find himself in a plain white tee-shirt and boxer shorts. He had a raging headache but did not remember much. He stumbled out of the room and into the living room, where Beil was smoking and sipping a cup of coffee.

"Oh, I see you're up," Beil said, trying not to laugh at the way Murray was staggering.

"How did I get into these horrible clothes?" Murray asked. Dory arrived with a platter on which perched another cup of jasmine tea and a cup of coffee. Murray grabbed the coffee.

"Too much planter's punch on the way up."

"But how did I get into these?" Murray said as he twirled around.

"You passed out shortly after arriving. The servants put you to bed."

"Well, give me a moment and I will change into something more like me," Murray said and went back to his room, only to emerge a few seconds later.

"It must be a bad dream. Now my bag is missing."

"Well, it can't be lost. It's not like the airline." Beil called out to Dory. "Where is Mr. Murray's bag?"

"We had to take everything out because he got sick on it and it leaked through. We are washing it up now," Dory said. They had already put Murray's clothes in the washing machine with enough bleach to make even black white.

"Is it ready?" Murray asked.

"It should be ready soon, tuan. I'll go check," Dory said and ran off, only to come back a few minutes later with a dejected look on his face.

"Sorry, tuan, I have some very bad news. The washing detergent got mixed up and all your clothes were bleached and ruined."

"Ruined? What do you mean?" Murray exclaimed. Beil stated laughing.

"They are all white," Dory said, showing him his beautiful and expensive safari suit that now looked like it was made of albino leopard skin.

"What I am going to do?"

"Oh, don't worry, Murray, I have plenty of clothes," Beil reassured him. "We are only here for a couple of days, and then you can go back to Jakarta and buy more. In the meantime nobody will be looking for you. Come to my room and let's have a little hair of the dog.

Mega Mendung was the perfect place to kidnap someone. It was out of the way, off the road, with a long driveway that was lined with thick lush bushes. The house was landscaped with privacy in mind. There was a long narrow swimming pool in the back yard, lined on either side with thick hedges of flowing shrubbery that hid it from the house. There were manicured hedges everywhere, so you could get close to the house without anyone seeing you. Then you could snatch somebody and be out in no time.

The only point of vantage where the house could be seen was from a plaster and stucco cabin that lay further up the hill in an alpine meadow. The Chinese team had arrived Saturday night. By the light of the full moon, they were able to find the old hut. From there they could spy down onto the main house undetected. To pass the time, they chain-smoked. One of them took out the photo of Beil and placed it on the window ledge to catch the moonlight. In the photograph Yang had provided, Beil was dressed in a Hawaiian shirt and long pants.

Murray woke early Sunday morning, slipped out of bed, and put on the outfit he had worn the day before. They were the only clothes of Beil that he felt even remotely comfortable in. Before he went to bed, he had made sure the servants wash the shirt and pants so they would be ready in the morning. He looked at himself in the mirror, feeling very self-conscious at being so underdressed. He was glad he was in such a remote place where he would not have to see anybody. When he had primped as best he could, he stumbled into the living room where Dory was waiting with coffee. Murray took a cup and asked if Tuan Beil was up. When Dory told him Beil was still sleeping, Murray decided to go outside by the pool to get some fresh air and have a smoke.

The Chinese agents saw him as he made his way to a lounge chair by the pool. There was their target. No mistaking the clothes. The same Hawaiian shirt and pants from the photo. One man pointed in silence. The job was going to be easier than they had imagined, because the pool was completely hidden from the house. There would be no interruptions. In their hurry to get started, they forgot to pick up the photograph of Beil from the window ledge. Stealthily the two men made their way down to the house.

The manicured hedges reflected off of the water in a mesmerizing light. In the lounge chair, Murray lit another cigarette and watched the reflection as he thought about the best way to get to Singapore to stock up on more clothes. He would have Beil's driver drive him right to the airport. Take the next flight out and be back before he had to leave with Sukarno on Tuesday. He took another drag then closed his eyes to bask in the hot sun. He did not see the men approach. The next thing he knew, someone had taped his mouth and thrown a hood over his head. The cigarette fell to the ground.

A few minutes later Beil awoke. In the living room, Dory was waiting with coffee. Beil took his black.

"Where is Tuan Murray?" he asked wanting to tease him more about his clothes.

"He is out by the pool, tuan."

Beil made his way outside, but Murray was no where to be found. "Murray!" he shouted, finding the still-lit butt; the cup of coffee on the table by the pool. Murray had left in a hurry, maybe to go to the bathroom. Beil went back into the house to find him.

Three hours later, and there was still no sign. No one in town had seen him either, but there had been a report of a tiger in the area. Beil began to worry. There was not much more he could do but wait until Umar arrived with the car.

169

Murray soiled his pants, scared shitless. All he could feel was the bag on his head His body was trussed like a pig. He had been pushed into the back of the trunk and was having trouble breathing. It was awfully hot. The air was stale. Thinking that he was dreaming, he started to lose consciousness from the confinement. His head ached.

The car had made it back to Jakarta to an abandoned warehouse by the industrial docks. They drove right into the building, closing the door behind them. They went over to the trunk and opened it. Inside they found the man passed out.

"Is he dead?" one man said.

"Impossible! Shake him!" Slowly Murray came to. He felt hands grab him as he was thrown roughly on the floor.

"Get up!" the man yelled in Mandarin, but Murray did not respond or understand. "Get up!" the man yelled again, this time kicking him. Murray started crying. The man kicked him again, this time in the face. He ripped off the tape. Murray started to howl.

"Shut up!" the man yelled, afraid the noise would give them away. The other man kicked Murray in the mouth, causing some teeth to pop out. Blood started to flow. Murray staggered to his feet. The man was yelling something incoherently into his face. Murray felt the bile come up. He threw up blood and vomit all over the Chinese men, driving them into a frenzy. One of them shoved Murray with such a force that he slammed against the wall and fell down. Just then Yang came in.

"What are you doing?" he shouted, seeing the slumped body on the floor.

"He threw up all over me!"

"Yes, some CIA agents have no manners and no will. Throw water on him and get him cleaned up. The boat is outside."

One of the men threw a bucket of water over Murray, but he didn't move. Yang came over

"He's dead," the man said when he went down to clean him up, checking his pulse.

"Dead? What did you do?"

"I did nothing. I just hit the fornicator for puking on me."

"He's dead, you idiot!"

"He's CIA! He must have swallowed a pill!"

"What are we going to do now?" The two men looked at Yang. He thought for a moment. They could leave him as a message, but then there would be an investigation. People would know. Yang made a decision.

"Put him on the boat," Yang said disgusted that all his effort had failed because of these two bumbling idiots. Now he would have to cover his tracks. He went over to the corpse to look at the face of the enemy, and was shocked. This was not Beil. They had gotten the wrong man.

Yang began to panic. Besides Kusdi and the agents, the only other person who knew about this was Umar the driver, whom Yang hated anyway. It would be good to get rid of him now rather than later.

170

There was no phone at Mega Mendung. Beil was unable to contact anyone until Umar arrived on Monday with Agnes and the kids. The Indonesian police were convinced that Murray had been eaten by the tiger. Beil had Dory arranged for them to come up and scour the land, but they were unable to find anything. The butt and coffee were the only clue.

The land around Mega Mendung was very steep, and there were some hidden gorges. It would take days to investigate. In the meantime, last night in a nearby village the tiger had stuck again, killing a woman as she got water from a well.

Umar spotted Beil smoking by the drive, waiting for the car to arrive. Immediately he felt a wave of relief rise from the bottom of his core and overcome him. It was all he could do to put on the brakes. The Tuan was alive! He quickly lit a cigarette to try to cover his emotions, all the time trying to figure out what had happened.

"Hello darling," Agnes said as she opened the door. "What's wrong?"

Beil had his worried little boy look on, which touched her. "Murray has disappeared. Maybe been eaten by a tiger, we think."

"What do you mean, disappeared?" Agnes asked.

"Hi, father," William said as he hugged Beil. "Is it OK that I explore the old house with the bullets?" he asked. Back in the fifties there had been a battle in the little house up the road. It was where a ruthless Dutch officer had been cornered. They said he killed twenty before they got him. The last time William was there he had found some bullets.

"Not today, son. There is a tiger about. Wait a few days and then you can. Stay around the house," Beil said, then turned to Agnes. "Make sure he stays in sight of the servants."

"William, come with me," Agnes said as she followed Dory into the house. When they had left Beil offered Umar another cigarette. Umar burst out crying.

"Umar what's the matter?" Beil said surprised by the sudden burst of emotion.

"Oh, Mr. Beil, we had heard that a tuan had gone missing. We thought it was you." The whole drive, Umar had been reliving his betrayal. He had heard from Kusdi that everything had gone according to plan. The CIA spy would never be seen again and once the Chinese were done with him he would be feeding the reef fish.

Umar had been so stupid to think that the Chinese would let Beil go, he thought. On the whole ride up he was hoping for a miracle. He had betrayed the only person who he loved in this world.

"Yes, Murray just disappeared without a trace," Beil said.

"That is very strange, Tuan," Umar said, still not fully recovered from his shock. Throughout the weekend Umar had prayed to a God he did not believe in, begging for divine intervention. Impulsively he came up and hugged the tuan. His emotion was contagious and Beil started crying too.

"Murray was out there by the pool having coffee. We found his lit cigarette but not a trace of him."

Three days later the tiger was caught and opened. Inside were human remains, which confirmed everyone fears. Murray had been eaten by the tiger.

Everyone was relieved that the tiger had been killed, especially William, who now could explore the old hut.

"We have done what you ordered, dukun tuan. All went according to what you said would happen. The tuan asked for jasmine tea. We dressed him in another's clothes. Then I went on the second night—Sunday night—by the light of the moon and dug in the corner of the hut and found the treasure just as you said. As soon as we did this, our daughter had the twins, one boy and one girl. With the jewelry inside the treasure chest we were able to give the village enough money to take the girl, who was given to a woman who had lost a daughter of her own. It was better than we could have hoped for. She took our granddaughter as her own, so everything had worked out, thank you so much," Dory said, handing William a box full of coins. "Here is what is left. It is for you."

"Thank you," William said, handing the box back. "Give it to Umar to give to Seam." He was more interested in getting down and exploring the little cabin. Along the way he asked more questions.

"Was there really a huge battle here?" he asked.

"Yes, tuan, back in the 1950's. The Dutch had soldiers operating in this area under the rule of Major Ton Van Derstock, who was known for his brutality. He would take pregnant women and slit their babies out of them. Then while the mother was still alive he would decapitate the baby and put the severed head to her breast. He was evil, tuan. The Indonesians trapped him here in this cabin and killed them all. Major Ton was the last left and each Indonesian man took his knife and cut him into pieces. They say that his remains are scattered over this area and he is a ghost that comes out at night."

"What an awful human!" William said, frightened but very interested. He imagined the scene as they walked to the cabin through the knee-high grass in the swaying breeze under the bright sun. He would have been one of the brave Indonesians fighting the Dutch in this high meadow. Soon they came upon the cabin on a hill. The cabin was painted yellow. The walls were plastered full of bullets holes, so many that it made the place look like it was thousands of years old.

"Tuan, if you look carefully around you will find more bullets," Dory said as they opened the door and went in. Inside the dirt floor was dug up in the corner, where the servants had found the treasure. William felt the past overwhelm him. He was propelled back in time able to feel the bullets ricocheting off of the building. It took him a while to regain his thoughts. He looked on the ground and saw a few cigarette butts and the pack they'd come from. It wasn't so old; he picked it up and noticed it had Chinese writing on it. He then made his way to the window to look out through the broken glass.

"I found a picture," William shouted. On the window ledge was a picture of a man who looked very familiar.

"It's a picture of my father. We need to go show him right away," William said. The two of them went running down the hill, not stopping until they reached the Stanvac house.

172

Two weeks later Murray's body was found washed up on the Jakarta docks, armless. They had been yanked from their sockets by the chains that had held him to the bottom. The police identified him initially from the Hawaiian shirt, and then a week later from dental records. The coroner determined that he died from blows to the head.

When William brought him the photo, Beil immediately knew that Murray had been kidnapped and that he was the intended target. He determined from the photo that it was only because of the servants' mix-up that Murray was taken instead of him.

The Chinese cigarettes made it clear who was behind the plot. He thought back to Yang, and the Chinese infiltration of the PKI. Then to the unthinkable: the only one in the PKI who knew he was going to the country was Umar. Since then he had refrained from confronting him, because he wished to study him for a while. Inside, he felt betrayed, though he did realize that they were on different sides. Like sort of with Hiu. Hiu had never betrayed him, but would he? Beil thought about human nature. How sometimes an ideal is worth more than friendship. It should be the other way around, but Beil knew that even he had done things, like the tape recorder in the lighter. Circles within, lies without. He needed counsel; so after identifying the body he flew to Singapore where he met up with General Jim, delighted that Tim Johnson was there also. They were meeting at a safe house owned by the jewelry dealer, an old lady named Fran Wu.

"Better him than you," Tim said, feeling bad for Murray, whom he remembered from the Sukarno mistress scandal.

"Yes, but what it means is that the Chinese are going after the operators," Jim said.

"I feel so bad for him; you know he was silly, but a good, kind heart. Not equipped to deal with this kind of thing," Beil said. "And of course I'm partly responsible."

"But it means that China is on the move," repeated Jim.

"They are on the move all over the place. No one is safe from their clutches," Tim said, not knowing the prophetic meaning of his words. Little did he know that he had been targeted, just like Beil, or that another Chinese team had followed him into Singapore and was outside the safe house at this very moment.

"They have asked Sukarno again if they can supply arms to the PKI militia as a counter to the regular military," Beil said. "Rockman has kept this at bay, but they push every day."

"You have the other plan in place?"

"Yes, I call it six hearts, but it is only if things spiral out of control."

"I understand, this conflict over the forming of Malaysia has complicated everything," said General Jim.

"At least they are not Communist. Or Thailand for that matter, but lots of arms come through Thailand into this conflict. How will it end?" Tim asked.

"In the end Sukarno will blink. There will be some face-saving formula and we will be on to the next crisis"

"Never ending. God, I need a game of bridge," Beil said.

"Well, you are in luck. Fran is a great player," Tim said. "Who do you think is the Chinese man on the ground in the Indonesian game?"

"The player behind all this is that friend of Haggard's you photographed, Yang Foo," said Beil.

"Oh, yes. I remember him, slight, intense eyes, very smart."

"He's advising the PKI's leadership. He is trying to purge them of nationalists. The PKI are the majority party. Strikes everywhere, anytime. There is a real danger that this could all go wrong, like its going wrong in Vietnam."

"Yes, that place is a mess," sighed Jim.

"Wish we would just cut our loses and throw in with Ho, before it is too late. Finesse the situation, that's what I'd do if I were president," Beil said.

"Don't worry about that." Tim and Jim laughed in unison. "You have too many skeletons for that."

Later that evening they were playing bridge. They had played for two hours straight and wanted a break.

"I'm going to get some more smokes," Tim said. He had run out at the start of the game.

"Here, have some more of mine," Beil said, passing over a Marlboro.

"Nope, I've had enough. No, it's Camels no filter or nothing," Tim said. "They will make me play better."

"I hope so," Beil said. Jim and Fran Wu were trouncing them.

"There's a store right down the street," said the jeweler. "Go outside and turn left. It's right there."

"OK, deal the cards. I'll be back in five."

Two hours later and Tim had still not come back. After the first half hour they had all gone outside and looked for him. An hour later and Fran had called her contacts in the police, who had soured the neighborhood going door to door but still no word. Tim had disappeared.

"Better for us to split up, just in case the Chinese are after us too. Nothing more to do until someone contacts us," Jim said. Both men felt impotent and sad.

Then Beil came upon an idea. "Why don't we intercept this Yang fellow and make a trade?"

173

Sometimes cowards can become heroes, and that is what happened in the case of Captain Puri, who returned home to a state welcome. Sukarno met him at the airport and promoted him on the spot to colonel, skipping the major rank. For the PKI to have such a high-ranking supporter in the military was unprecedented. On the day of his release, the PKI turned out into the streets in the hundreds of thousands to line the motorcade. All the papers told the story of his heroic stand in Sarawak.

"See, son, you are the future," Kusdi said over dinner at the Moon Palace. They were there with a few of Puri's friends, junior officers aligned with the PKI. They were all young, idealistic, and easily shaped. They had grown up in the years after the war and during the struggle for independence. All of them were sons of PKI members.

"Tell us again, Puri, how many our forces killed before they were overrun," one of the junior officers asked.

"We killed forty of them and two British soldiers, but of course there is no mention of that." Puri had told the lie so many times that he believed it. At first when he came back he had been ashamed, but when

Sukarno met him at the airport Puri had created his new story. He had not wanted to let his country down.

"I wish I had been there," said one of his friends. All of them met later that week and swore an oath becoming blood bothers as they had seen done in a movie about the wild west of America.

"Yes, we were pinned down, outnumbered. The rest of my men were martyred heroically. I was captured when we ran out of ammunition. That was when the American took the gun to our heads and started killing us. He wanted information, but none of us said anything. I was the last, but the madman's gun jammed and he walked away."

"What happened next?"

"Then I was taken and beaten, but still did not utter a word. Then our great leader Sukarno demanded that I be released."

"Yes, you young soldiers will be the future," a pride filled Kusdi said again. They were so wrapped up in the moment none of them paid attention when Beil entered with Carl Dremmer and their wives. Beil spotted them immediately. He recognized Kusdi and his son. Casually, he took out his lighter, pausing by them to light a cigarette, taking many photos.

He saw how young they all looked, and was glad even though Puri was the enemy that he had been able to save him. It made him think how everything was so complicated. How on both sides there was love of family, and there were good people and bad people. Momentarily he flashed on Haggard and on Umar.

It had now been over two months since Tim Johnson's abduction and three months since Murray's death, but Beil had still not confronted Umar. The two of them still went everywhere together. But something had changed and both men knew it.

"Edmond," Agnes called, bringing him out of his musing. He took a few more pictures and then joined them at the table.

"So, Edmond, we have been able to identify the other men at the table," Rockman said as they sipped on their bulls' eyes.

"So, what have you learned?" Beil said. It was a month later and Indonesia had entered into the New Year worse off than the year before. There was another crop failure. Unemployment was thirty percent. Prices were sometimes going up twenty percent in one day. The situation over Malaysia still consumed the nation. It looked like an all-out war would break out at any time. Most foreign companies had been seized and nationalized. Beil had to maneuver within this environment.

"Your hunch was right. They are all junior officers with PKI ties, eager to advance. I think they would be perfect for six hearts if it ever comes to that."

"Let's hope it doesn't," Beil said. Even so, he was satisfied with the final plan.

"The other piece of news I thought you should know," Rockman said, "is that Sukarno is very ill. He has been consulting all kinds of doctors, very hush-hush. It has something to do with his kidneys."

"Kidneys, that sounds bad," Beil said, contemplating this new problem. If this got out into the public, which he knew it would in time, then China would try and take over. Already they had coaxed Sukarno into limiting the press so that only pro-PKI papers were allowed to print.

"Yes, we must be prepared. Did you hear about the killing of the Chinese in Medan?"

"Yes, I heard from one of the servants who had relatives there."

"Well, it has spread to another city, same circumstances."

"Might not be bad to fan it a bit—could come in handy."

"Same thought as I have."

"Though once started it might be hard to stop."

"It is an extreme tactic."

"But what is better, Communism or Shariah law?"

"Bulls' eyes and bridge are better, but if we have to pick, then Islam."

"OK, but I have one more matter to discuss," Beil said. It three months and still there was no word at all about the fate of Tim Johnson. All the backwater channels had led to dead ends. What they needed was leverage to trade for information or an actual body for the switch. Beil took a personal interest, because of his connection to Tim and Murray.

"What is that?" Rockman asked, suddenly attentive. He didn't know what was on Beil's mind. but he knew that to mention it last, Beil wanted it first.

"I want your help in capturing the Chinese spy."

175

Umar and Beil were driving to Surabaya to go antiquing. It was a long all-day ride over rough terrain. Half-way, Beil finally broached the subject that had been on his mind for months.

"Umar, how do you think the Chinese knew that I was at the Stanvac house in Mega Mendung?" Beil asked in English, a language they had not used in a while.

"I don't know, tuan," Umar answered, almost forgetting to breathe. It was a long time since Murray's kidnapping, and sometimes Umar was able to forget all about it. For a few weeks afterwards he had expected to be fired, but as time passed things came back to normal. Umar knew one thing: he would never betray Beil again.

In the meantime, Umar got the impression that he was being watched. He found himself left out of many PKI activities.

"Strange, the only ones who knew that Murray was coming were you and me," Beil said as he lit two cigarettes with a Marlboro lighter, very much like the one that he had given Umar. Then he changed the subject.

"There shouldn't be any secrets between friends," he said as he took the lighter and opened it, revealing the camera. "Smile," he said as he snapped a picture. "Amazing what a lighter can do."

"Yes, tuan," Umar answered. "They can do a lot."

"Where is the one that I gave you?"

"I still have it."

"Yes, I know. I'm sorry that I gave you one just like it."

"You were spying on me, tuan," Umar said. The cigarette had done nothing to calm his nerves.

"Not on you, Umar. For you."

"For me, tuan? What do you mean?"

"These are very strange times when things are not what they seem. There is a larger game going on, a game in which Indonesia is a pawn. The PKI is very strong right now."

"I would not know of that, tuan."

"Umar, stop it!" Beil's harsh voice was like a slap. "This is not the time for games!"

"OK, tuan, the PKI is strong and we will win. Sukarno will come to support us," Umar said.

"Sukarno might not be the real power. There are forces, let's say rainmakers or little Gods that sit and decide."

"No, tuan you are wrong. This time the tide is strong."

"It appears that way because these Gods are still watching. Remember when we talked about the difference between Communism and nationalism?"

"Yes, tuan I remember."

"Nationalism for Indonesia is a good thing, though at the moment it is unbalanced because of outside pressure."

"Like the CIA and the United States."

"Like the Soviets but mostly the Chinese. Take your meetings. Think of the Chinese man who is always with you. It is like he is the puppet master of the wayang."

"But you are a puppet master too, tuan."

"No, not quite. I am more like the man who rides the tiger."

"What do you mean?"

"I mean that I will ride the beast as long as I can without falling off and letting it consume me. China right now is pushing to arm all of Indonesia and that cannot happen."

"China is a friend of the PKI."

"No, China is using the PKI for its own end."

"No, tuan, they are a friend," Umar said, though inside he was wary.

"They will betray you when the time is right." And then Beil let the words come out: "Like you betrayed me."

Beil then turned toward Umar, looking into him, seeing the hurt. Beil put his hand on his shoulder. "It is OK, Umar," Beil said compassion flowing out of him.

Umar started to cry. "Sorry, tuan, sorry, tuan," he wailed. "I did not know they were going to kill anybody."

"You were used, Umar. Who set up the operation?" Beil was now ready to gather information, as easy as stroking the cat.

"Yang and Kusdi. They insisted that I do it to prove my loyalty. They spread lies that I was involved in the fire bombing of the PKI headquarters. But it was not so—I was stopping it. They turned many friends against me."

"But that was no reason to—" Beil was going to say "betray," but decided against it.

"But tuan, I was angry at you for using me, with the tape recorder. Why do you do that, tuan?" Neither man noticed that they had slipped into Indonesian.

"For information."

"You mean spying, tuan."

"So that was a reason to set me up?"

"I will never do it again, tuan," Umar said meaning it. "I was so happy when it was Tuan Murray instead of you."

"Poor Murray is dead!"

"Dead, tuan?" Umar gasped. Another shiver came upon him and he started to break up. Beil ordered him to pull the car over.

Beil moved into the driver seat. "I will never do it again," Umar said over and over as he got in the passenger side. Beil grabbed him as a father might, just holding him, letting everything come out of him.

"Umar, I believe you," Beil said, "but betrayal is betrayal. How can I trust you again?"

"No, tuan you can trust me. I'll do anything to make it up."

Beil knew that Umar had been brought back, returned to him. Then he went for the kill.

"I want you to set Yang up for me. He is not good for the PKI and is leading it down a dangerous road. He is the enemy. China is the enemy, not the USA."

"Yes, yes, tuan, yes, tuan, I will do that."

"That's good, Umar, you are my friend. Now let's get to the antiques market before all the good barong is gone." Beil started the engine and drove.

176

The dukun had a strange visitor who arrived with a chauffer in a Rolls Royce but was dressed in rags. He was ancient with open sores covering his face. The old man was escorted by two young attendants, one on either side.

"I have come to see the white dukun," he said in a way that frightened Seam, who knew instantly who he was. It was Rodja, the king of the beggars, an elusive figure that controlled the begging throughout Jakarta.

"Of course," Seam said. "Please wait here." He ran to the main house to tell William. A few minutes later Seam led the king of the beggars into the servants' quarters, where William was sitting in his usual chair.

"I have a problem," the old man stated, looking at the dukun who was at least eighty years his junior. He felt more than saw the eyes of the dukun on his face. He was going to tell half the truth of what he wanted, but quickly changed his mind, deciding to tell the whole truth because otherwise the dukun would see through him.

"Tell me your problem," William said, fascinated with the sores on the man's face and by the car. It would seemed to him that someone who was driving that type of car would be very well dressed like his father or another of the Stanvac executives.

"Someone has put a curse on me," the man said.

A few months earlier, two beggars from a rival guild had arrived unannounced from China, wanting him to step aside and let them buy his operation. The old man had dismissed them. The next day the men came back, this time bringing with them a powerful Chinese mystic. They gave the beggar king one more chance to step aside. Only this time they said that they no longer would pay him for his operation, but that he could keep any money he already had and if he did not agree the mystic would put a curse on him. Again he refused, laughing it off, but as soon as the men left, things had started to go bad.

First the sores had grown all over his body and no Indonesian medicine man had able to relieve them. Second, for the past three months, constant strikes had erupted, making it impossible to run a begging business with thousands of angry poor people in the streets, keeping away the rich foreigners. No one had given anything, not even one copper coin. He related all this to the young dukun.

Once again William just said whatever came to him. Last week he had had a rash on his bottom. When his mother saw it she had Edmond fly to Singapore and get a huge tube of zinc oxide. In just two days it the rash was almost gone. He had the almost full tube in his pocket. "To combat this curse you need to take this tube and smear it all over your body to clean away the sore curse."

"Thank you," the old man said, already feeling better in this great dukun's power. He remembered the last thing the Chinese magic man had said to him—"You can not stop anything, not one man can stop it except…except a white dukun, and that is impossible to find." The mystic was mocking him; the old man had searched for weeks. Finally, when he was just about to give into the Chinese gang's demands….

William spoke again and he came back in from his reverie. "The second thing you must do is save a white woman and her daughter from an angry mob," William said, thinking about another batch of comics from his grandmother. In it his hero Dick Tracy saved a mother and child from being killed by a bunch of Russians that had come into New York City.

"Thank you, tuan," the old man said, confident that now the curse would be lifted.

177

The PKI took to the streets and gathered in large numbers at the gates of the US embassy. All day long the crowd grew.

Umar pulled up to let Beil out. "I'll be a while," Beil said.

"I do wish they would calm down a bit," said Agnes.

"You'll be fine. Where you're going will be a world away."

Agnes and Debbie, William's little sister, were going to the expo-center fair. There was a special exhibit that showed a movie in panorama in a new round theater where the screen was all around you and the sound came from all directions.

It was so exciting that Agnes and Debbie stayed for over two hours. When they emerged the street was jam-packed with people. Umar had gone back for Beil but they were nowhere in sight. Someone in the surge pushed against her. She almost lost her footing. Now she was fearful that in the crowd she might lose Debbie. Agnes began to panic.

Outside on the street-corner the king of the beggars had personally been begging. It was a month after he had seen the young dukun and miraculously all the sores on his face and body had disappeared because of the magic white cream. All he had to do now was wait for the opportunity to lift the rest of the curse. Normally he would not stoop to actual begging. He was sitting at his old corner where he had spent many years before the war when the Dutch were in control. An hour ago, the crowd started to grow.

"Merdeka!" the crowd shouted.

Everybody was furious that Malaysia and now Singapore were going to get their independence.

"Look, there is a white woman and child!" someone shouted as they passed by the old man who looked her way. Agnes was completely panicked. The swell of the crowd was like high tide on a rocky beach.

"What's she doing here?" another shouted.

"American go home. American go home!" The shout was taken up by the crowd. Agnes tried to press into the alley, almost losing her grip on her crying daughter. She made it into the alley but was surprised when she was followed by a group of teenagers.

The old man knew the alley well. It ended in a dead end, and unless you knew where the secret door was, you were trapped. The old man whistled a tune that pierced through the mob. Instantly a hundred or so of his beggar followers were with him, all were armed with sticks and canes.

"Follow me!" he shouted as he led them into the narrow alleyway. In front of him he heard the screams of the young girl.

"Americans are the problem with everything here!" one of the youths shouted in English into Agnes's ear.

"Please don't hurt us," Agnes said in Indonesian, trying to shield Debbie behind her. They were pushed up against the cement wall. Garbage was everywhere. One of the youths came forward and put a hand on Agnes, frightening her even more. Another was about to grab her wrists.

"Do not touch her!"

The youths turned, and were shocked to see a hundred or more beggars behind them.

"Get away," one of the teenagers shouted. But he was cut short when a strap slapped across his face. Enraged, he raised his hands, only to be met by a vicious slap to his chest. The other youths began to flee, but they had to run a gauntlet of beggars on both side of the narrow alley. By the time they got to the street most of them were bloody and beaten.

"I don't think they will be bothering you again," the old man said kindly.

Agnes let out her relief and began crying. "Thank you," she said in both English and Indonesian.

"Here, come over here," the old man said, motioning to an old piece of trim on the cement, with a barrel in front. One of his beggars pulled the barrel away, revealing a small opening. On the other side was another alley. He called for two of his beggars. "These men will lead you through to safety."

"How can I ever thank you?" Agnes asked reaching into her pocketbook to pull out what money she had.

The old man declined the payment. "You have already thanked me enough just by your presence," he said smiling with his remaining teeth, knowing that the curse had been lifted; that things would return to normal. Inside he marveled at the power of the white dukun, who had foreseen it all.

178

It was now the summer of 1965 and Sukarno's illness was an open secret. Over the last few months the PKI had cleverly used it to their advantage, along with the nationalist fever still surrounding the formation of Malaysia. All businesses had been nationalized, and now

Beil felt that his tiger-ride was almost over. With the mob attacks on foreign interests, Beil made the decision to send Agnes and Debbie back to the States. They were leaving in a week. He had originally thought to send William too, but the lad had pleaded that he wanted to finish seventh grade at the International School in Jakarta. After much thought, Beil decided that William could stay as long as there was no further escalation of the situation.

They were driving home. Beil was with Umar in the front seat while Agnes Debbie and William were in the back. Without being particularly aware of it, they were all speaking Indonesian.

"Well, darling, how long do you think it will be before we can come back?" Agnes said, nevertheless very relieved to be going. The riot had filled her with fear. No longer did she think of the Indonesians as children, but now rather as angry adolescents swept up with ideas like Communism that could spin out of control. But still she was sad, as most of the wives and a lot of the workers were leaving as well. She was looking forward to one more party. Perhaps another can-can party, where the theme would be going home.

"A good six months," Beil said having no idea. Everything was in flux. There had still been no word on Tim's whereabouts. There were many rumors, all leading to dead ends. But that was the least of his worries. The whole country was about to explode.

"Well, at least there is one good thing out of this turmoil," Agnes said looking out, glad to be in a car that was actually moving. There were no strikes today. The city was calm.

"What's that?" Beil answered.

"The farewell party."

"Yes, that is just the thing to get everyone's mind off the damned bon voyage."

"Yes, darling, and I have thought of the theme. Hawaii!"

"It will start to change when the big bird hovers in the jungle and you shoot it full of holes," William told the man in Indonesian military attire.

William really liked the uniform. It was like something from the set of soldiers that Beil had bought him in Jalan Surabaya. He had been playing with them last night on the full moon. He had led the first soldier over the fence in the light of the full moon. In his mind he was the general directing his troops from the old abandoned hut in Mega Mendung. He'd had an all-night battle which continued in his dreams. When he saw the soldier it triggered the reflection.

The colonel sat before him but did not comprehend its meaning. Puri now had a following of young officers. In addition he had been taken under the wing of an old general, one of the nationalistic old timers that Rockman had told Beil was part of the six hearts. Puri's reason for going to the dukun was that all the battles on the border were Indonesian defeats. They were being beaten by the Gurkhas with their British officers.

"When will that happen, tuan? What should I do next?"

"After you see the fence, then the battle will begin and what you were born to do will happen," William said, still inside his own battle world where his forces were winning. Winning what, he did not know. But there were sides and you needed at least two sides to have a war. "But first you will fight a battle by the sea," he said, thinking how nice it would be to have a battle on the beach.

"But when will this all happen, tuan?" Puri was caught in the power of the dukun's eyes. He knew his father Kusdi would not approve. He had told him many times that superstition did not belong in the new People's Republic of Indonesia. His father would be even more concerned by the dukun's whiteness, but Puri had spent much time with his Balinese friends, who had recommended that this particular dukun was the one to see.

"It will all be over by the end of the year," William said remembering what his father had said about them maybe leaving. All of them in the New Year.

"Thank you, tuan" the young officer said, confident he would now be successful.

180

Haggard was flying a new toy in the cat and mouse war going on at the border. It was very exciting to be piloting the helicopter. With it he was able to come in quick. Go out quick. No more need for a runway. He marveled that it was like a car in the air. It could turn on a dime. Go up, down, left, right, all that was needed to land was a pad the size of a swimming pool, which in a thick jungle was sometimes all there was. It also had machine guns that were controlled by the throttle sticks on either side of the control panel.

He was in the cockpit under the cover of night, flying low along a river on the Indonesian side of the border. It was the first cross-border raid, a preemptive strike. Intelligence had spotted the camp in a clearing a few days earlier. The Indonesians were using it as a staging ground for operations inside Malaysia.

Young Colonel Puri and his men had seen the helicopter from their observation post overlooking the river. The words of the white dukun filled his head. The bird would land in the field. Excited, he motioned for his men to hide.

Haggard made for the clearing about to set the helicopter down. When he got about twenty feet off the ground, he dropped the rope ladders. To Puri, they looked like the fences of the dukun's prophecy.

Soon the Special Forces came down the ropes, most of them somersaulting with guns drawn, just as the bullets began to rain down on them. "Back, back!" someone screamed as four more men fell from the ladders. A bullet ricocheted around the inside of the chopper, just missing Haggard. The next one struck the co-pilot. The blood flowed out of his head. Haggard steadied the ship.

On the ground Puri drove his men forward, guns blazing. The few left hanging from the fence ladder were like sitting ducks.

"Quickly, men, attack, attack!" he screamed at the top of his lungs, the adrenaline pumping through him.

"Now!" he shouted as the barrage let lose. Only by the grace of God none of the bullets hit Haggard or any of the fuselage. He twisted the chopper around. He had to get out. In the next barrage he would not be as lucky. He looked down; saw that no one was hanging from the ladders; he was the only one left. He pulled the throttle up. Quickly he brought the machine guns around, the glee evident in his face. He would get his revenge on these Indonesian savages. He pulled in the triggers on both machine-guns. They were jammed. He cursed his bad luck, banked left and got the hell out of there.

On the ground the young colonel and his men rejoiced. None had been lost; fourteen of the enemy were dead.

"See, the dukun was right!" his friend Kutuk said.

"Yes, for the glory of Indonesia." Puri said happily.

181

Yang was delighted with the successful raid and the quick promotion of Kusdi's son, Puri, to brigadier general. Now they had a high-ranking PKI officer that the junior officers looked up to.

"Finally on the inside," Kusdi said.

"Yes," Yang answered. Everything was going well. A few final maneuvers and Indonesia will be Communist, he thought. Now that they had people in the army, when the time came to move they would be ready.

"Since you have been away we have gained much," Kusdi said. Every day they enhanced their power. Sukarno had appointed a PKI chief of police. The PKI press was free to publish what it wanted. Sukarno had just given a speech explaining how Indonesia was entering a new stage where it was going to become Socialist.

"We have to be ready to move when the time comes. I hear that Sukarno is very sick."

"Yes, that is the case. He collapsed at the podium a few weeks ago. Since then there has been much speculation over his health."

"If he dies, that will be a time of great confusion. We will have to get your son in position to take over," Yang said.

"And that is the other thing. He is going to be stationed at headquarters with his own staff and office."

"That is even better than I thought," Yang said, his mind rolling through the next maneuvers.

He had come back to Jakarta to take another shot at Beil. This time he was going to set up the job himself, just like he had in Singapore when he and his team picked up Tim Johnson. They had extracted much on the CIA workings in Thailand. It had been regrettable that he had died under interrogation.

Now he had gotten word from Umar that Beil was going to the country again, to Mega Mendung.

182

"He is in Jakarta now, tuan. To capture you. I told him what you said, that you were going to Mega Mundune," Umar told Beil in the car.

He didn't feel at all bad about his decision to set up Yang. Part of that was to repay his debt to Beil for taking him back in when most would have thrown him out. But part was also for the friendship that he had betrayed for ideals that had seemed right at the time. Mostly though,

334

he hated Yang and the influence that he had over Kusdi and the PKI. Umar felt he had been driven out by the leadership, by the lies that Yang exploited. The story of the grenade, the meetings with Rockman, all those circumstances. No one really trusted him. And yet he was a patriot. He was angry that the PKI was losing its Indonesian flavor and embracing China. He hoped Beil could change that.

"Good," Beil said, remembering his last conversation with Rockman, when he had pleaded with him that not all PKI members were the same. That there were fanatical Communists like Kusdi and his block, but there were also the nationalists who were for a more equal Indonesia.

"Things are coming to a head," Rockman had said. "And there might not be time to separate the good from the bad. We have unleashed the Muslims." Both men knew that once a genie was released from a box it was difficult to put it back in. Already there were many mysterious deaths among the Chinese population.

"Yes," Beil had said at the time. "But do remember that unless you are prepared to kill millions, you need to be able to reel those people in. Umar for one is worth saving, and you will need people like him to rebuild."

"Plans can often go awry, Mr. Beil," Rockman had said, thinking about the past week. The situation in Indonesia was even more precarious that before. With the success of the brave young General Puri who had massacred the Malaysian troops, Sukarno had come even closer to the PKI and to China. "But I will take what you say seriously, as we have been friends for so long."

"That would be good. I have heard that Yang is now in Jakarta."

"We take him as soon as possible and as agreed we interrogate him and then give him to you."

"I thought the plan was I would be there for the interrogation," Beil said.

"Then we will need an out-of-the-way place to do it, so none of the PKI spies will get wind of it."

"I suggest we use the Stanvac house up in Mega Mendung as the base of operation. It is out of the way of everything. That's where they tried to get me."

"Good, then set it up," Rockman had said at the end of the meeting.

Beil, musing, was interrupted by Umar: "Tuan, I am so sorry for before." Umar couldn't bear to think back to his betrayal. Giving up Beil—but now he was giving up Yang. Nothing was black and white. He did not know who the enemy was.

"Apology accepted, Umar. Sometimes people do things that they are forced into," Beil said, thinking about Haggard now. How Beil had alerted Rockman who had moved the airplanes before Haggard could attack them. That had saved America from itself, he thought. If Haggard had been successful, Beil knew that they would have had another Vietnam on their hands. So much better the cat and mouse game.

183

Yang waited at the same hut that they had used for the first failed attempt. With him were the same two agents. All of them were armed with submachine guns. Their getaway car was parked at the bottom of the hill on the back path. Keys inside and ready to roll.

Earlier in the evening they had watched the car arrive with Beil and his driver. Yang was happy to see the two of them were alone. This time Beil was the only white person in the car. Through his binoculars he watched as Beil was greeted by the servants, ten of them, seven men and three women.

"Disgusting that the capitalist pigs have such waste," he commented to his men. By prearrangement, Umar was to signal which of the rooms Beil was in. Yang then focused his binoculars on the small window with the little blue card.

"He is in the upstairs north bedroom." That room was the most private, on the second floor with its own veranda that was only accessible from the room. More important, it was the nearest to them and their escape. Unlike the last plan to snatch him in the morning, they were going to get him in the room before dawn.

The only trouble was the full moon, but there was nothing Yang could do about that. They would work around it. The jungle was thick to the house and the hedges provided many hiding places. The men would have to be in the open for only a few seconds right near the house.

Silently, the three men slipped out of the cabin, hugging the underbrush. They made their way to the house, getting to the hedge by the swimming pool, using it to hide from all eyes. Soon they reached the shrubbery by the veranda and stopped. They would have to be in the open for twenty feet, with no cover. They waited for a while but detected no servants. Still, they all had their guns out with the safeties off, ready just in case. Yang looked to the sky; a cloud was about to go over the moon. As soon as the sky went dark, the three quickly crossed the patio making their way under the veranda.

There one of the men pulled out a small fold-out ladder placing it against the railing. Yang and one of the men climbed up and went over the side. As soon as they were out of sight, someone slipped a bag over the head of the one waiting at the base of the ladder. An experienced finger clamped over his windpipe. The man collapsed, was quickly brought inside and replaced with another.

Yang peered into the room spotting Beil sleeping under the mosquito net. The window was open, providing an easy entrance. Silently, both men darted in, hiding behind the curtain. The figure on the bed did not stir.

Yang had the tape out, ready to cover Beil's face as the other man slowly peeled back the netting. Then they froze. It was a trap. It was not Beil, but a dummy. Yang turned just as a bag went over his head. He felt a syringe pierce his arm. Then he went slack. The other man tried to raise his machine gun, but before he could shoot, someone grabbed it from his hands. He too was hooded and drugged.

"Which one is Yang?" Rockman asked Beil as they looked over the limp bodies. To Rockman they all looked the same. Beil came forward. He too was confused.

"I know he was very tall for a Chinese," Beil said. So they lined them up on the ground like pieces of meat. Now it was easier. There was only one tall one.

"That's him," Beil said. "What are you going to do with the others?"

"Oh, they will disappear in this anti-Chinese fever that is growing," Rockman said, both of them knowing that there was not much else to do with them. These agents were just bag men; dangerous to keep them alive. It was war. Still, Beil felt a touch of sadness that there would have to be a death. He thought of poor Murray who wanted to be a spy so badly that he had died a horrible spy's death. If there was a spy heaven, these two could be Murray's guards in the afterlife, like Inca or Aztec warriors.

When the two men were removed, Beil and Rockman focused their attention on Yang.

"How long do you think it will take to break him?" Beil asked, remembering the way Haggard had looked when he had seen him the first time after Rockman had got through with him.

"Oh, the best last a week or so, and he does look like the best. So we will start the wake/sleep cycle in the car ride to Jakarta."

184

The interrogation room was all white with bright lights that could become unbearably warm or else turn off and be pitch-black and freezing. There were no windows. The room had an evil air. For the last forty-eight hours the sleep/wake cycle had been alternated every thirty minutes. Rockman and Beil were behind the see-through mirror monitoring the interrogation.

"So far he has withstood everything," Beil said, in need of a drink. It was one thing to hear about an interrogation but another thing to view it. He was glad he wasn't Yang. He had been stripped naked.

The room alternated between very hot and dark during the sleep cycle, to freezing and bright during the "day." Calendars were placed all around the room with various dates and years. There was a vase on a table with a single flower, one of the giant pitcher plants that had been discovered in Java that could eat rodents.

"Yes, most have broken by now. Your friend Haggard was a blabbing mess by this point."

"He is not my friend," Beil said, nauseated. It was the part of the business that he hated. One he very rarely participated in. He preferred to bend someone's will by persuading them, having them want to change-like Umar

"When do you think he will talk?" Beil asked.

"Today, tomorrow, soon," Rockman said. They watched the interrogator shoot Yang with the wake syringe. He came to life.

The lights were overbearing. He thought he must be on the sun. But he could not be, because the air was freezing. The whole world was upside down. He had been here for days, how many exactly he did not know. Still he hung to his training. His trainers had told him that these cycles would come and go. He must endure them like a trip to the dentist. Part of his mind tried to understand where he was, why he was. The only thing he was sure of was the cut on his hand. It was the last thing he did just after the bag was put over his head and before the shot took effect. He had remembered his training; had felt around while he was being led out of the bedroom. He had found the sharp edge of a metal table. He gave himself a deep gash. It was his only salvation. Whenever he was about to give up he would open the cut, feel the pain.

Two days later he still had not broken. Rockman's interrogation team had brought in the most famous dukun in all of Indonesia. Rockman and Beil were again behind the mirror. Both of them on some level were very unsettled by the man's toughness.

"The Chinese train their agents better for torture than the Americans, Edmond," Rockman said, frustrated that so far no information had been obtained.

"Still, if I had not seen it myself I would not believed it," Beil said.

"We have a new interrogator today. One who is versed in the art of black magic. He is the dukun we use on these rare occasions," Rockman said as they watched Yang get the wake-up shot.

"You don't believe in that really, do you?" Beil asked in disbelief.

"This is Indonesia, Edmond, where all things are possible. This man is only used on the tough cases, not like that Haggard friend of yours."

"He is not my friend," Beil said again as the dukun entered the room.

Yang felt the bright lights and woke up from sleep, counting in his mind that now it was the fortieth day. He had dreamt of a river that was moving through the air. The air was full of evil and death. He waited for the questions to begin. Everything was the same as before except for there was another source of light in the room. No, not a light but a pair of eyes. They seemed to be everywhere.

The dukun saw the man before him and touched his forehead between the eyes, projecting a bolt of energy through his fingers into the inside of the man's brain, to get inside his thoughts.

Yang felt as if he were rising. There between his eyes was another eye of big light. Deep, long, grey, soul-permeating light. Yang felt that his mind was an open book. He fought the desire to talk. Quickly he tried to rip open his cut. But this time he was unable to feel anything but numbness through his body. "It is a dream," he said out loud without knowing it. He tried to concentrate on the harsh room light, but he saw nothing but the big mind light.

"What is your name?" the dukun asked.

"Kong Yang Foo." He felt he was unable to stop his voice. It seemed to flow by on its own.

"Where do you come from?"

"I come from Harbin," he said unable to stop answering. Beil and Rockman were riveted. It was the first time he had answered anything other than to deny.

"Why are you here, Mr. Yang," the dukun said, still holding his finger on Yang's third eye.

"I am here to serve China's interest."

"What are those?"

"To make Indonesia communist." The big light was reading his thoughts. He had to keep quiet, he thought, not knowing he was taking out loud.

"How will this happen?" the dukun asked.

"By overthrowing the government at the right time."

"Overthrowing?"

"Yes, when the time comes. Slowly. Already we have officers in the army. Waiting for Sukarno's death. It will be soon."

Beil and Rockman were amazed by the way he was talking. After thirty minutes the session ended with another shot to put him to sleep, as it was dangerous to keep him off his cycle. But both men knew that in a few more sessions they would get all the information Yang possessed.

Beil looked at his watch. He couldn't wait till then. He'd have Rockman brief him later.

185

The party started like them all, very early with the pre-round of drinks. Everybody knew that it was the last party for a while. They began with bloody marys at the Finns. They had just now moved over to the Beils, but his was still only the pre-party. None of them had changed into party clothes.

"Oh, I can't believe Camelot is going to end," Carl said as they were all sitting around in lounge chairs. He was going on furlough for six months, the whole family. They were going to be on the same flight as Agnes and her daughter.

"It ended with Murray's death."

"They still don't know who did it," Carl said, looking over at Beil who nodded his head. Rockman had kept it all out of the press until the body had been found.

"God, I can't believe we have been here so long. Seems like it was only yesterday that we moved from Sumatra," Agnes said. She had mixed feelings about going. She was wishing that Beil and William were going with her. She had told Beil the night before that she was afraid. Just yesterday a huge PKI mob had tried to storm the British embassy, even hurling fire-bombs into it before they were dispersed by riot troops. Foreigners were told to stay indoors and not to go anywhere that was not essential. The embassy had already evacuated non-vital personnel.

"Well, I can't wait to be home," Sally Dremmer said. "They don't want us here anymore." Her feeling was almost universal. The only ones who wanted to stay were the Finns.

"I can't believe all of you are wanting to leave," Dottie said, dressed in a sun hat to go with her long skirt and simple blouse.

"I can't believe you want to stay," Sally said. It was universal knowledge that the Finns use to hate everything about Indonesia.

"You're right, you know," Dottie said, thinking back on how she had despised everything about the place. That was until she got home and realized that life in the tropics was paradise compared to the mundane boring middle-class housewife experience in the States.

"Yeah, you really never know what you have until it is gone," Beil said, his mind full of thoughts. He had earlier in the day received a phone call from Rockman, who was going to come to see him at the party with important news. He took another sip of his cocktail and wondered what had happened.

"Speaking of being here a long time and things changing," Donald Finn chuckled. "I have been out shopping for the last few days and have come back with a collection of cans."

"More cans?" Beil said.

"Yes, and I paid almost nothing for the whole collection." Finn was very pleased with himself. He had been inspecting a transfer station and had stopped in an old abandoned Dutch market and had found them in a corner. Some looked like they were prewar or even from the last century. He clapped his hand and Talnor came forward with a silver tray of the very best and put them by Beil.

"So we started with a can party and we end with a can party," Agnes said, somewhat melancholy.

"Yes, this does call for another can-can party," Dottie Finn said, coming up behind Donald. She had been drinking heavily. "What a great idea, darling," she added as she pulled up her skirt and started dancing a can-can that soon changed into the twist, the new dance craze that had just reached Indonesia.

"Only if it has a twist," Agnes said coming out of here reverie. All of them laughed. She looked down at her watch. My God, it was almost time for the real party to start. She told everyone to go home and change and then come back, as the party would start at five.

Now in September, 1965, most of them had been in Indonesia for over fifteen years. It had been always safe, secure, but the series of events in the last few years, especially the last few months had upset everyone.

"I thought of them as happy children," Dottie Finn said. All of the others were in agreement. It was a little after five and none of the Indonesian guests had arrived.

"Yes, simple, but now things are different," Agnes said.

"It must have been so awful, being caught up in the mob like that," Sally Dremmer said. It was bad enough driving around. There were riots everywhere and if you read the papers all the news was about inflation, lack of food, the Chinese Communists trying to take over.

"Well, Sukarno did call it the year of living dangerously," Agnes said, still remembering the beggars who had saved her.

"There was another killing the other day by religious fanatics murdering another Chinese."

"And they are still so bent out of shape about Malaysia becoming free. Don't they know the British will make sure it is run well?"

"Yes, not like the French who gave us Vietnam," Beil said, full of worry knowing that Indonesia could easily and likely go that way. Everything was failing. There had been no choice but to begin six hearts.

He thought again about Murray Timmons, realizing how much he missed him.

"That will never happen here," Dottie said in a hopeful voice.

"It could if Sukarno lets the Chinese have their way."

"What do you mean?"

"I mean he is talking about a citizen militia."

"That would not be a good thing. Can you imagine the little children running around with guns, the servants, anybody?"

"I agree it would be complete anarchy," Beil said. He looked to the drive and saw Rockman and his wife coming up the walk. Immediately his stomach started to twist.

"Nasul, Mrs. Rockman," Beil said coming up to greet them. He could see by Rockman's face that something was up.

"Hello, Edmond, good to see you," Rockman said.

"Seam, bring Mr. Rockman a bull's eye and his lovely wife some champagne."

Just then Agnes came up and grabbed Mrs. Rockman by the hand. "Come over here with us girls."

"But what about the champagne?" Beil asked.

"We have our own," Agnes said as they walked away. Seam brought two bull's eyes to Beil and Rockman.

"Health," Beil said as they touched glasses. Rockman drank his quick and called Seam for another. The two men then went outside out of earshot.

"Well?"

"This Mr. Yang was very well informed."

"What have you heard?"

"For starters, Sukarno was secretly examined by Chinese doctors who confirmed that he has inoperable kidney disease and will soon be in complete kidney failure. The Chinese doctors give him at the most a year but it is more than likely he will go within the month."

"I knew it was serious."

"Yes, and with Sukarno so ill, the PKI is moving up its timetable. They now have their man in place at Army headquarters.

"You mean—"

"Puri, the hero of Sarawak. They are going to act through him. Yang did not think he was ready yet to seize control. But with Sukarno dying, they have to move. Yang says the Chinese and Sukarno have a secret pact. In a couple of weeks Sukarno will announce the formation of the peasant militia."

"That is bad news. Will the generals go along with it?"

"Normally no, but with the Malaysian situation there is so much pressure."

"We must stop that before it happens," Beil said gravely, both of them knowing that things had to stop before they were unable to stop them. Both were already worried that the Muslim youths they had allowed to counter the PKI were now on a killing spree that if left untouched they would not be able to stop. It was like gardening, where the fragile bud could be picked off but the big branch could not.

"We must finesse the hand," Rockman said.

"We can start by placing information, disinformation to the right people. Say I accidentally leave papers in my car with Umar...."

"Or even better," Rockman interrupted. "We can leave information for General Puri to see."

"Yes, claiming a coup by the military."

"Yes, we can name those six useless generals as the plotters and hope the PKI takes the bait and pushes for a coup of their own."

Both men inside felt it was like a game for the grand championship, only this game was real. They would all have to play it right or they would lose. There was no second chance; no room for failure.

Meanwhile the girls had been trying on clothes and makeup while drinking champagne and had decided to put on a peep-show for the men. Rockman and Beil heard all the commotion and turned toward the noise.

"Have you finished with Yang?" Beil asked.

"Not yet. Soon."

"Remember I want him when you are done."

"Of course, Edmond, of course."

"Then to the next play in the six hearts." Beil said as they clinked glasses, destiny entwined. It made their mood exciting. Despite the danger they felt so alive, as if they were playing bridge in the middle of a life or death rubber.

Just then the girls came out calling the men for the start of the can-can. All the women including Saya Rockman had changed into revealing outfits, short skirts and blouses that showed some of their belly and ample cleavage. The servants were all staring, especially at Mrs. Rockman, who had had enough champagne not to seem to notice.

"We thought we'd give you gentleman a show before we went for the cans," Dottie Finn said as the record player came back on, blasting "Twist and Shout." The women started moving their hips.

186

Beil, Agnes, and Debbie were on the way to the airport. It was the first day of autumn, September 22nd. Umar was driving them in a raging thunderstorm that had knocked the power out of most of Jakarta. The streetlights were not working. They had just dropped William off at school, where Agnes had said her tearful goodbye. In the car they were chain-smoking with the windows up, poor Debbie was surrounded by clouds of smoke that no one seemed to notice.

"Good day to be leaving," Agnes said. The storm and the power outage helped to reinforce the melancholy mood that entrapped them all for different treasons. Agnes felt the end of innocence, the end of a cycle. She felt the tears well up.

Umar was thinking about betraying the movement, about giving up Yang to save Beil. It was so confusing for him to hate people who were working for his own ideal, his own vision for the future. Beil was kind to him, but he working for the other side. Umar remembered the trepidation he felt at the next PKI meeting.

"Umar have you seen Yang?" Kusdi had come up to him after the meeting.

"No, I have not seen him."

"It is very strange not to see him," Kusdi said. Things were moving very quickly, with the people demanding weapons to fight the British. Yang was the liaison to the Chinese government, who would provide those weapons. So far Kusdi's PKI army could only fight with words.

"Oh, I am sure he will turn up," Umar said.

"Yes, but I wish he was here now. It's not like him to leave without telling any one. I have so much news. Sukarno met with me just the other day and promised Chinese guns soon, promised my militia, but now he is dying-We need those guns now to prevent the army from taking over."

"I thought the army was ours now—your son...."

"Yes, but not enough, and not quick enough. General Puri is only one man. He has enemies. We have to have more information."

"Yes," Umar had said then. Now, riding in the car, he wished to ask Beil about what had happened to Yang, but Beil had not mentioned it at all. Just then a water buffalo ran into the street and Umar had to maneuver the car to avoid it.

"Umar, I am going to miss your driving," Agnes said.

"It was nothing, Madam."

"Oh, I am going to miss everything about this place," Agnes said as she started crying. She thought back to the first days of driving from the airport where everything was new and foreign. It was like going into the ocean and swimming for years and years, until the sharks come. "I want you to take care of the tuan and William while I am gone," she said, speaking Indonesian, remembering her farewell to the servants. They had all been in a line in front of the house by the frangipani tree. They were crying, the tears pouring out. It was like leaving a family. The servants were all lined up, Seam, Eto, Ina and the twenty or more relatives of theirs who needed jobs and a place to stay. Agnes knew that this could be the last time she saw them. She had that feeling, that premonition in her gut.

On the side of the road ahead of them was a busy fruit market and Agnes remembered her first trip to Sumatra; the fruits that Umar had bought for her. "Pull over here," she said to Umar in Indonesian, feeling the need to speak it.

"Yes, madam," he answered back. Debbie started to cry for no reason. Beil and Umar both lit cigarettes to hide their feelings. Agnes soon came back with one piece of every fruit.

"Thought I'd bring them with me on the plane," she said. Why do all things have to end? she thought. It was like being on a carousel ride that goes round and round, everything taken for granted, and then it stops and you have to get off. She was forty years old.

The rest of the ride to the airport was silent. Each of them were in their thoughts, which for Umar ran in a circle. He was bringing the tuan's wife, the enemy, back to where she had come. But she was not enemy, and he did not know who or what he was. Finally they got to the airport.

"Umar, wait here while I bring Mrs. Beil to the plane," Beil said, looking at his watch. "My God, the plane leaves in just a few minutes!" He grabbed his briefcase, taking out the tickets and Anges's and Debbie's passports. Then he closed the case without locking it, leaving it on the front seat.

Umar got out of the car and opened the door for Agnes. She got out and wiped a tear from her eye. "I will miss you," she said, remembering his kindness. And then she reached up and hugged him, so unexpected. No one had ever done that in his life, felt sad for leaving him. It made him cry.

"Live life till we meet again," Umar said in Indonesian. The spell was broken when the porter came up. Umar watched as madam and Debbie went into the airport with Beil.

He lit another cigarette, and glanced down at the seat next to him. In Beil's hurry, he must have forgotten to lock his briefcase, something he never did. He had another cigarette. He looked at his watch. There were still fifteen minutes before the flight left. Umar knew Beil by habit would stay to the end, then have a drink at the bar. Umar had plenty of time. Finally he reached over, knowing he should not. He opened the case. On top was an envelope marked "Office of Nasul Rockman."

He closed the briefcase and slid down in his seat so that it would be hard for people to see what he was going. He kept the briefcase nearby, so if anyone approached he would have time to put it back in place.

Inside the envelope was a letter with the official seal of the Indonesian military.

Dear Mr. Beil:

> We fear that that things are moving too quickly and without our intervention Indonesia will fall to the Chinese. They have talked Sukarno who is very sick into forming a civilian militia. The arming of the civilian population is the arming the PKI. It is a direct threat to us. This dispatch is to inform you and your government that our officers will move on October 5th.

> Nasul Rockman

Umar's fingers were trembling the whole time he read. He read it again then lit another cigarette. His whole being was numb. There was going to be a coup. All of a sudden he became panicked by the information, feeling like the eyes of the world were on him. He quickly put the papers back and tried to remain calm.

Inside the terminal Agnes had cleared customs. The three of them were all sitting in the lounge. Beil had poured himself a bull's eye.

"Well, darling" she said to him, "so this is it."

"For a while, anyway," Beil said. Both of them knew that paradise had ended. There was nothing you could do about it except go on.

"Take care of yourself, Edmond."

"I'll see you in a month or so," Beil said, fighting the urge to smoke. He looked at Agnes and saw a soul mate. "When this is over, I'll come home," he said.

"Make sure William is safe," Agnes murmured, worried and not worried, crying more for leaving than in fear of anything happening to him. William was a unique boy and some of the older expat kids were staying, but the mob had unsettled her. It would only be for a few months anyway, as it was now the end of September and William's semester ended in December. He would be under the constant watch of the servants, so she put the worry out of her mind. Debbie started to tug at her hand. She was crying, too. Again Agnes remembered the servants all lined up, all of them crying. No one was paying any attention to Debbie, the girl.

"Seam, I'll need your recipe for fried peanuts," she had said, because there was nothing else to say.

She looked hard at Edmond. The call for the flight came over the loudspeaker. Beil walked her onto the tarmac. They paused at the foot of the stairs and he grabbed her in a hug.

"Agnes, I love you," he said, looking into her eyes.

"Sampai jumpa lagi—till we meet again, darling," she said, kissing him. He watched her as she walk up the stairs. She turned and blew him a kiss. Then she was gone.

He lit a cigarette and walked back to the car, where he found Umar waiting for him. He opened the front door and picked up the briefcase, which was in the same place as before. Nonchalantly, he picked it up and moved it to the back seat, only checking to see that the hair he had placed across the flap was now missing. Umar had read the report.

"Sad that the madam is leaving," Umar said, his mind still whirling with the information about the October plan.

"Sad on many fronts, Umar." Beil said. He lit two cigarettes, handing one to Umar. There was a slight drizzle as they drove. The fog made both men pensive.

"Yes, tuan," Umar said. Everything was moving too fast. Now this coup. He had to get that information to the PKI and quickly.

"The whole world seems headed to conflict. I don't know how things are held together."

"What do you mean, tuan?"

"Malaysia and Indonesia almost at war, even though they speak the same language as you."

They were speaking English. "Sukarno sick, China wanting to arm the peasants. The Muslims are killing innocent Chinese. It's all out of control," Beil said, baiting the trap.

"It is because the leadership is corrupt," Umar said, outraged at the idea of a coup. "Generals wanting power for themselves, not the people. No freedom."

"But it was the PKI who wanted censorship laws. It was they who ended freedom of the press."

"It was Sukarno who passed those laws, tuan," Umar said, though he knew it was because of Kusdi's pressure.

"And this push to nationalize all industries is causing huge inflation, and this war is adding to it."

"It is growing pains, tuan."

"Yes, but you are becoming what you don't want," Beil said, knowing that power corrupts and power is the prize. They were approaching downtown, where there was a huge protest in the streets.

"Those people want food and a better life," Umar said to justify it all.

"But are you better off now than five years ago? I mean, are you?" Their conversation ended when they got to the office.

187

Brigadier-General Puri sat back in his office, stunned by what he had just read. Earlier in the day he had been scheduled to meet with

General Solo, but when he had gone to his office, the secretary said the general would be late and for him to make himself at home.

Puri had never been in an office like this one. His own office was a small room with no view. He had thought it grand, having grown up in the slums of Jakarta with no house at all. But compared to his office, this was a palace. The air-conditioned room was adorned in fine teak carving. Old Dutch paintings hung on the walls. On one side was a long bar with every imaginable type of liquor.

Rockman came in. "I just wanted to make sure you give these to the general when he arrives," he said matter-of-factly, handing him the two pages that had come of out the telex machine. Rockman saw the young soldier eyeing the liquor and went over to the bar.

"The general is famous for his liquor collection," Rockman said, seeing the wide eyes of the youth. They became even wider when Rockman poured two glasses of whisky. He handed one to Puri. "Health," he said as he downed his. Puri choked on the hard liquor, but held it down. Rockman poured him another glass.

Puri's mind was reeling at this open taboo, this whiskey that had to be sucked down behind closed doors. Liquor was not allowed to Muslims like him and Rockman, but somehow here at headquarters the rules were different.

Rockman looked at his watch. "Oh, I'm late. Make sure the general gets these as soon as he comes in. Feel free to drink whatever you like while you wait."

"Certainly, sir," Puri said, even though he held the higher rank.

An hour later, the general had still not arrived. In the meantime Puri had taken a few more shots, really enjoying his good fortune. Soon he would be in charge of all Indonesia and have an office like this, he thought to himself. He sat down at the general's antique Dutch roll top desk. He settled himself in the fine leather chair. He then picked up the telexes and decided since that he was going to be the next leader of the country, there was no reason he shouldn't read them.

"Urgent Top Secret," the cover page said. Then the message: Be ready to assume your responsibilities by the end of the month. Sukarno is dying. You and the others named below will take command on the date selected. Let no one see this and destroy it as soon as you read it.

Just then Puri heard a knock on the door. He put the papers down and got out of the chair. The door opened, but it was not the general.

"I'm afraid General Solo will not be in today. Please go back to your office and come back tomorrow," Rockman said.

"Yes, sir."

By the way he walked out the door, Rockman knew that he had taken the bait. Before he left the general's office, Rockman picked up the fake telexes and shoved them into his back pocket.

188

Haggard had been contracted through the agency to fly covert missions for elements within the Indonesian military. He had no way of knowing that he was indirectly working for Beil. His flying skills had come to the Indonesians' attention. Since mercenaries have no sides and just followed the highest bidders, it suited Haggard just fine.

He had been flying a helicopter here and there, ferrying Indonesian VIPs around Java. It no longer bothered him that he had been shot down by the Indonesians. Only on the first mission had the humiliation surfaced. He had to fight the desire to push them all out of the helicopter. He had been flying in the same disputed part of Sarawak. He had gotten in and out, touching down in a clearing that was only the size of the chopper.

Today he was going to pick up some big-wig and fly him somewhere for a meeting. He put down on the pad at the outskirts of Jakarta where a big black sedan was waiting. As soon as he touched down, Rockman and two others came aboard.

"Welcome aboard," Haggard said, noticing that the Indonesians were well-dressed in civilian clothes.

Thank you," Rockman said, covering his surprise. It was the same pilot that he had interrogated. Luckily, there was no way Haggard would know, as he had never seen his face.

"Where do you want to go?"

"Here are the coordinates," Rockman said as he handed Haggard the map. He was going to a secret meeting that Beil had arranged with the British commander to try and come to some kind of an agreement. It was in thick jungle with very little place to land. Haggard spotted a break in the trees and set the bird down perfectly in a space that was only twice its size.

Haggard waited about an hour till Rockman came back and they took off, again having to go straight up with little room for error. Rockman was impressed; he had flown a few choppers himself when he was younger. When they landed Rockman turned to Haggard. "Maybe next time I can fly this baby, if that is all right with you."

Haggard nodded his head, knowing there was no way he would let anyone fly anything that he was on.

189

Yang was having a recurrent nightmare. A giant penis would come out of the sky and smother him, engulfing all of him, pressing into every orifice so that he felt he was suffocating. Just when he thought he would die, the penis would disappear, revealing Haggard's huge grinning face. Then Yang would feel that he was floating, falling from the sky, down, down. The dream would not end until the harsh lights came on and he would be back in living hell.

Every waking day was the same, the same room, the same voice, the same questions. The only thing different was the answers. Yang was chattering like a cricket, so he would not have to relive the dream. He was defenseless.

"We'll have him drained, soon. Not much information left," Rockman said to Beil. They were both in sober moods, watching on the other side of the mirror.

"Yes, I think you're right. Then I want him." Beil was hoping to trade Yang for Tim Johnson. Beil missed Agnes, who had phoned from New York to say that she and Debbie had arrived safety. She had told him that she'd had lunch with someone who knew the general. That made Beil think of his mentor and wonder what he would do. Everything was so dicey now. The bait had been set and all they could do was wait.

"Well, let us see if our young friend Puri has swallowed the hook," Rockman said. Beil had already told him about Umar. They were sure that by now the information was in the hands of the PKI.

"It is still no guarantee that they will act. Have you arranged for a meeting of the six hearts generals?"

"Yes, they are to meet at the base on September 30th. They think they are there to discuss Sukarno's health, and how to maintain law and order."

"That only gives you a few more days with Yang."

"Yes, and soon we will know whether we really have six hearts," Beil said, glad that everything was coming to a head, finally. "There is one last thing. I want Umar left alone, not touched."

"Sure, you can have your pet PKI, Edmond," Rockman said. They heard Yang whimpering through the window. Both men wanted a drink.

190

The anti-Chinese sentiment among the Muslims was at a fever pitch. The Chinese were all very frightened. Some had fled to Singapore.

They were caught between the rioting Muslim youths and the PKI, whose daily strikes threatened to drive the Chinese merchants out of business.

The Muslim youth movement was growing. Beil and Rockman knew that it had reached the point where it might be impossible to stop. That was the problem: These anti-Chinese sentiments were like an invasive weed that one planted to stabilize a hillside, unaware that it took over everything.

Gangs of young men dressed in black would go down streets late at night with machetes, looking for Chinese. They were like zombie assassins, terrorizing families that had been living in the country for generations. But at night under the cover of the dark, all things could happen. The Chinese knew that once the sun went down they had to hide.

There was a strike in Medan that had crippled the city. Thousands of PKI supporters had protested the high inflation and the lack of work. It had been a mess for days, and An Lee had not been able to open his shop. He was on his way to it to pick up some things that had to be delivered.

"Be very careful," his wife said.

"I always am," he said, trying not to worry her, hoping she did not see his eyes. He hid his face from her so she would not detect his worry. He saw the fear in her and in the children as he left his alley and turned onto the big street where there was a huge riot going on. He saw burning tires and angry mobs of PKI. He was about to turn around and go back, but some of the mob ran his way forcing him into the street. When he got his bearings again, he moved into the shadows and continued to walk to his shop. He was very thankful when the crowd thinned out. He picked up his pace, but was dismayed to see there was a small, vociferous crowd as he approached his block. He stood for a moment and waited, seeing if the mob would move. After a few minutes he realized that he was watching an anti-Chinese rally that was not part of the strike.

He had to walk through the mob to get to the front door of his shop on the other side of the street. He hunched over, looking at the ground, trying to be invisible. But just when he thought he was in safety, the mob spilled over him as he was opening the door.

"He's Chinese," someone shouted. Nearby was the brother of the little girl whose murder by the Chinese motorcyclist had sparked the anti-Chinese fever in Medan.

"He's the reason we have no money!"

"Yes, look, he is a shop owner!"

An Lee cried out as the mob pushed him inside his own shop. "Please, please," he squealed. They pushed him against his counter. All the merchandise went flying.

He was about cry out when a knife stabbed him in his arm. Then someone produced a rope and tied his hands and feet and tied him to the counter. Blood was seeping from his wound. He felt light-headed. He felt gasoline poured over him. Then the men left. But he was happy to be alive. He started to breathe better. He found he could move his hands and he was able to loosen the poorly-tied knots. He had just freed himself when the Molotov cocktail came through the window and set the place ablaze.

191

Umar arrived at the PKI meeting in the great hall of the old Dutch building. On the one hand it made him feel good that he no longer needed to sneak to a meeting or that a death squad would be waiting around ever corner. Those days were long gone. In the last months he had been confident that soon, finally, after all these years the PKI was going to take power. But that was before Beil's letter when he learned that certain generals were going to seize power on October 5th.

When he got to the hall, he saw Kusdi. "Umar, have you heard?"

"No, what?" Umar said, thinking the worst, but all he could see in Kusdi's face was happiness.

"Sukarno is going to allow for a people's army and make Indonesia a Socialist state."

"When?"

"Soon. He has ordered all businesses to be nationalized by the end of the year."

"That is good, but I have some news," Umar said. But before he could get it out, Kusdi's son Puri came running up. He was out of uniform.

"Father, the generals are going to seize power."

"Calm down, son," Kusdi said, and again repeated that Sukarno was on their side.

"No, father, they are already gathering. Here is list of them." On the list were the names of six generals, old, powerful, and corrupt.

"It does not matter. They do not have the power to do this," Kusdi said.

Just as he was about to say more, Umar interrupted. "Yes, Puri is right. They have told the Americans." Umar told them all the information he had gathered from Beil's unguarded letter.

"See, father, it is true. What Umar says collaborates my information."

"Then we will intercept them," Kusdi said, remembering what Yang had said about timing. That in the heat of war one had to be ready. Where was Yang? No one in China knew where he was either. He could use him now, but never mind. All this had been planned for, too. After all, his son was in place at military headquarters. The PKI controlled the press, the streets and the people.

"Intercept them?" Umar asked.

"Yes. We will act before they act. As soon as the generals gather, we will all act together, and Indonesia will be ours," Kusdi said triumphantly.

Rockman and Beil were together in his office, drinking and smoking, needing the alcohol and cigarettes to think clearly. They were aware that all their plans might backfire. It all hinged on the will of the army, which Rockman was sure would be with them. But anything was possible.

For Beil, the situation reminded him of the beginning of the crisis in Vietnam. He thought of Hiu.

"It's very dangerous here right now, Edmond," Rockman said. Those were the same words that Hiu spoke right before Haggard shot him at the start of it all. He thought of Umar, like Hiu in many ways. Someone he could work with. Now it was too late.

"Yes, very dangerous. I think I will take William to the Stanvac house for those days."

"That would be a prudent idea," Rockman replied.

He had arranged the meeting with the generals to discuss Sukarno's health, the PKI, and emergency powers. He himself would duck out at the last minute, not wanting to be anywhere near the base when the thing came down, if it came down.

"Yes, I can monitor the situation from there and take Umar with me," Beil said. He felt bad about feeding Umar false information, bad that all the seeds he had planted over the years would bear no fruit. Mostly he was furious that the Chinese had infiltrated the PKI to the extent that there was no hope for a peaceful transition after Sukarno's death. It was so much better to work change slowly. But time had run out. Nationalism had been co-opted by the Communists who were going to take over…who had to be stopped. After this they could begin again and hopefully get it right. Umar would be a big part of that. Beil knew Rockman would understand. Beil hoped Umar would. He would tell him when the time was right, try to explain.

"One last thing," Rockman said. "We are done with Yang."

"When can I have him?"

"Before the fifth. I will bring him to you."

"So this is it."

"To six hearts." The two men touched glasses.

193

The six generals were all over sixty. They controlled little ponds where they were the big fish. All of them had gotten rich on the spoils of power. Some of them were Rockman's friends, some even mentors. He felt bad about setting them up, but these were not normal times. Besides, maybe it would all work out and there would be no bloodshed. Even Beil did not know everything.

Rockman had been in constant worry ever since he came home a few days ago. He had just gotten out of the car when his son had excitedly raced up to him.

"Dad, come, we need volunteers. William is telling people random things that come into his mind. We all are. We are practicing for the talent show tomorrow—we are going to be fortune tellers. Come see if it sounds good. William is the best. The servants think he is a dukun, he's so good."

Andy was speaking English like a real American. "Sure son," Rockman said happily, going over to the table where William was dressed up in a turban with a false moustache.

"Good to see you, Mr. Rockman," William said locking eyes with him. Rockman felt the instant drain of energy as if all his being was sucked out of his body and into Williams mind.

"Tell me my fortune," Rockman said as good naturedly as he could. His eyes were still unable to unlock.

"I see a wall around you, a green high wall around some kind of army base." William did what he always did since he was young. He went into a space and just said things that came into his head. Earlier in the day he had been reading the latest comics from America. In the new Dick

Tracy, Dick was in Germany fighting the Nazis. A group of German generals were in a house around a huge table.

Along with the comics his grandmother had sent him a picture of her by a gas station with a huge flying red horse logo. They rest of the gas station was painted green. As he spoke, William changed from English to Indonesian: "You will be sitting with the generals staring at the green wall. You will all be sitting around the long table, and to save yourself you will have to fly over the fence before the red horses come over for tea...."

Rockman remembered how he had felt when William had mentioned the generals. He had tried not to let anyone see.

194

His terror returned when he was unexpectedly summoned back to the base on September thirtieth. His car and driver pulled through security just as the full moon was rising in the sky. When Rockman got out of the limo the first thing he noticed was the huge green wall that had been newly constructed around the perimeter. He went inside the building to the upstairs conference room, where a sentry was stationed at the door. The generals were all round the long table. Smoke filled the air.

"Oh, Rockman, you have arrived. Take that seat over there by the window. Would you like a drink?" General Yusto, his old mentor asked.

"Scotch and water, thank you," Rockman said, feeling ill at ease. He walked over to the open window and put his head outside to get some fresh air. He was surprised to see the top of the new wall was only ten feet below and ten feet from the building. His body tightened as he thought of the dukun's words—you have to fly over the fence before the red horses come over for tea. He tried to put the thought out of his mind. This was crazy. Then he spotted the road map with the flying red horse on the cover. His fear welled. He took his seat but could not help peering out the window every so often. Each time he was relieved that everything seemed tranquil.

On the other side of the fence, Puri and his men gathered. As soon as they had heard that the generals were all together, they had started their operation to save Indonesia. Conditions were prefect. The room was so secure that no one would be expecting this. The five men slid around the green wall, stopping by the willow tree on the other side. Silently they made their way to the entrance. All were armed.

Another group of men waited outside the communication facility, ready to take to the airwaves to announce that they had foiled the plot. Rockman looked out the window just as they were passing by and caught a slight movement of the willow tree moving when there was no wind. Involuntarily he got up and moved toward the window.

"Nasul, you seem rather strange tonight. Better have another drink," General Yusto said. Just as he finished his words the door was smashed in. "What the—" he said as someone started firing. One of the generals was cut almost in two by the machine gun fire. Another was able to extinguish the lamp, and then complete chaos took over.

Rockman did not hesitate when the first of the bullets came through the door, knowing he had to jump over the wall or he was doomed. Mustering all of his strength he leapt for his life. He was able to catch the top of the wall, pull himself up, and slip over the other side just as a rain of bullets thundered out of the window.

Inside, four generals were dead or dying. Two others lay begging for their lives. Puri shot point-blank into their heads. Then it was over, and the enormity of what they had done took over. They were now the saviors of Indonesia.

"We are in charge!" Puri relayed to the other team outside the radio tower. At once the other men stormed the communication center where they easily overpowered the guards.

Two hours later Kusdi joined them, very proud of his son. As with all acts of courage, they change you. Puri seemed more confident, taller. Kusdi knew that in the new Communist Indonesia, his son would be a player. He watched how the men treated him, with great respect.

"Father, come this way," the youth said. Very proper, very confident. He took Kusdi over to the radio room to begin his broadcast: "Comrades of Indonesia, the day is finally with us. The day of the imperialistic rule of the oppressors is over."

195

Rockman made his way back to Jakarta and to Beil's house. The servants led him to the porch where Beil was feeding the fish.

"What happened?"

"Six hearts," Rockman said, looking very disheveled. "I was there when they came in and started firing. They had a new wall and new security—I couldn't get away before. It was only by the grace of Allah that I escaped," Rockman said, aware that neither of them believed in God.

"What is the situation now?"

"At least three of the generals are dead. Maybe more. I thought it best to come here before I went back to report, before the news got to the streets. I need a safe car. Not an official limousine."

"You can use mine. Umar! Where will you be later on?" Beil asked, letting his mind roam. Umar came running in. "Take Mr. Rockman home. Then come back here."

It was best to send Umar and William immediately to the country in case there was any anti-American violence. Also, Beil wanted to keep Umar isolated, so he would not be able to join the PKI. Up in Mega Mendung, there was no phone in the house. In addition, Beil had disabled the car radio, and had installed a device to disable the engine after they arrived.

"I will be in the safe house by noon. Come and see me there," Rockman said as the car arrived out front. As soon as he left, Beil got William ready for when Umar returned, telling the boy that he was to go to the country and that Beil would follow later in a day or so.

By the time Beil arrived at Rockman's safe house, the news was all over the radio. Rogue elements within the military had staged a coup. The PKI had come out in favor of it; another general in Sumatra had also supported it.

Beil was led in by a young sergeant and taken to Rockman, who was with a number of other officers, none of them in uniform. Guards with semi-automatic rifles stood by every window.

"We have forces in place waiting to retake the army communication tower, which in any case is now blacked out. At the moment we are broadcasting from the Jakarta transmitter that six generals have been killed in an attempted coup," Rockman said. Both he and Beil needed a drink, but neither of them dared ask for one. Drinking would infuriate the devoted Muslims whom they needed now.

"We have put Suharto up as the public face in the counter-coup. He has gone on the radio saying Sukarno has told him to restore stability with whatever means are necessary."

"How did Sukarno take that?"

"He is very ill, incapable of making decisions. Suharto forced his hand. As always, Sukarno can blow with the wind and change. But at the moment he is bed-ridden and isolated."

"Then everything is going according to plan."

"Yes," Rockman said, but both men knew it was not that simple. The PKI had tuned out into the streets in numbers that threatened everything. Just then there was a knock on the office door.

"Sir, Kusdi has gone to headquarters and is meeting with members of the military. The Chinese government has come out in favor of the coup."

"Where is Sukarno at the moment?" Beil asked.

"He is in the presidential palace on the square," Rockman said. The palace was a few streets away.

"Do you have people there on the outside as well as the inside?"

"Yes, we sent a battalion. The PKI sent two. The square is surrounded," Rockman said. Each side knew they needed Sukarno, if only as a figurehead. At the moment there was a stalemate at the square.

"Let's go there," Beil said. In half an hour the two men were on the edge of a square full of soldiers. The PKI had surrounded Sukarno's palace. On the other side of the square the Army Headquarters was in the hands of Rockman's group. The sun was beating down, baking the pavement to an unbearable hundred-and-five degrees. It was so hot that it was hard to breathe, so much so that the never-sweating Beil was sweating. Everything had happened so quickly that no side had thought about supplies, especially water. By the end of the day most were feeling the first effects of dehydration. At dusk Beil and Rockman made their way back to the safe house.

"Very much in flux," Beil said, happy that he had dressed as an Indonesian and had bent over most of the time so his height would not make him stand out.

"No direction, nobody is willing to make a move," Rockman said. So far it was like a sea without a tide. The only battles were in the countryside where bands of Muslim groups were going on a massacre of anything and anyone Chinese. The other battle was at the army base where Rockman's forces under the command of Ures Jonas, of the secret death squads, had moved in.

"Well, the cards are played, so there is nothing to do but wait," Beil said, lighting a cigarette handing one to Rockman. They sat on the veranda near the square next to the palace, which was next to the army headquarters, which was surrounded by Rockman's people.

197

The next day was even hotter that the last. By eight in the morning the sun was baking the treeless square. The intense heat and lack of water was beginning to take to a toll on the soldiers who were at the square. During the night ten people had died of dehydration. Many others had collapsed from the claustrophobic conditions of so many people packed into a too small place. Yet nobody was leaving. The frustration and strain was beginning to show on all but the most hardened of the troops.

Throughout the night there had been starts and stops, but no side had made a move. Everybody was looking for a sign, for the defining moment. Rumors spread. Sukarno was either too sick to speak, or else something had happened to him.

Rockman and Beil had just returned from the square and were on the veranda of the safe house. Both men were chain-smoking.

"So you need to move," Beil said, weary. They had been up most of the night.

"So hard to make, Edmond," Rockman sighed.

Beil had gotten a few dispatches from Jim and heard about what the rest of the world was saying. China was for the coup, most of the world against it. The PKI soldiers were still in control of the main army base in Java and were still broadcasting from there, despite what Rockman had said. Maybe Kusdi was there also, Jim thought. He wanted Beil to get Yang out of the country now in case things went wrong. Something had to give.

"Were you able to get in to see Sukarno?" Beil asked.

"Yes but so did the PKI. This time they came heavily armed. They are furious that Sukarno has put Suharto in charge of restoring order and are demanding he put Puri there instead. Hard to say what is happening. He is scared."

"He should be. But I do know one thing, if something doesn't happen soon, everyone will have died of thirst."

"What did you say?"

"That everybody is dying of thirst."

That was the answer. It was so simple. Water, life giving water. They looked at each other, realizing they had the key to unlock the stalemate.

"Wish I were drinking a bull's eye, Edmond," Rockman said, savoring the realization of what would be a very fine finesse.

"Water. None of the soldiers have water."

"Who ever brings them water first will win."

"How long will it take to get someone out there with water?"

"Not long. Suharto is at headquarters."

An hour later Suharto, dressed in his uniform, came out of the building with a bucket of water and went over to the nearest soldiers. He offered them water, and he personally ladled it out to them. Then Suharto pledged loyalty to the army, saying he needed their support to restore order so Indonesia did not drift into anarchy. "Go home now, fellow Indonesians," he said proudly over the loud speakers. "Over behind the buildings we have water. I want to thank you all for coming to the protection of Indonesia. Everything is now in control. Thank you so much. Please come get the water. Indonesia salutes you for your support."

Beil and Rockman were watching from the veranda and saw the army begin to move and file out down the streets, even the PKI battalions. "Now we can crush those fools at the army base," Rockman said. He made a relay to the radio transmitter, and dictated the official announcement that Suharto has been made top general. He knew that nothing had been decided. But he decided to gamble that Sukarno would have little choice if Puri's coup was crushed as planned.

"Rockman, can you arrange a driver to take me to the country?"

"Sure."

"Good. Then I will go and wait for you to bring me Yang."

"Good. I will arrange as planned to pick you and Yang up in the helicopter and fly you both out."

198

At the base, General Puri and his fellow PKI officers were huddled in the conference room trying to figure what to do next. It had been very easy to kill all the generals, easy to grab hold of the radio room, easy to broadcast their message that they had liberated Indonesia from the corrupt generals that were going to seize power from Sukarno. But they did not know what to do next. Most of them had only a few years in the armed forces and despite their inflated egos they were at a loss.

A few hours after the raid, Puri's father had come to see him. "Congratulations, son," Kusdi had said, proud to see his son in command.

"What do I do next father?" he had asked, still fresh from the glow of the action.

"I'm not sure, son, but you are in charge and will figure it out. I heard that some of the army has moved to the palace to guard Sukarno. I will send someone to meet with him. But he is hiding, I think."

"Probably he is frightened of me," Puri said. That was two days ago and still he was unsure what to do. As far as he knew he was in charge of all Indonesia but all he could for sure be sure of was that he was in charge of five hundred men at the army base that was isolated from everything.

"At least we have good food," one of the officers said as they ate the ayam chicken in a brown curry sauce.

"Well, we cannot govern with food. Why is the communication still down?" Early in the evening they had lost all power, phone and radio transmitter.

"Must be a storm somewhere." They were eating by the light of some oil lamps. One of them was an old wayang lamp, decorated with a figure of Arjuna. It flickered in the little wind. Outside they heard a dog barking.

The assault team of five hundred commandos was ready. Rockman was giving last minutes instructions to kill all the leaders of the coup. They had just gotten word that the last piece of the puzzle had fallen into place. Suharto had met with Sukarno who had made him commander of the armed forces with a mandate to restore order.

Rockman had arrived at the base about an hour ago to find that the elite commandos that he had trained for this precise action were in position. The power lines had been cut. Ures Jonas waited for his order. With a nod of his head, the operation started; the commandos went over the green wall. In half an hour most of the soldiers had surrendered, and most of their officers were dead. Two were left alive. Rockman walked into the conference room to see them whimpering for their lives in the corner.

"Where is your father?" Rockman asked General Puri, the hero of Sarawak. When he did not answer right away, a commando put his gun to the other man's head and pulled the trigger sending blood and brains all over. They both looked like boys, Rockman thought, feeling bad in some way.

Again he asked, "Where is your father?"

This time the boy answered. "He is in Medan—" Puri did not see the gun come to the back of his head. He was dead before he knew it.

199

Beil arrived at Mega Mendung a day later, just after the commandos had retaken the army base, killing any officers with PKI ties. Prudent, Beil thought, though he did not like the violence. But it was wise to eliminate any potential opposition, especially Puri, who was a national hero—if left alive he could have caused major problems. Ures Jonas had been so efficient that some of the bodies of the dead could fit into a small box.

On the way into the mountains he had driven through many small towns and seen gangs of youths with pipes and rakes. There were dead bodies in the rivers. All day the radio broadcast the news that General Suharto was in charge and with the blessing of the president was restoring order.

"Father!" William shouted as he saw Beil get out of the car. Next to him was Umar, furious. "We are so happy you are all right," William said. "We heard there was a coup and many thousands were killed."

"Where did you hear that, son?" Beil said, keeping his face passive. He had hoped they would be isolated from the news. He glanced over at Umar, who was a ball of emotion. Beil saw the anger and fear.

"From a worker who came to change the doors."

"Oh it not so bad, son," Beil said, lying. The army is in control." And then to change the subject he brought out the sweets from William's favorite stand, coconut and sugar wrapped in banana leaves. When William saw them his mood changed.

"Thanks, dad," I said, and ran off, lest I would have to share them. When I was gone, Beil turned and looked at Umar.

"Tuan, what happened?" Umar said. He had heard only what had filtered through to him from the workers and a servant who had returned from Jakarta with supplies. He had been shocked to hear of the coup; very frustrated to be stuck up here in the middle of nowhere. He longed for details. All he knew was that six top generals had been murdered by the PKI, who had the taken power to support Sukarno. When the servants had left, Umar had jumped into the company car to head back to Jakarta. But as he tried to start the car, the engine started to smoke. Now he was very angry, hurt that he had no warning of this PKI coup, hurt that he had been left out of the know. He remembered back to the last meeting he had attended a few days before. No one had much to say to him, even after he had brought them the news from Beil's letter.

"There was a coup by the PKI," Beil said.

"So we have won," Umar interrupted excitedly. "Is Sukarno still in power?"

"Sukarno gave Suharto power to restore order. I am afraid I must tell you that the rebel PKI officers were all killed when the army took back power, including General Puri, Kusdi's son."

"You knew this was going to happen, tuan? Umar asked after a pause, the emotion heavy in his voice.

For the last day or so he had felt all kinds of things inside himself. What surprised him now was that deep down in some way he was relieved.

"Umar, there are things at play that are not in anyone's control," Beil said, taking a long draught on his cigarette, trying hard to find the words, where to begin. There was so much betrayal and deceit.

Maneuvering for the right words, he was glad when Umar broke his thought.

"Tuan, you knew. Tuan, you knew," Umar shouted again.

"Yes, Umar, I knew. Some, not all. I knew that the generals were going to meet, plotting a coup to take power from Sukarno...," Beil began, deciding on his hand, the one he had thought about for years. He had been trying to lead Umar into this position. "I did not know that those PKI officers were planning a coup all along."

"Tell me what happened, tuan, tell me all you know," Umar said, again feeling relieved to be away from all of it.

And Beil told him: how on the night of September 30th the generals were attacked by the PKI unit. "They slaughtered six old generals, old heroes." Beil did not mention that Rockman had fled over the fence. "For the next two days there was anarchy. Small fights broke out. Finally after that time Sukarno gave Suharto emergency powers to restore order. He ordered the storming of the base. All the perpetrators were killed."

"What about Kusdi?"

"I far as I know he had fled to Medan and has gone into hiding. Suharto has imposed martial law."

"Why, tuan?" Umar said, aghast.

"To stop the killing."

"Killing, tuan?"

"Yes of the PKI. Already there are reports of a mass killing in East Java. Hundreds dead, killed by the Muslim youth movement." Beil did not say he thought that government forces were behind the massacre, with lists that Rockman had supplied. He hoped that only the radical Chinese influences would be suppressed, not people like Umar.

"Tuan, I must get there."

"No, Umar, listen that is not the way to change. They are doomed. When this all clears up the country is going to need men like you who can bridge the divide."

Then Beil decided it was time to gamble. "Listen, Umar, it was not coincidence that they kept you out of the loop. Kusdi did not want moderates in their organization. Men of vision like you—"

"No, tuan, they did not trust me because I had to drive Rockman!"

"No, Umar, you are wrong. They did not want you. You know we captured Yang and interrogated him. He wanted you dead. It was only Rockman's protection that saved you. You do not want to throw your life away for nothing. You want to live for Indonesia."

"My life is over, tuan. They will get me."

"No, you are wrong. They will need you." And then he launched himself into his plan. "But it is wise for you to leave. I will be leaving, myself. A helicopter is coming for me in the next day or so. Come with me to Singapore for a few months. Then when this trouble has sorted itself out, then Indonesia will need men like you."

"No one will ever agree with that, tuan," Umar said, not knowing what to do. He needed to think. His whole world was turned upside down. If it had been two years ago he would have fled to join the revolution. But events had sidelined him, had kept him out of the loop. During that time he had had many conversations with Beil about the role of the worker, about modernization, freedom, capitalism, and found that he and Beil agreed more times than they disagreed.

"Rockman was the one who suggested it. He was the one who said they needed all good Indonesians, reasonable Indonesians, who can rebuild a democratic, modern free country. The Chinese were trying to take your country over and make you slaves."

200

Haggard set the helicopter down on the flat roof, a dicey landing. The chopper had no lights and there were no markings to give its origin away. He could see a figure standing on the roof. He picked up his revolver; set the safety off. His hand eased off the trigger when he recognized Rockman.

"Ah, Mr. Haggard, good to see you," Rockman said. He was on the roof above Merdeka Square, now mostly deserted expect for a few patrols. The drama was behind. The future looked more secure. In the last few days Suharto had consolidated power, having made it clear to Sukarno that he had lost. Still they could not risk killing or disposing of him, because there was a chance that the people would come to his side. They had decided to keep him isolated while they simultaneously shut down the PKI.

"You, too, Mr. Rockman," Haggard said, studying the man. All he had been told was that he was to extract some asset and bring it to a forward base, where he was to deliver his package to friendly forces. That wasn't enough information; the not knowing was what got you into danger. He fought the urge to grab Rockman and demand the details, lighting a cigarette instead.

"Mr. Haggard, you said I could fly the bird the next time we met," Rockman said, wanting to fly to clear his head. Already he had gotten reports that in the villages there were blood-baths. Reports that the rivers were full of bodies.

"I don't remember that," Haggard said.

"I do," Rockman said. He knew from the past that this man was a caged animal, who had been broken but was still wild and deviant.

"Maybe later, the next leg," Haggard said. He would think of another excuse and then another until the mission was over.

"Good, fly these coordinates," Rockman said, handing him the slip. The mission was to first fly and pick up Yang and then fly to Mega Mundune, pick up Beil, his son, and Umar. Then fly them out of the country. Rockman would go with them to assure the Americans that Indonesia was ready to be its greatest friend in stopping the Communist tide.

201

Yang had been awakened early in the night, and led out of his cell by a group of men he'd never seen before. For as long as he could remember, life had been the cell, the cold, the dripping water, and no light. Still he was all fear when the routine was broken. He struggled when they shackled him, bringing him to the showers, where he was washed and dressed in clothes for the first time in months. Then a hood was slipped over his head as he was led outside.

A few minutes later he heard an aircraft approach. He could feel the wind when it landed; could tell it was a helicopter. He felt himself pushed forward and when he hesitated he was shoved into the open door.

"Put him over there," Rockman said. The guards placed him on the bench, where they chained his feet to the railing but left his hands bound behind his back.

"Where to now?" Haggard asked Rockman. Yang heard the voice and thought it sounded familiar.

"Why don't you let me fly?" Rockman said.

"Maybe later." Again Yang found the voice familiar. They lifted off and flew fast at low height.

In an hour Yang felt the chopper heading down. He still had the hood on but the flight had invigorated him. Being out of the cell made him focus, for the first time in months he felt a fog was lifting.

Beil was waiting outside as the chopper landed near the swimming pool, beyond the hedge where there was some level ground. As soon as the copter landed, he approached.

"Mr. Beil," Rockman said pumping his hand. They had not seen each other for three days since the six hearts had been secured.

"Good to—" Beil stopped in mid-sentence when he saw Haggard at the controls. The anger surged inside of him, but he pressed it down. It had been a while since he had seen him, and the last time Haggard had been in hell.

"Now I am at ease with the best pilot in the Pacific," Beil said.

Haggard couldn't tell if he was speaking seriously. "Sergeant Beil." He used the term as a belittlement. "Fancy meeting you here."

"Are you ready?" Rockman asked.

"Yes," Beil said, for the first time noticing the bound and hooded figure slumped on the seat.

"Good. Let's hurry."

"Is that Yang? He looks so different," Beil said. The figure was much smaller and skinnier than he had remembered.

"Yes, here, see for yourself," Rockman said as he pulled off the hood. The face was scared, but Beil could tell it was Yang's. From the cockpit Haggard got a view. Rockman was about to put the hood back on but Beil stopped him.

"No, leave it off. The poor bugger is in a daze. Better that William see him without the hood," Beil said. Though it was sort of like seeing an apple with a bruise rather than having it covered up.

202

"Rockman, you can take the controls now," Haggard said as soon as Beil had disappeared into the house. Seeing Yang set off all kinds of feelings in him. But most of all, he was aroused. That was part of it, and the other part was Beil. He had not expected to see him. And then seeing the two of them together was overwhelming. He felt the hate well up in him. He decided he would rather not be at the controls, even though it was against every instinct to let a gook fly.

"Thank you. I was hoping for that," Rockman said. He wanted the freedom of forgetting all he had unleashed in the last few days. All the killings that he was unable to stop. He felt bad, bad for the six generals, bad for the misdirected youths that had staged the coup. He knew this feeling was the price he paid for power. He got behind the controls quickly sitting down in the pilot's seat before Haggard changed his mind. Rockman was familiar with the controls having trained on the very bird.

He did not see that Haggard had moved back into the belly of the chopper where Yang was.

Yang felt the fresh air on him but still was unable to open his eyes. His world of pain, cold, dark and light was still with him as he tried to focus his mind on his new reality. Where was he?

Haggard studied the poor bastard, transported back to his time in the Indonesian prison where he had been broken, just like Yang was broken. When Haggard had gotten back from being captured he had been told that Yang was an agent. Yang was the reason he'd been captured in the first place. Seeing the one who had set him up just lying there so helpless made him hard. Haggard felt his penis swell. He was consumed by the sick desire to slap the silly boy into submission.

"You don't look so good, little mealy mouth," Haggard said, shaking the slumped man by the shoulder. Yang heard the familiar words but still thought he was dreaming. Then he felt the shaking again; again the words. Slowly he began to open his eyes. This time someone had grabbed hold of his head and pulled him up. He felt hot air on his face. He opened his eyes and saw the face of evil. The face he knew so well from Singapore. He felt the stink of the rotting teeth, the stale cigarettes. He tried to move his hands but he was stopped by the cuffs behind his back. He opened his eyes again and saw Haggard with his mocking face; without thinking he spat into it—a mistake. A hand came crashing down across his cheek and forehead. The viciousness of the blow sent him reeling back. He hit his head on the wall of the copter and faded to unconsciousness.

203

Beil emerged out of the house holding William's hand, Umar behind him. He was a little unnerved when he saw Rockman at the controls with Haggard sitting next to him in the co-pilot seat. Beil saw the welt on Yang who lay with his head thrown back, unconscious. He would have said something if William had not been with him. He tried to put the facts out of his mind. Soon they would be in Singapore, rid of Haggard and his violence. Beil was looking forward to the long first-class fight to America. He could not wait for this flight to be over.

"You sure you know how to fly this thing," Beil asked Rockman.

"Yes, Edmond, this was the model I trained on."

"I'm surprised you would give up the controls." Beil turned to Haggard, detesting him. He saw the hate staring back at him.

"There are a lot of things that would surprise you," Haggard said. "Who is that?"

"This is my friend Umar, and this is my son William," Beil said. Inside his mind he flashed on Hiu, eerily reminded by Haggard's blank stare of hatred, the same one Beil had seen all those years ago. He switched to Bahasa, knowing that Haggard would not be able to understand him. This made Haggard even more enraged. He was sure that they were talking about him. He heard Umar laugh, and caught the asshole giving him a sideways glance.

"Yes, tuan, let's us hope Mr. Rockman can fly," Umar said. Rockman had always made him nervous. Inside a million emotions were going through him. He had never been outside of Indonesia before.

Rockman laughed too. Haggard was now even more convinced they were poking fun at him. He looked over to the corner and saw Yang had woken up and was looking his way. The only one not paying him any mind was the boy William, who was sitting silently, staring at Yang, fascinated by the huge welt that was forming on his face.

"What's so funny, Beil? Some faggot game to get your jollies off?"

"No Haggard, you pathetic bastard, nothing," Beil said, lighting a cigarette and offering one to Umar. Haggard grabbed the cigarette out of Umar's lips and threw it out the window.

"I don't want any gooks smoking in front of me," Haggard snarled.

"Well, it is not up to you, and he's not a gook." Beil said, coolly lighting another cigarette giving it to Umar. "Afraid you're the low man on this flight, old chap," Beil added in the most blue-blood manner he could muster.

"That's what wrong with you. You cuddle up to these gooks." Haggard again grabbed the butt and tossed it out of the chopper.

Over on the bench Yang had come to. He saw nothing but hate in Haggard, and felt nothing but hate himself. He wished he were not bound. He wanted to kill the son of a bitch.

"Little man like you can't get it up, little man," Yang started taunting. Haggard reached back and hit him, slamming him back against the wall where he remained slumped down. Haggard pulled the hood over his face.

"Stop it!" Beil shouted as a sudden blast of turbulence rocked the chopper. For a few minutes afterward they all rode in silence.

204

Thirty minutes later and they were over water, having cleared the Java coast. Yang was just coming to. He found himself dreaming. When he saw the eyes, he knew they were the eyes from the dream.

William was staring down at Yang. The welt that was now twice as big as it had been, dark red, bloated like a dead fish. He found it fascinating to watch the mountain of flesh grow out of Yang's pasty-white face. The months that Yang had spent in the darkness, deprived of sunlight, made the bruise seem much more extreme. William was so engrossed that he just had to touch it. He reached his fingers out and stuck it in the middle of the wound.

Yang cried out. He was back in the interrogation room. He closed his eyes, expecting to see the penetrating eyes come after him like before. Only this time the eyes did not follow him into the dream of the giant penis. Then he heard the voice, Haggard's voice. There in front of him was Haggard, the evil demon of his dreams. The demon was talking. Yang opened his eyes, but all he saw were those of the dukun.

"You don't know anything, Sergeant Beil," Haggard yelled at the top of his lungs. All the time he was watching Beil and Umar, who reminded him of Hiu.

"What did you say, Haggard?" Beil said, stopping the conversation he and Umar were having in Bahasa.

"I say you don't know anything!" Then he saw Beil's friend smoking again with that smug condescending smile on his face.

Umar looked back at Haggard, very worried about how open the chopper was. He had never been on one before and nothing about it felt safe. He was exhausted. All last night he had barely slept, thinking about the last ten years. All the twists and turns of the path leading to him onto the plane with the enemy who was really his friend. He thought about Indonesia that was now ripped apart, trying to understand how he felt and what he should be doing. He looked at Rockman, an Indonesian like himself. Were they on different sides? Could he work with him? Change him? Had he been changed? Was he a traitor?

"I told you, no smoking for gooks!" Haggard screamed, violently ripping the cigarette out of Umar's mouth.

"Haggard, stop it! I order it!" Beil shouted. He took out his cigarette pack.

"You can't order me to do anything," Haggard yelled back. He tried to grab the cigarettes but Beil blocked him.

"Haggard, go back to your seat. I am in command here, not you. You are a complete failure. The only thing you are good at is killing, nothing else."

"Well, I'll show you, you faggot," Haggard shrieked as he pushed Beil aside, slamming him to the floor. Haggard grabbed Umar by the shirt. "Watch this, you fucking bastard." Umar tried to break free but Haggard was much stronger and soon overcame him.

"Haggard, stop it," Beil cried, getting to his feet and scrambling over.

Beil was about to throw himself at him when Haggard pulled the pistol from his side. "Remember your friend Hiu," Haggard shouted. "I was glad I killed him! Glad I shot him!" Haggard moved the barrel to Umar's head.

"Haggard, don't," Beil yelled, impotent to do anything. Time stood still. Haggard pulled the trigger, but just as he did, Umar jerked his head away. The bullet missed him by inches, hitting the side wall where it began to ricochet round the cabin, almost hitting Yang, breaking the spell of the dukun's eyes. Yang turned away and saw Haggard clearly for the first time. He watched as Beil slammed into Haggard, knocking the gun from his hand, sending it skittering across the cabin, where it came to rest near the cockpit. The men wrestled, but Haggard was able break free. Instead of moving for the gun, Haggard darted towards Umar. Beil went for the gun.

Umar scrambled away only to be chased by Haggard who grabbed hold of him and forced him toward the open door in a full nelson.

"Well, the little bugger thought he got away," Haggard said, adrenaline pushing through him. Umar was struggling, but there was no way he could overcome the stronger man. Umar looked out of the chopper and saw the waves a few hundred yards below.

"Stop this!" Rockman said at the controls, "or I will crash the bird."

"Shut the fuck up, you Asian bastard, you don't have the balls," Haggard shouted, beyond caring whether he lived or died. He was going to get revenge.

"Haggard, are you crazy? Stop it now. When we get to base I will have you thrown into jail," Beil said, now with the gun in his hands. Slowly he made his way toward Haggard. Umar was limp in shock.

"Don't make a move or I throw this faggot out of the chopper," Haggard said, holding Umar over the opening.

"Haggard, it's over," Beil said, the gun now leveled on Haggard. He steadied the pistol, afraid to shoot for fear of hurting Umar. Haggard looked at Beil with the gun and knew everything was over, but then he saw Yang behind Beil and caught his eyes. The bastard was staring at him. Rage overtook him.

"Watch this, you mealy-mouthed whore," Haggard screamed to Yang. "I have not forgotten you." With that he picked Umar off the floor and hurled him out of the door.

"No!" Beil shouted and froze for a split-second, giving Haggard just enough time to dive at him, jarring the gun out of his hand. It bounced off the side and came to land by the door. Haggard picked it up.

"You're next," he said, pointing the gun at Beil. Just then Rockman banked the copter to the left, knocking Haggard to the ground. Beil lunged for him, but Haggard was able to thrust him toward the opening, where he ended up straddling the hole where Umar had just disappeared. Haggard turned towards Beil, waving the gun like a madman.

"Haggard, put the gun down!" Beil shouted. So many things were going through his mind. Umar was dead. He had to save William.

205

Yang knew he was part of a dream. A dream where he could end the evil. The thought took him back to the interrogation room, to his last session with the dukun when everything in him had finally been drained.

"When will this nightmare end?" he had asked.

"When you are numb and nothing is left but the chains, then you will cut off the tongue of the serpent."

William kept his eyes focused on Yang, afraid to look at his father, thinking if he did not look, then his father would be OK. Then something popped into his head. This chained man was like the wayang golek puppet on the stick.

"You can do it," he said in English, over and over.

Yang heard the words and turned back. The eyes bore into him. He was going to explode.

"Sergeant Beil, the time has come," Haggard said as he inched closer to the hole. He was formulating the plan in his mind. He would have to kill them all, even the little boy, but that was OK. In war there was collateral damage. The thrill of killing Beil's friend gave him the extra will to see this through. Killing Beil would be very pleasurable. He wished he could save it for last, but he knew that Beil would be after him the moment he turned away.

"Haggard, the problem with you is that you mistake violence for strength. You don't know how to finesse. You have the subtleties of a horse," Beil said, trying to buy time, looking around. He looked back at William.

"Son," Beil said in Indonesian. "Push him from behind on the count of three. One, two, three." William pushed Haggard down, allowing Beil to slip back to the safety of the wall.

"Why, you son of a bitch!" Haggard shouted, turning around but not seeing William who had scrambled back to his seat. He spotted Yang staring at him.

"So it's you, you fucking faggot." He went over to Yang and belted him again, this time with the butt of the pistol. Then he turned on Beil.

"I won't have the pleasure of pushing you into the ocean, but I will have the pleasure of killing you." Haggard spat, then started laughing. His back was to Yang.

"You can do it. You can do it," William said to Yang, this time in Indonesian. Yang judged the distance. It was around seven feet to Haggard, and Yang knew with the chains on his feet and his hands bound in back, he would only have one shot. Just as he was trying to figure this out, a large spider that had been dangling from the top of the copter dropped onto William's head.

"Ahh!" His scream pierced the cabin. Haggard turned around and moved a step closer.

"Shut up!" Haggard raged. He moved closer to kill the boy.

"No!" Beil shouted, causing Haggard to turn towards him to keep him at bay. This gave Yang the opening.

"AYYYA!" Yang shouted as he darted out like a snake, butting Haggard in the stomach. The momentum pushed him out the copter door. Only his quick reflexes saved him. At the last second he grabbed hold of Yang's head as he dangled out of the copter. Yang was stretched out on the floor, legs straining, with only his neck and head out of the helicopter.

Beil moved over to William. "Rockman!" he shouted. "Give me your gun!"

"I don't have one," Rockman said, looking behind him. Beil saw a pipe lying on the side of the cabin and picked it up and climbed over Yang's outstretched body.

Haggard still had hold of Yang's head. Yang was thrashing back and forth in an attempt to throw him off. The closeness of the contact brought back the nauseating smell and the vile breath. Again he shook hard. Haggard knew his only hope was to break Yang's neck. Then he would be free to climb aboard and finish Beil off. All of them off. Just the thought of the perverse pleasure of killing aroused him, lending him strength. He twisted his hands until he heard the pop.

Yang instantly felt a lightening bolt run up him, from the bottom of his toes through the top of his head. Then he felt nothing and was unable to do anything but stare out of his eyes. He saw Haggard's face. Now, face to face.

"So, mealy-mouth, thank you for saving me," Haggard said spitting into his face.

"Oh, give me a kiss, big boy, before I die," Yang said. It was like the dukun said. In a last act of violent lust Haggard put his tongue in Yang's mouth. For a few seconds he twirled it around in a fury. Then Yang was able to catch it with his teeth. With all the might he could muster he bit down.

"AHHHA!" Haggard gargled in pain. The blood poured out. Haggard hands around Yang's neck loosened and he felt himself falling, losing his grip. Frantically he threw his hand out, managing to grab hold of Yang's ear, but before he could get a good grip Yang shook his head.

"AHHHAA!" Haggard screamed as he fell to his death.

Inside the cabin Beil tried to pull Yang up, but there was no movement. He then felt for a pulse. "He's dead," he shouted to Rockman. Poor William was staring at him. Beil took out the key and unlocked the chains that bound Yang's feet to the floor. His body slid out and he was gone. In silence they all flew on. Just before they landed, Beil turned to William.

"That was good bridge, son. That was good bridge."

Epilogue

In the months after the attempted coup, Rockman and his group consolidated power. But they were unable to stop the mass killings that went on and on. Over a million Indonesians died. Kusdi was hunted down and executed. Sukarno relinquished power to Suharto and Indonesia became one of the United States' most important allies in the Cold War against Communism. Beil moved back to America and rejoined Agnes. Never again did he live in Asia, though from time to time he would venture to various hot spots in that area, especially Vietnam where he spent many months a year.

His son William went on to teach creative writing at Silvertown University where he stayed a dukun until his father's death, when this story could finally be told.